The Virgin Orient

The Virgin Orient
and Other Stories

by
Camille Mauclair

translated, annotated and introduced by
Brian Stableford

A Black Coat Press Book

ISBN 978-1-61227-502-4. First Printing. April 2016. Published by Black Coat Press, an imprint of Hollywood Comics.com, LLC, P.O. Box 17270, Encino, CA 91416. All rights reserved. Except for review purposes, no part of this book may be reproduced or transmitted in any form or by any means, electronic or mechanical, including photocopying, recording, or by any information storage and retrieval system, without permission in writing from the publisher. The stories and characters depicted in this novel are entirely fictional. Printed in the United States of America.

TABLE OF CONTENTS

*À Stéphane Mallarmé
avec mon admiration
et ma profonde affection*

Camille Mauclair

L'ORIENT VIERGE

Roman épique de l'An 2000

Introduction

L'Orient vierge, roman épique de l'an 2000, by Camille Mauclair, here translated as "The Virgin Orient, an Epic Novel of the Year 2000," was originally published by Paul Ollendorf in 1897. It was reprinted by Ollendorf, in a slightly revised version, in 1920, after the conclusion of the Great War, perhaps because the publisher thought that the fact that the novel anticipates a Franco-German war as a prelude to its own Even Greater War might add further interest to it, although the actual Great War had demonstrated very clearly that any war fought in the year 2000 would not bear the slightest resemblance to the one featured in Mauclair's novel, which is fought almost exclusively with the technology of the 1890s. The novel was brought back into print again in 1979 by Slatkine, that edition being reprinted in 1980, and it was reprinted again by Billière in 2000.

"Camille Mauclair" was the name used on all his writings by Camille-Laurent-Séverin Faust (1872-1945), who was one of the younger recruits to the Symbolist Movement that was a highly significant feature of the Parisian *fin-de-siècle*; he became one of the most fervent acolytes of one of the movement's figureheads, Stéphane Mallarmé. *L'Orient vierge* was Mauclair's first full-length novel, although it had been preceded by a visionary novella published as a book, *Couronne de clarté, roman féerique* (Ollendorf, 1895; here translated as "Crown of Clarity, a Fantastic Story"), as well a volume of poetry, a curious meditation, *Eleusis, causeries sur la cité intérieure* [Eleusis; Conversations on the Interior City], and two pamphlets, one an essay on Mallarmé, and the other a study of another of that writer's protégés, Jules Laforgue.

The preliminary pages of *L'Orient vierge* advertise four more volumes as forthcoming, including the author's next two books, the story collection *Les Clefs d'or* (1897) and another novel, *Le Soleil des morts, roman contemporain* (1898; tr. as *Sun of the Dead*). The latter is a quasi-autobiographical *roman à clef* which opens with the protagonist's first visit a literary salon run by an alter ego of Mallarmé, and is nowadays reckoned to provide a useful historical insight into the sociology and philosophy of the Symbolist Movement. Both books were presumably already complete, the dates of composition appended to *L'Orient vierge* indicate a significant gap between completion and publication, perhaps testifying to some hesitation on the part of the publisher. The list also includes *Parsifal ridicule, roman passionnel* [The Ridiculous Parsifal, a Love Story], which did not appear under that title; the alteration of the subtitle in the similar list includes in *Les Clefs d'or* to *roman contemporain* suggests that it was still in the process of evolution, and might well be the novel that eventually emerged as *L'Ennemie des rêves* [The Enemy of Dreams] (Ollendorf, 1900).

Mauclair went on write several more contemporary novels, *Etreindre* [Embracing] (1925) being his last, and also three further volumes of short stories, but the evolution of his fiction clearly illustrated the problems of adapting the techniques and philosophy of Symbolism to the novel, their much readier application being to poetry and to Baudelairean "poems in prose." Mauclair was by no means the only Symbolist whose later novels eventually abandoned all but a gloss of Symbolist theory and technique, and those of his generation who did not follow the example of Jules Laforgue, Alfred Jarry and Guillaume Apollinaire by dying young tended to followed the same trajectory as Mauclair, Gourmont and Henri de Régnier, inclining toward mundanity if never quite consenting to reach it.

Mauclair eventually dedicated himself entirely to nonfiction, much of it reflecting his journalistic career as a critic of art, literature and music, although he also published a number of travel books. His disenchantment with fiction, especially the kind of radical imaginative fiction that he produced in the first phase of his career, undoubtedly reflects the difficul-

8

ties he had in reconciling his literary ambitions with the prosaic demands of the novel—a struggle all too clearly evident in *L'Orient vierge*—but any desire he might have had to persist would have been obliterated in any case by hostile critical response and the increasing reluctance of publishers to repeat experiments of that sort, the prevailing wisdom being that too many readers found work of that kind too difficult to understand.

Symbolist writers in general were not renowned for the comprehensibility of their work, and Mauclair, as one of the most extreme, must have seemed to some readers to be the most difficult of all. Although *Couronne de clarté* is careful to include in its conclusion a detailed decoding of its allegory, some readers might have found the decoding as difficult to fathom as the visionary journey itself, and although *L'Orient vierge* is a much more straightforward text in terms of its presentation, and is deliberately cast as a novel of action, with elaborate descriptions of the key battles in the future war, it is not improbable that many readers sympathized with the stubborn practicality of the two villains, who cannot understand what the Idea with which the hero is so utterly obsessed actually is, let alone why it matters.

In fact, the attempt to graft an ideological quest, expressed in Symbolist terms, on to a future war story, creates a bizarre chimera that never comes remotely close to coherency, and the resultant novel one of many works of ambitious imaginative fiction whose reach manifestly far exceeds its grasp—but that is not necessarily a bad thing, however awkward the result, and there is no doubt that *L'Orient vierge* remains a fascinating hybrid. The author obviously found it hard to justify even to himself, and I have reproduced as appendices to the text the somewhat embarrassed apologetic prefaces that he attached to the 1897 and 1920 editions of the book.

The earlier preface seems surprising now in its apparent assumption that writing a book set in the future was a very unusual thing to do in the 1890s, even though the author was clearly aware of at least some of the future war novels whose

9

template he was borrowing. It is, however, possible that he did not read Jules Lermina's *La Bataille de Strasbourg* (serial version 1892; book version 1895)[1], the most significant "yellow peril" novel published in advance of his own, being content to borrow from newspaper reportage the alarmist tone that he adapted in order to modify it. His purpose is, in fact, to oppose the notion, albeit obliquely and half-hearted, by trying to divide its reflexive racism and reconcile one of the resultant fractions with the traditional French fascination with "the Orient" as a summation of lush exoticism and a repository of secret wisdom. That fascination had a particularly powerful influence on many of Mauclair's predecessors and contemporaries in the Romantic, Decadent and Symbolist movements, and his attraction to a project that might seem very peculiar from a more recent viewpoint, has a definite logic to it in the context of the *fin-de-siècle*.

The second preface vaguely claims credit for a measure of prophetic acumen, although any such claim is drastically undermined by the fact that Mauclair's image of the year 2000 includes hardly any technological innovations—none in everyday matters, and only enigmatic "gyroscopes" and aerostats firing "torpedoes" in the military context—thus remaining, in essence, a transfiguration of the 1890s only in a rather eccentric political sense. It is not obvious why that should have been the case, although Mauclair certainly seems to have been hostile to technological advancement, as evidenced by the mordant parable "La Mort mécanique" (in *Les Clefs d'or*, here translated as "Mechanical Death") and probably shied away from any elaborate extrapolation of that sort reflexively. He does claim in the first preface that his story is in some sense timeless, and thus not really futuristic at all, but that very claim calls into question the decision to employ the narrative device of a future setting.

---

[1] tr. as *The Battle of Strasbourg*, Black Coat Press, ISBN 978-1-61227-324-2.

The political history that the novel anticipates, in which a new Franco-German war is followed by the advent of a socialist internationalism that brings about a confederation of the European states, is virtually standard for the period in which the novel was written, and remained so for some time, although Mauclair's version is complicated by the assumption that socialism is a purely economic theory, requiring a further political sophistication by the subsequent triumph of Anarchism—a notion blurred by the conspicuous lack of any description of what Anarchist political organization might amount to, except for the somewhat surprising suggestion that it requires the appointment of a "dictator" and a council of ministers. In fact, by crediting Anarchism's accession to power to the strategic planting of bombs, the author seems to be pandering to the vulgar scarecrow image of Anarchists rather than referring to their actual political theories.

As with technological development, however, political development is not something in which the author is actually interested; his notion of progress is far more eupsychian than euchronian, and the point of his depiction of a European Confederation is not to map out its possible political evolution but to raise the question of what kind of ideology ought to provide it with a sense of identity and a spiritual goal. It is in that sense that the novel is still capable of striking a chord in today's very different historical circumstances, in which the crude and repulsive racism of Mauclair's attitude to the "yellow peril," the confused mysticism of his attitude to "secret India" and the flagrant nonsensicality of his notion of "Aryanism" are all manifestly absurd, and yet the nascent European Confederation that actually exists nevertheless seems vulnerable to the charge leveled by the novel that its domination by commercial and practical interests is both soulless and ultimately self-destructive. It is for that reason, rather than the novel's more ridiculous assumptions, that it was reprinted in 1979 and again in 2000, not simply as a historical curiosity or a specimen of Symbolist extravagance, but as a text whose manifest weirdness still retains a meaningful connection with ongoing processes of thought.

In order to set the translation of *L'Orient vierge* more fully in context within the author's output of imaginative fiction, I have included nine other fantastic stories in the present volume. Seven of them are taken from *Les Clefs d'or*, whose title story—first published in 1896 as "La Maison des clefs d'or"—is here translated as "The Golden Keys" The other two both appeared initially as books in spite of their limited wordage; *Le Poison des pierreries*, here translated as "The Poison of Precious Stones," was initially published in 1903, before being reprinted as the longest of the stories in *L'Amour tragique* [Tragic Love] (Calmann-Lévy, 1908). I have placed the stories from *Les Clefs d'or* before the three longer stories, not because I think that they were necessarily written earlier, although some of them surely were, but because they provide an easier introduction to the author's highly idiosyncratic mind-set, and thus help to illuminate aspects of *Couronne de Clarté* and *L'Orient vierge* that inevitably seem exceedingly odd to a reader approaching either without any advance warning of the central concerns to be addressed therein.

Like the prose work of many Symbolist writers, including Remy de Gourmont, Jean Lorrain and Marcel Schwob, Mauclair's short fiction took a great deal of inspiration from the work of Edgar Poe—or, more precisely, from Charles Baudelaire's translations of Poe—and his early work shows that influence clearly, as well as a determination—of which Poe would have approved thoroughly—to go further than any predecessor or contemporary in reaching for stylistic and thematic effects. There are few stories written in the 19th century that are more relentlessly peculiar than "Vie de la princesse Hérène" (tr. as "The Life of Princess Hérène") or "Le Démon du baiser" (tr. as "The Demon of the Kiss"), or which strive so hard for a novel *conte cruel* effect as "Lady Helena" or "Les Digitales" (tr. as "The Foxgloves").

The second of the two stories included here, "Le Regard dans l'infini" (tr. as "The Gaze into Infinity"), which was also placed second in the original collection, carries an author's note admitting that it is actually a variation of the first, and thus highlights the fact that although he was always striving to do something different, that had never been done before, there is also a sense in which he keeps doing the same thing over and over again, relentlessly pursuing the same quest to reach beyond the ordinary, groping for something that is essentially ungraspable within real experience, in spite of the teasing hints offered by art, music, and—above all—amour. Thus, there remains a sense in which *L'Orient vierge*, although it strives mightily for originality, not without success, is also, in a sense, a transfiguration of "Vie de la princesse Hérène." *Le Poison des pierreries*, which is the most conventional of Mauclair's Decadent fantasies, in its reliance on the standard theme of the eternal triangle and its conscientiously perverse eroticism, still retains many baroque images that recur repeatedly in the earlier works.

The most extreme of Mauclair's fantasies was undoubtedly *Couronne de clarté*, and although the Symbolist precursors most enthusiastically adopted by the Surrealists as their literary godparents were Jarry and Apollinaire, it is arguable that *Couronne de clarté* is the most obviously and intensely surreal prose work that the younger Symbolists produced in the course of their extrapolations. It remains stubbornly incomprehensible, in spite of its attempts to explain itself, but the sheer bizarrerie of the fantastic voyage featured therein has a definite charm, and its imagery is occasionally remarkable. The indicated dates of composition testify that Mauclair began work on *L'Orient vierge* almost immediately after finishing *Couronne de clarté*, and although he was clearly aiming for discontinuity in wanting to do something different, there are aspects of the novella that continue to haunt the novel in much the same way that the novel's hero is haunted, and the juxtaposition of the two works assists in the understanding of the psychological reactions that the hero of *L'Orient vierge* suffers in the course of his own fantastic voyage.

Although he was one of the more radical Symbolists in terms of his literary methods and concerns, the tastes that Mauclair displayed in his prolific art criticism now seem surprisingly conservative, never moving far beyond the work of the Impressionists and Symbolists who were already firmly established at the outset of his career, but that is not unusual. Whereas some of his other ideas now seem ahead of their time, others similarly seem to have been permanently stuck in the *fin-de-siècle*, although he did sometimes flatly contradict his earlier views in later essays; his view of women, in particular, seems to have been deeply confused and incoherent, some of his early essays exhibiting a blatant misogyny, while some of his later, more theoretically-inclined, ruminations on the subject of *amour* were applauded by at least some contemporary feminists.

The Anarchist sympathies that Mauclair displayed in *L'Orient vierge* attracted some criticism at the time, but any credit they won him on the political left was devastated when he collaborated with the Vichy regime during World War Two. He was old by then, and presumably thinking more about survival than political consistency, but the odd contrast does reflect a certain essential inconsistency and contradiction in his thinking. If he was not a convincing Anarchist, he was nevertheless a firm believer in the notion that the historical tide in Europe was flowing irresistibly in the direction of egalitarianism and libertarianism, and he is extremely unlikely to have sympathized sincerely with the Nazis on fundamental political grounds. *L'Orient vierge* clearly demonstrates that he had a strong sympathy with the ethnological racial theories that the Nazis adapted for their own purposes, but his interpretation of their significance is very different from theirs; he must have known perfectly well, although they might not, in claiming him as a sympathizer, that what he meant by the word "Aryan" and what they meant by it were two very different things.

What the works in this volume demonstrate very evidently, in fact, is that Camille Mauclair was a man apart, unaffiliated to any creed except that of wanting to rise above and go beyond what everybody else seemed to be doing. They demonstrate, too, that from the very beginning, he knew that he was not going to succeed, because the task was impossible—but he saw no reason why that ought to stop him giving it his best shot, at least to demonstrate and illustrate the fact of his difference, and his determination to sustain it.

The translation of *L'Orient Vierge* was made from the version of the University of Toronto's copy of 1897 Ollendorf edition, reproduced on the Internet Archive website at archive.org. The translation of the preface to the 1920 second edition of the novel was taken from the London Library's copy, which was also used in order to footnote some of the differences between the two versions. The translation of *Couronne de clarté* was made from the version of the University of Ottawa's copy of the 1895 Ollendorf edition reproduced on archive.org. The translations of stories form *Les Clefs d'or* were made from the London Library's copy of the 1897 Ollendorf edition and the translation of *Le Poison des pierreries* from the London Library's copy of the (undated) second printing of the Calmann-Lévy edition of *L'Amour tragique*.

Brian Stableford

THE GOLDEN KEYS

We are such stuff as dreams are made on,
and our little life is rounded with a sleep.

We arrived one evening in mid-September, my dear Fallea and I, having traversed the vast extent of heathland, salt-flats whose brilliant needles crackled beneath the hooves of our horses, clumps of pines strewn with purple-tinted rocks, marshes where the wind caused a population of reeds to babble, and irregular ponds, vestiges of a river drunk by the sandy ground. We were weary when we perceived the immense edge of the forest; a few bars of gold and rose floated nonchalantly in the middle of the humid sky, and the vapor of the late autumn was rising in the occident.

The avenue of poplars alternated in the canal with the series of its faithful reflections, and sinuously skirted the fixed mirror of the flat water all the way to the horizon, where the dusk inclined the indistinct faces of slowness of melancholy. Our inverted images were moving therein, already obscure; everything seemed simultaneously magnified and enfeebled by the silence, for our footfalls were muffled in the accumulated dust, and nature paid so little heed to us that our souls had difficulty breathing, and rose to the edges of our lips without daring to become visible.

But we had come into that forsaken landscape, whose very name was ill-defined, in search of solitude, after many passionate adventures and many harvests of pride; only ashen bitterness remained to us, and made us desire the simple fruits of a fresher and more intimate enclosure; we were in haste to descend into ourselves, to discover whether or not the prodigality of our blood had been totally ruined, and that nature full of savorous sorrows appeared alluring to us. When the chosen house appeared, at a bend in the canal, between the colonnades of poplars, we only experienced a confident sentiment before its façade, the placid desire for repose.

I only understood later, when everything was consummated, that the house contained graspable presages as soon as one crossed the threshold. But one never knows anything, and who can distinguish the real from the imaginary? Its aspect really was suited to our plans of retreat; situated in the depths of that abandoned region, it seemed to be its coagulated soul, concentrating its desuetude, even though it was not monotonous. Its windows, like circled eyes, the rich and undulating metalwork of its mildewed walls, its gallery filled with green-tinted shadow, and its dome whose sculptures had been thinned by time, gave us an impression simultaneously luxurious and extinct.

A semicircle of dark water branching from the canal bathed a part of the walls; they contemplated themselves therein, and the inverted edifice confronted the other obstinately, as if to reproach it for its ancient existence. The garden was disordered, and the arbors impoverished. Sunflowers, now rotten and black, swayed their leafless disks there feebly; the grayness of the sky had succeeded in extinguishing the insolent brightness of geraniums and tulips, and the flagstones of the cistern were disjointed among the mosses corroding the hinges and the pulleys.

The chimneys must have been cold for a long time, for the birds of the North no longer settled there, and fluttered around screeching. No one passed by, except exhausted and curbed haulers who only looked at the ground, and were already too weary themselves to feel sorry or the ennui of old neglected houses. That one had the air of a true widow, and was there to welcome the pilgrims that we were, disgusted by the routes of familiar life.

We went in, and as night fell, the lamps almost immediately sprang up like great luminous flowers, enlivening the woodwork and the gilt, stimulating sparkles on the fabrics for which they no longer hoped, causing the crystal to glitter, awakening a joy from the torpor of mortal shadows, with the consequence that the intimacy of life commenced for us immediately in that place. It is born more easily of artificial light than the light of the sky for beings who are their own confessors, and for those disenchanted dreamers, the lamp is a more familiar, more consoling and less severe witness. In any case, the necessities of life were not lacking; concerted cares had organized everything for a sojourn; we had specifically requested that only the exterior of the house should be left untouched, for we did not want to offend in any way the natural work of the weather and the autumn.

When Fallea and I found ourselves alone we sensed that, since our entry, a new period of life had begun, and we did not say anything for a long time. Every day, side by side, we had thought about what that refuge would be, and that insistence in representation had rendered us mute. For the time being, finding it in conformity with our wishes, we were already imagining what we would make of it. But they were interior projects that speech elucidates poorly, and we looked at one another violently, as if to refer only to our faces.

Fallea's was careworn, her tawny hair surrounding it heavily, and her fingers played slowly with the curls, while her eyelashes quivered over eyes that were not gazing anywhere. Eventually, however, she smiled, got up, came toward me, and, understanding that it was unnecessary to talk, kissed me like a child and headed slowly toward her room, looking at me over her shoulder. Her small head was inclined in the warm torsions of her abundant free-flowing hair, through which her eyes and mouth shone. Thus the first evening concluded.

In a few days, a regenerated existence developed for us, full of both force and meditation. We had until then overexcited our souls in the fêtes of the crowd and the thousand noisy and illusory events that are a parody of real life; but here, abandoned to themselves or put in the presence of a composite location, one might have thought that, purely by the choice of silence, they regained their purchase with an unexpected fervor and became almost material. We believed that we had reached a compromise, and they awakened more decisively. We drew them behind us like double shadows, glimpsed them on turning round, sensed their opacity rising like a vapor along mirrors, and our conversations were addressed, at the same time as one another, to those souls whose ornament and amour was our unique solicitude.

Fallea always displayed a passionate taste, abnormally beautiful in a woman, for the things of dreams and everything that is emblematic; speaking of mystery as a garden, and flowers and kisses as abstract arguments, she mingled the mental and the physical, and touched everything composing life with a little soul armed with tact and presentiments of an infinite subtlety.

For myself, in the disorder of a youth occupied with studies and elegantly profound lust, I had never forgotten to consult, behind the most seductive appearances, the essentially holy visages of life and dream that are the reference points of well-born souls, and which nothing can distract them from perceiving in hours of solitude. We had, therefore, singular conversations that would have disconcerted any fortuitous witness, so ardently were our metaphysical tastes satisfied therein. We brought the same fever to them as to pleasure, and often went so far in hypotheses that the words were too slow to catch up with the superhuman verity we were pursuing. We overturned them, we aided them with shivers, inflexions of the voice, and then rejected them impatiently, and the supreme palpitation of our thoughts swooned in a gaze.

In those superior games, Fallea contented a strange intellectual perversity; I believe now, when I look back at what happened, that we went too far and that she truly tempted that which is hidden too much. When one has her hair, her eyes and her youthful flesh, one does not descend with the insolent flower of voluptuousness into the crypts of meditation, which require visits more veiled and offerings less provocative. Happiness requires more cunning, more precaution in the sciences of thought; one does not constrain them, and around spirits devoid of modesty, drunk on the joy of understanding and the hope of knowing everything, incalculable reprisals are concerted by the immanent force of worlds...

But does one ever know when it becomes fatal to interrogate destiny, and can one foresee at what moment misfortune will enter with the science?

We rarely went out, the house and the water being almost sufficient for us, and what we could perceive of the sky when we leaned on the balustrade of the gallery. We lived, above all, with the lamps. Our strolls, however, sometimes took us along the canal, toward the plain, or into the first avenues of the forest. Only an ancient set of railings separated it from the thick bushes that terminated our garden; it was vast and very somber; its luxuriance offended us slightly, and we preferred to lose our gaze in the verdant half-light from the height of the windows. It limited our minuscule world, and we would not have dared to go deeply into it. Our slow and idle conversations unfurled more complaisantly in accord with the grassy banks and the reflections of the poplars, the geometry of which, troubled by great frissons, represented with exactitude the mixture of our reasoning and our passion.

Sometimes, too, we went out alone. At the end of the day, Fallea liked to distance herself. It was a girlish sentiment that gripped her; I believe that she went to weep, that she did not like to be seen, because she would not have found any words to express what she had felt. She communicated with the evening, and her enfevered soul, weighed down by presentiments, eased itself voluptuously in tears.

She came back from those confrontations with the dusk like a galleon laden with treasures and balms, of which one dream returning from the Orient and anchoring in an imaginary port. She was full of thoughts, and pale, and she often walked more rapidly on seeing me on the threshold, as if to tell me some news without delay. Then she threw herself into my arms without speaking, and for the sake of that delicious moment, I never opposed her isolation.

One evening, she stayed out late; I put a lamp on the per-
ron, for it was already dark, and she might have stumbled in
the garden. Finally, I saw her coming, indistinct and yet still
visible, and when she placed her head on my chest, I felt a
great tremor, and she murmured, so faintly that I could hardly
hear her:

"Perhaps I have been unfaithful to you; forgive me."

She was sobbing so forcefully that she fainted, and, in
the warm and luminous room into which I took her, was still
chilled by dew.

After a brief interval she calmed down.

"I had an encounter," she said. "Yes, a real encounter,
and yet there was nothing. How poor we are! We don't
know...."

And she resumed weeping.

I moved the light away and drew her to me, gently.

Then, her face turned toward the shadow, she spoke.

"I've seen Autumn this evening, like a child," she told
me, in a low voice. "I encountered him in the forest, as I was
coming back. A garland of bronzed leaves was leaning over
his forehead, and golden curls were tarnishing at his neck, and
there was born in his mysterious eyes an immense lassitude
and a supernatural desolation. But his lips were bloody and
alive, like the sun of the fortunate isles, and their gleam of life
cast a strange charm.

"He dared not say anything to me," she told me, "and I
dared not say anything to him. So we stood there motionless,
not knowing whether we existed or whether we were dreaming
our own shadows, black forms rising in the dusk. The red and
gold beacon wasn't trembling over the lock-gate; the towpath
was abandoned, the grass and the rock were mute. And we
considered one another fixedly. But in the end I understood
the meaning of all that silence, and that it was not an anxious
child before me but the profound Autumn himself, the taciturn, pagan and pure Autumn that one never sees.

"And then, as no one was present and he was so beautiful," she told me, "a singular desire came to me. And doubt-

less, he also wanted it, for he approached gently, caressing my eyes with his desperate eyes, and the leaves on his forehead quivered, and I was exquisitely chilled by anguish and by the evening. But as I awaited, my eyelids closed, the kiss of handsome Autumn, I only felt him lean over to place his burning lips, as bloody and alive as the sun of the fortunate isles, on my open hand.

"When I raised my eyes, I no longer saw anything; doubtless he feared my real lips. I heard a light flight in the darkness, and then I ran toward the threshold and I saw you waiting for me with the light. And since my hands have known the warm and moist kiss of Autumn, it seems to me that I have touched a mortal flower of flesh, whose ungraspable poison has desolated my entire soul—my entire little soul, my love—and I'm very afraid," she told me, in a whisper.

The shadows driven back by the lamp appeared more solemn, and I know not what supernatural chill entered. Fallea remained inert, and I, troubled by a special horror, drew her into the apartments and laid her on her bed. Her hands hung down; one of them was closed, and as I took it, in order to place it on her bosom, I saw something shining between the fingers.

It was a little golden key in the form of a crumpled leaf; it did not come from the house, and we did not know where it had come from.

After that, Fallea did not go out alone. The influence of the autumn had touched us, and I feared for the child as for myself the languid enervation of the reckonings and degenerations of nature in October. Everywhere, the tawny intensity of its colors was exasperated, and the great veils of the mist trailed over the singed and bright treetops. The leaves descended rather than fell; their light gilt-work floated in accordance with the wind, or tore away from espaliers like dead birds. An odor of damp and silence was born of the forest and the canal; between the illuminated branches the tarnished sun was like a forgotten fruit, and indecisive forms appeared at the extremities of paths or inclined over thresholds. The spectacles of the sky were delicate and fragile; the azure paled, and one saw a slight rosiness in the water, of clouds wandering transparently.

We went some distance from the house, at a slow pace, like convalescents, talking about the nonchalance of the late autumn and that sort of universal forgetfulness that distinguishes it. Everything—water, leaves and clouds—goes away gradually, toward one know not what; even the sun seems to be leaving, and souls have a desire to imitate it; one would think that nothing can any longer hold in place, that everything is descending to the other side of the earth in search of other dawns and unknown abundances.

Meditating on all that, we sometimes reached, by following the banks, a building whose toothless, jaundiced and almost human physiognomy captivated us, not without pity. Dislocated buoys lay beside it on the sand.

One afternoon, forgetful in the radiance of a feeble daylight, we sat down to watch a barge with rounded flanks that was coming along the canal. It was heavily laden and submerged to the level of the deck; its cabins, painted green and white, were pretty, and flowers were enlaced on trellises there. It advanced slowly, dragged from the shore, and silken patches deformed its image in the heavy rippling water.

Little girls were playing on the deck—but when they saw the sad building, they stopped, and they watched the ruin pass by, silently, with a finger over the lips and eyelashes troubled by the wind in their bright hair, as if they perceive a malevolent figure. The light died away, rain began to fall unhurriedly, and we returned.

That day, we had a sensation of forgetfulness. The bleak lake, the indifferent boat, the anxious eyes of the little girls, the leaves, the bare walls and the scent of exile impressed us; everything was truly going away, and we no longer knew whether we might have emerged from ourselves slightly, to be a little absent ourselves. We spoke very sparsely, and Fallea, who had been feeling ill for several days, was more feverish.

I spent the night by her bedside; she was slightly delirious in her sleep. Toward daybreak, she opened her eyes and I kissed her—but she looked at me with astonishment and said to me: "How changed you are! Is it still you?"

Her voice had changed itself; she was interrogating me as if in a dream.

"Nothing has changed in me," I said, smiling. "I'm still the same, and I love you."

"No, no," she said, "there's something...it seems to me that I've forgotten...truly forgotten..."

"What have you forgotten, little innocent? You're still asleep, you're not seeing clearly."

"Oh, yes, I can see clearly, but I've forgotten, forgotten...I don't really know...I believe that I'm not very well. Everything is spinning like a ring...forgetfulness has the form of a ring..."

She went to sleep as she said that; the light of dawn made objects more distinct. I took a few paces in the room; I looked outside; then I sensed another presence, and I came back to the bed.

At the instant when my eyes descended toward the thick golden hair that divided over Fallea's forehead, it seemed to me that I saw a jewel scintillating there. My fingers moved a curl aside, and I touched a little golden key surmounted by a sculpted ring.

An indescribable depression stunned my soul. I went out without making a sound and went to put the unfamiliar key with the first one, in a hidden casket. I walked in the garden for a while, not knowing whether I was alive or whether I had died of fright.

The trees were very visible now, and the cold morning air was shivering in a pink mist.

The late autumn advanced, the presages of the end increasing implacably. What more can I say about my destiny, what commentary can I add to the evidence of woe? That day, I understood everything that was going to happen, and the health of my beloved would have told me if I had still been in doubt, for her decline was rapid.

When she awoke, she told me that, at the moment when she had gone to sleep again, she had felt a kiss of her eyes. I told her that my mouth had touched her, and I did not mention the key to her. But I knew full well that possession of her eyes had been taken by the same invisible lips that had previously brushed her hands in the forest at nightfall, and I knew that someone had come, immaterially, into our solitude and our dreams, and I waited in secret.

With the days of the glacial November, Fallea appeared more diaphanous; her pure and passionate visage attained expressions whose harmonious subtlety cannot be revealed by words. She was united with the crystal of the landscape; her eyes no longer gazed and her hands no longer grasped, but something vaporous was born in her, and even the designs of her dresses were no longer differentiated, on her body, from iridescent ornamentations of frost. She was an apparition, a pretext of the spirit that was in progress, and whose presence was gently benevolent. She was silent, as if knowing everything, and in her infinitely distant gaze particular certainties were reflected.

Sometimes I contemplated her almost without sadness, so confused was she with nature and the hours. But sometimes, too, I choked with sobs and turned away in order to go and cry to the walls of my closed room the immense incomprehension and the furious revolt of my sentiments...

It finally came, the day when my Fallea vanished into death. And everything happened so simply! It seems that those crises would drive emotions to a paroxysm, disrupting everyday life, and suddenly, the disaster itself arrived without fuss, and everything settled like a cloth, into a kind of exhausted calm. I saw the child's supreme gaze, I seized its gleam, her lips stirred as if to summon mine, and I leaned towards them without dying of despair.

All my senses, on the contrary, were intensely alive, and the fatigue of the nights had excited them further.

When my lips were about to touch Fallea's for the last time I felt a light breath, but it was not hers! It was a breath that interposed itself between ours, and which came from the invisible. And it stole my kiss, because I stopped momentarily, retained by I know not what diabolical force, and in that instant Fallea's mouth was touched by that other breath, and her life went away with it completely, and I only brushed, a second afterwards, the lips of a corpse...

I straightened up, and, by virtue of an inexplicable counsel, my hands wandered mechanically over the face, neck and breasts of the woman who was no more. As my fingers disturbed a pleat in her corsage, something slid within the silk directly over the heart, and my fingernails collided with a hard object, which suddenly gleamed. It was a little golden key, in the form of a cross.

I quit the house of love and death when the candles had been extinguished. In Fallea's tomb the three golden keys were placed, by my wish, as an obol was once placed to par for entrance to the eternal darkness.

At present my life can become whatever the monotony of hazard pleases, and a singular indifference is somnolent over all my thoughts. But I also know the meaning now of those three keys of Autumn, Forgetfulness and Death, which entered the soul of my child of bounty, and I know how the three emblematic specters, by way of her hands, her eyes and her lips, by way of her forehead and her heart, entered impatiently to steal that sweet little mortal existence! I have buried in her coffin, with her dear body, the keys to her life, the autumn leaf, the ring of forgetfulness and the cross of paradise—and perhaps, with her, they will open the Invisible.

As for me, I remain on the edge of myself, contemplating my stolen happiness drawing away, like a jewel descending very slowly in exceedingly dense water, gradually fading, and circling in successive spirals and rings toward the somber, infinite wells of despair and silence.

THE GAZE INTO INFINITY[2]

The house where we came to savor autumn and solitude was situated on the edge of a great forest, he said to me, one evening, and it was Nora that had desired it thus. From the wooden balcony our gazes lost themselves in the half-light of foliage or floated toward the violet plain, according to whether we were leaning on the sill of the eastern window or the western, in such a way that a verdant obscurity filed the rooms turned toward the east and those lit from the west were bathed in a bright light. That disposition pleased our souls; following their joy or their penchant for sadness, we reposed in the light appropriate to our thoughts. The windows were their confidants ad sufficed to signify the extreme dissimilarities of our passions and our dreams.

You have never come to that house, he continued, and I am almost unsure as to whether I ever really lived in it. But it is such a vain fatigue to want to be sure of what is real! One knows nothing. At times, I believe that the house did not exist; at other times, I hesitate; but I always see it with clarity.

In the grounds, the old woman who served us walked with precaution; bent over, she slipped between the flower-beds, along the paths, skirting the hedge. The pulley of the well was mute; the espaliers were heavy, seemingly full of lassitude, and the flies danced, quivering, against the windows. The masses of red and golden fruits no longer attracted them; one might have thought that they had ended up loving something other than the light. The crystals in the penumbra lit up their little braziers of tremulous enchantment, and scintil-

---

[2] Author's note: "This story is a version of the previous one, briefer and more exclusively intellectual. It appeared to us that it might not be without interest to juxtapose these two versions sharing the same idea."

lated like eyes devoid of thought; the designs of the carpet led our dreams into sinuous forgetfulness, in incessantly complications endlessly curling back upon themselves and repeated in restricted ornaments.

At the hour when the eastern rooms were dark and those of the west allowed the long horizontal rays of the ailing sun to enter through their bays, the lamp, with its luminously tender gauze, brought more joy. It was the moment when Nora's ashen hair commenced to be admirable. She let it fall feely over her shoulders, in such a way that, when she picked up a book, all I saw of the dear inclined fringe was a stream of pink gold.

We very rarely went outside; the view of the plain sufficed for us, and the violent vitality of the forest troubled us a little.

Nora was strange, disposed to philosophy with a rare and subtle power, such as one never encounters among women, and you know that I have always had a taste for what is hidden. Thus we lived, edifying our happiness on inconceivable affinities that the amour sufficient to fill ordinary hearts does not provide. Our conversations were astonished. I loved Nora in those moments of exaltation when the gaze alone reveals the upheaval of the soul, when the course of the dialogue, aiding with its mutual replies the elucidation of something difficult, leads to the glimpse, in a flash, if a truth that words can never sketch. While gazing at me, her eyes, supported by mine, penetrated the shadow of another being beyond me, which one might have thought concealed by my self.

She had the double vision of veritable mystics, the gaze that seems to live between two pupils, one of which considers clearly the visage of life, while the other, the more remote, contemplates, though the first, with an unknown disturbance, the immaterial visage of pure ideas. Nora also mingled within her, like the mystics, voluptuousness and dreams. She could not separate them; in her, the most violent physical enjoyment was entirely mental, just as she brought to the sensuality of the mind an intuition aided by extraordinarily keen senses. She was one of those for whom the physical and the mental are two indiscernible elements dissolved in a single harmony, and our conversations were terminated by love-making in which nothing appeared to us to be shocking or discontinuous.

I believe that we went too far, he said to me, in a whisper. I believe that we went further than is permitted to happiness, and that is the cause of what happened. Solitude left our minds too fee; there is no durable peace without some banality and some disturbance. I had certainly thought about that during the first weeks, after certain evenings when the union of our thoughts was pursued in our kisses with such force that we were left exhausted, as vibrant as violins that are about to break. But Nora was simultaneously so ardent in those emotions, and so normally equilibrated in her mind and her body, that my presentiments faded away.

If only there had been a rupture then, a discord or a malaise! Fear would have stopped us. But nothing happened, and truly, I was able to believe that it was given to us, among all beings and for ourselves alone, to touch surprising beauties. Truly, I am not responsible...

Listen now to how Nora died in my autumnal house, how the greatest injustice, or at least the most enigmatic will, of nature demanded that she die, he told me, dejectedly.

Our constant solicitude was for the sky; we spent hours following the play of the clouds in the light or watching descend from the zenith and rise from the horizon those violet tinted mists and those gardens of gold and rose that unite in mid-air slowly to efface the declining day. The combinations of the clouds were familiar to us, and their lines, in which we had first learned to divine the next day's weather, had then revealed images to us and unknown analogies with the things of the earth, mirages and bizarre duplications of objects and material beings, of which you might perhaps be able to read in the notes we made in a few albums, if I have the courage to collate them in order to publish them some day.

But it was, above all, the empty nocturnal sky, with its brilliant fires and its lakes of sapphirine obscurity that impassioned us. We considered it long into the night, and often got up again in order to look at it. She, above all, awoke with a start, as if the stars were summoning her, wanting to be seen.

I perceived increasingly that Nora had the malady of infinity.

I don't know whether the words I've just pronounced are intelligible, but I can't speak any more clearly. It was a hyperphysical illness that left no trace, and which was not madness, but which wore away internally. I divined a perpetual, mute, unconscious and immense effort of that soul to escape the body and touch the universal object of its thought. It was a hidden struggle that rendered her, in appearance, more calm, and on those days her beauty attained heights of serenity that I had never seen in her. At times, I doubted that I had before me a being made of the same particles as us, even though she was very much alive. But that impression mingled within me with an increasing dolor and admiration, and I resolved to be sparing with amour in order to conserve it.

The most dangerous precaution of all! We never know what it is necessary to do in the presence of the soul, and Nora's spiritual malady was only augmented. I could not prevent her from dreaming and attaching herself to the spectacle of the sky and the night. She arrived at the point of living exclusively through her eyes, of acting mechanically in all the rest. But all that was extremely dissimulated, ungraspable; it brushed my ideas without precision, for you might be astonished that I didn't take her away, and deliver her for her salvation to the beneficent contact of the vulgar. I only saw all that later...

That evening, the evening when it happened, there had been nothing extraordinary, until everything was suddenly accomplished. She was standing on the balcony, and I was sitting next to her, holding her hands, while she was gazing at the stars. The weather was very clear, and it must have been a long time that had been absorbed in the rotation of the infinite, when, not daring to break the silence or make her any reproach, I kissed her hands and kept them on my lips. But she didn't move, and, after a moment, I raised my head. She was stiff, and her forehead was turned upwards, and she was so motionless that I was afraid.

Finally, I said: "Can't you look at me, Nora?"

Then I sensed against me, coming from her entire body, a strange, violent, mortal, interior tremor, as powerful the stirring of a world. And it seemed to me that her voice came from millions of leagues away, her unknown voice, which replied in a whisper:

"I can't, any longer."

Oh, what a terror there was in that voice, and yet, mingled with I know not what inexplicable ecstasy! My lips returned to her hands, and I remained leaning over thus, still listening to the uncanny tremor that was passing from her flesh into mine. My tears flowed over Nora's fingers.

"Can't you feel that I'm weeping over your hands?" I said to her. "Look at me."

"Why won't you come yourself, my love?" she said. "I want so much to kiss your eyes, but I can't, any longer. I know that your tears are wetting my fingers, but I can't stop looking up there! I believe I'll never be able to—they'll never come down again, my eyes. My gaze has been stolen...*and it's in the process of being taken.*"

Penetrated to the depths of my soul by an icy horror, I surrounded my beloved with my two arms, and I leaned over the balustrade in order to look up at her eyes. They were staring and immense, and all the stars were reflected therein as in the polar lakes, but there was no longer anything in their gaze known to humanity.

Then I stood up before that insensible statue, in order to put my presence between her and the thief of the infinite, but, at the instant when the opaque show of my visage covered her luminous face, and when my gaze placed itself on hers, I sensed a fracture...yes, I had just broken the double golden thread of life and dream that linked my Nora's eyes to the heart of the eternal sky!

And between my futile hands, at that very second, she dissolved into death.

MECHANICAL DEATH

I want to retrace, he said to me, what happened to me on the Isle of Wellbeing, which caused me to flee therefrom. Now that I have rediscovered faces in which a simple emotion appears, and I can breathe under natural suns, I can think about it without terror.

Imagine—for this participates in dream—a land where avid human genius has been able to stand up against death such as your race has always known it. On the Isle of Wellbeing, the scientist could cure all diseases, and repair damaged organs; even old age, reanimated by irresistible cordials, no longer extinguished. All wounds were closed, all wear and tear compensated, any weakness of the body divined by translucent rays remedied without delay, with the result that the return of humans to darkness seemed driven back beyond the normal time, and matter no longer seemed to want to become inanimate again.

Nature was humbly domesticated; machinery was the uncontested master of life. Chemistry and the science of magnetisms possessed all the sources of force, and analysis decomposed the unknown. In minuscule volumes, extraordinary engines ensured nourishment, prevented desire, banished fatigue. Thought, acting on the instrument, was the sole human force that had to be employed, and the brain watched in the body alone, led the universal entente of mechanical forces alone.

Everywhere, silent electricity intervened in the name of the individual. We had in our hands all the wellbeing that the enslavement of terrestrial powers can offer to an ideally scientific humankind. How can I give, by means of metaphors, an idea of those vast cities of steel, where metallic vegetations, of a greater tenuity than that of real leaves, distributed a delightful shade, unassailable by the seasons; those cities where even the propensity for reverie was encouraged by secret aromatic inhalations born at will from the walls of those aluminum palaces; of those evenings enriched by artificial stars; those triumphal domes where heat, light and perfume sprang forth by mans of industrial refinements; of those vast unknown fleets that soared in rapid and luminous flight in the highest spheres of the sky?

Such quotidian prodigies cannot be described, and humans, in the Isle of Wellbeing, would have rediscovered, by dint of art, the veritable Eden, if the perfection of their souls could have followed that progressive conquest over the mute resistance of miserly nature.

But it was not to be thus. Some of us hoped that that refinement of life, pushing back the limits of hideous misery, would give birth to a greater mental energy, and that, by means of the admirable aid of science, humans would feel freer to occupy themselves with their souls. Alas, beneath the material triumph that exalted under the star and the clouds the dominating and subtle genius of inventors and intellectuals, the cancer of ennui and decadence was wearing away, as among barbarians in decline, the morality of crowds. Material enjoyment carried everyone away, and under the ostentation of the supreme civilization, an abominable stagnation extended.

The soul of the people believed that it had nothing to do, for people had not consented thus far to put their minds and their energy to work except to procure external comfort. With that, the goal of life appeared to be attained, and we flattered ourselves vainly that people would finally recognize that the conquest of matter was a means of progressing spiritually. The national soul remained inert; but it began to feel strangely sick.

The deadly odor of moral decadence oozed through the richest spectacles of the cities. Even the covetous, who had once created interested actions, a competition that was perhaps beautiful, felt oppressed by Wellbeing, and ennui stammered its monotonous and bitter complaint in the depths of hearts. Even lust and debauchery were no longer sufficient to delight ordinary souls, and none of them turned toward books and dreams. The rare thinkers felt more alone than in any other place on earth.

Humanity was somnolent among the machines that made everything for it; through the thick slumber of quotidian life, strange shudders were felt. Crime, no longer inspired by immediate interest, took on unusual and disconcerting forms. Wars could no longer occur, the island being inaccessible and possessing everything that it might have usurped from foreign nations. The consequence was that everything began to spin in a circle of futile affectations, a deplorable and paltry game of bizarrerie and lassitude.

People approached one another, saying: "Do you lack anything? We don't know what to demand? We'd like to give ourselves difficulty for some reason or other. How do you pass the time?"

Or: "It's funny how one feels that there's a lack of something when one has acquired everything. Is that progress? We're confronted by the void. Something has to happen. It's not amusing to have nothing to do except to think about nothing. What do you think? The shadow of the end is prowling the land."

And the yawn became the ruler of faces.

At length, a perversity was born, demanding its share of pain, voluptuously disturbing the intolerable Wellbeing. The flood of machinery created beneath our feet a terrible ant-hive of forces, a scientific volcano ready to erupt—and the temptation to provoke it grew with the ennui of souls, in order that at least something would happen about which one could care, which would reanimate sobbing or laughter, which would bring back to mind the mirage of great blind fatalities.

That infantile perversity, of ruining the plaything ardently desired, developed secretly, without anyone daring to talk about it. The bankruptcy of material wellbeing was decreed in the silent collapse of individual dreams. And suddenly, little accidents began to occur. Electric wires were found linked to others, by error or malevolence. Dosages were falsified, mechanisms paralyzed, explosions and breakages cast long sprays of human blood into the city.

No serious search was made for those responsible; the people were impassioned for a few days, and drank the horror as well as the catastrophes, as an intoxicating wine that their blasé souls could enjoy.

Gradually, however, the disorder increased, and the hatred of the anonymous machines, whose quivering mastered the nerves, also increased, with a intensity that no longer calmed down. Humans, embarrassed by their innumerable slaves of steel and fluids, lost their heads and their direction, no longer wanting to make use of them.

At that moment, strange prophets began to penetrate into houses and speak to passers-by in the squares. With violent and obscure images, they preached a grim faith in simplicity, they spoke of a retrograde religion, and launched anathema against the machines that instilled sloth in the heart and disorganized the genius of activity. They came from the country and had passed over rivers and seas. They cried that wellbeing is an interior and mental flower, and that it was necessary to break all the bonds that attached humans to the earth. They seemed powerful and beautiful.

The women followed them first. The desire for debauchery had left them with a voluptuous animality and preserved their soul from scientific desiccation. With the prophets, they ran to the apparatus that centralized force. A tumult and a horrible confusion followed.

The magnetic network that acted in the houses and underlay the streets, attained in many places, burst with a sinister frenzy. One by one, the accumulators exploded, and the lights went out in the immensity of the city. An unforgettable night passed among the conflagrations, the vibrations of the unleashed electricity and the howls of joy and terror of revolutionaries who perished in thousands in torrents of blood and fire. Colonnades of flame oscillating in the darkness sustained above the capital the illusory palace of dreams of the new dawn, flamboyant on the clouds.

Humankind, braced against its own fatal genius, stumbled over like into the oblivion of that single night. Books and works, the keys to the detested inventions, burned with the rest in the irremediable folly of the deliverance. The mechanical world collapsed from the full height of its prodigious elevation by virtue of the convulsive fury of humans reverted to their primitive nature.

In the morning, the gigantic skeletons appeared of the factories, and amid the rubble, the gaping ditches, the desperate arms of machines twisted by the fire, the heaps of cadavers agglutinated by streams of molten metal, the chaos of chains, of wires, of beams and wheels, we fled toward the vegetation beyond the suburbs, toward the peaceful streams, toward the forests and toward the seas, and in order to go back to the simple the simple life we freed our panting souls from that lugubrious memory, considering, with the fervor of the first man and the first woman, the immortal sun that was rising into the middle of the sky.

THE LIFE OF PRINCESS HÉRÈNE

A frightful storm burst over Vallyria, the capital of Tauronesia, on the day when Princess Hérène was born there. Fiery signs surrounded the parks, turbulently, and an entire population of unknown terrifying lights descended from the sky. A molten bolide flew with grew velocity over the surface of the grand canal, setting fire to ships, and disappeared under the arch of a basin that plunged underground; it was heard smashing in the obscure depths, and the city was convulsed by it.

The tumultuous rain lasted for six hours, and the red rays of an unusual sun mingled its vertical sheets with blood. Many Tauronesians were killed; it was a day of celebration, and the bewildered corteges were dispersed, abandoning cadavers still flowery and clad in white, the faces of which, seared by fulgurant sulfur, were horrific.

The shock of the scourge was so sudden that the followers fled in the first moment of panic, leaving the queen alone in the depths of her apartments. She lay there exhausted, the vast and sinister lights giving her delirium, and when they came back, they did not find her. She had dragged herself out of bed; she was perceived, diaphanous in her lace, at the extremity of a terrace; she raised her arms, emitting bursts of laughter; the downpour chilled her; her tawny hair twisted like a crazed flag. When they took hold of her and brought her back to her room, she died after a brief interval without having recovered her reason.

Little Princess Hérène remained in the care of her uncles, for her father was already deceased. Those lugubrious presages inaugurated her life with a pitiless warning; it was observed that she was strangely pale, and the roses of infancy and joy were never seen in her face. She was like ivory, with gray eyes that were incessantly veiled by eyelashes inwardly curved like a bird's wing, and there was, in total, something forbidding and reticent about her.

As soon as she could be suspected of consciousness, she manifested a violent taste for solitude, and she could not be persuaded to interest herself in games or take pleasure in the company of little girls.

Her desires were mysterious and rare. In the vast galleries of the palace she was a familiar and omnipresent shadow. She was perceived on balconies, with a finger over her mouth, gazing at the crowns of the trees in the park, or the horizon of the sea, which could be seen from the opposite façade.

She loved the stairways of the towers, the tortuous spirals that led through obscurity to the blue sky burning the balustrades of terraces. She composed strange soliloquies; she was heard talking at night in the unconsciousness of sleep, and in the morning her eyes often seemed to have reflected that which does not belong to the earth.

Because of these indications, her uncles, who hated her and coveted the throne, believed her to be mad, and did not imagine that a murder, anticipating the work of dementia, was necessary to hasten their projects. Thus, Hérène grew up without menaces, and her soul educated itself without human involvement.

Her taciturnity served her well; she lived nearer to things than to people, and learned more therefrom. A familiarity immediately mingled majesty with the counsels brought to her by the forest, dusk, the sea, silence, and all the things that are weakened by the commentary of words. She sensed that she was part of them, and progressively came to know their special life, concentrated by will in their apparent impassivity, the mysterious tissue that links them to what we perceive.

The parks, especially, touched her. Their visages, changing with the seasons, were divined by her own. Spring with ringed eyes, summer simultaneously welcoming and imperious, tender autumn, when the springs spoke to her, and unquiet and ailing winter summarized exactly the periods of her adolescence, which accorded with them and found their example therein. The watercourses, capturing the symmetrical reflection of branches confronted by them, taught her an interior tranquility, which a sudden sadness could nevertheless trouble as rapidly as a gust of wind can break up the images on the surface of a canal.

For long hours, lying in the grass or beside the water, the young Hérène studied the thousand tragedies whose enormous and minuscule landscape is a clump of reeds, and of which scarcely perceptible insects are the ferocious and active princes. When the last ray of horizontal sunlight mingled its soft fatigued roses with the crystal of the corners of pools, and slowly caressed the narcissi and the nenuphars, the entire nascent soul of the princess filled with a voluptuous and enigmatic melancholy. She remained immobile and attentive, anxious on sensing enter into her entire being the supreme sigh of the nameless and free life that is the supreme inspiration of noble souls. She returned paler, her lips quivering, as if her heart were about to appear there, finally surging from within her for an unknown revelation. Then she calmed down and sat down without saying a word.

By night, the mystery of the windows and doors that one passes by, behind which there is everything and nothing, and which allow alternate dreams of terror and pity, the mystery of simple objects and natural things, penetrated her to the depth of her dreams. She sometimes went out in the moonlight; she did not fear it, even in its most fantastic interventions; the unusual forms that it reveals at the extremity of deserted pathways, the bizarre faces it animates in the blue-tinted mist, the mirages and the metamorphoses that it provokes, represented for her a flavorsome life, light and unthreatening.

Hérène often went, through a labyrinth of lawns and bushes whose ancient order charmed her, to seek afar, in a little pavilion, favorite peacocks that could only tolerate her presence. They were seductive and extraordinary fêtes, those evenings of golden moonlight in which she was alone, frolicking with them. The great sacred birds displayed their tails in the taciturn light, and came to her without screeching. The living and sumptuous orb of heir plumage displayed ocellate pupils to the mystic star, which shone like precious stones endowed with thought. From everywhere, those vast tremulous and silky expansions surged forth in response to the princess's appeal. Lying back in the flowers, bathed by diffuse light, she let her hands wander in the plumes, her fingers collecting imaginary jewels there, and the supernatural fans of their circles soothed her face with the warmth of the nocturnal summer. It was an aristocratic and rare coquetry that suited the girl with the pale cheeks.

One night, when she was asleep in her room, leaving her windows open, a singular rustling woke her up, and she saw great shadows around her, mingled with patches of light made by the reflection of trees. It was her peacocks. They had finally come to her, having crossed the balustrade and come in; and around the bed, and even on the wooden bed-head, they silently unfolded their glorious shields of aquamarine, silver, sapphire and nacre, like a royal guard, an elite among all the armies of the land of enchantment, to protect the slumber of the precious child with magnificence.

Such were the spectacles that ornamented the childhood of Princess Hérène.

Later, music and books impassioned her. The languor of oriental melodies described to her more delicately the landscapes she had loved. She learned, in that art in which silence is painted with sound, to link her thoughts with nature. The tales that she read revealed existences and passions that she had not yet envisaged, and informed her that beyond the blue mountains that limited Tauronesia, the cerebral world continued in accordance with vast and changing caprices. She communicated with the horizon and the sad and admirable spectacle of the extent.

The dominating blood that she had inherited from a long cortege of princes murmured within her its immanent desire for distant conquests; the instinct that had pushed her, as a little girl, to climb to the top of the towers and to wander by night far from the counsels of the palace, grew and become violently precise. She dreamed of seeing high and far, and creating a sumptuous and solitary life of voyages; in a few months, that idea made surprising progress in her, but no one knew anything about it. Her pallor, her haughty expression, her reserve, a childhood devoid of smiles and kisses, and the latent peril of her conspiratorial uncles, all collaborated in enveloping her soul and her designs in an impenetrable obscurity; from the very first hour she had accustomed her soul to secrecy.

Books, after the tales, touched her intelligence; she entered into them without hesitation. Their alchemy seduced her armed thought, the dreams of philosophers fortified her own dreams, defining them, and all of her will went in a single direction. It was at that moment—she had reached her sixteenth year—that the ritual distancing of child princes customary in Tauronesia came to an end for her, and she was shown to the people.

She appeared in Vallyria with luxury and sustained a hundred thousand impatient and ardent gazes; the crowds hastened to see her from the crests of hills. Her galley floated over the canals in the sunlight, amid the banners, the censers and the fanfares. Clad in black, in memory of the late princess, her mother, but sparkling with silver ornaments that further increased the pallor of her beauty, the mute Hérène felt herself touched by those innumerable eyes, remembered her peacocks darting their pupils around her, and, smiling, suddenly opened her curved eyelashes wide, and subjugated the breathless congress of her race with that single flash.

The cold and shiny sculpted corselet that undulated over her bosom almost made her a warrior; her strange adornment of blue-tinted stones, mingled with the gleam of metal armor and her nacreous and icy flesh, revealed her as a conqueror, looming over Vallyria, over the sea, over the Tauronesia that she inclined with a gesture, a dominatrix with a smooth forehead, in which the thrust of eagles exalted. The public acclamation was like an age-old awakening: a visage of flame incarnated the glorious faces of ancient kings; one sensed that the celebrated sword of the Tauronesian princes had been taken up again for the astonishment of the world.

The girl who had been born under such a sinister star seemed, by the effort of her solitary will, to have rejected the fatality of her existence, and tamed fate. In the dusk, hope irradiated the oriflammes of the sovereign galley, and made Vallyria sparkle with joyous flames; triumph burst forth in a barbaric and sonorous pomp, and a future grandeur was presaged thereby.

That same night, the uncles of the predestined penetrated into the palace in order to kill her, but they did not find her in her apartments. She had fled through the gardens, and they heard a great clamor to the north of the city and the blast of trumpets. By the light of torches they were seized themselves and dragged with a party of nobles through a furious populace that invaded the palace. They were thrown at the feet of Princess Hérène, grim and armed.

Divining their project, she had taken the living genius of her beauty, and the burning gaze that contained the word, to the crowd, still impressed, and all of them—soldiers, women or priests—had returned with her to her criminal kin. In the darkness traversed by torchlight, the revolution sprang forth, a battle was engaged between the partisans of the princess and those of her uncles, who defended themselves desperately; it was necessary to massacre them, and thus death intervened in the birth of the sovereign's glory, as it had intervened in her first birth.

On the throne, the victorious Hérène crowned her will.

Tauronesia knew, thanks to her, a prosperity and order for which it had never dared to hope. Ambassadors appeared; Oriental fleets announced, among the homages and the offerings, the fearful respect of distant archipelagoes. Promises of splendor made by prophets were brought; illustrious swords and invincible standards inclined.

One day, the watchers on the high towers of Vallyria saw the cavalries of Scythia galloping in a golden dust. Thomyris, who had vanquished Cyrus, was mandating to Princess Hérène the elite of her amazons of the terrible arrows, and she called her sister.[3] Caravans, from the Persian Gulf to Taurus, brought her the sumptuousness of their presents. Everyone bowed down to her renown.

She remained pensive, soberly dressed and pale. Finally, she made up her mind; the blood of the ages and the race spoke more loudly than anything else, and she orientated Tauronesia toward the conquest of the North.

The unknown of the icy plains haunted her. They alone could still seduce that virgin soul, which the languor of odorous dusks and the soft sumptuousness of the fatherland had not touched. The preoccupation of the North and the Occident, where the seas took on a different hue, triumphed over the seduction of the eternally blue sky. Its azure penetrated Princess Hérène with the special sadness that prolonged serenity engenders; she dreamed of distracting herself before a variable nature. She assembled armies on her frontiers, constrained allied populations, and bristled in the center of Asia an immense union of blades and flags, and finally departed with that cortege of peoples to find an unknown intoxication.

For some time she followed the ancient roads trodden by the cavalries of Timur and the Amurats, brought into subjection the cities of purple and the cities of nacre, lingered on the Persian promontories, and led her horses toward the Caspian regions, in the monotonous extent of which humans are sparse.

---

[3] Although Hérène's realm is an invention of the present author, Thomyris was allegedly an ancient empress of the 6th century B.C., who was indeed rumored to have killed Cyrus the Great, although even Herodotus, who initially recorded the datum, suggests that it might be apocryphal. Her association with the amazons, of whom she was sometimes represented to be the queen, was an elaboration added by much later writers. Mauclair would have seen Gustave Moreau's painting of Thomyris, which might have inspired his own extravagant exercise in fakelore.

Then she turned resolutely toward Europe, and after many mountains and many plains, she finally encountered the Barbarians.

Her weapons shone in the forests of Dacia; they knew the flights of arrows of the Arimaspi, the breastplates of whose captains suddenly sounded.[4] The cold wind that made the pines shiver and convulsed the surfaces of sad lakes awoke a new vivacity in her heart; after the capture of lacustrian cities she swam with her soldiers and whirled her ax without knowing the fear of death.

The burning forests dressed her with gold and blood, colored her ivory flesh and hallucinated her eternally lucid eyes, when she galloped therein on the evenings of her victories, hurling torches at the retreating enemy. The gray dawns paled, in a sinister fashion, over the ruddy smoke rising from wooden cities; over the interminable roads, across the violet heathlands and salt-marshes, among the sandstones and granites with eroded faces, rolled innumerable squadrons driving captives and carts. From the tenebrous bosom of the oaks and beeches of Saxony, melancholy oracles stammered at the passage of the Oriental conquest. The rumble of battalions on the march troubled the bleak and anxious landscapes; potholes impregnated with rain caused the catapults to swerve. The taciturn sterility of Pomerania appeared to the Tauronesians as an impoverished and somber imitation of the luminous deserts of sand where the sun is master, which they had crossed in Asia.

By all that, Hérène was impassioned. What complex dreams visited her great soul during the evenings when she wandered on the shores of the Baltic, in the mists, keeping watch over the narrow straits for the fleets to be chartered that

---

[4] The Arimaspi were a legendary people of what was, to Herodotus, the far north; their battle against the griffins in the Hyperborean lands was apparently recorded in a poem by Aristeas of Poroconessus, which is only known through Herodotus' second-hand account of it.

would carry her toward the Pole! No woman had ever been so glorious, but glory was already insufficient for her dream. Strange desires to overturn the order of things penetrated her; the power of her sword caused her to disdain the victories, the assaults seemed tedious to her, the triumphal entrances and the hymns of the army on the evenings of the surrender of cities left her indifferent.

The attraction of the North signified to her a struggle with the elements, the unprecedented audacity of an abnormal empire over natural laws. The union, under her scepter, of the sun and the snow seduced her. The veils were not parting rapidly enough for her liking; the indispensable delays irritated her fever.

Finally, they came, those fleets so much desired, and on them, Princess Hérène embarked for unexplored lands.

The isles and mountains of Norway were submerged by the flood of her battalions. On the high plateaux, bloody combats stopped them; since the sea, the Orientals had wearied. They no longer understood where the implacable princess was leading them. Alternations and success and reverses used up entire months; the permanent snow, the vertigo of the icy plains, the isolation and horrible majesty of peaks, and the lugubrious midnight aurora made a tragic décor for the supernatural folly of the warrior woman.

When she reached the icy sea beyond which no living being has ever set foot, the army considered the limits of the habitable world. Obscurity reigned; the irrespirable cold gave birth to a universal counsel of lassitude and death. It was then that Hérène understood her destiny entirely.

She had been born too virginal, too icy and too pensive for the sensible world, and that of which she dreamed could not be found at the horizontal extremity of the universe, but above the gaze, in the open sky, and in the soul.

One by one, her favorite peacocks, which had been brought in cages at the price of incredible difficulties, behind the troops, had died. The last one perished, and its pride died with the pride of its mistress. In her the memory rose up of the perfumed nights in which, under the admirable moon, her childhood had played with the plumes constellated with eyes.

The baneful presage of her mother, dead in the storm, the lividity of her complexion, everything, appeared to have decreed since the beginning the vanity of her effort and the supreme failure of her dreams. The evil spell of the birds had not been vain; the deceptive eyes that they had opened in their fans were the inanimate eyes of the innumerable cadavers strewn along her victorious route, and the coveted North offered such a void to her dream that she no longer knew what it was she had come to seek. She sensed within her a realm of pallor and death.

The thought of returning did not even occur to her; amour, languor and flowers were not made for her, and she was penetrated by a sad serenity and an eternal silence.

She had a translucent basin hollowed out in the ice, and came there to dream. The image of the sky appeared therein; the aurora borealis shed a surprising blood therein. No one knew what she was contemplating in that mirror of unreal blood by night. The giant figures engendered by the mirage of the Pole appeared to her; she learned from them the inanity of effort, the unsatisfaction of active life, the seduction of the void.

She perceived that even the sentiment of her fatherland and her race did not exist. Vallyria was absent from her memory, its blue and gilded domes, its palm trees and its pink walls no longer returned to her memory, and the world seemed confused to her. She mingled in a similar mist the conflagrations and the victories that had illustrated her immense pilgrimage; all of that was an indistinct vapor that rose from the bloody mirror; and on the edge of the diaphanous crystals that enclosed her, she raised up in its pensive whiteness the visible image of her unsmiling soul.

She had been born septentrional and meditative, nothing had been able to distract her from returning instinctively to the sterile land of that second and essential nativity. The ice and the blood summarized so absolutely the whole of her heroic attempt that she had nothing further to seek.

The army was murmuring, however; the harassment of the mountain-dwellers became more pressing and more terrible. The gaze of Princess Hérène no longer counseled those who gazed at her. The captains sensed that an unknown magnetism was gradually ebbing away from them. The useful reality of this race of conquest toward the pole escaped them.

They came to ask her intentions, but she made no rely. The ennui of existence had seized her; the world no longer tempted her; the profit of empire no longer solicited her. The murmurs increased then, but she paid no heed to them. Obscurely, the idea was born in her of her responsibility toward the soldiers that she had led into the incomprehensible. She admitted their resentment, but there was nothing more she could do; it seemed to her that she had exhausted her will by virtue of satisfying it.

She thought about abdicating, of remaining in these solitudes alone, but she would only have ceded power to subalterns; the heritage of her race was concentrated in her, and with her, the line of mad kings would perish. If she had spoken about her dreams, no one among the men of war would have understood her.

In these alternatives, her reason became more luminously desperate. Finally, one evening, the officers approached her, and in the name of the army implored her to return to the Orient. She responded, violently: "Never! Never! I shall stay here; I shall force the secret. I am here, I sense it...it's necessary that I force the secret..."

They asked her what secret she was talking about, but she remained silent.

Then, suddenly, she became irritated. "You wouldn't understand!" she cried. "You don't have my thoughts, you don't know! I've come to the limits of the world, confronting the permanent night, in order to discover how far power goes, what purpose does the sword serve, what imagination wants, and where the contentment of the soul is to be found. Your homelands of effeminate sensuality, your petty, comfortable and miserable existences, weary me. Here, in this pure and icy air, is perhaps congealed the invisible revelation of which I have need, and which your odious sun enervated. Do you think that I disturbed myself and dragged you across the world for the vulgar pleasure of devastating and subjugating? And what do you, my subjects, want to comprehend in the very hesitation of your queen? I've employed you all, with the destinies of the empire, to satisfy a caprice so unprecedented and so immeasurable that your minds can't grasp it. It pleased me to make a people under arms the breathless witness of my melancholy. Now, leave me alone!"

They withdrew, with a silent fury. A conspiracy was formed. The madness of the sovereign seemed evident. The rumor born of her mother's death and her strange childhood accused her, after many years, of the strange dementia that her triumphs had caused to be forgotten. It was decided to seize her and take her southwards by force.

One night, after doubts and dreads, the trumpets sounded and the army descended the slopes of the glaciers to the place where Princess Hérène was camped. The funereal aurora that mingled its sinister roses with the full obscurity illuminated from the middle of the sky the bloody mirror next to which the central tent stood. The officers rushed upon it; then they saw the sovereign, entirely white, with her arms extended, rise up like a polar enchantress and challenge them. Through her veils the roseate rays shone feebly; she seemed to be a supernatural statue. And when the midnight sun was directly above her head, crowning the ill-fated madness with its enigmatic divinity, she bent her knees and fell backwards into the sheet of glacial blood.

When they were able to reach her, the conspirators saw that Princess Hérène, dead, retained the diaphanous pallor that ornamented her beauty so singularly since childhood. She was not distinct from the snow; her transparent eyes remained open and implacable. The boreal light was extinct; the mirror had become pure and colorless again.

The conspirators sensed then that the genius of conquering Tauronesia had just withdrawn from their midst, and that a grandeur of the Orient had been abolished. Piety touched all souls; the army wept, the hatred disappeared; for a while, they forgot the frightful solitude, the tenebrous future and the peril.

Around the cadaver, the superstitious respect of the generals caused them to dispose, for the funeral, the remains of Princess Hérène's sacred peacocks; they had been kept on her orders. Their ocellated plumage was the ornament of her supreme bed, and the last crown of her forehead. Her hands, which had touched them while she edified her first dreams in childhood, touched them again in death.

No pyre was built; it appeared to all of them that the incorruptible body, whose soul had brought them to the conquest of the superhuman, would be the essential safeguard of the return. And in the midst of the snows and the darkness, extinguishing the fires and furling the flags, to the sound of barbaric music, the innumerable hordes of the army turned southwards and commenced the immense exodus.

LADY HELENA

The corrosive hours.
Poe.

I am going to reveal an abnormal invention of my brain, or perhaps simply a spectacle of my life, if you think with the poet that existence is an incessant combat against the monsters that inhabit us. I cannot affirm whether or not I encountered the circumstance in what is known as real life. I have never been able to differentiate my deliria and the accurate usage of my senses; I don't even know if the distinction belongs to us; since my childhood, living with the passivity of a plant, I have limited myself to feeling violently without reasoning. I am bringing you, as one exhumes a terrible old engraving from the dust in which it was buried, a vision, a venomous seed of doubt and fear: a vision, an adventure, something that I dreamed or that someone cried out to me from a window in some city, something, in sum, that existed, since I'm thinking it, considering it and then retracing it, but of which I can't reconstitute the before or the afterwards—a real thing, but in what world?

It is not, alas, a pure hallucination that unfurls in my mind at any moment that my will evokes them, of the years in which I conceived time in reverse, the hasty course of the minutes flowing backwards. Those years, in which I witnessed a slow and fatal mental anguish born of an unusual ordering of nature, are perhaps not evidence of an illusion, but a revelation of an order of things that can suddenly reign in certain souls. And if they were the effect of an unhealthy obsession, why, instead of an abstract reverie unable to take on substance, did I dream at such length, so insistently, with the clarity of normal memory, the pallid and voluptuous face of Lady Helena

Glenor? Can delirium really be so precise? Or, rather, can authentic events seem do contrary to the course of existence? I don't know, and I'm speaking to you in that doubt.

It was in a vague time of my life, filled with mists and nostalgias, that I suddenly regrasped the memory of the room in the castle where I saluted Lord Henry and Lady Helena Glenor for the first time, and I cannot explain the origin of our acquaintance, or how I became their guest and their intimate, or even in what fashion I behaved, having no memory of my life with them. But I found myself endowed with an extraordinary knowledge of all their actions, and although it is impossible for me to see myself again throughout that lapse of time, at the point at which I'm conscious of having lived uniquely for the observations I made then, I remember with the greatest clarity everything that does not concern me.

Certainly, in that vast ancestral castle, all sonorous with solitude, I can contemplate at leisure the passionate face of Lady Helena and the haughty profile of Lord Glenor. I can easily see them again in the late evenings, or in the motionless foliage, amid the idleness of the afternoon. I spent calm vacations in that domain with discreet and taciturn hosts. Long silences allowed our souls a mutual exchange in a subtle language, and we lived without thinking of troubling one another with distractions and dialogues, until the day when a new guest arrived in the dwelling: a young man, whom Lady Helena introduced to me as her cousin, Lionel.

From that day on, the communal life was animated by laughter, and I have the memory of long months during which I saw effaced from the visage of that woman, young and possessed of an ancient beauty, the melancholy spread therein by the isolated childhood of an orphan and a premature union with a spouse with a careworn soul. How did I succeed in grasping those imperceptible signs? How did I acquire the certainty, one evening, that in the depths of mute apartments, Lionel felt the languid body of Lady Helena swooning in his arms? That adultery was known to me in spite of the most absolute secrecy, and everything that followed alloys in me the horror of a tragic scene and the immateriality of a dream.

Shortly afterwards, Lady Glenor became pregnant, and in the anticipated period she gave birth to a male child. I shall always remember having read clearly in Lionel's eyes an indescribable expression: that of a father opposing his enthusiasm by means of a horrible prudence when he kissed, within an artificial delight, the son that Lord Henry was hugging as his own. From then on, an incredible dissimulation, a perilous implication, the flutter of a somber destiny, was mingled in the quotidian life of the castle with that exterior joy, and the noise familial emotions that the advent of a child brings.

I saw Lady Helena, her beauty further enhanced by the make-up of her charming lassitude, combining with exceptional tact, in her bruised and profound eyes, the love of a happy mother and the perversity of an adulterous woman. I saw Lionel going crazy between the woman whose secret lusts snatched him out of his mind, and the child—his child!—torturing himself in order to look at both of them with the calm eye of a relative in the presence of the unsuspecting husband.

I divined the most tenebrous fevers in those hearts, and the intrigues whose convolutions those three individuals were following, by force of circumstance, were continually revealed to me.

My memories darken again over the existence we led in that great castle of unconsciousness, and I believe that we awoke abruptly from a dream of prolonged melancholy on the day when the child of the adultery died: that autumn day when Lady Helena stood upright, livid, next to the candles and the little florid bed, crumpling infantile lace between her fingers; that day when we came back in mourning from the Glenor crypt, me retaining and torturing cautious words, Lionel his exasperated grief, while Lord Henry, stiffer, sustained his wife.

The horrible night next to the empty crib! It inaugurated the period of obscurity that I mentioned; it caused me to witness the thing—you know?—the birth of that monstrosity, life in reverse! It was from that night, in the mists of a dream with a real exterior, that I saw the years go backwards, returning inversely toward their commencement the gestures and the words governed by the times and placed before it. It is from that night that the inexplicable existence in question dated.

For know that, after a profound despair, when the date and the minute returned in which the child was born, Lady Helena, seized by a delirium that seemed inconceivable, writhed in the convulsions of a woman about to give birth. And when she had calmed down, she never ceased to counterfeit the gestures of a woman reaching the limits of her pregnancy, although she offered no apparent trace of it.

The following month, she seemed similar to a woman eight months pregnant. It was the same in the weeks that followed, and a bleak dolor, shadows of dilapidation and finality, weighed upon Lord Glenor and Lionel, weeping silently for the woman they believed to be afflicted by the most irredeemable madness.

But I, by virtue of a clairvoyance whose supernatural nature frightened me, tell you that time had been going backwards from that accursed date! Attentive to Lady Helena's delirium, I recognize the words that she had pronounced on anniversary dates. She said them again in the reverse order, by virtue of a horrible deviation of the mathematics of things. Time was flowing backwards in her soul!

The following month, and the one after, she complained of the symptoms of a pregnancy of six months, and then five—and the days succeeded one another without the natural order of the hours recovering their natural harmony and inexorable time ceasing to retreat toward its origin even once, so far as she was concerned, while for us and other beings it pursued its normal course!

In truth, was Lady Helena mad, or simply conscious of the frightful anomaly? I could not discover that in the gleam of her cold pupils, but I never ceased, when everyone else thought her demented, to sense in her that tumultuous reflux of years renascent of ancient nascence.

Every month that victim of a heaven devoid of forgiveness pronounced in her strange state the words once pronounced on a parallel date; she imitated the actions, and gave evidence of the singular tastes that we had known without surprise on the anniversary. She lived—how else can I put it?—her anterior existence in our midst; traveling toward hr past as toward a future, and her beautiful pale face gradually recovered the cheerful colors and the spirit of perversity that I had seen animating her for some time after her sin.

Thus was the pregnancy relived. And when the day finally approached when she had sensed her lover's child stirring within her, her calmer face and the near-disappearance of her lassitude made Lord Henry and Lionel anticipate a miraculous cure. What they had judged to be a madness was a reality—inexplicable, but aren't they all?

And the terrible evening arrived; for a long time I knew that it had to come, and under the accumulation of inalterable fatalities I waited for it, nor daring to flee and desirous of seeing, counting in the equal notches of the calendar the resolute steps of the mystery...

It finally sounded, that crepuscular hour when Lady Glenor, swooning in Lionel's arms, had conceived the adulterous child. It came, that hour, it was born, that redoubted minute, I recognized it, time had not suspended it! I saw everything again, in a fog in which my being was annulled, everything, in the great hall where fate reunited us with that moment; I can still feel my heart beating with muted shocks in expectation.

Ah! At the very instant when the act of old was consummated, Lady Helena, stiff, calm and frightening, stood up, marched toward the bewildered Lionel and, gluing her mouth to his, tore off his garments, while gasping in great surges of lust. And, deaf to the clamor of Lord Henry Glenor—who, *perhaps having understood*, was convulsed with rage and horror on the carpet—by virtue of I know not what order of vengeance fallen from the tenebrous heavens, possessed by her own conscience, she cried out under the fecundation of yore, relived the initial instant of the sacrilegious insemination, expiated the adultery and spat out her shame, all the way to the spurt of its seed!

THE FOXGLOVES

Luc. Seigneur d'Avraines, had three daughters: Simone, Hérène and Fallea. He was a bitter man and inclined to solitude, and there was gray weather in his soul, as in the region of pines and crags in which he lived, for the heaths and the skies there were immensely sad and mute. In the paths felted with moss and desiccated pine-needles footsteps made no sound, the foliage was devoid of birds and the holes in the rocks remained arid, with the consequence that no one spoke cheerfully and the silence was as much seigneur as the man. Luc accepted that taciturn counsel, and his three pale daughters lived without smiling, with few gestures, which were similar in all three of them, for they loved one another dearly.

At the edge of a vast forest, toward a cold sandy plain the dull lilac color of heather, the chatelaines d'Avraines gazed at the decent of the blue evening and the diffuse autumn mist, as odorous and subtle as a poison. They languished, leaning on the dull windows, or went into depths of the pine-wood, all the way to a distant and rare spring, green-tinted and faded, full of rushes and irises, and they gazed into the water.

Their father, returning from hunting, found them there, and they went home with him, holding hands in the dark. Thus their frail life flourished. Simone was the eldest by a year, but Hérène and Fallea were twins, and were thirteen.

The voluntary secrecy of the dry solitude insinuated vertigo into Luc's primitive soul, and he desired his daughters. And as soon as that idea had occurred to him, everything took on the appearance of an ancient crime and turned toward the intention of evil.

The sky in decline was as pink as an infant's flesh, the mist loosened tresses, the leaves rustled like belated women, and the shadow of the house counseled deadly fevers, with the consequence that, for Luc d'Avraines, the sky descended, things change their significance, and demons took pleasure in looming up before him and dancing in accordance with the hidden movement of his blood. And he knew in increasingly precise forms the route of the phantom of his sin.

In the autumn, his soul devoid of courage did not go toward the violence of instinct and egotistical desire, and as he was aware of the unconscious modesty of his daughters, he thought that after what he was meditating it would be necessary for him to live alone—and he decided within himself that the sinister event of his destiny could not be long delayed, for he was marching to meet it with heavy steps.

And one evening, on the edge of the green-tinted spring full of irises, as the three sisters were sitting there and three pale faces were leaning toward them in the water, languid in the silence and the determination of mute things the Seigneur d'Avraines approached in the thickness of the wood and made them a sign to stay. And they knew by his gaze what he had decreed in himself, but they stayed.

And when he had violated all three of them with a sad ardor, as no leaf quivered, and no trees or rock was moved, the three weeping and pliant children, Simone, Hérène and Fallea, believed they divined that their destiny had not caused pain to anyone, and that nature had not even perceived it. But all the horror that they did not feel entered into Luc's soul, and, as it was necessary for him to go to the extreme horizon of his sin, he stood before them as before the hinds he hunted, with the knife that prolongs the silence of human beings in the absolute.

Then all three of them said, with a poor soft voice: "You are the father and you can do as you wish, but you are our father and you ought to grant us something before we die.

And, Luc, Seigneur d'Avraines, having responded that he would, Simone got up and said: "I pray that you permit me to touch my father's forehead before dying." And she touched it.

Hérène said: "I pray that you allow me to touch my father's hand before dying." And she touched it.

And Fallea said: "I pray that you let me touch my father's heart before dying." And she touched it.

After that, Luc killed all three of them, threw them into the depths of the glaucous spring, and went away, having accomplished that which was marked. The demons ceased to appear before his eyes and the indecisive hour of dusk, because his temptation had been realized and he no longer desired anything; thus he seemed as calm as the objects.

But in his memory, and however meek the faces of his three daughters appeared to him, he thought that perhaps their supreme wish concealed a malevolent power, because he could not explain it, and he remained anxious, as if he were awaiting some accident.

One day, when he was hunting, he emerged from the forest and entered the plain, into the heaths of heather and rocks. The sun suddenly became so terribly hot that he was afflicted by it, in spite of his rudeness and his habituation to the caprices of the sky, and he came home ill, his head seized by a red vertigo. An ardent delirium took hold of him for several weeks, and when he had recovered, still unsteady on his feet, he recalled that his daughter Simone had touched his forehead, and he was afraid, somberly, thinking of the danger that he had it escaped, with great difficulty. The wing of Death had agitated over him, with a draught. And he wondered, with anguish, what evils might be sent by the other two dead sisters.

He began to frequent the church and its priests, previously scorned. He said long prayers, looking anxiously at his hands and listening to the muffled beating of his heart.

One day, he begged to be allowed to touch the pyx, hoping by that means to sanctify his hands and thus confer an incorruptible health upon them. But as he took hold of it his fingers froze and stiffened, inertly; the golden vase fell on the marble and the precious stones fell away, as well as the hosts. And Luc d'Avraines saw his hands dangling like those of a corpse for a month, without any physician being able to supply a remedy—and he often remembered the wish of his daughter Hérène.

Then he did not want to wait any longer in his solitary castle, among the shadows and the silent cortege of curses, for the message of punishment that his daughter Fallea would send him. He went to shut himself away in a cloister, where, as a white-haired monk, he weeded the earth of the orchard under the holy shelter of high walls and espaliers.

He lived a repentant and humble life for a long time among the monks, and many years passed, during which he got up three times every night to await the punishment of his daughter Fallea, but nothing happened to him, and he lived in uncertainty.

It was one morning in August when the prior who was Luc d'Avraines' confessor declared that he had seen him absolved in a dream by the angels before the tribunal of God, and gave him, weeping, definitive remission of his sins. Luc conceived an infinite joy therefrom, but that afternoon he was afflicted by a strange malady, a profound weakness of his being, as if seized by a secret warning.

At the approach of evening he seemed close to death, and the monks around his bed did not know what care to give him, when one of them remembered a flower that cured, and which he had recently observed on the edge of verdant springs, and he went out in order to go and pick some.

When he came back, Luc looked at the flowers and asked for them to be given to him. Then, when he had held them in his hands, he knew that the message of his daughter Fallea had finally come, and he said: "I sense that these flowers with truly cure me of life, and will provide me with a real safeguard, if three of them are placed on my heart."

And as they were placed there, he closed his eyes and died.

The flowers were those that are known as fingers of death,[5] or foxgloves, and their power is to kill or cure, according to circumstances. Thus Luc d'Avraines was marked until beyond death by the fingers of his three daughters: except that when his soul had been conveyed to eternal salvation, it no longer existed.

---

[5] I have translated the French *doigts-de-mort* literally, in order to preserve the double meaning within the story, which the equivalent common term in English, "dead men's fingers," would not do.

THE DEMON OF THE KISS

Ah, that my mouth for Muses' milk were fed
On the sweet blood thy sweet small wounds had bled!
Swinburne, "Anactoria."

There is a little god that presides over every one of the petty actions of our life. There is a little god for each of the things that have the air of being unimportant; and of those things the god makes an empire, and he extends himself therein and refines his power with an ingenuity of which we would be forever unaware, if those minimal events did not sometimes take on a significance in our existence that shows them to be linked to the very essence of our greatest designs.

On the mouth of a young woman whose smile was touched by the sun, I have seen the invisible little golden god that presides over kisses. He sleeps between the shiny teeth; the flesh of the lips presses him tenderly, and when two other lips approach, thus hiding the light, in the warm and sugary obscurity where soft, fondant and avid tongues grope, seeking one another, the little god slowly swoons.

I have seen him! He is a demon; his smile is cruel and ironic. For the kiss is an evil thing. Souls do not pass in that breath; even the most fervent souls are deceived in the purest and most sincere love, in thinking that they are penetrating one another by that route. Souls are only exchanged via the eyes; the lips can do nothing, either by sound, by breath or by moisture, to link souls to one another. What emerges from the kiss is another kind of soul, which is demonic, and lust is an art that the veritable soul does not admit, of which it can make no use.

Thus, the little god of the kiss is a malevolent god. For the breath of beings is never sufficiently prolonged for the perfumes of mental amour to be carried thereon, and the ecstasy of the kiss is not even the little warning shudder that those individuals who are destined to love one another experience, of perceiving one another for the first time. The little god of the kiss knows that full well, and he smiles maliciously, because he is content to live between lips that take one another, and that his invisible body thus prevents souls from traversing the flesh in order to join together.

I have to talk about an evening whose significance is full of mystery. Who I am, you don't know, and it isn't important to the story: I am a mouth that loved another mouth. How I came to know Clarisse is a story would be long in the telling and futile. She was a very virginal young woman, and when I came into her life, she seemed to have been waiting for me. Although I was immediately attracted to her by a singular force, I don't know whether it was precisely by desire as it is normally understood. That curiosity, when I meditate upon it, was attached to a mute and nervously-observed faculty that seemed to want to reveal itself at any moment in Clarisse, but which remained in suspense.

I know that it seems almost absurd to materialize a faculty in itself, and to lend a consistency to the soul, but it is quite true that within Clarisse, and from within her, something abstract and essential was born, which murmured on the edge of the lips but never emerged on the wings of speech. Extensive frissons circulated incessantly in the nervous networks that surrounded her lips and designed their contours, with the consequence that she always seemed to want to say something, and that she was retaining a secret between her teeth.

The impression produced by that perceptible tremor almost demanded that a question be asked to determine whether Clarisse's silence was simply a want of the exact choice of terms; one would have helped her to explain if her calm, almost unconscious eyes had not belied with their coldness the stirring of her parted lips, and made one think that one was mistaken.

I observed with solicitude the discord between the upper and lower fractions of her face, and eventually convinced myself that it was not the eyes that manifested her soul, but uniquely, and authentically, her lips. I no longer looked at anything but Clarisse's mouth; it obsessed me to the extent of dolor.

I ought to mention that, since my adolescence, a hereditary sensuality had given me the intuition of physical amour to the extent of deregulating my thought and obscuring all reason within me to the sole profit of instinct. For me, voluptuousness has not been the appreciated and joyful distraction of a few vain hours, but my chosen study and my great, my only means of comprehending the spectacles of life, art and sentiment: a lucid passion in which everything that I could collect in my heart of delicacy and charity was renewed.

Thus, in Clarisse, nothing touched me except for the contemplation of her lips: neither her virgin eyes, nor her body, nor her hair, nor aroma, nor the confidences of her youthful speech, nor even the charm of her hands; nothing, except for her mute quivering mouth, in which some unknown desire was babbling; and I understood that nothing except for that mouth could tell me anything true about Clarisse.

The form of her lips was particular. Beneath their living, undulating and excessively mobile flesh—perpetually moist and oozing the rich interior lust of virgin blood—beneath their doubly sinuous flesh, ripe and seemingly ready to open the heart of the fruit over the sharp teeth, it seemed that a minuscule being lived and agitated—yes, a being! A being, or speech, or I know not what force, voluptuously parted that fondant warm flesh or tightened it upon itself, alternately. The presence of an invisible living entity behind Clarisse's lips was certain, and I had an intuition that it was neither her breath, nor the natural play of the muscles that extended around that part of the face, but truly some unforeseen possessor established there without her being aware of it.

That attraction was so strong that when I touched Clarisse's lips one evening in the garden, it was not with the precaution, the sentimental ruses and all the artifice that a young man uses to approach a young woman gently—and I cannot comprehend how my cautious nature was abolished at that moment before a visage as calm and an attitude that offered me no provocation at all. I suddenly kissed Clarisse, having looked at her lips for a long time; mine seized hers without my being capable of thinking about what I was doing, about the surprise, the possible anger, and a thousand other hazards. It happened abruptly, and by virtue of a natural force, as the fable says of the nails of ships that, while the vessel is skirting a magnetic mountain, fly out their holes to attach themselves to the magnetic stone.

And yet, Clarissa made no movement to push me away, nor to draw me to her either. One might have thought that she did not even perceive my action. Her mouth acted immediately under mine with a cold frenzy, the mouth that I sensed had been waiting for me. But the rest of the face did not move, and I, frightened by my action, did not dare not say anything more, or to look at her—with the result that we were soldered by the lips while leaving our souls absent and without even trying to move our hands.

For a long time we drank the elixir of life that was warmly born in that obscure and nervous flesh. We drank for a long time, avidly. And I penetrated profoundly into the beloved mouth to seize the breath and the soul borne by the breath, for love as finally born within the kiss. But neither the breath nor the soul emerged to be yielded by the virgin.

I tasted her, I aspired her, I modeled her, and bit her to the point of dryness, to the point of pain, and I impregnated my kiss with all the immodest moistures that prostitutes know, and she welcomed them and returned them to me in silence, but I sensed clearly that I could not obtain her soul and her breath: that between her and me, on the barrier of the teeth and the lips, something was creating an obstacle.

We came apart, pale, and Clarisse's eyes revealed to mine that she accepted between us all the things of a man and a woman. But her lips palpitated and trembled as if still waiting. And I leaned forward to look at them, and as a fugitive gleam illuminated them—was it a hallucination or a real vision?—it seemed to me that I saw *a little ironic being* slipping away into their shadow.

Instantly, taking Clarisse's lips again without saying a word, I tried to seize that being with my tongue and my teeth. And we exhausted ourselves for a long time in a violent contact, a wearying, deceptive, insipid contact, chewing the inanity of the kiss and amour on one another's flesh. And that went on for a part of the night.

As our thirst possessed us, in spite of the fatigue and the desiccation, we threw ourselves upon one another indefinitely, and I finally seemed to feel that between our two souls, risen from our hearts to our lips and all the way to the teeth, trying to enter into one another mutually, a veritable being was lying, voraciously intercepting our breath and our love: a little being exactly as large as the interval between four lips can be; a malevolent playful being that was usurping our nervousness and the obstinate labor of our embraces! And I knew full well that Clarisse and I were not embracing, but that he was stealing our embrace and that it was to caress him, the intermediary, that our mouths were joined. On them, as if we were each eating one side of an indestructible fruit, he remained swooning, and as the amour of our souls rose up tumultuously, he, the little demon of the kiss, was intercepting it and gorging himself upon it, while mocking us.

It was him who was agitating beneath Clarisse's unconscious lips, and Clarisse would never be satisfied, and her lips would eternally reach out toward other lips in order that the emotion of amour might descend by way of them into her young, desirous and strong soul, and eternally, the little demon of the kiss would steal that emotion in passing, and eternally, Clarisse would be the unconscious instrument of his pleasure.

We are the servants of amour; it plays with us when we want to play with it. That is what I understood while swooning into obscurity against my beloved. And when, finally extenuated, we ceased to embrace one another, we had no more penetrated into one another than into marble. Clarisse was alike and I was alike, and between our dry lips, where the dying aspiration had caused the bitter blood to pearl, we sensed that the demon of the kiss, satisfied and fortified by our illusory effort, was sleeping insouciantly, leaving our souls, which we had not been able to bring forth, to sob in our breasts.

Never, never can one take or give souls and desires by way of the flesh; everything always has to be recommenced; one is always working for another; the mouths that squeeze one another crush between them a fragile and essential thing, amour itself; the barrier of the flesh is insurmountable; one exhausts oneself, in vain, one feels ill; one has done nothing but dream...

And Clarisse fainted as the pallor of the September dawn was born; and when the first ray of morning shone on her poor enslaved lips, I glimpsed the *other*, enjoying himself there like a simple golden statue; and I heard him mingle his dormouse breath with a little eternal snigger. And I went far away from my sad and impotent accomplice, and the state of unsatisfaction and death convulsed my heart.

CROWN OF CLARITY
A Fantastic Story

I will so trust that what is deep is holy,
that I will do strongly before the sun and moon
whatever only rejoices me and the heart appoints.
R W. Emerson[6]

We undoubtedly have as much foresight as memory, because, incessantly becoming, out soul is orientated toward
what we do not know, enthusiastic to modify the attitudes previously known; and orientation absorbs it essentially. The light
soul looks at memory over its shoulder, compassionately; but
it is necessary that it does not linger. Only extinct souls are
seated by the roadside or the river bank, looking toward the
bend or upstream. So, I cannot decide whether this book is a
commentary on my past or measures some of my hours to
come; I have, in writing it, mingled reminiscence with invention, antedated hopes, or envisaged with mystery and desire
things that have happened.

And truly, it is permitted to us to consider clearly and to
describe as exact visitors the events that will happen to us; and
it is also permissible to reform as dreams that which will happen to us, in periods that we have not yet seized with the force
of events. For we do not know very well how time will dispose of the eventualities that compose our lives; and the order
that we give them is perhaps not that which it will attribute to

---

[6] The quotation is from "Self-Reliance" (1841). I have substituted the original; the French translation on the cover of the
Ollendorf book is slightly abridged.

them. A dream does not distinguish between invention and memory, and all that the soul can say is that it likes the future better. Facts and judgments are not always ordered in a chronological progression; often they are juxtaposed without dates, and remain suspended in the environment of time. Certain lives, entirely interior, are thus incomprehensible; it seems that nothing of them has yet arrived, because the observer only sees surprising and unusual things arising there, but if one had looked more closely, one would have discovered something, dormant since the first day in the depths of consciousness. And the life in the present book is similarly disposed, for the facts that will be encountered there do not hasten to trouble it, but were contained there, and one discovers it at a glance.

There are beings and mirrors in this tale that would not be dissimilar to nothing if they did not signify, in various forms, my own reflection. They are mine; I am contemplating myself for a long time therein. And if I call my book a memorial of phantoms, it is because the purely subjective life of my fictitious characters does not pretend to what we call reality, and only desires the equivalence of my dreams. Commenced in the evening, under my lamp, it strays in a few hours of reverie, and finishes, pales and dies with the artificial light in the morning light; it is the chimera of one night, I know no more than that. Does this memorial truly differ from a hypothesis, will hope and regret not show, to whoever dares to lift their veil, and immutable and similar face? In any case, I pray that I might be absolved if I do not know anything about the extent to which truth and invention are confined here, except perhaps that invention itself is surely a thus-far-neglected truth.

Real, unreal: I don't know. Any then, what do you call real?

For me, it's *the profound*...

Prelude

I have illuminated my soul with my lamp, and I abandon myself to confront a few phantoms.

Perhaps I was born in a country that will never be explored. For we have an infinity of births, and if time and human reason are satisfied to know one, our dreams choose their own, and they are the masters of the choice. The land of my memory is beautiful. Eternal espaliers ripen there in an ideal autumn of vine-branches; the setting sun is extinguished there over marbles, and in the pensive foliage one can hear the sea breeze; but the horizon mists over the depths, and over immense and supernatural forests. The worn face of the rocks is revelatory; and the sand conceals pure shells in which the equivocal dolor of the waves laments, fixing in the nacre of their chambers both the echo of their appeal and the ornamental memory of their voluptuous fugitives. The charm of these things is great; but a river winds sleepily from the forest to the sea, born in the shade of slender pines, where the roseate bracelet of solar light rises and falls in accordance with the hour; nympheas and narcissi hide the mystery of the water, black swans are the sole galleys, and no one has ever come. That is where I have lived, and where my mind appeared to me in the first moments of voluptuousness and silence.

How I have known that secret place, and what road led me there, I do not know. It seems to me simultaneously that my being awoke like a reed, and that it only arrived there after years of pilgrimage; a man who passes a bend in a path, staff in hand, makes me think of a self who must have wandered for a long time, on gravel where my feet must have bruised their infantile flesh, and thresholds, with the smoke of the evening, make me tremble and astonish me like a perpetual stranger. But all that is so distant, all that is so advanced in memory, so close to the moment in which one is surprised to find oneself, that I dare not think about it anymore. I cling to the belief that there is no road to reach my country; the old Exile himself

71

would renounce it, and the pathways too, and perhaps the gaze of angels.

From the rusty balcony of the dwelling, I have not seen anyone; the discreet sun hardly dared to call the faithful heliotropes, and the fruits of the orchard were velveted by the dust of centuries, ignorant of baskets and sickles. The apartments were those that Melancholy would choose if it ceased to be ideal. No door-frame there depicted painted amours, no tapestry there wove a décor of hunters and mares, no picture-frame enlaced with golden snakes the attracted mystery of prorates; only virgin nature abandoned its images there and art recreated there the spectacle of windows, for the forests and the sea entered the house by the crystal of bays to lull on the walls the illusion—silk, wool or pastel—of their inert magnificence. And those waves of those artificial thickets, comparing themselves to their natural models, presented to the contemplation singular sketches of fixed features, the innumerable and ungraspable faces that strive to emerge from the objects of customary life; I thought I understood the ancient physiognomy of time, and those landscapes impassioned me like women; I no longer doubted the interior life so long as they were speaking...

Perhaps one only learns and only loves nature by means of the artificial, for if one is not a faun or a blade of grass, nature inspires fear. I have worn away long hours thinking about that.

The mirrors have only contemplated the sky, and I have thought that I divined there at dusk the real form of the stars, which danced slowly above me. Luxurious reflections assembled enigmatic synods of faded gleams on the pendants of the chandeliers. The curtains had no loops—who had taken them away? Personally, I did not exist. The chairs were not awaiting anyone, and the faiences of the dressers immobilized, under the dust of inappreciable time, a cold orchard of faded blue flowers.

Oh, my soul, how pure we have been! We were as pure as the very years, as the ether, the snow, the lilies. Oh, my soul, we were as pure as the silence.

On a jet of stone, somnolent poplars cast a swaying violet shadow. The wind lifted up the short vegetation, like a hand running through unkempt hair. The clouds were not crowding the sky, but moved away without having waited too long. The sluice of verdant water wrinkled, the clusters of black moss were etiolating under the flat stones of the crofts. Over these things a damp sky was somnolent, and the idle sun leaned palely over the occidental groves. Old fatigued voices, old voices that did not come from humans, grieved in the depths of enclosures, the long yellow rays setting obliquely over the disjointed threshold; they were hours of ideal confrontation with everything that is simple or extraordinary.

The days probably did not exist anymore; time had forgotten them, having sowed them in its wake without turning round, and if the curious clocks had begun to chime they would not have been understood; those old hearts with the even rhythm were sleeping meekly in their prison of glass, and the figures on the dials had not numbered anything for a long time. The clepsydras were devoid of water, the sand-glasses remained stable, and the blue flies murmured alone against the windows. Everything seemed abolished and discolored by gentle hands; existence wove a blurred design like winter frost, and the air was so impregnated with quietude that one could have believe that one was seeing calm crystallizations; the evening mists were like the changing veils that emotion causes to quiver on the pupils, and everything seemed to be passing within the eyes.

I have had irremediable impressions there. The majesty of autumn leaves has left heaps of sumptuous dusk in the soul, and I have often known what the water, the heliotrope and the things of the placid earth are thinking. I rarely went to the sea shore, imagining it too insolent to my great desire for peace. But how friendly were the fruits and the pale rays of six o'clock! I confided to them almost all my sadness, and they have not betrayed me. All my sentiments have played thus in their adolescence with simple forms, and the spectacles of the sky, foliage, horizons and hours.

I went down under the rosy pines as far as the near bank of the river to see the swans. They were fighting in the vegetation, their black wings deployed over the crimson evening; the water shone in necklaces of droplets, iris petals torn up in the battle were flying, and the large nympheas undulating in the current. A few swans were fond of those flowers and were sailing toward them. Their sparkling necks imitated the curve of calices, swooning in the poison of golden pollen; but everything calmed down at the heroic cry of peacocks, and I plunged into the thicket in order to avoid them, for the eyes of their feathers were malevolent; perhaps they are the ones that we see in our dreams, gazing at our hidden thoughts, the jewels of hypocritical fatality.

My heart was touched by the birds; they have taught me almost everything. The phrases that their distant flights inscribe in black triangles on the azure have probably decreed my entire life, with the form of clouds that have informed me of passions and forgotten them. The obscure maxims that the bewildered pigeons traced on the ground of the sky entered into my memory with the shadow, whose suave counsel descended from the treetops; and a few moments before the nascence of the lamps, I meditated those prophecies of the forest, which the song of the sea solemnized with confused choruses, broken into prayers on the foliage.

It is thus that I grew up with Pity in grave eyes and Tenderness in soft eyes, until the evening when, descending toward the river-bank, I saw, standing facing me in the darkness, the form of a woman.

I had not raised my head, having seen in the reflection of the water a strange patch of gold coming toward me, and I thought I was following, leaning over, the last memory of the sun. But as that light became motionless, I opened my half-closed eyes, and I perceived Maia.

The golden patch was her hair, and her violet eyes were considering me in the twilight. One finger was touching her lips, the other hand signaling to me. The birds ran away into the blue banks, and I alone knew, amid the waves and the calices, the new form of my Destiny.

We contemplated one another for a long time without saying anything, because the words that we knew would have broken before our thoughts; then we came back to the house together, and from then on the ancient mirrors knew two faces coming to meditate there in their twin solitude before the fixed torsion of the golden serpentine frames.

Maia's soul made my landscapes jealous; it summarized them with splendor. When our walks took us toward the forest, the plain or the sea, the song of her phrases modulated their real inflections, and I knew by her silence what the night would be. Her hair was my entire sunset, her hands collected in the empty air all the flowers I had chosen, and her presence simultaneously charmed my desire to be far away and my desire to remain, because a pleat of her dress signified the beach of many distant heavens, whereas the quivering and glaucous water for which I had wished slept in its inert satin. And I did not think that one could flee and further then the exile opened by her eyes.

Those eyes of Maia's hid even more dreams than memories. Their golden flecks shone in a minuscule and unexplored sky; phantoms and flowers lingered there; entire autumns, and perhaps perfumes, perished there. I loved to follow the luxurious agony of my dreams there; they spun there softly, hesitated, then plunged into that sad water and did not come back again. The lashes, trembling reeds, leaned over the ideal spring, and a pageantry of veiled stones rose up there vaguely, shone, and sank back down into the darkness. Then there were blue skies, arborescences, luminous waves, and ineffable silks heightening a black diamond; or, finally, unknown things, abstract forests, which antique Folly herself would never divine...

We both went to the edge of the woods, and considered one another without saying a word, but at the moment when there was only a single star in the sky, Maia suddenly spoke, and sobbed like the foliage and the water. Her dolor seemed to me a white plain, and I guided her sobs like ewes toward my melancholy, seated on the horizon. One evening, I wanted to know why the ewes had emerged, and I put my lips on Maia's eyes, and I heard her murmuring in a low voice, murmuring as if nature were about to die.

"Alas," she said, "we do not know ourselves."

Then I stepped back and I said, fearfully: "Why descend into ourselves, Maia, and what will we find?"

"I want to know what we will find," sang her voice, and tears ran down her cheeks.

"It's not necessary, Maia; perhaps it would be the end."

"I no longer see myself in mirrors, I no longer see myself in nature, my hair no longer comprehends the sun, and the light no longer loves my eyes," she said. "Where are we? Where are we, alas, and what is it that we are? We're dying, as ignorant as the gardens of autumn, my friend! The odor of leaves saddens me, and my swans have secrets. We didn't descend into ourselves when we were alone; how can we descend there together? It's necessary to know our interior skies, the forests of our thoughts, the seasons of our desires, the espaliers of our hopes. But we don't know anything..."

That evening, we came back without saying any more.

I took Maia's hands in mine and I said to her: "I've consulted the house and the flowers. I've consulted the gravity of life. We'll go toward it in order to know ourselves, and we'll be happy forever. We'll wait for a clear night and we'll go. It's not good for a man to be happy alone; you've come to take me away; come, we'll seek an undeniable testimony, if there is any on the earth.

"Oh, Maia, that's enough of dreaming in the dusk, signifying nothing. It's necessary to depart into the supernatural dew of the Orient. Out there, our white soul is waiting for us on the hills; it's necessary to reach it. Its diaphanous reflection descends toward us with the dawn, but we can't see it yet. And perhaps it's praying, and sad that we aren't coming. This is a land of shadows; we're too easily satisfied with indecisive forms: that which dies, changing water, black swans; but out there, out there, Maia, there's a land of light; let's not die without seeing it.

"What we'll see there might perhaps be frightful. Perhaps we'll discover fateful inscriptions in the desert of ourselves that will chill us with terror. But you've wanted it, Maia, and we're going to look for it. Happiness hasn't entered here; it's prowling around the house, waiting to enter until our souls are open. An immense sea of passion and frenzy is rolling around us, but our hearts can't contain it. Even music has only scintillated over us with the distance of the stars, and if we've wept, our eyes alone have perceived it.

"Hyperion is illuminated over the infinite forest, the air is screaming sensuously, the obscure foliage is crystallizing diamonds, the evening wind is dancing over your heroic hair; it's time. Tomorrow we'll attempt the fortunate isles where one finally encounters one's real face, and we'll kiss it on the lips and our souls will melt like oranges. Let's launch forth on the mysterious voyage, dream the landscapes of our eyes, and weave garlands of joy for the threshold of Truth.

"As I saw you one evening, bathing in my solitary spring the reflection of your golden curls, so perhaps we shall see ourselves leaning over, at the bend of a sublime path, the interior being that counsels our sobs and our smiles. In the hazards of crowds and foliage, in the tumultuous population of waves, perhaps it with spring forth like a flash of lightning, and then, and then how luminous our love will be. Maia! All our life will be resplendent in that flash, our kisses will savor an incorruptible fruit, and we'll each pick ourselves like eternal grapes."

The child raised her eyes toward me and said, softly: "Let's go to sleep beside one another, and we'll go together toward the bright light of our selves..."

Her head leaned over my knees; she fell silent. I sustained her warm hair in my hands; a glimmer emerged therefrom and went astray in the darkness. In the nocturnal sky, the fixed fires of the stars contemplated the sea. Solitude touched our brows, and we drifted slowly into inexplicable forgetfulness.

The Road to the Orient

"Narcissa!"
"Perdita!"
"Dea!"
That suddenly sang in the forest; the day was declining.

How many hours had we remained immobile? A dusk had quit us, and we found ourselves in a dusk again, listening to a concert of chattering supernatural birds.

Leaning over the branches, suspended like ripe fruit, they were crying out the names of courtesans, gemstones, flowers and poisons; then, suddenly trilling hectically, they launched themselves from one tree to another, swimming in the air like crimson fish. With their beaks they split pomegranates, making the bright seeds spurt out, and drops of red amber oozed from the foliage; then they leapt into the heart of enormous roses and scattered golden pollen with thrusts of their claws. Striping the colonnades of oak-groves with multicolored joy, they clamored frenziedly. Some, their wings outspread, remained there, beaks open, fiery larks singing for all eternity, while the greater number spoke, predicting bizarre destinies, the adventure of naked goddesses with terrible eyes, and numerous significances of fate. We had considered their astonishing crowd, our souls, accustomed to solitude, marveling, and since our departure we had heard nothing else. But who had just pronounced loudly, beside us, in the darkness, those three women's names?

"Dea!"
"Perdita!"
"Narcissa!"

It seemed to come from the trees, and the three voices were calling out. They became very distinct.

"Let's call too," I said, in a whisper, to Maia, "for we don't know where we are."

"But who will see us coming?" she said. "This is an impenetrable sacred forest; perhaps God doesn't know everything that happens here. These trails, both tumultuous and motionless...that shadow...will we find beings here that understand what a road is? For only those who are desirous worry about roads. Those who have obtained limit the horizon to their minds and remain turned toward themselves. Alas, these thickets are as bushy as the minutes. They're dense, multiform and yet similar, leaf imitating leaf, the grains of sand in an hour-glass, each sliding alongside the others, and all similar, all living confounded in the same isolation. Perhaps we know enough about humans by the example of blades of grass. Who is coming, and what will they say to us?"

"Are you afraid?"

"No," said Maia, "but I'm pensive. Call if you want to, and let them come."

We were about to call out the three names we had heard in the darkness when a kind of blue light appeared, and the faces of three children were illuminated by it. They were gentle beings of immemorial appearance, little girls with wide eyes, whom we thought had seen already, and who were looking at us without speaking. Their hair was flowing over their shoulders like the minuscule rivers of gold that one sees sparkling confusedly in mirrors. Those delicate sinuosities isolated their faces less, one might have thought, than their own nature, so inattentive and distant did they seem, beyond life, with the last clouds rusting above the trees.

Maia, leaning toward me, said in a low voice: "I'm glad that our first encounter is with children. Don't you like that pledge of purity? We don't know where we are; we've never known it, or even where we've come from, in the identical obscurity of these fanned-out pathways. And now our uncertainty will be addressed, firstly, to these fresh and happy memories of what we have been. Perhaps we'll come back thus to our past, becoming tender as we think about ourselves before these children. Look, they have flowers in their hands, beautiful hair, and carry the memory of an evening with a noble melancholy. Ask them the way, for we need to go toward the sea; and discover what dream they're imagining among the trees, and whence come those names they were singing in the distance just now, which the wind seemed to repeat with a smile..."

And I asked the little girls what Maia had told me to ask.

The blondest of them spoke.

"Why ask us the way? You alone know what path it's necessary to take. The goal is known to you alone, and everyone goes toward the sea and the unknown under different stars. As for us, we don't expect anything; you knew us once; we're the three children who appear in legends, the lost children, those who fall into ponds for having desired water flowers, or those who sing rounds, or those who go into the sky with the angels. You've never encountered us outside stories, because you didn't believe that the stories were true, but now you're no longer telling them to your soul to distract it, you're going to live one of them yourselves. So you've found us this evening for the first time.

"My name is Narcissa, because I love the flowers with the golden hearts that emerge from the dark water; they're the image of my love. I'm the collector of flowers. And this sister to my right is named Perdita, because she was lost one day among ancient rocks, and always seems to be lost where she's found, and absent from her own presence. She's the collector of tears. And this one to my left is named Dea, for she maintains herself with the birds of the sky, and she's the one who says a prayer for us when the hour has come. She hasn't been lost in the rocks or been thoughtful on the edge of a pool, but I think she's come from above us, because she sometimes says things that we can't understand. She's the collector of stars. You've known us, you've known us! Our smiles have illuminated your dreams, and you've imagined us in accordance with your childhood.

"There are no words to determine the meaning of your life. Your Destiny, however, inhabits this forest; go toward it in silence. It will collect you without speaking, but some emblem that it offers you will tell you the meaning of your enigmas, for those who confront their Destiny never leave with empty hands."

"And where do we find it?" I said. "It's dusk. Who will be the guide? The stars, the leaves, or you?"

"It will happen of its own accord," said the three little girls. "We're only children."

And suddenly, they were no longer there...

Destiny, sitting on a milestone with figures worn away by time, gave us red flowers, black flowers and blue flowers without saying a word. And when we had touched them, we knew what they signified.

The red flowers were poppies and roses. We shall love the sun and blood, we shall dream of murders and tenebrous descents into the abysms of forgetfulness and death. We shall reach Truth and the Light after those two countries of oblivion, where human thought has been able to venture thus far, and that which will not be abolished or somnolent in us will be able to spring forth as a virgin shoot in the lily-fields of Paradise.

The black flowers were asphodels and heartsease. Alas, Maia, Maia, shall we weave them in your hair, those petals of darkness? Will it be necessary to cherish the night, converse with shadows, design our desires according to the funereal velvet of those corollas, to know an invincible trouble in a pale lunar light in which the plaintive agony of jets of water will die...?

But the blue flowers were irises and convolvulus, and I have recognized you, Maia, my water flower, my beloved with honeyed eyes! Those pools closed like eyes where you appeared to me, similar to one of those flowers, the dormant pools that have just renounced with an insensible frisson the sobbing kiss of the sun, shall we see descending therein, as I perceived the famous golden patch of your hair coming toward me, the entanglement of our realities and our appearances...?

The port in which we are about to embark for the Orient is at the center of a profound gulf; not far away are the ruins of a dead city that it once enriched. Today, rare vessels come to dock there, and seem only to have strayed there in order to report to distant nations whether the face of Time and Neglect is always similar to its own ennui...

This morning, the quays are warmed by the sun; the grass insinuated between the paving-stones inclines toward the light; large blue shadows are asleep on the roseate stones. It is mild beneath a clear firmament; it is the dawn of the eternal departure.

Maia and I walk at a slow pace through the ancient streets. At their extremity one sees masts, or the sea. Their houses are faded, expressing sentiments maintained, and as if purified, by solitude. They are aligned around little oblong squares, where beautiful trees rise into the azure, joyfully deploying fans of sunlit leaves. Among the branches one can see the painted windows and their regular panes. Sinuous espaliers are shedding the blossom of their garlands there. The drinking-fountains with moldy bronze masks frowning amid the sandstone, which wear has illuminated with gold, sing the hours drop by drop.

Canals traverse the streets. Their still water captures the dreamy image of deserted dwellings, and caravans of clouds inflict the fleeting and negligent illusion of their vaporous swirls upon it. Humpbacked bridges are doubled therein into rings of shadow, through which swans pass, contemplated pensively by the sculpted monsters that seem to be leaping from the prows of motionless barges moored to the banks awaiting an imaginary cargo. The anchor-chains sway over the water, silky with flocculent algae and lacy lichens; life seems as slow and solemn as the prayers of the humble.

Old bells hang on portals, and everything listens for their absent song. White birds pass overhead, crossing one another's paths; heavy satin curtains mirror in the bleak canals the valueless armory of their emblematic fabric, and their embroidered eagles open there impotent wings, which they no longer animate, to the morning breeze...

All these symbols remind us, with a singular beauty, of the life that we are about to quit. We have wandered in their midst for a long time, and I glimpse tears in Maia's eyes.

She is walking with an undulating slowness that I have never seen anywhere else but in her. Her visage is like that of thought itself, all that is conscious animating a perpetual landscape there. Her contemplative pupils detain the secrets of precious stones; her mouth, which swoons against mine with such child-like lust, is nevertheless the purest of proud and living roses when I gaze at it beside me like this, and her surprising hair flows in waves that truly summarize for me all art and all beauty.

I am not intoxicated by passion; placidly, I admire Maia with the serenity befitting a statue; she is a perfect thing, who is animate and present; she astonishes in me the old belief that Beauty cannot be touched. And above all, there is a universe of emotion between the Maia that I am contemplating and the one that I possess in the dark. Every time there is the ineffable impression of seizing that which cannot be seized, and at every awakening the immutable stupor of seeing it became intangible again.

It is doubtless thus that sentiment possesses our immortal souls; they drink it in with delight and yet their exile leaves it intact and fresh for further kisses. How the entire world that sings within Maia frightens me, when I make contact with it! I seem to be pressed against the wall of a crypt in which unsuspectable and frightening ceremonies are enthroned; it seems, when I sense her close to me, that I hear within her processions armies that have been marching for millions of centuries...

And all that expires on her serious lips, between her lashes, and I know nothing, and God will perhaps never know anything. And I, however, sense myself dissolving in voluptuousness and am aware of my starts and stumbles, toward that universe enclosed within Maia, and I can no longer divine whether I am possessing her or she is taking me, whether I am descending into her or she is rising up within me. My entire interior universe burns against hers, our phantom cohorts and cavalry fall upon one another in the never of nocturnal lust, and perhaps our embraces are abstract and purely cerebral, so far has our flesh been exceeded by those prodigious collapses...

And all that, all that is held in the two tranquil forms of strollers, the little hand of my beloved resting on my arm, the delicate light dissolving our negligence in a double shadow swinging its bizarre blue patch behind us on the pink paving-stones...

Thus superimposed enigmas light up in my soul with the hours, like golden torches in a forest. Shall we know the secret of what we are, and shall I understand this fiancée who is with me and far away from me, a statuette of void or a living bust of the invisible truth?

We have to go back toward the quay where the sea is splashing. Groups of sailors are assembled there, some letting their legs hang over the edge, while the surf leaps up to their knees. They are surrounding a strange old man who is showing them sharpened knives, rings, bloody fruits and little metal figurines. He is setting them out on the paving-stones in unexpected arrangements, and sometimes, in the series of juxtaposed objects, the sense of a destiny edifies an ideal architecture, in which human life enters head bowed. We have not dared, like the sailors, to consult the old man who speaks in accordance with the daggers, the rings and the other things; we have only bought a necklace, which we have thrown into the sea.

The tall masts charged with sails are swaying. The rigging spins the web of a gigantic spider against the sky; the curved anchors rising out of the water stripe the woodwork of the prow; the triangular jibs ripple and then stiffen; the multi-colored pennants perpetuate a reflection of the fire of the dawn on the yardarms.

We have decided a step in our lives; we are aboard, and the first surge of the swell has promised us within a second the supreme conquest of the Orient!

By the channels, the gulfs, the appearances of promontories, by the magic of the ocean and the sky, we are going forth! The stars of Lyra and Cassiopeia, Rigel and the grandiose Sirius, are glittering in the crown of our dream. We are being conveyed to the multiform fête of the elements. The sun has initiated us into agonies whose horrible magnificence we do not suspect as yet, and the sea has refracted for us constellations and rainbows for which our dreams were hesitant to hope...

We are going toward a large island where it is said that one of the visages of Verity is visible. Perhaps we shall land on other islands before that one; it appears that one cannot call there right away. For how long have we been sailing thus?

But time has never existed...

The stars...

At dawn we sighted the trireme of Ulysses! He was standing at the prow, his helmet resplendent, the light setting its golden plume ablaze. The great galley leapt over the white waves with its living oars, a blue monster twisting and extending its neck toward the sea beyond the triple spur. An alternating song laughed over the Hellenic flutes and fluttered over the masts. The bronze bucklers radiated along the sides a hundred images of the sun, breaking up into flashes. A sumptuous wake snaked far behind it, all the way to the horizon. It passed heroically while we were awake, and we shouted, but the sleek warrior did not want to turn his head, and we found ourselves alone on the ocean again.

A long time afterwards...

The stem of our ship hissed in the contortions of foaming waves, while a great crepuscular light colored the air, the sea and our obese sails, and the golden breasts of the rigid siren at our prow, and, all standing in the supernatural blood of the sky, we were aware, even before the cry of the watchman, of the approach of the Bloody Isles. It was an evening of fatalities and autumn, on a princely sea, and the beaks of the soaring gulls shone as if they were holding gems and pink pearls.

As prophesied by that etheric conflagration, by the redness of the perpetual waves, we knew the abstract magnificence and architecture of our destiny. And first, emerging from the waters, there were three pyramidal islands of porphyrine rust and ancient congealed blood with their coralline grottos open like lips, flowers, vaginas or wounds. We pushed our vessel toward one of them, to shelter it from the winds of the open sea, and with our masts with great yardarms changed with white sails, with our sonorous rigging in which birds were perching, with our winged oriflammes, by means of the powerful and smooth thrust of the high woodwork of the mizzen stem, we entered into the singular channel, into the heart of the rock rippled by undulations and smooth folds, like a wasp into a corolla.

Our souls were proud, exalted by the glorious adventure of touching, in that indubitable fashion, those haunted islands, whose celebrated and untroubled pomp had only dazzled the dreams of our somnolent wakefulness as yet. Full of desire to tempt their legend, we lifted our hearts to real courage. However, consenting to our haste to reconnoiter before nightfall, dusk did not fall as usual, and, bathed in the red ether, we saw that the stars were not going to come out this time; for the bloody color of the land, the sky and the waters seemed ineffaceable, and beyond time.

Mounted on the rocky escarpments and reaching the oriental slope, a red-gold plain burst forth, luxuriant with sumptuous orchards and crazy flowers, which none of us picked, although all of us, holding the enormity of the world to be nothing, had known Java, the Hindu palms, the mystery of the North and all the vegetal treasure of the archipelagos.

More wonderstruck at every step by the vivacious and eternal flora, we were thinking, forgetful of our destiny, when the inhabitants came running from all directions. They were men and women scarcely emerged from a rich adolescence, admirable in their beauty, slenderness and strength. Their clear faces marked a humanity so essential that it elevated them above any particular type; in a word, they seemed to be show-ing us universal faces. Their language was comprehensible to us, although for a number of our companions, the sun did not rise over the same continents. They were ardent, and voracious for the truth.

We love the stars without understanding them, and they are the same, but while arguing furiously about their wake and their course; their hypotheses struck us with their audacity, and a host of others, regarding the earth, the sky and the as-pects of Nature. They burst into passionate proclamations, in an indefatigable desire for analysis, interrogating us even as to the forms and the timing of our dreams, with the consequence that, frightened by that overflow of cerebral faculties, we con-sidered our simplicity with regret, and we savored the ideal orange that perfumed the speech of that people.

Thus, living on the first of the Bloody Isles, where the air is impregnated, like the ground, by constant blood red colora-tion, we were exalted by the fever of knowledge, to such an extent that, in single day—if that word is appropriate to a place where an even and supernatural light reigns—it seemed that fatigue was burning our temples, drying our hands, mak-ing out fingernails painful, and putting rings around our anx-ious eyes, like those of the young men and women of that paroxysmal island. We went down to the shore and bathed in the frigid water; the wind of the departure reanimated us. The sails inflated and, as we prepared to depart we asked: "Have you divined the cause of this terrible redness, and can you also tell us the name of your homeland?"

"I cannot explain the light," said one, "and nor can anyone else here. I think, however, that you might learn its cause on one of the other islands. We have never communicated with them. It is claimed that a singular order makes us forget one another, and I don't know any more than that. As for the name, we call this land of congealed blood the Isle of Knowledge."

Our ship began to cut through the celestial reflections in the water, and we agreed among ourselves to call the island the Isle of Fever.

As we touched the sand of the second supernatural land, several of our traveling companions felt their excitement attenuate; everything advertised a more temperate vegetation, the illusion of a return to the fields gilded by the mild sun of the western lands. The inhabitants commiserated with us. They were less exuberant and nearer to us mentally, even though they demonstrated in their repose and slightly disdainful middle-aged beauty that they too were exceptional. A melancholy slept in their eyes and disenchanted their silence; it softened us, evoked the beautiful sadness of the abandoned young women who grow ponderous in the dusks of ports, by virtue of so much languor and divination of their eyes, turning toward the sails promising exile. A similar languor was communicated to us.

Those people were even milder than the young folk of the previous island, but they spoke with more reserve and their gestures sometimes revealed a lassitude of life, the ideal burden of their knowledge. Like them, on casting our eyes over ourselves, we saw ourselves dying and declining in strength. The redness of the sky and the land, the eternal calm of the water, appeared to us less of a dawn than a sunset, and, thinking about the hour when the white stone quays were a tender pink at their summit and a somber violet at their base, when the European sun lies horizontal to the chambers, we thought bitterly about the enormity of the world, which had previously counted for nothing.

The shadows came to fall upon our foreheads and kiss our cheeks. The countryside was the color of iron oxide, old blood and ocher. The inexplicable redness weighed upon us, as well as the regret of knowledge; we recalled legends, with tears in our eyes, which the sea wind no longer dried up.

We said: "It's time to go." Our fever for exploration was extinct, our curiosity blunted. We no longer looked at the stars; having meditated on their nature too much, they no longer amused us. The hours were animated like training flowers and bent over tiredly in our dreams; their regular faces revealed tears, their troubled eyes were immemorial; already we could no longer distinguish them any longer, but they all seemed to be our sisters weeping: "Tell us, is it necessary to go?"

Pale dock-workers, shadows of sailors, the disorientated hectic flight of the gulls! When we begged our sad hosts to tell us the cause of the redness and the name of their homeland, the response was: "None of us can explain the light. You might, though, find it on the third island; for we have never communicated with it. It is claimed that a singular order made us forget one another, and we no longer know why. As for this island, it has always been the Isle of Doubt."

Our prow was soon cleaving the foam; the strand disappeared. Pensively, we said: "Let's call it the Isle of Misunderstanding; that's what suits it best."

When he set foot on the soil of the third Bloody Island, we found a faded land. Little pathways led us to little starlit orchards; the mosses wearing away the walls were black, and the paltry huts long out of date. The trees, as powdery as old bones, bore withered leaves and small, sickly fruits of an ancient sweetness. The shade of thickets hung over our heads in a debilitated fashion. Everything seemed to be filled with a green-tinted and age-old memory.

We encountered sluggish individuals. Their limbs were devoid of strength, their extinct eyes ridiculously circled with wrinkles. No beauty resided in their eyes, and their dusty souls, devoid of virtue, saddened us. They talked with assurance about the uselessness of all things, and listed them with scorn, affirming that they served no purpose at all. We protested internally: *Can one talk like that about Nature?* But they enlaced us with arguments and axioms. They took dreams like moths and tore away their legs in order to see them hop or writhe. Their knotty and meager fingers suspended a lacework of spider-webs in the air, which imprisoned our silence. Their swaying hands thus became weavers with the detestable shuttle of sophisms; they caught our enthusiasms on the wing like larks, in the mirror of negligibility and futility, in which our lives were reflected. Between ourselves, not knowing what to think, we wondered whether our life was ruined, as if the blood in the veins had dried up.

"Humans," we said, "you who know and deny everything, tell us the name of your island, and why it is this uniform color of red given to the earth, the sky and the water—for we are living in that doubt."

"This," said the old men, "is the Isle of Certainty, or Disgust, for those two names are equivalent. The red color is the reflection of the red rust fecund in these parts, and that fixed red is the eternal blood of the inhabitants of our three islands, which streams perpetually from the wounds in their heart, and is gradually sterilizing it. They spread it through their lives. Those of the first island have rich veins, heirs to beauty and desire, and their flowerings are opulent. Those of the second isle already have paler and depreciated blood, for the struggle of the truth is rude there. And we, who have learned, have blood that is clear and exhausted; see how it flows a pale ocher. For know that the earth is only nourished by blood. So, increasingly absorbed by the knowledge of things, we proceed tranquilly toward the minute when, knowing everything, we have to renounce our flesh. But why ask for the recitation of a fable? Have you not, like us, accomplished the three voyages, outside time and immemorially? Are you amusing yourselves by having us recite a conjecture as well known to you as to us, poor blind men? Or are you becoming blind in body and soul, unable any longer to see your hair, your wrinkles, your minds and your blind and abolished selves?"

Then, having looked at one another, there was not one of us who wanted to sound the same words within himself, and did not see that his body was extenuated like the bodies of those men. The blood in our veins was congealed and annulled, our voices broken, our minds faded and feeble. We repeated in the bottom of our hearts: *The Isle of Wrinkles*.

And we turned toward the sea, in a surge of despair, in order to go back to our ship on our feeble legs, and perhaps—perhaps!—to flee.

We saw that over the immutable sea, an invisible current had caused the vessel to drift, and that the inert waves would not carry us back to her, even swimming, and that, with her great wings immobile in the absence of breeze, she was asleep like a swan in the middle of the red ocean...

We were no longer anything but meager little old men, like toys; we felt very sorry for ourselves.

That is what happened to us, in the unfolding of the Supernatural, by virtue of having made landfall in the Bloody Isles, where the sea is calm. Is there no remission, Lord, and recommencement? Shall we no longer know the deafening tempest, the cloud where the chattering veils are as livid as chalk, the mortal gesture of celestial sulfur, and the howling omnipotence of the Ocean? Or will we remain, Lord, in the sickness of this pink land, forever renouncing the misty quay of the native inlet, the mildness of Northern mists, the cherished frisson of the vast sea, silk with algae and tresses?

Oh, to live again, to suffer, ah! To live under Cygnus, Orion, the tenebrous Night and the lucid stars!

...When we opened our eyes the stars still loved us.
Such was our first dream,

The Pale Hands

The high colonnades of black marble rose into the somber sky, veils of silk stretched over the bays, and no one ever saw the stars. A population of terrible forms wandered confusedly in the metallic garden, and an odor of flesh advanced toward us.

We entered into the city of Voluptuousness and Darkness.

A stairway opened over a pit of shadow. On the first step, warm tears touched our foreheads with a kiss, and invisible lips drew away; perhaps it was modesty...

On the last step, lips touched ours, and that kiss had the taste of Oblivion. Perhaps it was lust...

Since then, how have we lived? There was an immense weakness, and silence and time appeared to be a single immortal spasm.

A gust of warm wind, extinguishing the lamps, stirred the foliage; they rustled with a confused life, abnormal fruits colliding; they stiffened in sky opaque with shameless and singular silhouettes. Their shadows elongated like bridal trains, snaking along the pathways, disappearing into others full of petals and benzoin fumes. We wandered in those odorous by-ways; our feet brushed quivering beings; hands rose up toward us from the bases of hornbeams, surging forth alone and clenched; the arms were invisible but warm breath rose up with them, and fever stretched their fingers into strange images.

It was a country with no digestion of open hands, and a double hedge bristled with the promising fingers in the darkness. Vague glimmers caused Maia's face to shine within her golden hair as she walked, upright and rigid, her hands dangling and her staring eyes raised high up, in order not to see the croaking couples, and beside her, my heart was bitten by a vague bitterness, for we were swaying like flower-heads, emerging from the waist up from a universal stupor. A divination caused the liquid eyes of my beloved to scintillate in the darkness...

When we finally fell, mouth against mouth, into the warm annihilation of the city, we resumed in an embrace the frenzy of long sobbing centuries; and although we did not know everything, we had anticipated everything. The cherished one, tight against me, inclined her long lashes over her drowned pupils; her neck folded like an alga, and I thought I was sinking into a deep pond.

We waited, breathless, for the moment when the bewildered soul opens like a furnace and crumbles into the infinity of death, and with a great frisson we went with the universal flow. Armies of specters poured obliquely across the road of our reason in a red tumult, cataracts of thunderbolts rumbled around us in their luminous foam, and projected our will far outside of into the chaos.

The spasm of the fall increased the agony of others; we heard their hissing voices whispering in the friction of fabric, and the sigh of the amorous breeze upset is delightfully with the plaint of violins. Delirium threw us across the opaque depths of the ether, hammering our limbs, deforming us and transforming us.

We became things or thoughts again, or singular spectacles: a field of wheat bleeding its poppies toward the crazed azure; a group of wild animals bounding over charred rocks; a wave breaking against a great ship; the face of a man looking down into a fire from the height of a tall tower. The colonnades commenced rotating like a vast wheel; they spun more rapidly, insensately, and the pillars of porphyry saw their capitals, like beacons or the great sails, flew away like blind eagles, exasperated by the spinning, the disrupted equilibrium collapsing into the improbable, the mingled colors striping the obscurity with frantic rainbows.

We swam in a sea of inconceivable hues, the ultra-violet burning our pupils; and in the utmost depth of a firmament of enchantment and wrath, a silent face smiled at us behind a rain of gems, diaphanized by the hectic flight of doves...

The awakening: Maia's eyelids slowly raised, like aquatic flowers, the blue of fugitive eyes, glimpsed, then veiled by tears, then thoughtful and then infinitely soft. And her dear lips were murmuring, while we descended toward life again and reality entered into our souls again in the beating of our hearts with the regular and soporific rhythm of waves desirous of the sands...

Our souls were like strands lying nonchalantly alongside the dunes, and the tide of passion rose there, leaving behind in its ebb a few precious objects that remained embedded; at each embrace there was an infinity of visions of spiritual jewels, with which we augmented ourselves in the darkness. Slumber embalmed them with slowness.

Around us, an immemorial orgy was perpetuated. We never saw the faces of our companions, but only their pale hands with the illuminated brushing fingers coming toward us. The women's hands parodied cut lilies.

We sometimes dragged ourselves, like convalescents, all the way to the thresholds of nocturnal porticos. The gardens of steel and bronze were asleep without a frisson, and the air bathed our faces. A meditative moon drew blue silk over the palm trees, blanching the steles and the polished corners of upright frontons. A violent and sexual aroma was rising from basins of perfumed oil, disturbing us; and we remained hesitant, in the heart-sickness of voluptuousness, leaning on the marble columns. They rose up indifferently toward the sky. In the distance, the orange lamps and the braziers of an imperial fête were burning, and illuminated galleries were ablaze over the sea.

That embalmed warmth exhausted us; our fermented spirits became more lucid in the fatigued satisfaction of our flesh. They lamented, and sometimes quit us. Many a time, swooning devoid of strength on the wide bed, I saw above us the chaste soul of Maia mingling with mine. It was like an enlightenment; we had never seen ourselves thus. It seemed that the exhaustion of our bodies had caused the vivacious flora of our contrition and our silence to spring forth, independent and virginal.

Knowledge wandered toward us and possessed us. Augmented and dissolved together, we contained the entire universe, the planets obeying the beating of our arteries, the most distant voyages not going beyond our confused gazes, and we listened to the pulsation of the world, harmonized with our fever. We knew neither day nor night.

Under the influence of lust, our brains exalted, and our thoughts of old contemplated us with a new visage. Visions obsessed us.

Naked people descended to the banks of a great black river. They played there, and linked their waists together with interlaced reds. They were seen jumping, their arms raised and their heads supported by the shoulder, or diving like dolphins and rising up again with livid faces. The caress of the water enervated them, and they went to sleep on the bank, lying next to one another, while the youngest ran anxiously between the trees, their eyes moist with desire.

Dancers approached and drew away from one another, coming back only to depart again, in a cadenced and mechanical movement. Their faces were masked, their breasts jutting from diamond-studded corsets, their legs joined and their feet in sharp, inward-turned sandals, fluttering toward one another. They were perfumed and mute. Their hair brushed us, and they bent their arms languidly.

Above us rose warm and living statuettes, stretched toward the flowers that their extended arms were offering to the heavens. They stretched themselves smoothly, or remained immobile, as if waiting for something. They leaned over their supple loins, contemplating some hidden and impure object whose charm shrank their pupils. Their feline eyes peeked at us from behind the silk of the mass, and already they were snaking toward something else; a crazy impulse struck them and they turned round. Their hair, as straight and smooth as a fabric in the wind of the dance, drew away from the nape, mingling as it threw great shadows into the room, and then, at a pause, falling back in heavy waves over the shoulders and the pale breasts—with the consequence that the bare flesh was alternately revealed and concealed.

A crouching negress extended her nipples over a mandora; a child clad in colorful cloth clicked castanets, and we were penetrated by melancholy.

On emerging from the bath we kissed with so much force that our lips seemed desiccated and worn. The form of our mouths delighted us, and we talked about them with earnest gravity: their taste, their sweet softness, their moisture penetrated with amour. The intoxication gave us so much pleasure that we were both carried away by gratitude and devotion, stammering and confused. A little blood pearled and our mouths parted momentarily. We took one another's heads in our hands and looked one another in the eyes. Then, without detaching our gazes, we drank the blood, drop by drop, from one another's lips, gently and fearfully, as if absorbing a venom. It appeared to us that we were tasting a little death, that we were, in a sense, entering a little way into it.

The fever rendered us an almost normal calm. Lying down, we exchanged weary words, torpid, like peasants taking a siesta in the wheat in August. Their eyes are burned by white clouds, consumers of warm light, the black sky weighs upon them, agglutinating their eyelashes and cracking their parted lips; the trickle of flesh water no longer flows under the stones and leaves, and exhaustion is great. Thus we were stagnating in the somnolence of a discouraged afternoon.

They were hours of penetration and analysis. Life was audible within us, making a slight crackle, like fire-crickets quivering on the logs of the heart, in the silence. That sizzling delighted us; it was the only sure sign that we were not extinct, and we savored its presence bitterly in the solitude.

How well we sensed it, life! Even our flesh did not prevent us from seeing one another. Through it we perceived the movement of the blood, a minimal gesture deployed for our study an infinite network of nerves, and the hymn of our accorded thoughts alternated its double harmony on those material awakenings. Our decomposed ideas fell asleep in spiritual designs, and the carnal orgy gradually ignited a metaphysical fête. Immodesty appeared to us as the veritable purity, the enchantment of the nocturnal city limited our belief to perfumed kisses that one gave to the person one wanted to know, and the ignored seems to us bound to dissolve thus between the lips, like a woman ceding to the hour of shadows.

We knew one another in the dream; our mouths opened simultaneously to respond mutually to their demand. Maia was entirely my imagination, I was entirely hers, and we imagined almost everything. Voluptuousness was an enormous country, where forms were modified fantastically, and wherever we touched one another was the center of the world.

I believe that those great crises enabled us to be understood even to the sensuality of heaven. In demanding pleasure from everything, we loved everything with discernment, for pleasure is the essential means of knowledge. We had never communicated so recklessly with fabrics, the darkness, or flowers. Their interior life oozed, through the velvet folds, the vaporous swirls of palms and incense; the satined petals of corollas impregnated us with their special moisture, penetrating us, animating, testifying to occult desires, and their existence, finally understood, created new phantoms for us.

We knew what an aroma or a touch was, we could almost see them, we detailed their various phrases, their attitudes, so strongly did they seems to us to be affirmed. The universe was populated, for us, as much with abstract ideas as objects, and we became sufficiently accustomed to it no longer to be able to envisage anything in isolation. For us, the world was not a confusion of multiform spectacles and simultaneous sensations, but an order of reciprocal harmonies, evolving without hazard even in their breakages, an edifice of nobility and meditation in which we wandered respectfully; and no event or object ever appeared to us as an accident, of which we had not envisaged piously the evidence of a centuries-long descendancy, the conclusion of a family or a form, and, like the bas-reliefs of destiny, the visible molding of our ideal.

Such was for us the real meaning of voluptuousness, which is not lust, but which arises from it and is the precious and pure reflection of it; it appeared to us an art of knowledge, and by way of desire we came to cherish nature disinterestedly. We found in the delirium of our bodies an aliment for our minds, and passion burned us to purify us, for we awoke more loving.

Is it not reason, we thought, to be intoxicated by love until the dazzling moment of death? And what is more comprehensible that a creation of nature, when she offers herself with a smile? She presents, like a bouquet, all the bounty and charms of which she is capable, and if she did not desire to do so, she would never reveal anything...

Thus our thoughts wandered in the monotonous ecstasy of the city in which we languished. They were born and fortified during our walks. We went all the way to the promontory through supernatural gardens. Their immutable metal loomed up in beautiful forms around us, and we leaned our foreheads delightedly on the fresh leaves...

Amorous goats were running hither and yon, and their velvet eyes troubled us; they breathed in the sea breeze and bleated ingenuously. A little violet shadow fluttered behind them...

And we envisaged with a hidden dread the universal instinct of touches and caresses. We saw them impregnating the world and becoming its mainspring. Everything coagulated and was orientated in reciprocal unions, and the same antique fury constrained flower and animal, tree and human, perfume and obscurity.

We never saw the faces of the inhabitants of that kingdom. Only their hands emerged, pale, long and caressant, from the shadow of padded beds.

One might have thought that only their long fingers were alive, and that their eyes had abdicated all desire to add precision to embrace by contemplation. Their quivering hands frightened us. Their fingernails were gilded, appearing to us as refined and special instruments, and all the vitality of their possessors descended into them. Sometimes we glimpses the confused forms of human beings standing up, tottering, and voices muffled by debauchery calling to them softly from the mass of cushions and drapes. They had the appearance of phantoms; toward the colonnades of platforms they reached out wearily with those strange hands, scintillating with jewels, only those fugitive flashes revealing their existence...fire follets in a poisoned atmosphere...

The voluptuousness of music was the most heart-rending, and perhaps the most delicious. It embraced our flesh and our sentiments simultaneously. When symphonies unfurled their sobbing tempests toward us, a spasm gripped the heart, without our being able to know whether its dear exhaustion was physical or mental.

At those moments, most of all, we no longer existed for ourselves, but were instruments played by the hands of an unknown god. They strayed over us, they brushed us; the violins streaked our dolorous skin, the howling of the horns made us bristle, the vivid liquid spurting from the flutes made us delirious. We paused in the midst of the music like a shepherd beneath the sky, and everything rotated around our isolation. The song of the oboes rose up alone, and its shrill monotony exasperated us with melancholy...but already the frenzy of the cellos was croaking slowly, clarinets were sliding and biting us like vipers, and the entire invisible and formidable orchestra stiffened like the undulating sea of crops toward the sun. That arid imaginary ocean bowled us over; we fell into its gulfs, rolled from one weave to another, until a supreme appeal of trumpets emerged from the melodic hurricane like a haloed hero.

The great exhaustion of the music transposed landscapes in slumber. Its nature continued for us in dream, and the sounds were colored to the extent of burning our eyelids. The gesture of the bow traced real lines upon us, the measure determining entire planes; an andante figured unerringly fields descending from the mountains toward the plain, an allegro painted golden and violet skies, and the capricious finale undulated like the shiny river extending to vanish at the horizon...

Songs, again, enchanted us in a beautiful garden through which pure weeping forms were passing; or there were isolated notes, almost broken, in which we were suspended in the collapse of our vanquished nervousness...

It seemed to us that we were lying against the wall of the universe, and that we were hearing a din behind an invisible and yet impenetrable wall. Those spiritual orgies subjugated us; we never tasted with more violence the nullity and all the prestige of annihilation. Inebriated, we went into gardens singing in loud voices the tunes that had charmed us, and we were moist with those transports. Our eyes were ringed, our temples throbbing, all noise became harmonic for us, we improvised regular hymns on the waves, and the cries of birds lacerated us delightfully. The intoxication of song fused with that of the flesh ad that of metaphysics, and we dragged out a dazzling and defeated life, a miserable and magnificent existence in which ideas, songs and intercourse extenuated us with a similar inclemency.

We had perceptions so sharp that we conceived everything in their orders and expansion, and supported all the weight of the world. We were sick with the knowledge of memory. We arrived before one another like two ships returning from the Orient, gilded with treasures and supernatural balms; thus our courage buckled under the burden of familiar things. But fatigue gripped us, nothing seemed fresh to us any longer. Intuition killed ingenuousness within us, examining every new object with piercing eyes, so that its properties sometimes penetrated us without our being able to enjoy them. Distaste ate us away like scurvy, and we considered the sea with the desire to forget and to leave,

We waited for a long time, so weak were we. Around us, the lustful fête of the sectarians of Voluptuousness was exasperated. We saw them running into the dense woods at dusk with torches, and their clamors resonated over the strand. Perfumed wood fires burned with great straight blue flames, and frightened snakes launched themselves into the undergrowth. Troops of wild beasts howled and hugged the trees; obscene monkeys threw flowers, and pursued goat-kids fled over the rocks. The entire island was agitated by a feverish tremor.

We hid in an abandoned palace. One evening, we went down to our ship. We saw the sailors arriving one by one. They were as thin and wan as ourselves, and were not thinking about anything but flight. We were so debilitated that the sight of the waves frightened us, and we thought about staying. But our destiny was alert! One of our companions came running with terror; he emerged from a sandy eminence from which the city was visible.

"Let's go!" he howled. "Hordes of men and women are running toward us!"

A great light rose up behind him, and he hurled himself aboard. The moment of peril caused us to cast off with an unexpected vigor, and within a matter of moments we were at sea.

Then, from the open sea, we contemplated the most terrible of spectacles. Undoubtedly, the torches of the celebrations had set fire to the city, for its high incandescent colonnades were crowned with enormous sparks, and the metallic vegetation was sizzling like a hellish rod. The desperate clamors of the inhabitants reached us with the odor of cellars of molten perfumes, and red gleams inflamed their faces. They leapt on the water like supernatural fish, and it was with the crash of a gigantic, inconceivable thunderbolt that we saw the city of Voluptuousness and Darkness collapse in an abominable cataclysm.

Scylla's Song
Scattered Fragments of a
Voyage to the Land of Amnesia

...and of extinct blood that no longer knew life. Ancient figures appeared in our dusk, and we were unable to determine whether they had been born during the day—for we were at the end of our memory or our foresight—or, alternatively, without discerning from what direction they arose, from the depths of the taciturn night when we leaned over that void in anguish. We were unable to discover whether, beyond the miserable frame in which our effort was agitating, memory and presentiment were reconciled in the illusion of infinity, or floating separately in the darkness.

The figures that rose up that evening defied all the names with which humans can stigmatize their phantoms. There was sometimes a dance of aureoles like crescent moons on the surface of the troubled water. We dreamed of strange, and yet sad, prides, not knowing whether we ought to deplore past royalties or caress future dreams.

...the Isle of Migraine is populated with beings who are composed in unity, not in duality; they have one eye, one nostril, one leg, one arm. They do not distinguish right or left, and go straight ahead, hopping. They have no idea of environment, but throw themselves to the right or the left when an obstacle presents itself; thus, they are constantly the center of everything, without knowing it.

They wear iron crowns on their heads, which they tighten with pegs, and never ornament with other jewels. Their country is weighed upon by thick, low clouds, which drag their mist-sweating blisters almost along the ground; roads strewn with the pyrites of various metals lead via difficult networks to oxidized mountains where vertigo strolls over pale grass, the malevolent odor of which grips the temples.

We perceived Vertigo. He is sad, and reaches circling clenched fists toward the sky, or folds his arms and leans over rocky abysms, nodding his head, and then extends his hands into the depths and brings them back, as if capturing an imaginary flower, and becomes immobile. His robe swirls in the wind; he prophesies everything that Fear has promised Thought and his shrill voice screeches like a rusty trap. When he saw us, he came toward us, and we were recoiling when, having looked over my shoulder. I saw a gulf open at our heels and cried out. One second, and we fell down before the white figure; but already it was no longer advancing, and, leaping over us, disappeared.

We retraced our steps, and the inhabitants offered us metal diadems like their own, but we could not...could scarcely tolerate the heat of our oriental curls. They seem, however to experience a supreme enjoyment in tightening those strange crowns to the very last peg, and it gives them the illusion of being at the bottom of the sea and falling recklessly into unchained maelstroms. They love the unstable whirl passionately, and dolor replaced lust for them, for they are pure and live for a long time.

Their faces are as blank as an autumnal landscape at daybreak, their eyes revealing an insomnia...

That morning, Maia was dreaming, still somnolent, and she said, softly: "This is what the melodious bird called Chalcis by the gods and Cimidis by humans will sing...Chalcis and Cimidis, musical notes..."

And so saying, she awoke. I retraced her dream for her, but she smiled without any response. We dream so often and with such fervent love of things that do not exist that they have become our veritable and essential existence; we no longer live except in dreams, and it would not serve any purpose for us to remember them, for we find a firm support in that which is no longer there.

Maia, in particular, exalts thus toward the future, and she is, above all, sympathetic to phantoms yet to be born. It seems, on seeing her divining the future, that her golden hair inscribes her with a more undeniable crown, and that little silken princess, whose life is made of diamonds and birds, hides an interior light that has not yet risen.

Perhaps, light, you are what we seek? The dawn and the sunset have not yet revealed you; we have desired you on the terraces, we have appealed to you on balconies at dusk, we have traveled the seas…I am weary of sands and rocks, I have confronted gorse and heather, bushes and linden trees, without discovering you either in the Orient or in the Occident, without seizing you, without drinking you, without absorbing you, golden river!

And as for her, the very dear one, the lover all tremulous with the great heroic frisson, whom the morning awakens, babbling, I believe her silence is closed over an interior aureole of your essential glare. Yes, in her, perhaps, is the goal, for in myself I know nothing…but in her, when I embrace her, I hear something like a marching dawn…

The plain of sand is incredibly immense. It is months since we landed here after our return from the Isle of Migraine, and the journey through the desert does not seem to promise us a renewal of the ocean breeze as yet.

Footsteps leave no impression. The route is strewn with bleached bones; objects, weapons and jewels lie nearby, and, recognizing the style and form of some, we believed that we had unknowingly reentered a region of memory, but we were suddenly unable to attribute such jewels or arms to any ancient civilization; their very substance was unknown to us, and we thought that perhaps they were only reflections of objects to come, and that the mirage in the deserts of Amnesia only presented travelers with future spectacles. And, indeed, architectures were edified on the horizon of which we had no idea; our descendents will invent them, and their enchantment impregnated our minds in order that we might transmit them. Thus, only prevision truly exists…

Finally, having encountered cadavers, we recognized ourselves among them. They wore the brilliant necklaces that ornamented our necks, corroded and tarnished, and their ragged clothing was the debris of ours. Other, young cadavers seemed to be those of our children, and others, even more distant, testified to a descendancy.

We slowly visited our future. Since memory had been taken away from us, what could we think about, except the future? For nothing is present, the raised arm has already been lifted up and is about to fall back again, so infinitesimally is the gesture divided, and only God sees everything entrapped in the frame of eternal immutability...

We have contemplated the faces we will have when dead for a long time. They are calm and happy. Their eyelids sleep heavily over watery blue irises. One might think they the crystals of a congealed sky; and the ashy mouths have tasted dolorous fruits. There are also the hands alongside the bodies. They dangle limply; they are open; they no longer take the trouble to grasp anything; they have renounced everything— but perhaps they are full of dreams. Some of their fingers are still supple; one might think they were caressing the silk of a slow and caressant dream, and those raise themselves up toward the eyes in order to extinguish them—one might think— while others drift away like cut reeds, and others signify an embrace concluded in the depths of death.

I have seen one finger over a smile, one hand searching for a sword, another princely with immortal sapphires, and two white, long, pale, frail and terrible, gripping like convulsive birds, crushing mallows and jonquils

Maia wanted to lean over and kiss those poor hands, which resembled hers, but she straightened up again, astonished, for she had kissed the sand.

Night has fallen on that country of magic spells; we entered it more than two hundred nights ago. The stars, fixed...

This interminable voyage presents us with difficult aspects of our destiny. We cherish the presages, and that which is not annotated. When something does not surpass our speech, we like to judge it negligible, but that which penetrates our silence charms us.

Our silence is like a marine grotto; currents of lukewarm passion ripple there in concentric circles, propagated all the way to infinite concealment, and we rotate therein slowly on a solitary skiff, lost in the darkness, mouth to mouth, retaining of the memory of youth only what is necessary to divine our burning eyes and cold teeth, when we release one another momentarily. Our silence is a warm and odorous cyclone; we rotate on the spot in its perfume, living as if between lips that disdain speech and only love in kisses. Objects enter that strange current; they do not touch us but they float and whirl around our boat...but we have forgotten who we are, and have no need of anything...

Thus, events are spectacles and symptoms, but we do not participate in them. We leave them to signify what they contain, and would not dare to modify them. They bring us varied and singing reveries.

This morning we passed a corroded galleon laden with old armor, which was slowly moving against the current. Its haulers were stiffened their muscles; they were young and bright-eyed. But how bleak the old vessel was! Chipped and faded, it dragged its stripped mass and its dishonored prow, ironically ornamented with a fragment of a siren whose head and conch-shell had been carried away by an ancient cannon-ball. The worm-eaten hull still supported above the waves the vain thrust of two draped arms, over which a coating of gilt still flowed in clots, and the two fists clenched above the severed neck and the bruised breasts sketched an obscene gesture at the pink sky. The portholes gave the impression of empty eyes; the sculpted hawse-holes opened futile maws from which chains no longer sprang, and stupid birds were screeching on the stumps of the masts.

That long cadaver, ornamented like a monster of nightmare, went past our vessel; thousands of ancient suits of armor filed her hold completely and encumbered the deck. Repulsive rust made that abolished nobility ridiculous; helmets without visors rolled against bucklers, still dragging limp plumes whose bouquets were broken. The armpits of breastplates yawned like pits of shadow, gauntlets renounced slaps and a few spear-heads stole dull gleams from the dawn. A heap of chain mail was folded up like a damaged fishing-net.

An ancient grandeur was extinct in that vessel. We followed it with our eyes for some time. A few slender boatmen ran over the gunwales with poles, rhythming indifferently the interminable exodus of haulage against the flow. Gleams strayed over the yellowed and parted morions. That rusty magnificence appeared to us to be attenuating with majesty, like our life; the sinister noises of the metal debris parodied the clash of swords sparkling over heroic flesh, like a caricaturish echo A child standing up in the bow put on the plumed helmet in play, strapped an oversized breastplate on his torso, whose double shell grated as it danced, and we thought, sadly, that our dream was attempting in the same fashion to gird itself with the invisible, and covet a nimbus with the same vanity.

At a bend, the galleon disappeared behind the reeds, and we remained pensive, as if slightly diminished. Maia's smile supposed singular melancholies. I touched that smile softly with mine, for a moment; it retained within it an odor of autumn leaves, the perfume of a bouquet of faded and solitary glory...

We are descending the river of time. A double hedge of eternal trees inclines over the banks. I imagine my dreams alternating with them. Trophies hang from those trees, and one can see old blood burnishing the weapons and the trunks, hanging down in dense crystals. The grass on the bank is trampled, rising stepwise in jaundices strips toward the plain. A blazing sky is agonizing behind the hill, and the wind is making the clouds tremble. A cold azure is dreaming over the summits of the poplars, its unstable similar reflections breaking up in the eddies. The west is striped with colors that influence one another reciprocally, as the year surrenders to the irremediable diversity of the hours, and fades with the last into a luminous and nonchalant radiation.

A yellow road snakes between the blue banks, swallows cry shrilly and martins amuse themselves in rapid and irritate flight; a slight breeze in the branches plays with the first rusty leaf, and the old song of obsolescence sways the naked birches and willows; they are nodding off into a light slumber; it evening. A mist, suddenly risen, lazily extends is blue-tinted tresses toward the shores. The tall reeds are black, and pink moonlight quivers in the water.

Meanwhile, indifferent clouds lead a few sleepy stars, in the smoke and lace of their opaque flotation, toward the sullen horizon. A stand of pines coagulates in the darkness. Nothing is audible.

I remember coming down here once, through the wheatfields, on horseback, on emerging from the forest. We had wandered under the covert in the cool green shade, and had headed back toward the plain at dusk. Suddenly, we emerged from the foliage at the top of a hill. The orange-tinted crops and the blue grass extended their declining squares all the way to the violet distance; a firmament of heroic gold loomed up to seduce us with famous architectures, which crumbled into an extreme and horizontal furnace. We descended at a rhythmic pace; the wind pleased us; the smoke of nearby roofs rose up amid the vegetation; the bend in the river mirrored a fugitive flash among the trees. The landscape, warm and voluptuous in color, embalmed the pines and the wild cherries...

A simple soul rose from the fatigue of the evening, wandering dazedly toward the small houses emerging from the verdant swell. The shoes of our horses clattered on the hardened ground of shadowy hamlets; the occidental radiation was already hesitating on pink-tinted chimneys.

I looked at Maia, upright in a green and silver dress, and thought of an Armida before that slim upper body and that dear imperious head, aureoled with an exquisite gold by the dusk's farewell.

I do not know whether we had ever emerged like that from a real forest, like conquerors, toward a horizon, and perhaps it was only a picture once seen; but whether it was dream or reality, as we sometimes sensed it violently, instinct traced the black and beautiful gestures of a celebrated sword, crowned by a flamboyant tournament, on a fiery firmament. Unhealthy bulwark rails from which one gazes at the shore or the sea! We had departed in search of light and we were only encountering ennui. We had, in the meantime, attempted many things—legend, lust, and the Bloody Isles where one learns the three ages, and the pale sensualities that are consummated marvelously in the storm of an enervating and obscure disaster—but now we only find headaches or ironic verdure.

Melancholy on such evenings, on the terraces of indolence, we have raised our white forms toward you; we have drunk you in the cups of tombs like the birds of the sun, we have sent our souls toward you like doves! Now we are descending a dismal river that detests aquatic flowers, and our overripe hearts are suspended in our breast like a disdained fruit; a little ash has insinuated itself therein...

The lake is surrounded by sheer cliffs of glaucous and violet-tinted basalt, vertically carved and reflected in very clear water. Things sometimes scintillate in the depths. Our nets have brought up gold rings and opal necklaces, which were sleeping in an immemorial dream down there, and crosses too, and silver blades figuring the moon. Who had come to abdicate those jewels?

In the utmost depths of the lake, one is hidden. They have been worn there by the dead, in their graves. We have not dared to take possession of them, but threw them back into the water, and they fell back into the palace of damp oblivion, for we never found the same ones again in our fishing expeditions.

All night long it seemed to us that the hair and hands of women were brushing our faces. The disdain of centuries had flowed through the holes in those rings...

Maia utters a cry; she has found an hour-glass on the bank. The sand that fills it is strange. Yes, that substance really is the dust of time. How many thoughts, burned by the infinite sun, have confided their cinerary adieu to that useless timepiece? There is no more past, there has never been a present, and perhaps it is the ashes of our imminent dreams that are warning us of their vanity now, in that lobe of impenetrable crystal.

A city at dusk. Lights in the rain. Poor grass growing among the debris of factory chimneys; the voracious furnaces of bloody forges agonizing in their smoky enclosures. The violet collieries are deserted, the astonishing skeletons of pitheads standing out stiffly against a neutral sky, O cities widowed of drapes, how ennui multiplies within you! It is a voracious lichen, or some unhealthy octopus.

There are a certain number of motives for ennui, or rather, in every conjuncture there resides a cause. But will we ever know them as anything more than the fire behind a grate, the lock of a disused door or an incomplete drawing? I have seen pastels of women lying on the ground in the street. Carriages threw stars of mud over their lace and their cleavages, their hair and their lips; one, with her eyes splashed in that manner, was gazing with eyes of filthy mud.

I still dream about the old gods, who exhausted themselves brandishing stone torches, from which stone flames emerged, on the ledges of an abandoned pavilion. They incarnate the languid stupidity of stability, and it is perhaps only fluidity that goes running from one dream to another, from one island to another, from one corolla to another, from the pupil of one eye to the pupil of another, indefinitely...

Cities wound us with their aspect of *installation*. Meanwhile, the clouds pass, crowning them, releasing them; their bridges attempt in vain the clutch of a metal claw over the water; the river flows, and the souls of the inhabitants flow toward the darkness, the moon and death, under the breath of dreams, and the houses remain, like empty coffins...

Maia does not like, any more than I do, that which is established. It is necessary to *discover*, and noble souls only know that pilgrimage. A man who puts his faith in the present is unhealthy and devoid of elevation, let us say, and the countries of Amnesia teach us only to look to the future for courage. We are traveling in order to discover ourselves, but I am beginning to see that we will not encounter ourselves in landscapes traversed. They do not tell us the essential, they are merely décor. We exist, whereas they appear, and the main thing is that we are heading through them toward our future; for we constitute ourselves with time, and the last minute is not the one that finishes a life but the one that completes it.

Maia's eyes sometimes seem to me to reflect the firmament of the chosen life; they contain everything fugitively; one might think that they had glimpsed the end of the voyage. At those moments I sense that she no longer exists, that she is in advance of me, that she is like my detached imagination, dancing before me with a smile. I almost no longer love her...or rather, I love her like myself; there is very little difference any longer between the two of us, and by the beating of her heart, mine has been decreed for a long time.

One sees children with beautiful eyes leaning against walls. One does not know what they are waiting for. Only the mud and hunger know, but they do not speak; then, on certain days, they should very loudly, and those are terrible days, dark with blood.

Those waiting children are no longer hungry. The suck emptiness and negation with their lips, old lips monstrous in twilight, on evenings when it lies drowsily, like a moribund, over the cities dirtied by black sweat. I like those children; perhaps I will discover myself entirely in them, and each of them is one of my souls—for if I only had one soul, it would hate me, but the others keep me safe...

Some of them have eyes as terrible as the song of the lark behind a dead man's door. Hyacinths and nympheas faded between the lashes of others, and such eyes are moist fruits; others have a patina like green pommels of bronze. One sees in others the tones of ancient leather brightened by the net-

111

work of veins of a nubile breast. Those are indefinable, resembling axioms more closely than living things.

The hand of those children, too...they plunge them into their poor pockets. They make their fingernails screech on the last little coin in the bottom of those miserable canvas bags warmed by the head of their virgin sex organs. And their feet seem to be born from the mud. Sinister peddler's trays adding to the infamy of their meager flesh and their rags, they languish, lost children, between the icy bars of insistent downpours. We love them without knowing why, having pity, fundamentally, only for that which we might be. They huddle together in the shadow under the light of crazy windows, like huge scarabs with burned wings. They have no particular form, and it would not be useful to them to have one more precise than misery itself; but they are all that the rest of the living have disdained of avatars of rags and chlorosis. They fill the corners of doorways; a few play a sad music, and their falsetto voices propagate a menacing and punctuated cry along the walls. Emaciated Insomnia smoothes their hair, and makes them beautiful for the hour of solitude. Famine, idleness and the troubling rain prepare them to cough to the staccato rhythm of their footsteps in the deserted streets, while their belated heels press the asphalt with a soft sound and the gas-lamps turn the oily reflections of the gutters yellow, tarnished by the obscure rancor of the silence.

I hate cities.

We left the land of Amnesia this morning. It disappeared abruptly behind us. A sailor was singing, and we suddenly remembered with a great tenderness our ancient and secret house. On the shore, birds were playing and chirping. In the grass dotted with red and gilded flowers, placid sheep came to drink. And from further away, when he perceived us, a young goatherd came running and dancing; he leapt as if his heart might burst, his head raised in laughter, naked and pink in the lovely morning light.

A head emerged from the nenuphars and gazed at us. Amid golden hair, bright eyes opened and closed.

Another emerged from the irises and gazed at us, another from the jonquils, and another from the asphodels, and others still from the reeds and the rocks—everywhere. They floated like medusas, and we considered them in silence. Then we perceived on the stones, and hanging from the branches above the water, lyres, swords, diadems and gems scintillating among fabrics. All of that was abandoned, and we understood that we had before us the sirens, for a light song rose up in the placid murmur of the sea.

"Whoever wants to know oriental sweetness, the secret of the reeds, the song of kisses, to give a precise meaning to the modesty of the dawn and the lusts of the night, let him come toward our lips and our eyes, laugh in our smiles and sob in our hair!

"We shall love him like a fruit, we shall cherish him like a bird, we shall lull him to sleep like the summer clouds, we shall cradle him in our souls as on autumn leaves!

"His joy will be gilded like the summit of a tree in the sun, his pride will raise hollyhocks, his nonchalance will float like seaweed, it will dissolve in a dusk!

"Has he not time to know and to rest from the voyage? Many have pursued stars, circled their destiny with the fire of a divine blade, rocking their anxiety upon the sea!

"And yet they will not discover themselves, and will die while waiting for creation to recommence! They will sit down in the evening to see the future race pass by, and put an ear to the ground. But they will not hear anything rumble!

"Never have they seen the white kings standing up among the manes, the bronze, the catapults and standards! They have not seen the tranquil men descend from the glaciers of the Pole into the confusion of the seasons!

"They have shivered in the wind of doubt and decay, they have fled their own pride, they have sensed themselves cowards like a thief in broad daylight, and they have died as negligible as branches in December.

"Only those who have entered into our grotto have listened, amid the echo of the waves, to the sentence of river Ocean, curbed and sonorous as a barbaric buckler. He summarizes everything; he is a sagacious and eternal serpent!

"Nothing escapes him. He coils slowly around horizons, he penetrates the meaning of countries, he lists the meditations of rocks and the immemorial sadness of snows when the sun goes away!

"And turn by turn, the sickly Spring, with its verdant convalescence, which disturbs the slumbering trees, crowns him with new leaves falling upon his hollow eyes.

"Summer, with its mild corteges of singing hours, its flights of alternating oars over the warm water, and its warrior nudities beloved by luxurious light.

"Autumn, sliding like dead flowers over the silence, orchard of vines, bruised garden, with its dear blue-tinted fevers upon the red reeds.

"And Winter, which goes forth like a hunter with muted footsteps to force the wolves in their lugubrious forests, with its bright fire, its jealous crowd and the horror of the sterile mantle that it spreads out toward the taciturn sun.

"Turn by turn the seasons present themselves, with their dangling girdle of poems and their robe of years, before our father Ocean, who enveloped the Earth, like a child, in the epoch when she rolled in the sky, with a body of clouds and sandy cyclones devoid of consistency or skeleton!

"Then he squeezed her, coagulated her and sustained her, soft still; and he is like a blue ring clenched about her, contemplating her with his innumerable secret visages; and she hides nothing from him.

"We know the abstract things that given the seasons and humans. They shine like divine gems in the darkness of that lair. And we dance joyfully in the happy water, a few paces away!

"We will give them to the man who comes close and imposes his lips on ours, to the man who is not afraid to feel the marine freshness of our virgin arms around his neck, and who will belie, with a simple gesture, the eternal fear that isolates us!

"Oh, dear unknown, will you finally come toward the redoubted and bloody Scylla, toward our lips and our eyes, laughing in our smiles and weeping in our hair?"

They were no longer singing, and between their golden curls their glaucous eyes opened and closed alternately. And we, sensing that a visage of our decreed destiny was about, to reveal itself, solemnly, steal away or confound us, we listened in our hearts, very softly, so softy that they scarcely survived...

We took a step toward the grotto, and then we began to walk. And as we came closer, the gilded heads surrounded us in greater numbers. On the threshold, we darted a long last glance at the sea, and it appeared to us, in a flash, that innumerable sails had been fleeing madly toward open water for an eternity.

We went into the darkness.

And when we had penetrated far enough for the feeble light of the opening to have disappeared, bathed in humid and glaucous darkness, we thought we were about to faint in madness and vertigo, for a small, poor and frail voice rose up, which said, very softly: "Why have you come in? No one ever comes in. Why have you dared to come in? Are you not like the others, then? But if you are singular enough to have been tempted thus, alas, how have you not divined that there is nothing here?"

And other poor, small and frail voices whispered around us. They spoke very quietly; their breath touched our faces. "Alas, alas! We have nothing to say, and there is absolutely nothing here! You know the whole secret in advance; it is you who invented it. Why have you dared to come in? You are killing us with lies..."

The voices seemed to fade away; they fell silent. A little light having been made, we no longer saw anything but disgusting dead medusas, with algal hair, rotting in pools of water...

Instantly, the scales fell from our eyes, and we fled from that venomous cavern, nauseated. On the threshold, the sky was fresh. And, Maya having considered me without speaking, we started to smile at one another softly, our eyes full of tears of disappointment and ecstasy.

The Island of Closed Eyes

At our small windows, diamond-shapes of extinct glass in a frame of leaves, we wait for autumn for hours. It is pleasant to relax in the dusk. The street is shiny under the fine rain, and the houses contemplate the inversion of their prolonged images placidly, on the age-old paving stones; one might think that they are absorbed in their doubles, so gravely are they considering them, and the image of moist roses descends with charm in the tremor of puddles. The corner of the street is deserted, few chimneys smoking at seven o'clock, and sometimes, in the gentle rain, a pale gleam the color of ancient and fugitive gold, rises up and dies down.

Pensive faces, pure foreheads under headbands or tulle, can be glimpsed behind the ornate grilles of low casements. The blue eyes of embroideresses are as cold as the convolvulus of trellises; amber napes undulate with a sad grace, hands extract themselves and imprison themselves in alternate tangles, and the back of the room, where some worn and sumptuous marquetry is illuminated, dissolves into the darkness.

Long gray walls extend, the foliage of a rutilant park, verdant and denuded, on their crest; a little solitary door is enclosed in the middle of stones, placed at intervals. No lock is visible there; one might think that time alone enters. It falls from the shadow with the leaves, and the shadow and the leaves accumulate in a corner of the doorway, immemorially. Footsteps are stifled beneath those walls in the thick carpet of dead twigs, and one can lean on the frame of the postern for a long time without hearing anyone walking on the other side; for the gardens are abandoned, and those who lived there are

116

abandoned themselves to destiny and silence, and no longer emerge.

The gallop of a horse sounds; a rider suddenly bounds forth in the black wrapping of his warrior cloak; the harsh face is visible, the tarnished steel of the damp helmet, the rigid line of the long sword under the fabric. He disappears, and the calm, momentarily disturbed, become torpid again. In the evening, women in mourning walk with little lamps, and sobs are audible beneath their veils; one hand hangs down alongside their dresses, and its fingertips swing the copper lamp. Its red reflection shimmers on the ground, and the tall trees are deformed over the obscure houses. At intervals, at the end of a street, the countryside can be seen, or a crenellated portal, a canal with red and gilded lights trembling in the water, or clumps of cypresses; through the branches the crescent moon is revealed, and a few discreet stars palpitate above the poplars.

On the bridges where an image of a saint stands, whose tortoiseshell aureole and palm are broken; on the quays where bronze balusters are aligned, our nonchalance has taken for its example the matinal indolence of the green-tinted water. Shiny plaques of vegetation are floating there; reeds emerge from it; it is cold, dense, transparent and motionless. It reflects smoke and birds; and when a kingfisher streaks it with a furtive thrust of a wing, it scarcely trembles, so many forgotten and fixed spectacles are steeped therein.

When women lean on the pilasters of the bridges, their exact and mute specters can be seen rising from the depths toward them. One might think that they are making the acquaintance of their sadness, and are slightly astonished by it; those who are young still hesitate to draw away; they consider themselves anxiously, their lips stammering muted and unconscious requests. Then, the similar lips of the inert reflected image are seen to quiver in the ironic mirage, and the words descend toward that reflection like withered leaves. They sink into the water and do not reappear. But old women only look at themselves mechanically, and never speak.

A cold wind twists the mantles of the strolling women into beautiful pleats. Hoods frame the frail hair in which belated and fearful eyes shine, and hands lift up heavy sleeves. The pavement seems to have renounced all sound. Carts are very rare, and life is only announced, very nearly, by the appeals of barge-haulers.

A galley comes into view, which glides over the rippled water at a bend in a canal; its rigging ablaze with armoried pennants dominates the roofs of the houses. Its flags flap in the air with a soft sound; its prow cuts through the heaped-up nenuphars and throws them back upon its curved flanks, over the pendant chains, with the consequence that the sailors hoist those velveted and leafy nenuphars aboard in long streaming trains, mingled with rings and pulleys.

That vast apparatus of wood, gold, ropes and masts passes the buildings thus, one window after another; and the pensive faces behind the panes contemplate that oriental vestige. The odor of roses and spices floats like silk, embalming the mist. Talking birds can be heard chattering; some are surprising. In their wicker cages, they seem like multicolored captive lightning-flashes. They pronounce foreign phrases volubly, hop on to the fists of sailors, and people assemble in corners of the bank to listen to them.

Meanwhile, the holds of ships are emptied, bales roll over the ground, and piles of beautiful silver or green fish can be seen in places, bulging like sculpted and bloodstained breastplates. Staved in baskets let out small shiny sardines; one might think them freshly-sharpened knives. They are the armor of unknown hosts at the bottom of the sea, poured out as pillage after the victory.

But that agitation is rare, and the streets that extend from the harbor are deserted almost immediately. Old men are sitting at the feet of trees, with mute children; grass grows, ignorant of the sickle, and the faces of the houses are blissful. The towers of cathedrals parade their blue shadow over the crossroads, regular and gigantic; it moves with the clock-faces, and rotates around the sunlit squares, with the consequence that the morning shadow alternates at each of the corners with the evening sun, forever. The glare of twilight maintains the chimeras of golden steeples for a long time, and the song of the bells, it is said, idealizes them in an eccentric and supreme sonority.

The entire city awaits autumn passionately. It stiffens with it; its carillons seem to be listening for it, to be anticipating it, measuring out its placid approach. In September, everything slows down; the fountains wear away the stone more slowly, their drops of water hesitant, receding rather than falling. The face of things pales with regret and desire. Then, muffled footsteps begin to be audible in the silence, and something akin to the friction of a sled.

The faces and the windows look down, with a slightly more vital melancholy, and in the evening, groups of women stop at street corners and look without speaking at the timid sky dying behind the hills; one would think that they could see something. Some have their fingers on their lips, others raise attentive hands. That friction, almost mingled with the wind, is that of autumn. It is on its way, like a pilgrim, coming like pity, in brief stages.

Every evening, one thinks that it is going to enter the city, the sky fades a little earlier every day, and the green trees seem astonished by their leaves. Meanwhile, the taciturn season draws closer; at the ends of the long avenues that draw away from the ramparts, it is glimpsed in the distance, passing behind a cloud; or the poplars bordering the deserted canals appear to see its tall and indescribable form, for their attitude is special.

Suddenly, amid the murmur of the thin rain, one senses that it has entered, and at that moment, the shadow and the light overlap. The voluptuousness of the half-light fades in a great abandonment, and an interior clarity renders faces transparent. Autumn enters, with its landscape of gold and tears, its trailing magnificence and its mild unreal head, which nods and inclines with the hours. The erosion of bronzes illuminates a morose fire on the statues that watch it pass; it advances like a child of dusk, touches the dwellings, groping a little with its long pure hands, and an odor of dead foliage of flowers comes to the far horizon behind, around and in front of it.

Then that aroma penetrates objects and beings; all gazes are veiled; all eyes close piously, in order not to see the parks and the clouds dying, which murmur softly and whose agony is theirs alone. And in the odorous souls the leaflets of abandoned branches also begin to fall obscurely; one falls, and then another, little interior falls of branches of thought and anxiety, which defoliate, dissolve, no longer holding any place; and the depths of souls are muffled by all the faded things that accumulate there. Nothing any longer remains but isolated and bare beliefs, as stiff as stripped trunks, and the rust and the moss gradually deaden forgetfulness there.

The souls doze like old men; they go to sit down on ancient benches at the corners of gates, gazing at the exile and the decay stepping an unhealthy gold, devoid of prestige, in the puddles; its sinks, folds up, covered with water, becomes almost nothing, and then nothing more, and a light mist persists. It is becoming slightly cold, in souls rather than really; a great nostalgia for repose commences to rise, and sensibility becomes torpid. It is like an ideal fête, totally internal. Closed eyes contemplate it, and the ecstasy of descent into oneself grips the dreamers at the ancient casements.

It is thus that we listen to life in the peaceful city we have chosen, and it is so delightfully similar to our dreams, that we accept it like children, to whom the place of their birth is inconceivable. Those statues, those pathways of water and shadow, those opulent or ruined foundations, those ostentatious galleys outside the ages, and that calm population of embroideresses with closed eyes do not astonish us at all; but we like them in ourselves, they are ours, and our life, going meekly before theirs, has embraced it, smiling. Together we wait for the purification of the dusk, and our soul, similarly, consents to the abdication of the autumn.

Perhaps there is no neglect, and that which is forgotten is necessarily that which is present, for everything in the universe is simultaneously foreseen and forgotten. Thus, painted faces are perhaps worth as much as real ones, and the man who puts on an immutable mask does not diminish the effect of his face so much as increase it, with an inanimate and yet living shadow.

The city where we are resident now is without precedent in our voyage. One might think that exterior facts do not exist here in themselves, but are concerted with a view to another objective. They take place in the mind at least as much as in the atmosphere. Scarcely hatched, they are absorbed by an omnipotent soul; they dissolve there, are recomposed there, and become their own models.

Events no longer have the appearance of accidents; they are no longer surprising, but present themselves by turns, amalgamate with one another and are fixed in a gallery of imagined spectacles in which one amuses oneself by visiting it in memory. Art is a fluid absorbing facts, and the inhabitants of the city are its mysterious masters. Thus, they possess by thought alone a part of the most inconceivable natural forces, and even the one to which they seem to defer is found to be the essential exercise of their power.

We did not anticipate that art until today; we saw things alternating their appearance like moths around a lamp, while admiring them, but they did not enter into our minds. We did not think of retaining them, and it appeared to us more prudent to let them develop and they go away. Our souls passed through life like breezes, savoring fugitive aromas and forgetting the balms of yesterday for future incenses. We lived before life, and none of it became our flesh and our thought.

Here, however, we have begun to comprehend something else; and it is as if we have entered into a long avenue. In the Isle of Voluptuousness we enjoyed the various forms of sensation greatly, but we were their servants, and we obeyed sensuality tremulously; later, we fathomed the secret of time guarded by the sirens, and that secret, consented and dreaded by multiple waves of human beings, bequeathed nothing to our persistence but the sudden sentiment of its emptiness. The world appeared to us as a mass of brilliant colored vapors; we passed through it; but here the verity appears transparently more real. That verity, feverishly pursued, I had already foreseen; it is within us, and it is necessary to look inside ourselves in order to grasp it.

Stripped of unnecessary details, it lies dormant in the crystal depths of our thoughts. It seems that events are transformed in coming to us. They cling to us by a thousand invisible bonds, they penetrate us like balms sweated by the glass of a seemingly-impenetrable bottle. They become torpid in our soul, and they become sumptuous with that continual infusion. It is like a universal bride; everything comes to her in caravans of meditation, and she smiles with tranquility.

Art is the philter that accomplishes these incessant alliances. It elaborates nature; it appears like a young god to violent eyes, it floats and insinuates itself. Between pity and death it stands upright as between two sisters. The beings that live here are masters of the art, and their eyes are closed. They gaze at their own serenity, and only see life in order to penetrate that which is behind life. They stroll without ever considering anything in itself, and they pupils are, veritably, turned inwards. They hoard forms and images with a subtle avarice, and enjoy what happens without participating in it.

This nation of artists is unusual and singular. Their morality is limited to beauty, and they ask nothing more of anything than an attitude in conformity with evident destinations. What they call virtue can often be nothing but vice in the eyes of other people, but complete and logical, and they measure the elegance of a gesture by its propriety alone. They only admit that which is composed and harmonized. They live, meanwhile, in an environment of the excessive, for they take all ideas to their conclusion, demanding the plenitude of good instincts as of bad ones, and often finding more advantage in protecting all the developments, no matter in what direction they are orientated, than restricting everything to a medium morality transportable anywhere.

Their essential tribunal is their work; they only respect other people to the degree of their comprehension. They are unaware of inequalities of condition and posses nothing but their dreams; the rest seems to them to be accessory; they put in common the things necessary to their subsistence, suffering and enjoying extremely. For them, equilibrium is not the half-measure, but the absolute exercise of all the sentiments, in going to good and evil; but crimes are no more frequent in that society than in others, for the right to anger balances the right to charity, as prohibition and permission balance one another in other countries. They admire initiative and hate conformity.

Those characteristics bring the elite closer to the cosmopolitan crowd; and, in fact, they place relationship in the background and have established a preeminence of intellectual sympathy. Affinity is their guide, and they never inquire about birth, but only admit into their midst those passionate individuals who desire to live in an endeavor. An extreme solitude surrounds them, because they have never sought to get closer to other nations. They travel though them and observe them without mingling with them; their language and their vision are distinctive, and do not always come from the land. They do not worry about whether its essence is incomprehensible to traders or soldiers.

The span of life does not appear to them as it appears to others, and their sign of recognition is that they are dissimilar everywhere they go. They arrive, announce special things about which one never has time to think, inspire in their audience disturbance or enthusiasm, mildness or energy, sometimes hatred and almost always incomprehension, but never ennui because their eyes are beautiful and significant; and then they leave, and the placid man of transactions, who scorns them as useless disinterested individuals, shaken momentarily, only addresses himself to the dust of their footprints, which take away the irony of his smile.

The life of these people is probably orientated in a parabola contrary to that of others. They are eternal passers-by, they touch their brothers in humanity momentarily, and then seem to be drawn elsewhere. Their artistic intoxication does not explain itself, appearing superfluous and even shocking to the immense majority of crowds. They pass over it, and that sentiment of the abnormality of artists is universal. Often, their own relatives let them go, sadly, no longer understanding them, astonished by the sudden bizarrerie of their descendancy. They are phenomena, dangerous to the understanding of societies; their silence is a protest and their effort unutilizable.

It is said that they tire themselves out building toward the firmament a Babel that is never terminated; they are like the prideful and impious honor of humankind, exceptional monuments, and they make use of languages in a restricted fashion different from ordinary uses. Their endeavor is beyond public reasoning and consent, and the muted jealousy of active men tolerates it with displeasure, waiting for it to collapse, encircling it with isolation and disdain. But they are occupied with their passion, and only think about themselves.

We loved them immediately with a great fervor, because they opened up to us by their example a new world, rich and flavorsome, and their concerns were in accord with ours. They came to us simply, and in a few words awakened amplified and progressive echoes in our minds. The notion of time has fled, we have known ourselves forever, and the unexpected aspect of an object brings similar phrases to our lips. They see the differential character in everything, which truly contrasts it with something else. And the world, seen thus, seems indefinitely renewable.

Painting, above all, tormented us. It unveiled strange visions, it created multiple hypotheses, and we went astray in it without wearying.

The representation of the face in paintings plunged us into troubling reflections. The mere fact of taking a blank sheet and tracing the lines of a head there, a mouth, eyes and hair, penetrated us with fear. We thought that for centuries, millions of humans had only merited the name human and appeared different from other creatures by virtue of the sum of those few signs. The face thus arranged had always signified that race, one thought of it when one thought of them; they were inseparable, and the life of a human being announced itself in those particular features. The act of reproducing them thus seemed to us to be almost a birth; it was impossible that one could evoke the face—the eyes above all, those terrible eyes of paintings!—without a little life emerging from the shadow, drawn, constrained and coagulated at the tip of a brush and fixed according to the painter's caprice.

That rapid representation of a face, tormented or illuminated from the origin by so many heroisms or by august horror, could not be accomplished with impunity; it was necessary that a consecration of life should be added to it. And from then on, that animate thing had commenced to live and to think what it wanted. And what did it want? And did the artist know it? The unknown of that free existence, formulated and suddenly installed in a forehead, eyes and lips, struck us with terror and sadness.

We imagined the little soul condemned only to express itself by a single and immutable contraction of the features. What if the image in which it was imprisoned had imagined the eyes closed, and yet it ardently desired to see? What if, able to think according to its own whim, it was afflicted, but remained forced to smile eternally? Those unsuspected captivities left us dolorous, and we saw around us legions of errant phantoms, slaves of an illusory liberty, desolated by their form and dreaming about the storm of a cataclysmic salvation. By what right had they been subdued and deceived by a hypocritical offer of self-expression, while stagnated unconsciously in the marshes of chaos?

But we preferred to think that those painted faces were sufficient, that they were only adjoined to a soul, or a parcel of soul, in conformity with their features. And that idea drew us into a diversion of even more singular conjectures. How bizarre that atrophied life, limited to a single gesture, a single physiognomy, must be! The exchanges of those atomic existences by night, in the dark and solitary museums, would be like replies of inverted conversations, and if they detached themselves to mingle with one another, it was doubtless the sterile agitation of disorganized and sluggish beings, miserable confusions, a loquacious realm of unintelligences wandering in poverty...

We amused ourselves by imagining those dialogues and those ridiculous caresses, suffering them by mingling an irony therein. And we continued our logical deductions regarding those specialized lives for a long time.

A painted figure, for example, colored and shaded, offered the absolute appearance of a real being. However, it only had two dimensions, and had no depth; artifice alone created it and modeled it on a flat surface, and could only conceive of life by its own example, in only two dimensions. It had to see, judge and imagine everything as a décor without depth, the sense of perspective, space, the fatigue of journeys or the idea of exile; even the idea of looking behind itself was essentially lacking, and it retained nothing of the universe but width and height. It was a life entirely transformed, rendered incomprehensible to us, and an enigma born for the artist of his thought itself.

By contrast, statues offered to the spectator the three natural dimensions, but they were not colored, and only saw in nature a white light, gray half-tones and shadow; the suppression of color threw them into another dream, equally fantastic. That chalky world must be one of desolate monotony, a geometry without repose. And if one imagined painted wax models, seeming as complete and organized as living humans, it was sufficient to turn them around to see their empty head. That irregular and dusty hole, traversed by metal wires, was the seat of their thought; when one had seen that miserable cloaca, one could no longer be amused by the expressions of faces, no longer be moved by them; and the Nothing, hideous and almost materialized by our dream, leaned over us like an abominable and sarcastic dwarf.

Those thoughts occupied us during long evenings. We planned them as games, but the detestation of matter gripped us. Art was only in the mind; the act of the painter or modeler served to testify to another what one had already thought, and it was almost a satisfaction of self-esteem, or the relief of boredom, nothing more. All that made us doubt, and irritated us a little, and we turned increasingly toward ourselves.

Isolated in the middle of the sea like a chosen fatherland, the Island of Closed Eyes, with its dream, its memories, its contemplation, its paroxysm! Thus art was revealed to us as an ideal refuge, inaccessible or exceptional, one of the most noble, the most monstrous, the most illogical renunciations of destiny and mystery...

One day, going toward one of the gates of the city, in the direction of the countryside, we arrived via deserted streets at a small, very ancient cloister, which we did not know. The walls were covered in ivy, broken capitals were scattered in the grass, and the arches of doorways were split. Blue florets with fresh foliage were growing in the cracks, and stunted apple trees were twisting in the breaches.

We went down a few steps toward a gate barred with worm-eaten planks, and entered beneath damp arches. An odor of cadavers and incense gripped up; we walked slowly, stepping over brambles. A stone knight stood at a corner. Leaning against the wall on his broken legs, he considered us with frightening hollow eyes. His fists were clenched on a fragment of a broadsword, and his rigid face with dead lips projected sharply from a hood of mail and moss. Spiders were climbing over the gorget of that sentry of the afterlife; we passed on.

A square courtyard, like a shaft, opened abruptly. Enormous ruined walls rose up to a great height; through their cracks one could see the blue of the sky, and patches of luminous cloud. Broken arcades bristled on the suspended denticulations; blocks of marble with raised inscriptions still remained embedded in the cement; agglutinated brick pavements were about to fall, holed colonnettes remained rigid. From gray and pink vestiges an extraordinary vegetation sprang: hectic vines were strung from one doorway to another, large trees crawled and reared up in the windows, a mass of foliage and multicolored flowers filled the corners of buildings.

Red, violet and gilded patches lit up in the vivid verdure, bursting forth everywhere with an insolent richness; one might have thought that they were crying out in that dead place, glorifying an intensive and animal life there. They took up so much room that the memories and the shadows did not know where to hide, and garlands plunged into in the bays of enormous subterrains, too heavy for the daylight, falling with their venomous fruits and large leaves, fecund, encumbrant and transgressive. One had no idea where they were going; perhaps they wanted to reach the depths of obscurity, to burgeon in the darkness.

Blue insects were flying in all directions, urgently, and swallows could be seen circling. The place was simultaneously austere and luxurious.

Under the open arches a quadrangular galley extended, the walls of which were covered in pale frescos. And as the daylight was very bright, we approached them in order to examine them at our ease. We hardly existed that day, and were scarcely superior to painted figures; it pleased us to visit them; they were like a population of calm brethren, and we would probably discover ourselves among them.

Those frescos were very beautiful, and considerable. Sculpted trees with symmetrical foliage framed them, and in the blue-tinted stone their tender colorations were fading harmoniously. Some had a golden background, other turquoise, others silver, and they retraced legends, several of which had been forgotten. On one lawn of tender and charming green, Noah, still irritated and tottering, was cursing his son Ham. The old man was displaying his bare and robust chest, a wreath of vines still would around his neck, but his beard was full of majesty. Ham was seen dressed in red, turning his head, and his blue-clad brothers seemed fearful and imploring. Children pursued woolly sheep behind the scene, and seven pointed mountains rose above the horizon in the background. Between them snaked an endless river, and the colorless sky was tarnished and flaking.

A blonde woman in a black dress advanced under the orange trees. Her right hand was raised, her left held a fold of her dress; she was smiling with perversity at a young woman clad in violet veils of a delightful transparency, lying in the grass and playing with a bouquet of plumes. The young woman's head was slightly turned, her eyes dewy and full of dreamy. Through a gap in the trees a plain was visible, in which a young archer, completely nude, was asleep. His hand held a bow and his leather helmet was open, like the rind of a fruit.

Small emerald-green lizards were running over the ground; a golden trellis allowed glimpses of sheep and goats. The sun was rising to the middle of the firmament, and a hill bore a fantastic fortress. The Assyrian turrets were ornamented with oriflammes, which hung down to the ground; the sculpted drawbridge had the form of a dolphin, and a troop of soldiers in striped coats was reentering at a gallop, sounding a horn. Red and yellow clouds crowned that singular landscape.

In the third fresco one discovered the festival hall of a great château. An immense table extended, laden with golden tankards and ewers, but no one was eating there and everything had fallen into a prodigious disorder. A green and blue dragon was lying over the dishes, the dressers and the seats, from one end of the feast to the other, and its tail was twisted in scaly spirals all the way to the depths of the galleries. Four terrible vipers were emerging from its neck and radiating around it.

A small child was hiding under a heap of rugs, over which one of the folds of the monster was sliding; forgotten or abandoned, he remained frozen with terror, suppressing a scream. Meanwhile, lords and ladies covered in velvet and gemstones were leaning over an interior gallery, wringing their hands or covering their faces. A few of them had seen the child, but none of them dared do down to combat the intrusive Desolation.

In the background, a round window opened on a luminous horizon. Through the panes once could see a yellow road, the edge of a blue wood, crops, and on the road, a rider racing toward the gate of the château. He was wearing armor of black steel; his head, covered in blond curls, with bright eyes, was surrounded by an aureole; he was clutching his raised lance, and making his large house bound. In the sky, four white angels with multicolored necklaces and wings were pointing out the gate to him, dressed with palms and steamers.

A forest of pines extended to the edge of the sea. Carts were passing between the pink or violet trunks, escorted by horsemen armed with axes, in the shade. At sea, red-painted galleys were sailing toward a white city perched on a promontory. In the foreground of the fresco, a spring was born among tamarisks and irises; a young woman in mourning was weeping beside it, her head in her hands, and a robust hunter with a sad and regal face was leaning toward her, interrogating her.

The little princess' dress was torn, her white foot emerging from beneath a frayed gold-braid hem, and droplets of blood were pearling on her ankle. In the water of the spring a golden crown could be glimpsed; and Mélisande sobbed without wanting to reply to Golaud,[7] leaning on his arbalest and considering her ecstatically. A wolf was fleeing beneath the foliage, and dusk was descending over everything.

A vast chaos unfolded in the fifth fresco. One perceived a cavern opening in an enormous rock, and a host of amorphous, grotesque or repulsive beings swarming within: men with the heads of turbots, women without eyes and almost devoid of flesh, birds with only one wing or flying with hands,

---

[7] Mélisande and Golaud are characters in Maurice Maeterlinck's Symbolist play *Pelléas et Mélisande* (1893).

an obese king with a face the color of agate with a wooden diadem, dwarf with pendant and jagged ears, dogs with crocodiles' tails and a host of other absurdities that surprised the imagination.

Above that cavern, however, guarded by silver unicorns, set against a spiritualized and exquisite sky, stood a tribunal of fresh foliage where naked women of an incomparable beauty were holding hands and dancing. Nearby, a goatherd was throwing gilded grapes into the air and frolicking with his goats; a troop of satyreaux was climbing a large colossal oak that dominated the entire landscape, and in the vaporous and paradisal distance one glimpsed children playing with doves. Green-tinted tortoises were crawling in the grass, and a vivacious laurel framed the entire allegory.

In the sixth fresco, a terrible Pegasus was lifting Perseus and Andromeda above the ocean in a spray of tumultuous foam. The hero, streaming with blood, was holding the virgin tightly, the white body swooning in the iron-clad arms, and her golden hair, soaked with water, unfurling over the blue-tinted armor. Medusa's head was hanging from the saddle-bow with a curved sword, beneath the outspread wings of Pegasus, and the fabulous destiny was rising into a sumptuous firmament amid architectures of starry clouds and cataracts of lightning.

The seventh fresco depicted the Virgin surrounded by saints, against a blue background; she was seated beneath a flowery awning, and Saint Cecilia was at her feet, languidly playing a lute. The infant Jesus, clad in red, was laughing, and playing with an ivory casket and a book. Behind them one could see Jerusalem, and groups of she-asses with their drivers, emerging from the city and pausing to chat. All around that composition the frame itself was painted with various legends. In a mauve and white landscape a slender executioner dressed half in red and half in green was cutting off the head of a saint, and the blood was spurting in a vivid jet the color of geranium. A cloister of colonnettes, with yew-trees, opened on a room where a martyr was sleeping, and an angelet was entering quietly. Saint Francis of Assisi, sitting next to a bush, was summoning the birds and the wolves. But in all the frescos we had not recognized our faces, and we went away regretfully.

Suddenly, in a shadowy bay, we perceived a very old painting, to which we had not paid any attention, and when we had considered it, we looked at one another in silence, our hearts beating faster, for we had finally recognized ourselves, and all of our dream appeared to us:

On the bank of a river over which the twilight was fading, one could see Narcissus lying in the reeds. His divine body was stretched out indolently, diaphanous in the half-light, and his profound eyes were contemplating himself in the water. But the current had carried toward him a lyre and a supremely beautiful severed head; they were the lyre and head of Orpheus. A black laurel was mingled with the black hair, the pure lips were parted, the pupils veiled; and Narcissus, taking in his hands that august face fixed in destiny and death, kissed it slowly...

Narcissus' face was similar to mine, and Maia's head was that of Orpheus. The silence, the increasing obscurity, the superhuman disturbance of the symbol, the visible advertisement of our destiny suddenly gripped us so terrible that we fainted, mouth to mouth, into the unknowable, bewildered by enigmas, fears, presentiments and darkness.

The Impalpable

After that evening, a life commenced for us that was entirely similar to the envelopment of a great train of mourning rising over a mysterious horizon: a starry veil, the descent of an august shadow, the dream...

Maia is entirely my imagination, and I love myself too much; the revelatory fresco has shown me my lips kissing my dead beloved. And perhaps she is indeed nothing but my poetry, my unreal exaltation, that elect who came to me one day; she passes like the lyre and the head along the steam, I kiss her as she is passing, and I resume my endless contemplation of myself. A horrible enigma!

Yes, many a time I felt transparent and inconsistent, as if dissolved in my thoughts, not a living being but an echo; and that uncertainty desolated me; I accused myself of misunderstanding my sister. But always she seemed to me materially dead: my imagination taking form, and nothing more. She spoke to me from the depths of my own voice, by virtue of an intoxicating and inexplicable sortilege, and the words she pronounced signified so perfectly what I wanted that I surely had not heard them pronounced before; I collected their sonority on the lips of my own mirage, without knowing it.

But then, what if she were not my mirage, born of me and pliant to my caprice: if she were a woman, if she were only a woman, some phantom?

I formed a different idea of a companion; I had dreamed something else: the loyal and reflective accord of two wills, each one going in the direction of its sex, and within its special empire; the alliance of two powerful liminal states sharing the multiple horizons of sensuality and knowledge...but not that doubling of a man before himself, that perpetual non-contradiction. Maia did not appear to exist...

Slow hours, similar to the insistent dripping of a tap, descended penetratingly into my thoughts on that subject. That phantomatism haunted me. The further our voyage went, the more Maia lightened and immaterialized. One might have thought that she was gradually dissolving into my progressive experience of the contemplated spectacles.

If the woman is only the imagination of the man, I said to myself, there comes a moment when the sage who knows everything no longer has any need to imagine anything, and from then on he can be alone; the bewitching and deformative woman can disappear, reabsorbed into him; and the more he knows, the more his invention is restricted, for the lie is reduced day by day. So the woman vaporizes day by day; and perhaps I shall see Maia die at the moment when I know, and perhaps I shall die myself at that moment, for I shall have reached a plenitude, and every plenitude excludes duration, destroying time; there is no longer thereafter any but one point, and one moment...

Those reflections gave way at a glance from the beloved. She too arrived overburdened with dreams and melancholy, and as soon as her poor eyes looked up and rose toward mine, I forgot the cruel laughter of reason and drank the trickling tears fervently; that was my necklace of predilection, my chagrined treasure; they were my jewels of repentance, and I no longer thought about anything at all but the suffering of the being quivering in my arms.

The goal of our voyage remained the same, but we approached it with renewed hearts and different pride, ennobled by a spiritual dolor. Maia had no apparent reasons to weep, but I divined deserts of desolation behind her eyes. She had understood solely by enervation a host of destinies of which I could not comprehend the joy; and art, instead of restoring her serenity, only caused her further despair. That which I sought in the universe methodically, stiffening against the night and hiding my adolescent reason, she sought with passion and without awareness, her dear living sensibility colliding with the immutable angles of the laws and geometries that are the foundation of events.

I accused her of being unconscious, of being my reflection, of being the deformation, magnified and dancing before me, of my reasoning—but how unjust I was to accuse her of that! How did I know whether passion and illusion were not closer to happiness, with their broken wings than the robust and limited organism of reason? She was preparing a rout full of splendor, and I was not even sure of a petty victory...

Where, then, was the certainty with which desire made us vibrate? What was not illusory? Did there exist in the transitory universe a suspended and solid point, or was it always like the middle of the sea? That point, when we imagined it together, sometimes took on substance; it formed a kind of spot on our sun; we desired it; we drew ourselves toward it by invisible threads. Sometimes it seemed to us, by means of a mental effort, to be hauling us toward it, to be drawn through a great tumult of sensations all the way to its stable spur; then the threads broke, one after another, became confused, forming knots that we patiently worked around, and breaking again; and a wave carried us out to sea.

Oh, truly, it was miserable, the quarrel between my sad logic and my deplorable imagination; they were as void and vain as one another. That obscure point of anchorage we had already sensed and we had said that it was necessary to seek it within ourselves and there alone; but when we leaned over that interior abyss, we could not see any bottom to it. It was as vast as the land where we had wandered, and how could we undertake that voyage? Where could we land in that imaginary archipelago? Reason and fantasy remained impotent to know it.

And on examining the matter more closely, was I any more alive than Maia? Was the man any better armed than the woman? Was he more likely to come to the end of that abstract struggle by making use of his cold reason than the woman making use of her passion? I was probably a shadow too, and that was another bitter irony of the old fresco: Narcissus and Orpheus, both painted faces. Maia and myself, and the innumerable host of human beings, we were all therein, and I had a symmetrical, simplified and desolating vision of the universe as an interminable wall, on which, by the play of a muted lantern, cohorts of ruddy specters oscillated, seen from a carriage moving through the night in the back streets of a village...

The tangible! Nothing possible without it! The tangible is the second title of happiness! But a tangible interior, a repair, a fixed place of mental forces and reflections. Our body not even being that place, it was within it that is was necessary to go: and we would be deflected toward the evocation of psychic forces that gave us the power.

Our solitude saw us absorbed in singular analyses of the occult. Among the artists who surrounded us, many had thought like us, and, weary of forms, had interrogated the mind. The intoxication of the absolute had taken us with them, the tension of our associated wills multiplied our enervation a hundredfold, and materializations soon followed.

Lying next to one another in closed rooms, we saw the air illuminate with blue flames that emerged from us, and vaporous being glided through objects and people. Some were opaque against a bright background, as if made of real flesh, but diaphanous against a dark background. They considered us sadly, and sometimes, when we spoke to them without fear, they drew closer and placed their luminous hands over our lips. They all seemed to want to conceal that which we asked of them; they obeyed us in everything save for that one point, and we ended up understanding that there was no more certainty in their world than in ours, and that they were probably searching, just as we were.

Two of them that we saw once made an impression on us; they almost had our features, and seemed to be weary voyagers. Doubtless they too had traveled, in an unexplored universe, the mountains and the oceans, known the emptiness of Amnesia and the irony of the sirens without a secret. They seemed to like us; we evoked them before the fatal fresco in which we were painted, but as soon as they had seen it they brushed it, became confused with it, entered into it again; and we went away, enjoying our own hallucination once more.

Those phantoms were still outside of us; they duplicated objects, they were an aspect of the other side of existence, but we did not contain them, and their magnetism was just one more servitude.

The holy hysteria of cathedrals did not want us. In vain we prayed under the solemnity of arched windows, in the blaze of violet stained glass, in the apocalypse of flowery stones, in the maze of cavernous crypts, in the radiation of angelets with distended cheeks, florid with symmetrical and luminous wings, in the delirium of organ music twisting amid the incense a giant and tortured lamentation. The man with open arms remained ivory, our knees became callused on the flagstones, and we felt nothing within us.

The absolutism of faith did not address itself to us, and did not want it to. The impalpable, in all its forms, enwrapped us and it was necessary to believe that the critical moment of our lives was marked there, for we remained devoid of strength and with a great heartache.

Why should I extend myself on our efforts toward the occult and toward God? I no longer have the courage to recount what we had to live. There is a moment in every life when the bow of robustness loses its tension, when the muscles and nerves of the soul relax, and everything weakens at its limit, like wet hair that can no longer curl; there is nothing to be done; it is like the first trial of the renunciation of death, and, having departed with a white and burning ardor, we hesitate at the last stage. Legend and voluptuousness, forgetfulness and illusion have not beaten us, but here we feel overloaded by an immense burden of autumns and intuitions.

The final pause in that city had sunk us in art, and the essential season, placing its cool hands the nape of our neck, had pressed down gently and pitilessly, toward the depths of despair. It was the miserable instant in which our souls, long constrained, felt themselves torn and dislocated by the sudden development of internal trellises, and the intellectual orchard, long warmed by the suns of heaven, finally cried maturity, throwing themselves with an insolent and tumultuous flowering into the etiolation of our mind...

We really were very low. Everything offended and fatigued us. The disproportion of intellectuality in paroxysm and a body devoid of vigor crushed us. Around us, the accumulated notions finally assembled to liberate themselves and avenge themselves; they arranged themselves like massed and regular armies and launched intolerable legions and cavalry against our irritated nerves.

We were mentally ill. Dragged to the window, we considered the eternal rain, and only began to understand. It was like a silent form of punishment, its gray or blue stripes, symmetrical and serried, descended slowly, with composure and perseverance; we called it the wicked lady with the grey eyes. It paraded over the city and the harbor without pressing down; we encountered it continually; it followed us, and we could still see it through the windows. We shivered with unsatisfied anger, and threw ourselves back into the half-light. Wrapped in the curtains, we remained motionless for entire hours, and the hoof-beats of horses made us shiver. Faded roses sometimes fell from the foliage ornamenting the windows above ours; they suddenly appeared at the top of the window, brushed it in a hesitant descent, disappeared into the emptiness, and we leaned over to see them soiled on the pavement; but in the morning, when we went out, we found them heaped on the threshold. Sometimes the wind blew them into our room, and the damp, cold petals touched our faces like nocturnal moths.

Everything took a direction of ennui concentric to ourselves. I do not know whether that expression is comprehensible, but in any case, I cannot put it better. In truth, we felt a kind of universal disappointment propagating toward us in regular waves, and objects too closely studied took on the most indefinable aspect, for us. How many times we felt, distinctly, the implacability of things that refused their freshness and their character, the ill-will that made them banalize themselves, become their own grimace, as it were, lacking all interest, and yet letting us divine that they had one, but were hiding it deliberately, with peevish, infantile, ferocious determination!

Those heart-breaking walks toward a destination that made us yawn with disgust, at which one arrived without joy and from which one returned without knowing why! The impalpable in truth, the absence of proofs, the lack of a bottom from which to rise up again with a single thrust to the bright surface of visions and enjoyments! And all our lives to lead us there...

It is neither voluptuousness, nor faith, nor art, but the ensemble of all of them that can create harmony, endow the fixed point and deliver the intangible, we said to ourselves one day. But all of that is confused within us; it is necessary to be able to step back outside ourselves in order to consider it. Perhaps the harmony is there, but we cannot perceive it, because we contain it. If we were able to duplicate ourselves spiritually, perhaps we would see harmonies realized in our own presence?

Harmonies! Perhaps, in fact, they can be realized. We have dreamed so much, reflected so much, possessed so much, hoped so much that we might have reached the desired point without knowing it. But it might be necessary to duplicate ourselves, to retreat outside ourselves...

A mirror.

The old myth included in the fresco definitely signifies our entire life. We have ornamented the beauty of our Narcissus sufficiently, it is necessary now, in order for him to enjoy his own spectacle, in order to know himself, to have a mirror! And we—Maia and I—are like Narcissus. The beauty has come; it is only necessary for us to reflect ourselves in the universe, and we will encounter ourselves.

Finally...

We departed in a pure morning, like two pilgrims, toward the center of the island. One might think that a limpid spring has been born in the middle of a great forest, which is the fountain of youth. On sees things extranaturally there. Its property is to reflect not only real forms but also future forms, and no one has ever completely known all that can be discovered there.

Another adventure to attempt: the supreme one.

We departed like pilgrims, like paupers, holding hands, and we held the other two out toward the horizon like questors. Our eyes were ringed and blue-tinted, similar in every respect to those of people who have come from far way and have renounced almost everything. My poor Maia was trailing her worn dress along the roads; only the gold of her heavy curls consecrated to her shoulders the scintillation of an ancient prestige. As for me, my knotty staff burned my hand, and life weighed as heavily as the clouds upon my brow; but our hearts were firm and we went fearlessly toward the last station.

We saw great spaces covered in violet heather. Hillocks of sand loomed up; midday burned them tranquilly; their mica sparkled. Then the immense heaths extended monotonously; they could be seen rising to the horizon, a few tufts of grass quivering in the nascence of the moist sky, seemingly uncrossable; one might have thought that they were defying the march of time. We pressed on. We thought about stopping in a clump of trees from which a blue shade descended, but it was necessary to get there and we continued walking. However, the ground began to rise toward the lower slopes of a hill, and the light was declining; we went up with haste along the ridges. When we reached the top, it was seven o'clock; the forest suddenly appeared to us, vast, undulating and black. On its edge we turned round to consider the valley, the distance we had traveled, the sea that was perceptible on the horizon like purple silk. Then we went into the trees.

In the heart of the foliage, the bloody globe of the sun appeared through the lace of the pines, descending. Its reflection ran over ground and died in a tranquil pool languishing between the rocks.

We leaned over the spring, but already, we could no longer see anything therein.

The Mirror

The pallor of the stars was gentle, and we sat there without speaking, considering one another through the shadows. The fresh air of the foliage came to us and calmed us. Renunciation entered our souls with the obscurity, and the solemnity of the hour and attitudes penetrated us with a supernatural repose.

We had only climbed hills, and yet it seemed to us that we had reached the highest summit of the highest mountain in the universe, so violently were we gripped by the lightness of the solitude and the sentiment of our decision. The simplicity of children, the candid and light simplicity, we had suddenly recovered in its entirety, and the burden of our dreams was sleeping at the bottom of the rocks. Suddenly relieved of our immemorial melancholy, it was as if we were empty, and an embalmed confidence floated within us. It was a spiritual rejuvenation; we seemed to perceive one another for the first time, and the idea that that supreme vigil would complete our cycle buoyed us up with a definitive liberty.

We were finally about to know ourselves and to be conscious of ourselves; and there was no thought of a disappointment, for that effort was final; there would be nothing more thereafter, not even the lassitude of imagining something else. Everything would be finished with those brilliant stars, and the dream of life, commenced in a dusk, would be completed at dawn with tranquility.

As happens to those who are about to die, everything that we had seen came back to our memory, and interior images appeared with their veritable meaning and the connection of their harmonies. We had not known anything without searching for its significance, had never enjoyed anything for ourselves but for the enrichment of our minds, and in that hour of justice when we contemplated one another face to face, no reproach haunted us.

We had not been bad priests, and we had not deviated from our worship; having chosen a faith from among all the errors, we had served it piously. The appreciation of another had not troubled us; we had stiffened our will like a rudder, and envisaged the goal fixedly. We had set out to be, in accordance with our birth and form, complete and personal human beings, and to approach as closely as possible the ideal representation thereof, with the consequence that in the event of the annihilation of the race, our couple alone would conserve ancient humanity, able to recognize itself entirely and regret nothing. What we had wanted was to be human beings in accordance with their nature and their destiny, in their development in all directions, as the duty of oaks is to be oaks, that of birds to be birds and that of the sun to be, immortally, the sun!

If we had only added to the order of phenomena a single miserable vestige, at least a consciousness would have been revealed therein that did not wish to die without testimony, and we would not have deigned to diminish ourselves by any of the sentiments of solidarity, charity or modesty that are only the inter-collision of weaknesses, and which attenuate, by a condescension and a reciprocal renunciation, the original vitality of living beings.

Our character as solitary individuals was not belied, and having selected in existence an extremely rare and unutilizable concern, we had plunged into our attempt without involving anyone else in it. We had sought to retain nothing but the essential, and to be displaced from time and death in a metaphysical vision in which there was no longer anything exact.

We had invented a world of our fantasy, and if it was not veritable, at least other humans had not known a certainty more valuable than ours; thus we had repudiated their conception, dealt straightforwardly with the events confronting our thought, and by virtue of that, had truly lived in the full measure of our power, if life, for the human mind, is the recomposition of the universe.

The first advertisement of our exodus had been the encounter with the children of legend, and thanks to them we had already obtained the presentiment that life is merely a fable of which the images are given to us, and of which the meaning can only be deduced a long time afterwards. And the three Bloody Isles had also shows us, in a rapid prediction, the periods of our future; by then, knowledge and doubt had been successively announced, and then the final certainly of which our present exhaustion had come in search.

Meanwhile, the land of Voluptuousness offered us the initiation of the senses. We had explored therein a whole universe of surfaces, of apparential enchantments, and with the satisfaction of desire had come other more internal joys. It was then that the immense countries of Amnesia had unfolded to our eyes, with their espaliers of multiform spectacles, their dusks and their sands, their foliage and their dawns. We had learned there to live solely in the future of our dreams, to renounce ourselves in the present among chimerical encounters and to hope for nothing except ourselves. The ancient secret of the sirens of Scylla had dissipated before the violation of its shadow, and the terrors of our humanity had been abolished with it.

Ripened henceforth by knowledge, in the Island of Closed Eyes, Art had revealed a philosophy of phenomena to us. By virtue of it, we had eventually discovered a meaning and a superior utility. But voluptuousness, like philosophy, art, like legend, still had need of the external world to complete us, and now we were finally sitting down in darkness next to pure, interior knowledge, free of things and beings; that was what was about to awaken, and we would finally enter into our authentic thought, as the disinherited of the dusk whose docile misery makes its way slowly toward the cradle...

Those dreams and realities collided in our minds. Maia remained motionless and rigid, and we no longer dared speak. She seemed to me really and increasingly to be a shadow, my vacillating imagination, beside me like an Antigone, and I had all the desperate and pacified soul of the blind king. Our thoughts had melted into one alone, our hearts alternated in their beats, and there really was no necessity for us to be separated into two bodies. Even desire no longer touched us in our solitude; what would we have desired, already being entirely within one another? And our bodies hardly existed any more, about to be spiritualized, to rise up like the mists before the dew...

Meanwhile, the profound avenues became less black. Glimmers trembled fleetingly there, and the stars consented to leave. We followed them with our gaze; one was effaced, and then the other. Suddenly, there was no more to be seen in the foliage itself than a strange violet redness; and an entire constellation dissolved, and a triangle of fire was dead, and the lyre was no more.

The celestial deviation drew away majestically and fearfully into the impenetrability of the azure. A frisson ran through the thickets; the lace of summits began to be clearly visible over the mauve sky. The heather of the sun was discernible, the stumps of pines stood up with a visible symmetry, innumerable and slender, grouped in desert colonnades. The rocks emerged from the ground with their mosses, the palpitating ferns; icy droplets covered us, and from a compact massif of oaks a roseate fire suddenly sprang forth, almost indistinct, which burned the flash of a bar of gold; the sky was irradiated by purple and blue clouds, the great night threw itself entirely into the Occident, and we watched the definitive dawn with eyes moist with tears.

Upright, hands trembling, we waited for the light to be entirely resplendent. It descended through the branches like a cataract of dream, steaming in cascades of gold and turquoise in the forest, and that gold and that turquoise, clarified and pure, ran all the way to our feet and fell in great gushes into the tenebrous blue-tinted pool where we awaited our Destiny.

Now, feet braced on the ground, terrified by the Instant, we veiled our faces with our hands, not daring as yet to cast our life into nothingness with that single glance...

But suddenly, without touching, without speaking, with a dazed accord, our hands fell back, our eyes closed, we leaned over, tightened the lashes, until they brushed the fateful water, and when the moral mist of the surface chilled the face, both of us opened our eyelids and the same time, with terror, over the Mirror.

There was no reflection therein.

"Maia!" I cried, then, in an inexplicable delirium. "Maia, look, the Light is surrounding us, bathing us, penetrating us and transfiguring us! Our bodies no longer cast a shadow on the ground, and I can see all of the sky within you and through you!

"We are finally the sovereigns of certainty and the masters of the enigma, Maia! Everything is our invention, everything that we have seen, and even our bodies, is our invention, and it does not even have a reflection! No more than the sirens had a secret, we have no reality, and the fusion of our souls is completed in the nothingness of that impenetrable water!

"No knowledge is exterior. We have sought to know ourselves by visiting the world, but we imagined it according to what we already were, and it has taught us nothing about ourselves. The mind contains everything and thought is the sole sovereign of the universe! Everything is fantasy, and the empires and the deserts, with the horrible Ocean and all the faces of old chaos are mirages of our melancholies and our joys!

"We sought the light and we had it in ourselves, Maia, and could never reflect ourselves any more than a flame can illuminate itself, for it is in us and internally that all mirrors come to create one another!

"Everything emerges from human being and returns there, to the realm of interior things. Thought permits and encapsulates everything. Everyone is a total and terrible planetary system! I see human being without fraternity, kissing the lips of its own solitude, setting in progress, with a sad gesture, and entire unsuspectable universe of which it alone knows the meaning. Thus we have been isolated in the middle of everything, and we have not been understood by anyone!

"The understood human is inferior, for what others understand is not him, nor completely born of him; it is the exchange of depreciated ideas and spectacles, which escape him go into neighboring souls like transfusions! But the person who knows how to shut his frightful ideas up in his aviary, like stone birds, is the absolute human! He cannot condescend, he has no need of the charity of others, but his sovereignty is universal. The world is merely the décor of his summarizing thought; he concentrates entire countries in a smile, condenses the polar icecaps in a gesture, so his conversation is amusing, and he triumphs over the plant and the animal, over the rock and the cloud, over everything the blossoms or falls asleep, with an insouciant beauty.

"There is no meaning of life, Maia. There is no meaning in the sea. We have come to climb an imaginary mountain, the highest summit of which would reveal to us in an orderly fashion the horizon of our existence, but the horizon and the mountain are already in our dreams, and we have not attained any goal, because the only goal was not to have one, but to seek one while smiling for the sole joy of animation and hope.

"We are becalmed in the middle of the universe like crystal galleys, everything is coming toward us from all directions and we are not heading for anything. The center of the wheel is not heading for the rim, but all the spokes originate from it and come toward it without it ever being displaced; thus we believed that we were going toward something, but we were carrying everything with us; and having arrived at the mirror we have not seen anything, for our body too is a mirage of our thoughts.

"The mind exists and is sufficient. Everything gyrates like a thunderous cyclone around it; even the idea of God depends on humans, and the Clarity that we desired to kill, all the way to the derisory god that we have just contemplated in the spring. Narcissus has no need of his double; he *is*—and the innumerable forms of the firmament will not be when he is no longer!

"And you, Maia with the golden hair, now you are dissolving like a resplendent vapor. You have never been anything but my dear imagination, my dream; but this is the place of pure knowledge, and the imagination no longer exists, since we are at the center of everything imaginable.

"Oh, the flamboyance of truth convulses as it burns my breast! All this dawn is streaming over my forehead; I am idealizing myself in an immaterial lust in which all light is an aroma of kisses!

Let it triumph, then, that apotheosis of Life! Come, definitive Clarity, run like a great luminous bird flagellating the heavens, and overturn Sirius, Betelgeuse and all the grandiose Milky Way with its immense wings! If the human of the ages beyond is incarnate in me for an instant, adjoin to his delirium the wild testimony of your conflagration! Ornament your king with the Diadem of the sun, and if his realm and his crown are entirely interior, attest at least by a visible sign the granted prayer of that prince of solitude, delirious in his blaze! Be helpful to him, come as far as his forehead, burn his hair, surmount him with a flame spinning beneath the azure of his unforeseeable paradise!

Come, materialize yourself, miracle; emerge from the depths of the unknowable, prove that a man has not belied his own power, but has gazed at the universe as a sovereign, has squeezed it in his clenched hands like an eagle and will precipitate it with his final gesture into Oblivion and Nullity!

"But I sense it! It's coming! Squeeze yourself against me, enter into me again, disappear within me, Maia, dear phantom! It's coming; something sublime is approaching, and the torrid sky is saluting us majestically, for the known Truth shakes the universe to its most tenebrous skeleton, and old Hades himself is chilled by fear, considering it as a grim presentiment!

"We can do no more than accept the supreme and the paroxysm of all things; we are born for the realm of Clarity!"

Swooning in the eternal light, we raised our pale foreheads at the same time. Maia melted into me like a perfume and in the vertigo, and immense dazzle appeared.

It was a diamond crown sparkling in the middle of the sun. And at the instant when the miracle touched us, we ceased to be.

Bruges-Montigny,
January-August 1894.

THE VIRGIN ORIENT

He will dream everywhere of the warmth of the breast.
Vigny.[8]

Book One: The Forces

I. The Solemn Gathering

That evening, toward the darkness accumulated in the high corner of the architraves, with the flames of candelabras, the ardent and devouring voice rose up of the dictator, simply clad in black.

And above the silent legates, the bellicose words collided and clashed violently, like golden swords.

"…The depositary of a heavy grandeur of centuries on the shores of occidental seas, a strange body vivified by all bloods, a profound soul in which all souls are purified, Europe, Messieurs, seems only to exhaust destinies in order to awaken new ones. A tradition of beauty visits its summits, and that giant and complex being, with its meditative or violent forms, signifies in its very configuration a vivacity and an inexhaustible nativity. Corteges of dreams still surge forth infinitely from that continent, toward which rears up, from the depths of the Pole, the great emblematic lion of Scandinavia; and, over and above the necessities of everyday diplomacy,

---

[8] The quotation is from Alfred de Vigny's "La Colère de Samson," from Dalila's monologue proudly explaining her role as a *femme fatale*.

the whole of politics is adding to those dreams a new subject of amazement for future generations.

"I attest, Messieurs, to the force that wells up from those countries of the Germano-Latin race, finally united, of which your presence here summarizes the mission and the history: the sublimity of politics is to lead States through events and indispensable and immediate precautions toward a new legend! It has required enormous periods of time for so-called dreams to become the essential goal of applied intelligences, the final desire of manipulators of ideas; for science, once considering them with inimity, finally to have a sufficiently high intuition of its true role to grasp them, to legitimate them, and to renew them by means of its own conquests, to dissolve them in itself and to dissolve itself within them, to utilize for one unique knowledge the precious and exalting power that is born from the gift of illusion! It required centuries of metaphysics devoid of foundation and positivist science devoid of a general idea, hollow dreams and equally detestable receipts, for humanity to arrive at no longer separating its material efforts from its meditations, and mingling them together in a single logical harmony.

"Previously, people seemed to consider the imagination and dreams as pernicious sensualities; they had recourse to them secretly after having labored, but they would have blushed to mingle them with their labor, they did not admit that one could ever employ oneself in fortifying dreams; and they did not enjoy anything perfectly, their morality being timid and restricted. But when, instead of disavowing their ideal by experience, they supported one by the other, people united science and consciousness, they became great living and perpetual poems, and thus rendered poets—which is to say, the only individuals that intelligence had previously been unable to declare futile by virtue setting before humankind the concentrated and purified effects of its own genius—useful.

"Those august recorders of human effort, those revealers of the true mental world, those embalmers of the soul of crowds in elixirs of imperishable beauty, artists, no longer had

149

a social role on the day when the liberated individual could be his own confessor and poet, and had no need of anyone to show him the promised land, because he had already entered it. On that day, the experimental age of science, psychology and politics gave way to an age of results; on that day, and on that day only, civilization commenced on earth.

"You are the children of those who saw that unusual evolution, and already it seems to you that it is as eternal as the logic of climates and stars, and that everything before was merely murky barbarism, traversed by lightning-flashes of presentiments. The modern genius is the free and total exercise of the faculties; with the feudalism of the mind fell one of the great despairs of souls, and everything was raised up for humankind. That elevation of humans to the envisaging of their own results drew all morality with it.

"Messieurs, it will have been our recent honor, that of people of the year 2000, to have understood and permitted that supremacy of the dream, to have made it no longer the inane abandonment of the soul in the vague and inexact, but the comforting and lucid sentiment of the unity of all knowledge before the individual mind. We have made the dream the goal of the experimental sciences that once oppressed it: obstinate in despising or hating it, even though the sensed themselves incapable of contenting the heart after the mind, they wandered in the immensity of intellectual realms like blind queens, colliding, impotent and furious, with the impenetrable door behind which imagination was sleeping as peacefully as a baby!

"In the end, the threshold opened, and the extinct and closed eyes were touched by an equal and just light. The science of dream was created, everything was concerted to produce more happiness, and the old threats of the prophets, which predicted with the increase of knowledge a parallel increase in sorrow no longer signified anything and died with primitive errors. We have finally conceived that the labor of all the scientists and the exaltation of all the poets were only made to ornament a constant harmony in the mind of the free individual, no longer to differ but to unite that that result.

"That blossoming, we have seen! Its renaissance is so close to us that I need not remind you of it any further. It is becoming merely history, and it would not be necessary to dig deeply into the soil of our capitals for the deplorable blood that it cost to appear. Those who did not understand opposed it, and disappeared in the surge of the revolution. It was necessary, and it is good.

"The progress of the social creature toward true humanity amid cadavers has led us all, the heirs of the centuries of authoritarianism and lucre, to this great, this unaccustomed political and moral notion of the identification of dream and knowledge, of the fusion of the logical sciences and expansive sensibility. It is on that philosophical idea that our confederation will live; it is therein that the divorce of ideology and analysis of which the age-old actuality presently seems so deformed, so absurd, has been reconciled, to open the new era of the reign of the individual, whose isolated consciousness is the generative image of worlds.

"I can, therefore, no longer astonish, in speaking here about these abstract and simple things, ordered like everything that participates in logic and the abstract, those among you who, whether as legislators or diplomats, study with curiosity the speeches of that abolished period when Parliaments existed, and when 'the eloquence of numbers,' as the people of that poor era cynically put it, was in honor, along with the strange 'sobriety of images,' in which our lyrical vision no longer sees anything but paltriness and platitude.

"I cannot renounce a certain irony in thinking about the scandal my words would cause if eventuality had placed me among them, and if I had stood up to say, as I am saying to you, to those stupid and base assemblies of technicians and speculators: 'Having reflected on the supreme goal of politics, I believe, Messieurs, that with the means at my disposal, I can propose to our State that authentic luxury, *the realization of a dream'!*"

The grandmaster of the Germano-Latin Confederation fell silent momentarily, and leaned over the crowd. The bouquets of immobile flames were radiant; the shadow of the solemn pulpit descended toward the raised faces. A rumor filed the halls, weapons clinked. The scintillation of embroideries undulated and sparkled against the backcloth of scarlet drapes. Groups of Alliance ministers, clad in black, were massed in the embrasures of the colonnades. Hands and faces tensed by expectation emerged from fabrics and bright spots. The rumor of the night over the city was born at the threshold of the vestibules.

Silence fell again; the tall form of the orator straightened, and his prestigious voice rang out again.

"To be sure, those sterile people of a wretched extinct epoch would not have failed to laugh on hearing me pronounce, in their coarsely immediate debates, those words of meditation and dream, of which their skepticism and their abject elegance could not admit anything but the sounds.

"Today, we find it natural to satisfy our consciences with what was neglected by those unfortunate parliamentarians, those bastardized advocates of democracy, who perished without confessing the force of the ideas with which we live! It is a dream that bears us; and if I have come to speak to you this evening, having consulted the generals and the ministers, having spent months revising my project with the collaboration of their technical expertise, it is a dream that I want to expose to you urgently. It is a new legend that I want to propose to you, to feature in future memoirs!

"Messieurs,[9] ancient Europe, I repeat, has not yet accomplished all of her destinies. She has survived the strangest

[9] In the 1920 edition this is the second paragraph in the text, all the interim text having been cut. The deleted material is, in fact, inconsistent with the eventual argument of the story, which assumes that the synthesis to which the dictator refers is still far from achievement. Further cuts are made to the remainder of the speech to make it terser and most focused. The

political cataclysms; her fecund earth is robust with bloody sap. After having killed the barbaric world, it was necessary for her to kill the Roman world. Feudalism died thereafter, and after that it was necessary to kill the kings. And we, after the kings, have killed the bourgeois, who had confiscated revolt to their profit, and soiled life with a putrescence of egalitarianism, mediocrity and stupidity veritably more hateful than everything else! Civilizations have agglomerated and overheated on this extreme continent, art has taken refuge here, and all the sciences of idea. Metaphysics has sanctified the territory where the tyrannical Germany of militant emperors was. The balance of forces has been displaced, the state of armed peace that paralyzed everything has ceased.

"The concert of European efforts was assured, after the last Franco-German conflict, by the socialist alliance of the German and Latin races. Under their combined action, the Anarchistic revolution has triumphed over the parliamentary Republic in France, the Italian royalty in fief to Prussia and Austria; the individualist English constitution was unified with ours after the exile of the last prince. The Russian Empire, installed in Constantinople, having turned almost exclusively toward Asia and becoming semi-Oriental, has ceased to have direct communications with us, and if our evolutions of thought have not influenced its secular authority or suppressed there the ancient error of divine right, at least it has disinterested itself in our transformations in order to occupy itself entirely with its eastward expansion. Those of you who are grouped around me, therefore, represent a rejuvenated and free Europe, occidental guardian of the supreme conquests of the human mind!

"Here we are, Confederates of Central Europe, grandchildren of Carlyle, individualists before the single cult of Superhumanity, aristocratic Anarchists. I, the dictator of the Occident, have just sketchily summarized our recent birth, our

---

occasional deletions in subsequent chapters are much more sparing, usually only removing short phrases.

spiritual awakening, after the indescribable volcanic convulsion that, from Berlin to London and Paris to Rome, crushed the capitalist assemblies and monarchies in an unprecedented shedding of blood. Well, Messieurs, that destiny, finally edified, the course of events is compromising by the hour. Something formidable is born, which might ruin that which impassions us! In opposition to the unified Occident, the Orient is rising!

"The Orient! It is preparing an obscure and terrible vengeance, and its brutish black peoples are trailing immense and oscillating machineries toward us over their anthills.

"For a long time, the pretended slumber of those enervated races has no longer deceived me. While we were constructing our work and edifying our era, the people out there were slowly stirring as well. But it was an obscure agitation of subterranean beasts, the babbling of embryonic consciousnesses, an indistinct and formless rumor, the stretching of a pug-faced ignorance couched against the topics. We were too absorbed in our own thoughts to pay any heed to those distant symptoms. They have been germinating there for years.

"In its sands and its woods, depressed Tartary began to think; on his reed boat, the Chinaman raised a barely human head; the Indian fisherman ceased to roast in the sun unconsciously; the puny Annamite acquired cunning again. A bizarre birth of who knows what reprisals! The continent of fatalism dreamed of action. Everything changed on the day when, profiting for the revolutions of Europe, the alert Japanese race, having adopted our weapons and tactics, pushed its victorious armies into the depths of the Celestial Empire and commenced the civilization of its stagnant hordes. In their wake came the spirit of precise organization and the classification of forces.

"By means of the omnipotence of method, Japan appropriated Asia with a single surge of its devouring genius, and the danger began to concentrate against us. The successive annexation of all the countries of the Far Eastern littoral, the expulsion of the English hordes from India, the revolts in Burma and Annam, the treaties of the Rajah with the Yellows, and a hundred events of that genre were welcomed here with inattention. They were scarcely mentioned. It was the epoch when the capitals of Europe were burning, when bombs were annihilating in a single agreed night the parliaments of Paris and Berlin, when disarmament threw the rebel hosts out of their barracks, when civil war hurled the provinces against the functionaries, the salaried against the employer, the vagabond against the gendarme, the free man against the magistrate, all the independencies against all the authorities! The Orient was so far away!

"Now, the work is complete. That immense marriage has coagulated.

"Facing us, Messieurs, a unified society is standing up, and it is impossible for us to coexist. An eternal instinct of hatred stiffens against us those masses of men, and suspends above our continent an abominable invasion. The pullulation of those beings is terrible. Superstition, fatalism and somnolence have changed their face; the presentiment of our resources has haunted the Orientals, needs have been born therefrom; they are imminent on our frontiers, and tomorrow, a Timur or a Genghis Khan might arise again and hurl innumerable cavalries upon us. But the scourge will be a thousand times worse! Their armament is already almost ours; the numbers have learned tactics, the locust mentality is no longer sufficient for them.

"No one can imagine what that lugubrious cataract of men with brutal faces upon our provinces and our capitals would be like. The ancient world, fragmented into a hundred nations, no longer admits any but two reigns, two incompatible souls. That cannot last much longer. The Occident in heaped up against the Atlantic, its back braced, its face turned toward the Orient, ready to pounce. One of the two will die.

"You know that the first symptoms have already become manifest. The cables inform us that consuls have been seized and killed in Indo-China and Benares, simultaneously. Every demand for explanation or reparation has been rejected insolently; just now, the latest dispatches have confirmed that those troubles and others are suspected.

"There can be no question of remedying the evil once again within the precise limits of its extent, of limiting ourselves to an envoy of troops, to some partial colonial war that will ignite at a hundred successive points. What is necessary is a simultaneous action; it is to take up arms, before that enormous mass of humans has taken complete cognizance of what it might dare.

"What is necessary, Messieurs, let us say it, is a unanimous rising of Confederated Europe before the yellow peril!

"We can do that. I have thought of it; everything has been anticipated, and it is necessary that it takes place without any delay, that we anticipate the cyclone by cutting the very base of its turbulence with a lightning suddenness. Every hour lost aggravates the concentration of those hordes. The accursed spirit of Asia is agglutinating repulsive masses of armed slaves in camps and on the oriental plateaux. Neither conciliation nor pity can be anticipated. The situation is clear.

"So, this evening my speech must create a decisive resolution in you. The dream that I have come to propose that you render real is the one that pushed Europeans for centuries toward the Far Eastern seas; it is the one that took Napoléon to Egypt; it is the backlash of the civilized against the afflux of Barbarians, the revulsion of the West against the East: something more than a conquest, Messieurs; the affirmation of a law of salvation! But it is necessary for us to go further than Napoléon and all the colonizers; it is necessary for us to depart for a total subjugation, a methodical destruction of every attempt at yellow civilization.

"This is no longer a political war, it is a war of ideas. We can sustain it; everything has been anticipated. America, occupied with its extension and its struggles against the insurrectionists of the South, leaves us every initiative this side of its commercial neutrality. The Russian Empire is reserving for itself an action in Mongolia. Although no veritable sympathy links us to that autocratic empire, its situation makes it the advance guard of the civilized against the barbarian peril; it understands that, and its interests cause it to acquiesce to the will of Central Europe. All diplomatic measures have been taken to assure it the benefits of Asia in exchange for its neutrality in Europe.

"We can therefore act freely, in confederation; and if the Germano-Latin soul, in the presence of the Russian oligarchy, African obscurantism and American indifference, remains alone in condensing and fortifying itself, if it rejects the old threat of the end in order to get a grip on itself, once supreme, if I have come here to tell you that I have prepared everything in order that the immense effort should not be wasted, at least it is necessary for us to succeed in dissociating that which we have allowed to combine, in throwing these recently-armed troops back into a definitive barbarism. Otherwise, the day will come of filthy and ferocious inundations of men!

"It is a matter now of violently turning the face of destiny around: a mission of intellectual enlightenment is incumbent upon us, in the name of the arts, of the philosophical mind, of the plastic or abstract thought that was born here a long time ago. The intellectual nullity of the Orient is the condition of the Occident's existence!"

The dictator fell silent, abruptly. His arms raised, his eyes bright and fixed, he seemed to be raising over the breathless congress the visible image of war. Everyone bristled, but no one budged. The moment seemed vertiginous.

And suddenly, the master's arms fell, and in the clear voice of a logician, he pronounced:

"I, Claude Laigle, man of the people, become by the advent of Anarchism the responsible dictator of the Confederation of Central Europe, propose to the legates, as a glorious, unparalleled and immediate necessity, the declaration of a merciless war against the yellow race!"

The silence broke in a flash. A clamor burst forth; black-clad ministers ran toward the tribune,

"War! War! It's accepted!"

The undulation of the crowd pressed against the walls, beneath the electric chandeliers. The sentiment of a supreme and extraordinary decision seized the throats of hundreds of men.

"War! War!"

The terrible word, with a raucous rip, sprang outside souls like a shiny blade, before a living being, bounded among the colonnades toward the stairways, toward the street, toward the world; pale faces became crimson, mouths remained open in the cry, a convulsion shook the palace, and in the flux of the crowd the grim proclamation went forth.

Near the dictator, descended from the steps and surrounded by generals, feverish gazes shone, adieux and cheers sounded, and suddenly an appeal burst forth:

"Vive l'Aigle! Vive Claude l'Aigle!"

The favorite nickname with which the people, deforming at pleasure a predestined name, saluted the master, ran over the lips like a fanfare.

"Vive l'Aigle!"

Calmly, he saluted with his hand, and slowly went out, svelte in his black garments. The stormy assembly broke up; the doors filled with busy men rushing toward the city; bells rang: ushers hurried; the last members of the audience disappeared, and under the vaults, along the ramps, the decisive word—"War! War!"—resounded over their footsteps and accompanied them to the threshold. It was prolonged for a long time yet in the silence of the great gallery, solemn and deserted.

And then the lights of the chandeliers went out, one by one; the last palpitated and died, and the echo of the murderous word remained, face to face with silence and darkness...

By means of a door opening to the gardens, a man, Claude Laigle went out and headed for the boulevards. The street-lamps were blue-tinted by the mist of a recent shower of rain. It was a little after midnight. Luminous posters poured multicolored joyful gleams into the fog; masses of people were emerging from the dazzling exits of theaters, the terraces were overflowing, flowers were heaped up in peddlers' trays, diamond-clad women were iridescent on silks and furs, the steam of vehicles filled the streets. A great tumult of laughter and confused words rose toward the pale green metallic crowns of aligned trees, where fiery oranges and quivering letters designed their unreal specters.

The dictator allowed himself to be carried along by the human current. He liked annihilating himself thus and seeking solitude in the very din of life, passing unperceived and devoid of prestige, because no one looked at him. He followed the vast avenues, his soul of a logician and an ideologue delighting in feeling itself free and immense in a body protected by its very evidence against any inconvenient curiosity. The sentiment of only being a man of narrow form, a banal and fugitive unit between backs and breasts, in the jostle of a boulevard, delighted him. He bore his soul like an interior fire, which no order of precious stones, no embroidered torsade, no visible sign at all, had any need to symbolize externally.

The cold air touched his forehead deliciously, the formidable odor of life teased his entire being. Within himself, the decision of omnipotence that he had just announced bounded like a magical secret; his lips, previously open to the flow of his great sovereign voice, were now closed upon *the word*, but his mind was growling. "War! War!" it murmured, as he brushed past laughing women and elegant groups, and the sentiment of everything that that single word could do made his heart expand gloriously.

He walked firmly, without anyone paying any heed to him. He glanced mechanically at his hands, and the idea that those two white patches, similar in that night to a hundred thousand other white patches, would set a world in motion tomorrow, penetrated him with obscure thoughts about the nullity of the body before the moral will. He sensed that he was very much a modern man, living only by the brain and renouncing any decorative gesture, any uselessly theatrical

159

custom, the black intercessor of the destinies of a crowd that his gaze alone was sufficient to dazzle.

At one moment, he experienced the need to communicate even more closely with those existences that the force of circumstance confided to him, and, in a corner of the noisiest terrace he could discover, he sat down calmly, and ordered a drink. Without him paying any attention to them, his fingers sketched a map of Asia on the table, and he could not help smiling at that image, studied so many times for months. Those few hasty lineaments were the writing of the entire future. He thought about the new race, about himself, absorbed.

Suddenly, though, an immense rumor caused him to raise his head. Shrill clamors rose up, men brandishing telegrams and newspapers with enormous headlines, still damp, were running along the boulevards. Everyone stood up, jostling one another.

"War against the Orient!"

"Vote of the great Federal Council!"

"The dictator's speech!"

"War!"

"The yellow peril!"

The cries succeeded one another frenetically, from one end of the street to the other the conflagration radiated in outbursts of howls and appeals. Clusters of men climbed on to tables, multicolored pieces of paper flew over heads at the end of griping hands. Women in ball dresses threw themselves into the middle of the crowd in order to find out more, asking questions at the top of their voice in the tumult.

The storm of anxieties swirled in the illuminated night.

"War declared!"

"The Council has voted!"

Passengers leapt out of vehicles; the bearers of news struggled in seething groups, songs burst forth, soon broken off by the exasperated clamor of a furious human tide, which disgorged thousand of haggard faces everywhere.

Claude Laigle stood up, threw down a coin at random, slipped into obscurity and reached less populous streets. But the mad and delirious acclamation echoed in his ears: "War! War!"

"Yes, yes, war" he repeated to himself. "It's necessary; they know everything; I've finally unleashed everything."

The flamboyance of pride and resolution invaded his thoughts, which he had wanted to be calm. He turned up the collar of his coat, and lowered his head, fearing that he might be recognized, and marched toward the quais, where a relative solitude reigned. He leaned over the parapets to consider the long trails of blood, lunar steel and gold with which the reflections of street lights broke the black water—and it appeared to him that everything was ornamented by glory and sumptuousness beneath the enigmatic face of the nocturnal sky.

Behind him, however, the cry was running like a fantastic wild beast, devouring the city.

"War! War!"

Tomorrow, the monster would devour convulsed Europe, would raise its glittering cry over the entire world.

"Yes, war," the dictator repeated, pensively. He pronounced the word very quietly, against the placid trees. And, a thin, indistinct silhouette, the little shadows of which vacillated on the ground behind him, he came back along the quais toward the bleak Palais, and rang the bell at a secret door. And the dry click of the batten closing behind the master leapt into his thoughts with the echo of the eternal cry of death.

II. The Faces of the Old World

When Claude Laigle came back he went straight to a simple drawing room where four men were waiting for him. They rose to their feet; a gesture made them sit down again in silence. The dictator remained standing for a few moments in their midst, then, curtly, said: "The Council is open. Let's talk."

After a moment he added: "I wanted to go out to see the crowd, to feel it at close range. It's not good to keep ourselves to our own thoughts. The magnetism of the crowd is salutary;

between the public council and our private meeting, that aspiration of fresh air and living souls has fortified me. I've seen the city convulse under the news. I would have liked you to see it, you Mènieres, who like the movements of men! The street and the fête bounded.

"It reminded me, Médion, of the evening when we were walking together, waiting for the moment when the Chambre was about to blow up, thanks to you, fifteen years ago. I haven't seen since then an evening so magnificently upset. You remember how attentive we were, and how, all of a sudden, the distant noise of the explosion, the irruption of the crowd, and the clamors of the revolution, made us raise our heads— us, silent passers-by who might have been anyone. It was a moment of extraordinary life, a voluptuous bath of cerebral emotion.

"The cry of war, just now, caused me to vibrate in a similar fashion. To be a man, a thin form, that a carriage might crush in a moment of inattention, to say nothing, to have the appearance of being nothing, and yet to contain that in one's head, to be *the cause*, is quite beautiful and very tasty. Truly, the chiefs of old, with their mania for decorations and exterior signs, were maladroit. It's that anonymity which truly signifies power, which delightfully accentuates a secret."

"Yes," said Médion. "The mentality is everything."

The person who had just responded was a man of forty-five, thin and stiff, with a face framed by a short-cropped back beard, an impassive face striped by hard wrinkles, in which opened two dry bright eyes whose mineral blue was astonishing. The two hands placed flat on the table extended square, tightly-packed fingers; from the thin lips emerged a voice as precise and stiff as the features, and the entire man.

Médion was the foremost sociological intelligence of his era. A physiologist, mathematician and economist, his intransigent hypotheses, equally valiant in general ideas and marked by a gripping intuition of analogies, had frightened the routines of the institutions to which he had one presented his papers, always written with a rigid arrogance whose attitude of abstract conviction alone had displeased. The Anarchist revolution had found in him a terrible and glacial adherent. The silent energy of the scientist was effortlessly transformed into actions like the one that Claude Laigle had just recalled: ideological murder, in his engineer's hands, had become the striking and mysterious fatality of a concluding era.

Sensibility did not count for Médion; he was, according to the expression of his friends, "a living number." Today a Minister of State, he lived on nothing, ignored women, watched over everything, and still found means of innovating in chemistry, in spite of the crushing burden of his responsibility. The sole weakness of that antipathetic and admirable character was perhaps an authoritarian mania of the logician, an abuse of violent and curt formulae on all subjects, emerging with disdain, falling mercilessly in harsh words in which the humanity of the heart never trembled.

Raising a placid face, he repeated: "Mentality is everything. The examination of facts in the brain, the communion of the brain with the facts, the exact exchange: that is the whole of life. You'll come you that, Claude Laigle—you've come to it already. Sensibility is only an error of calculation, a false solution in the permanent mathematics that the mind develops in the presence of phenomena. Just now, in the meeting, I listened to you with interest; you were lyrical, you know how to speak to crowds; but I always have the impression that the eloquence is a means of seducing inferior beings. Your words sound within me without touching me; I only enjoyed the minute in which you squarely proposed war. That's a fact: the rest is smoke.

"I don't like lyricism any more than stimulants. I believe, definitely, that art and all matters of fantasy, of décor, as means of elegant illusion, are bound to disappear. They were yesterday's forms; we won't keep them for long. We'll go on to something else, to an ideal of mechanical harmony in which humans will no longer amuse themselves by making a god out of each of their faculties. It was very good, your theory of the illusion that leads the energies of State, obviously very good to excite the assembly, but I don't believe in it from the scientific viewpoint. I believe in a cohesion of the machine and individual orders; I believe in the present, and I detest metaphysics."

"Even applied to the science—not the sciences, but *the* science, unified in a single search for knowledge?" said Claude Laigle, slowly. "Even metaphysics linked to the psychology of races and considered as a very broad ethnology?"

"Even that," said Médion. "You've constructed the new society, in spite of everything, on the ruins of the past and faith in the future. Personally I attach myself to the present, and you don't. You all remain ideologues: Girondins or Montagnards, if you like; but you still count on instinct, on the sentiments of exception, on the dream. The dream! Oh, Claude Laigle, I'm astonished that you count on that word: poetry, poetry…in truth, an old song! Personally, I call all my desires a universe of chemistry, as Emerson put it."

"Reactionary!" murmured a voice that was simultaneously slow, sonorous and veiled.

"Reactionary? You say that to me, Ménières?" said Médion, turning round. "Well, if you like, yes: reactionary to your humanitarian ideas, I am. You've founded a society on the union of science and morality: an intelligent concept, but inviable. You've falsified both, and that's all. I intend to put those two incompatible forces back in their place, and elevate science—documentary, physiological, analytical intelligence—above the debauchery of hypotheses and dreams that you're all inclined to allow to grow. That's good for nervous minutes in which we need to draw the masses along; I know, of course, that your eloquence, your continual allusion to abstract verities, are excellent means, and that people only decide on dreams—but afterwards? We can do nothing serious without a scientific mind. We've suppressed religions; let's not replace them with a sociological fatalism—for that's your idea, isn't it, Ménières?

Blond, pale, raising his long musician's hands, Ménières straightened up and relied, serenely.

"Yes, Médion—sociological fatalism, that's a sufficiently accurate formulation. I, you know, am of the race of the unsatisfied, as much by dreams as by actions. I'm there, between you and Claude, without taking sides. I hold that art is a necessary form of cerebral expansion, and that metaphysics, although it was for too long a cloudy construction alongside life, can become a science of generality, a very precious force of synthesis. In that, I'm with Claude, and when he said just now that the essence of politics is the realization of a dream, I approve wholeheartedly.

"I think that you're a reactionary, my dear Médion, because you've retained a utilitarian, not ideological, conception of science, and because your 'universe of chemistry' is still a religion, as inconvenient as those we've swept away. Our attempt at a lyrical and logical State hasn't convinced you. You hold to the present—personally, I have a horror of it. On the other hand, I can't share Claude's opinion when I see him thinking that there is progress in the state we're in, and I readily admit that you doubt it. You know that I don't believe at all in the idea of progress, and you, who appear to limit yourself strictly to facts, have your little corner of intimate idealism even so, in believing that your regimentation of forces will lead to a superior condition.

"Life, as Claude understands it, is one life, and you understand life in another fashion, equivalent if not similar. That he's lyrical and you're exact is your right, both of you, but don't quarrel, and above all don't touch the soul, either to exalt it or to deny it. It doesn't concern you, and only develops covertly, without any preoccupation with progress."

"Don't touch it, except with the conviction that one is acting for its benefit," said someone, loudly.

Ménières looked at the man who had spoken. They considered one another.

Ménières was a childhood friend of Claude Laigle's. A poet and essayist of a delicately profound charm, he enjoyed a desperately amorous and quivering soul; great enthusiastic successes and equally violent chagrins had divided his life.

Famous adventures, and striking and desolating amours, had illustrated his name. He had been trailing through the world a luxurious and disenchanted existence, tearful and admirable, when the revolution turned him around, perhaps counting on finding an excitement sufficiently grandiose for his capricious and fatigued genius. The dictator adored him, incessantly kept him close to him, and took his advice, even though Ménières had refused any definite attribution in the new State. For Claude's ardent and feverish soul, there was no more refreshing company than that of the extremely subtle dilettante, ready for anything, intellectual to the point of suffering. Claude's mind was both exact, by virtue of his sociological studies, and innately poetic; Ménières counterbalanced Médion fortunately in that regard, and the three men, linked by an amity fortified by unusual circumstances, loved and esteemed one another while always contradicting one another.

The man who had just interrupted Ménières was Dessort, a thin individual, almost beardless, with a Caesarian profile, singularly feminine eyes, and a wide mouth, creased in a smile that was both ironic and charming. A throaty, slightly guttural voice seemed surprising in that frail person, elegant in the English fashion and sober of silhouette. Before the foundation of the Occidental State, Dessort had been the socialist orator to whom the international congresses listened most readily, the most persuasive of all. He it was who had prepared the mass desertions, had aborted the last Franco-German war by means of a general disarmament, and powerfully aided the establishment of the Anarchist government by bringing it his hosts of indoctrinated workers, when he had understood that socialism could only be an economic movement without a political future.

Dessort was an active force of the State. Claude Laigle did not like him much, but he had a marvelous understanding with Médion. The scientifistic mentality of the one and the communist spirit of the other were associated in a similar version for the rights of sensibility. They regulated public interest perfectly, leaving Claude Laigle to occupy himself with morality and ideology; those were domains in which they never intervened, while nevertheless having a secret desire to intervene in them. Médion desired to unify even souls in a universal mechanics; Dessort thought that a system of ideas might be useful to the crowds, albeit imposed. Both of them believed in Progress, and by force; they imagined that the ingenuity of the mind can aid in the elaboration of the soul of races, and that the elaboration in question is not accomplished freely and mysteriously by laws above human force.

Dessort, stared at by Ménières, stared back. "Yes," he said, "one can touch the soul of others for their benefit."

"What do you call their benefit?" replied Ménières, "and how do you know that a notion, however ingenious it might be, will create benefit in someone? No one is like anyone else. You're forgetting the human factor. The mystery of souls is individual."

"The word *mystery* annoys me, in sum," said Dessort.

"And I find it intolerable," added Médion.

They smiled.

"Regulate hygiene, commerce, material wellbeing and the employment of forces as much as you wish; that's the benefit that it's praiseworthy to augment," replied Ménières, "but leave the rest alone: the interior vibration that your chemistry can't analyze, Médion; the emotion that your economic theories and your satisfaction of stomachs cannot, Dessort, bring to the surface. You really are the democrats of old, with your belief in progress, your wounding pretention to systematize. The spirit of science and the spirit of socialism are, in sum, old sectarian spirits; the union of all that in the spirit of humanity escapes you. Human being is all of that and something else; a human isn't a machine, but that and more! I'm already not happy in demanding of all inventions of genius, in all branches, that they can offer me subjects of meditation, but if I restricted myself to your barracks-State or your laboratory-State , I'd wonder whether we were right to go to so much trouble to shake up Europe, only to leave it there."

Médion and Dessort had stood up abruptly. Ménières, still seated, considered them calmly. There was a silence.

"Enough," said Claude Laigle. "I don't like such divergences of opinion to be manifest in loud voices in the council of fellows. The State is founded on the unification of ideas in one alone, the science of knowledge, both mental and moral. The Occident needs a vision of intellectual verity. Enough systems! I affirmed again, at this evening's meeting, that that entente was the basis of the Confederation; if there's dissent among us, let it only be manifest internally. I don't want our theories to clash here, especially on such a decisive night. I've just seen the eternal conflict in you. We're going to act, let's not argue any more. We're not in Byzantium here; we can do metaphysics when the war is over."

"The Barbarians aren't at the gates," said Médion, smiling. "We're not at the stage where Byzantium was. In any case, I scorn debates, but if someone brings them here, I don't recoil. This is between us, Claude, there's no harm done. Modern humans do everything by cerebration, they're inclined to quibble. Tomorrow, we'll no longer have time; let's amuse ourselves for once before going to face the Barbarians."

"Perhaps it's us who are the Barbarians," said Ménières.

The remark fell heavily between the four men. Ménières' seemingly negligent voice gave him a strange relief. Claude Laigle stiffened, a trifle pale.

"That has no meaning, what you just said, Ménières. Have you even been paying attention?"

"Pooh!" said Ménières, softly. "I don't know. I said it, yes…anyway, I'm the most Byzantine of us all, I have no protest to make. The Orient is a great danger, Claude, you've done well, having charged souls, to raise up one half of the Old Continent against the other. But it's still an invasion, in the eternal fashion…and that can also be called Barbarity.

"It's called Civilization," replied Claude Laigle.

"As you wish," Ménières responded.

"No! Not 'as I wish'!" cried the dictator. "As is correct! As is piously and nobly just! How nervous and bizarre we are this evening!"

He sat down, and then got up again, went to a window and opened it. But he suddenly recoiled; a rumor rising from the nocturnal avenues quivered through the gardens. And like a sinister bird on the wings of a frigid wind, the fateful word entered the room:

"War!"

The four men listened momentarily.

"How they shout!" murmured Dessort.

"Yes, they're shouting almost as if...as if they weren't..."

"What?" said Claude, abruptly.

"Civilized," Ménières completed, with an almost imperceptible irony.

Claude Laigle started violently. "Ah!" he exclaimed. "Is this today or yesterday? We've made the material and moral revolution while holding a few verities to be certain, and now, at the first result of the power we wanted to obtain, the words of doubt come back, as if all that weren't agreed, and firmly agreed. Now you're contesting eloquence and sensibility, Médion; we have, however, made plenty of room for your scientific ideas. Stick to that! You, Dessort, are starting again to advocate intervention is the happiness of others with ready-made principles—but we founded the Occidental State on Anarchistic Individualism, which doesn't admit the intervention of the collectivity in subjective morality. Limit yourself to codes of hygiene and prevention, and don't resuscitate the specter of social religiosity. And you, Ménières, with your undulating, charming and fatal dilettantism, are putting in question, with any airy remark, the very legitimacy of what will be tomorrow the capital effort of the twentieth century!

"So, between you, what do you want me to do? In the epoch of parliamentarianism, oligarchies and constitutional or despotic monarchies, when we were preparing the revolution and, as unknown young men, we were dreaming during nocturnal strolls of the future State that would spring from the bomb—*then* was the time to raise these doubts and debate them. But at present, what are you thinking? The desire to argue is rising again from your heart to your lips. Is doubt, then a recurrent disease? What I affirmed before the legates just now as the very of that State, you no longer think, at the moment when it's necessary, in order to live?

"For myself, I no longer have any hesitation. The superior human of whom I have dreamed, whom I have described, is one who unites science and art in a single intellectual clarity. One who is a character first before being a technician, one who is his own confessor and poet. That human being I can see, I can sense; he exists, even if I'm not him completely, and you refuse to become him. That human being will reign and vanquish, the one that must—must, you hear—be revealed in every individual in the confederation. And if I have decided this war, it's less because of the danger of the Orient's weapons or the peril of its industrial competition than because of that very revelation.

"The unprecedented war that has virtually commenced at this moment is the proof, the purchase of consciousness that I want to give the crowd on the individuality in which I believe. It is in this effort that the still-hesitant consciousness in question will solidify. Oh, that human being, that intellect no longer fixed but living, will not be, if you cannot or dare not. For myself, I know that he exists, I want to draw him from our race, force him to appear, and I shall seek him if he cannot yet be found!"

"He isn't viable," said Médion.. "He's hypothetical; I refuse to believe in him."

"He is viable," said Dessort, "but in dreams."

"He exists," said Ménières. "Claude's right. But..."

"But! Always a *but* in whatever you say!" cried the dictator. "But what?"

"But...perhaps he isn't here," Ménières concluded.

"Where then?"

The four men looked at one another.

"Perhaps among *them*," pronounced Ménières, serenely.

"You mean those we're going to fight?"

"Yes—because you don't know what their soul is, fundamentally. They're ancient; they date from the night; they completed their self-realization in the era when we were still prehistoric. And who knows whether they haven't formed, in the midst of those obscure and seething masses, a being like the one you describe?"

"But the consciousness," Claude interjected, violently, "and the sentiment of moral autonomy, is a notion of ours! It's finished, out there! You know full well that those people have nothing in common with us, nothing but economic theories learned in our schools, weapons, an industrial socialization, a means of practical life and an apparent modernism, that's all! Beneath all that burns a barbaric and voracious soul, bogged down in atavistic fatalisms, heavy with passivity.

"You know full well that the odious Sino-Japanese race has retained the cranium of the beaver or the hamadryad, a terrible cranium with the jaws of a burrower, with polished and finished brows, the cranium of a predator and brute with devouring senses! We're not going to war, we're going hunting, in running against those thousands of militarized anthropomorphs! Do you think that the superior human of whom we've dreamed is there? Nothing, nothing, I tell you, but an animal parodying our usages.

"In sum, Ménières, you're too poetic, if the others aren't poetic enough. The mirage of the name Orient, I don't know what seduction of Bibles and Vedas, has deflected you from the truth. Personally, I envisage it in the real, that Orient, as an ideologue and as a Head of State, and I firmly believe in the intellectual supremacy of the Occident. I see nothing out there but a force of exaction and base enjoyment contained for centuries by obscurantism, awakened by Japan and rushing upon us to rob us, devoid of a goal, dreams and beauty.

"You know what an industrial war we've been fighting against the yellow race for two hundred years; it pours waves of emaciated individuals into our ports, as clever as monkeys, living on nothing, killing the value of European money by their unsustainable competition. Already, the monarchic and parliamentary states were infested by them; already, there were massacres of Chinese workers in various places, fifty years after the opening of the Orient to commerce—and that has multiplied a hundredfold since. If the American State has promised us neutrality in the present war, and the Russian Empire has agreed to join us and operate for its part on the frontiers of northern China—an acceptance of which I obtained a definite assurance this morning—it's because of that economic peril. But I'm acting in the name of higher and more general ideas than those.

"As I said this evening, I'm proposing a dream to the desire of the energy of the Occidental Confederation. I'm proposing to monopolize here, by the crushing of those masses, the intellectuality of the Latin races. We've used the bomb to suppress the governments that were fragmenting us, we've used the cannon to save what the bomb created. And you're now putting those two ideas in doubt? In the name of what? In the name of some pantheism, some benevolent egalitarianism? No, no, I repeat, enough dreams! The intellectual nullity of the Orient is the condition of the Occident. Médion likes formulae, I give him that one; more than any other it's true, urgent and essential! It's the pivot of the future system!

"In sum, I'm weary of these doubts, these reticences, these backward glances, these pities, these hypotheses! Do you know what you represent to me, you three, one with his exaggerated poetic dreams, another with his dreams of exclusive science, and the third with his utopias of the collective education of the race? Well, you represent three synthetic forms of the spirit of yesterday, the spirit that we wanted to kill, and which is trying to be reborn. What are you, this evening, on the eve of the creation of the future? You're dilettantism, intolerance and indoctrination, the faces of the Old World!"

He fell silent, out of breath, his face contracted by anger. For a few minutes, no one spoke. And suddenly, on the long table, stiff and wrinkled hands shifted plans and papers and the dull voice of an old man pronounced:

"If the metaphysics is finished, we're going to work, Messieurs."

They all looked at the man who had not yet said a word. The old generalissimo Luxeilles de Trénan smiled disdainfully, lifting a glabrous and ivory-tinted head from the heap of maps, in which gray moist eyes gleamed, bulging like the eyes of mystics. With his elbows on the arms of his chair, taciturn as ever, he had waited without a muscle of his hard and frozen face having stirred. Only an occasional frisson of impatience had caused him to turn his spectacles over nervously between his fingers.

He was a tall, thin individual, shaven like a priest, with mannerisms that were both unctuous and precise. He was dressed in black, like the others, simple gold torsades at the neck and sleeves signifying, strictly, that the master of arms was there; and one would scarcely have supposed so, on seeing that ecclesiastical face and thin mouth, the aspect of a pastor both troubling and benevolent.

Beneath those glacial and methodical appearances burned the commander-in-chief's great military intelligence. The Marquis Luxeilles de Trénan, retaining without coquetry in the anarchistic state a title that summarized a race, was a tactician without ostentation, less reminiscent of a Maurice de Saxe than a Moltke, implacably exact, speaking little, truly made to lead black armies to whom heroism in the ancient fashion was incomprehensible. He was the logician of death, the tranquil destroyer, the engineer and strategist acting by means of artillery, marches and the commissariat with the surety of a chemist in his laboratory. What Médion had done in the civil war, General de Trénan had done in the last continental wars, his campaigns in Franconia and Bohemia, where the power of imperial Germany had been broken, and thanks to which the social unification of the Germano-Latin race had been able to take place, remained models for the future, perfect mathematical operations systematizing and orientating massacre.

In the superior council, facing Claude Laigle, haunted by lyrical visions of history, Ménières, haunted by dreams, Dessort, preoccupied with fraternary theories, Médion and he were the stiff and violent faces of force, the missionaries of the dynamic modern world over which it seemed that darkness had passed. But in Médion's soul a scientific ideal remained; the soul of General de Trénan was simple. It was a feudal soul, demanding supremacy for itself, exaction for exaction, ignorant of the scruple of attacking a race: a brutal and grandiose soul, savoring war, inaccessible to everything that was not destructive effort.

"I have what will put you in accord here," he said, softly. "These are the estimates of the war. I have reviewed them. They are as exact as your chemistry, Médion. They are, Ménières, rich enough in deployments of energy to surpass your poetic ideal; these stacks of paper, Dessort, contain the wherewithal to put the forces that interest you in motion. And you, Master, will find here a power of certainty that will allow you to avoid rising in anger against doubt. Fortunately, there is one force in the service of the Old World that will give the new one all the time to develop and to modify its morality and hypotheses other than on paper. I bring here the palpable domination of shells. I rely upon that messenger to deliver ideas. Speeches first, that afterwards, to conclude."

"We have spoken," said Ménières slowly, "And you…"

"I, if you wish, will conclude with that," General de Trénan finished.

"It is indeed you who will conclude," said Médion. "The Occident of the future is founded on the shell and it will triumph by the shell."

"The shell is, then, an idea for you, Trénan?" said Claude Laigle, bitterly.

"It's a fashion of pronouncing the word *idea*," affirmed Dessort, sarcastically. "Anyway, you were talking just now about bombs. Means for means, my socialism wouldn't want to choose."

"The bomb was an idea," said Claude Laigle, getting up, his eyes shining. "It was necessary—you hear, Dessort, necessary! Like everyone else, I have my interior cemetery, and I think all that is terrible, when I'm alone. But it was necessary! I don't regret the civil war. But I sense that Trénan likes the shell for its own sake—and oppose that to my fashion of killing if you like. There are various meanings of death. The shell isn't an idea, it doesn't carry anything but our material defense, because our moral defense is in ourselves..."

"Let's say that it's only a guarantee," the commander-in-chief rectified, placidly. "It's already that, and that guarantee, Master, your ideology needs." Smiling, the terrible old man added: "Besides which, I too am an ideologue, since I calculate the energies without occupying myself with the matter. In your rationalizations, you suppress the material being; personally, I too rationalize my art—for it is an art—by suppressing it...once and for all, and seriously, that's all."

"Let us," said the dictator, "allow the principle of death give life to our race, this time as before, in accordance with the eternal decrees. To our new race..."

The end of the sentence expired in silence.

And the five men, three of whom symbolized the three great moral heresies of the modern world, while the fourth was devoid of faith, and the fifth was imploring one, pored over maps, their precise hands touching electric buttons in the calm of the nocturnal council, preparing until the pallor of the imminent dawn the impact of the Civilized against the Barbarians.

III. The March Eastwards

The declaration of war was notified to the ministerial cabinets of Tokyo and Peking and to the Rajahs of Delhi and Hyderabad—which is to say, to the four official delegations of

175

the Asiatic Alliance, early the following morning, The concentration of European forces commenced immediately.

It was already prepared. For months, the active genius of General de Trénan had been coordinating the Confederation armies, getting the arsenals and supply chains ready. The colossal enterprise had germinated in the mind of the dictator as soon as his election to power, and although the first years of his administration had been devoted to organizing the new constitution and erasing the traces of the frightful civil war, Claude Laigle had never escaped his obsession with the Orient. He had been examining it as a logician, analyzing the industrial and military peril, since the conquest of China by the Japanese, and the autonomy of India, reestablished after the expulsion of the English in 1950, had only confirmed him in the sentiment of a terrible future.

That fusion of Hindustan and the Far East had become the obsession of his politics; it was there, at that junction, that it was necessary for Occidental civilization, with a decisive and mathematical stroke, to cut that stormy and barbaric cloud like a lightning bolt, to scatter it into a rain of men permanently disarmed and inoffensive. With the sociological and assimilative genius of the Japanese, a force of cohesion had really been born in those vast stagnant fatalisms; the danger of a Timur leading regiments with equal arms was inevitable; the leader had only to appear.

Claude Laigle evaluated the historical situation with the intuitive clarity that is the prerogative of sentimental individuals, and which as easily makes them diplomats as poets. Claude Laigle was a lyricist and a dialectician; he did not hide not from himself that the extraordinary moral and mental effort by means of which anarchism had triumphed had as good as exhausted the active force that overcome the power of reflection of the Occidentals. A crisis of sociological moralism had then occupied, almost exclusively, twenty-five years; philosophies had undulated furiously over the crowds, and energy, in those restricted nations, crushing one against another, had been polarized, in a fashion, toward pure abstraction.

The complication of the modern mind had become extraordinary and, amid all the intellectual research, hardly any attention had been paid to foreign politics. Russia, especially after its occupation of the Bosphorus, had lost interest in the politics of Central Europe. Its autocracy accepted anarchism without welcoming it; there was, between the Occident and Asia, an immense intermediary territory, not at all disposed to encroach upon the West, extending eastwards without meeting any obstacle, And since the Russo-English conflicts in Afghanistan and Kashmir, since England's reversals and the loss of India, Russia was only occupied in a slow advancement in that direction. It hid the view of Asia from Europe.

However, an almost analogous evolution had been accomplished out there, and sooner or later, Russia would have to make a decision between the Occidental Confederation and the Asian Confederation. The egotism of its diplomacy would have to come to an end or become a veritable dementia. Claude Laigle knew full well that the gigantic antagonism, if it was not openly declared, was brooding; and he glimpsed, on the far side of the world, agglomerations of beings of primitive morality, having the enormous superiority of brutality over the intellectuals, and stiffening it with the two or three sentiments that are sufficient to convulse a race: the instinct of eternal westward expansion, hatred against colonial occupation, and the lure of booty conquered from fatigued peoples.

The alternatives had become increasingly precise. The dictator had never ceased to think that it was the capital question of vitality, and that after having, by means of a libertarian explosion, nullified the perils and conflicts of nationalities within its own bosom, Central Europe would only have repose and faith by throwing itself into the most terrible war of all against the obscure and immense yellow peril, increasingly coagulated. The establishment of scientific intellectualism could only ensure quietude after being liberated from the threat of that Barbarism.

He repeated that to himself for years; it was for him an absolute reality that took on the amplitude of a dream. His lyrical vision warned him that everything was bound to end there, that the unification of Europe, coinciding with the unification of Asia, clearly demonstrated the future war, the true and beautiful ethnological war, no longer playing out only in frontier squabbles and annexed provinces, like the paltry conflicts of old, but clashing as much in thought as with swords, setting two irreconcilable worlds against one another.

Asia! Claude Laigle did not only hate it as Head of State. He hated it as a thinker, fond of scientificism, having reforged an idealism above religion and worn-out metaphysics. Asia was the symbolic name of fatalism, of obscurantism, of hereditary hierarchies, of everything that the burning soul of Anarchist philosophy had seen melt in the brazier of the recent revolution, with intoxication. It was the recommencement of feudal dominion, the annulment of three centuries of liberalism. Claude Laigle feared those mental reprisals even more than the material dangers. And as soon as unlooked-for events had clearly delimited the situation, reduced the war to a single motive against the Old World, the ideologue had concentrated in himself and had begun to envision coldly the supreme assault that no nation of fragmented Europe would ever have dared to attempt first.

For long years Claude Laigle had waited for a pretext, and sounded the Occidental soul. It was necessary not to fail. The alternatives of war for diplomatic motives signify little and are reparable, but an ethnological war can only terminate in the extinction of one of the parties, and if it failed, the prestige of the civilized would be ruined, fear would set in, the hope of one day succeeding would vanish, to go foment Oriental ambition. Claude Laigle had let the situation become clearer, so lucidly that there was no longer any hope of a third solution, and the truth appeared evident to everyone. The dream of being the man who would terminate the great struggle haunted him.

Once, as a very young man, before the triumph of Anarchism, he had been, with Médion, one of the first to talk about that problem, and he found himself, going gray, still thinking about it, and having by force of energy, multiplied its importance a hundredfold in the eyes of the crowd. Industrial conflicts, bursting out with increasing frequency, between white and yellow workers, had served him even more than colonial revolts or acts of war.

Claude Laigle knew that nothing excites people more than evidence that results from financial questions, and that in spite of all the individualistic ideas that, in Europe, had penetrated the masses and elevated their moral degree, money remained the great motive of human force. All his genius had been extended to placing at the center of that impulsion, instead of a simple promise of immediate benefit, a profound notion, the very thought of the race: a dream, in truth. That lyrical man conceived a dream, not as a nebulous construction that turns the mind away from ordinary spectacles, but as the highest reality of energy, the intellectual reality *par excellence*.

The most striking mental conquest of the new State had been making everyone admit—for the first time since the beginning of the world—that the reality of subjective beings is as valid and as palpable as that of objective ones, that it is as realistic to meditate as it is to eat, that they are two equivalent actions of life. And truly, Claude Laigle hoped for everything from all those fatigued races, from the moment that seemingly elementary concession had been obtained.

He had known for so long the bitterness of the intellectual in the midst of capitalists that he had been seized by an immense hope on observing that Anarchism had created the people the notion of the active utility of pure cerebration. Thus, it had appeared to him to be possible to present the war—his war!—in its true sense, and from the day when he had obtained that assurance, he had considered the work as half-done. The material preparation did not seem to him to be insurmountable.

Long and detailed conversations with Médion had planned its economics, and the unexpected good fortune of General de Trénan had brought the dictator a further assurance. During the Franco-German war, two devastating campaigns in Franconia and Silesia, deciding the ruin of the house of Hohenzollern and permitting socialism to impose disarmament, had revealed to the world that a surprising tactician had been born.

The French language and French influence had remained preponderant, the movement of unification had departed from that victory, the international electorate had granted to Claude Laigle the dictatorship of Paris and General de Trénan had become, by virtue of the clear-sighted will of the ideologue, the master of strategy throughout the domain of the Confederation. The two of them, with Médion, had elaborated the campaign, down to the smallest incidents, until the evening when, all measures having been taken, finally decided, the dictator had summoned the legates in order to present to them officially the project of the declaration of war.

The order of mobilization ran electrically from one end of Europe to the other on that very night when the five friends, still vibrant with the decisive acclamation, had stirred the intimacy of their souls, enfevered by general ideas, one final time, and, by virtue of a heroic coquetry, inclined their energy and their certainty before the abstract and eternal doubt of the cherished philosophical dreams that their minds contained.

It was like a supreme adieu, that hour given to pure mental speculation before the action. One final time they had interrogated one another, feeling themselves keenly to be civilized, anxious, modern, free men united in effort but each one privately retaining a different conviction. And when they separated, no trace remained of their secret antagonism. There was nothing more in presence than the organizers of a fact.

The acclamation of crowds broke out all over Europe as the armies passed by. Ancient patriotism was dead, the conflicts of nations no longer existed, but a true ethnological patriotism had risen on the ruins of the other, and no longer had anything absurd about it. The defense of illusory or arbitrary frontiers no longer occupied anyone, but the defense of the civilized soul appeared sacred to everyone. The great eternal cry: "Death to the Barbarians!" traversed the Occidental lands, and there was no one, even among the most rustic, who did not have the sentiment of a sacred necessity.

When Claude Laigle, black,[10] simple and pale, appeared in cities in the middle of a human ocean and raised over the thousands of howling people that proud head whose luminous eyes fascinated to the point of delirium, he seemed more than the dictator and the master; he incarnated the entire race of the Latin Occident, a fugitive vision leaning out of the caleche that carried him toward railway stations, toward army assembly points, toward the unknown and toward hope.

His farewell gesture signified the immense stir, and beside him, leaning on the cushions wearily and thoughtfully, inclining a delicate and pained face beneath gilded hair, Claude's adviser and friend, Ménières, showed him, smiling, on the balustrades of balconies and the arches of avenues, the symbolic black and yellow pennants that the people had suspended to summarize the great struggle. The black people against the yellow people! Black and yellow! The two fateful colors decked windows and edifices everywhere, simplifying thought terribly, opposing the shadow where one meditates to the sun of unconsciousness, the Occident to the Orient, science to fatalism, always and implacably.

Ménières said these things in a low voice while Claude Laigle, lucid, saluted the human floods, his soul convulsed in their enormous cry, feeling himself carried away in the whirlwind of the Adventure...

It was Dessort who, with his supple eloquence and his prodigious instinct of simple sentiments, stirred enthusiasm in

---

[10] The symbolic employment of the color black in this passage, which has already been invoked with regard to the clothing worn by the dictator and his associates, but whose significance becomes much more obvious from here on, reflects the fact that the symbolic flag of Anarchism was black, frequently wielded assertively, often in opposition to the red flag of Socialism, in Parisian political demonstrations.

the heart of the masses, embedding there the two or three general ideas sufficient to create opinion, suppressing futile complications, illuminating the magnetic blaze, heightening the distinction of the two patriotisms. In the name of the vanity of the old, the orator had preached disarmament once to the international syndicates of which he was the soul; in the name of the intellectual novelty of the new, he preached merciless war.

From city to city Dessort moved, from city to city the dictator sensed his secret influence, his genius for persuasion; at every step the idea, explained and synthesized by the agitator of crowds, appeared to Claude Laigle with a new force. He read on the faces of the spectators who rushed around his vehicle or at the decent from his railway carriage, that the dispatches, the articles and the manifestos of the special press inspired by Dessort had fundamentally insufflated the confederated countries with the evidence of the great war and its destiny. All were unified in the same determination.

By night, in the vibrations of the express carrying him across the plains of Germany, Claude rediscovered the rhythmic sensation that intoxicates, which gives a kind of mathematical certainty to effort, and that mastered his insomnia. In the brightness of the narrow saloon, his eyes, after being bathed in the infinite obscurity of landscapes through the windows, returned to the table where, impassive and ignorant of fatigue, General de Trénan was writing, calculating, putting the final touches to every detail of the plan of campaign, his bony head, white and shaven, leaning over his golden collar.

And, absorbing himself in that contemplation, Claude Laigle thought about Médion, who had remained for some time in Paris. He too had a power, but occult; confined in his study or his laboratory, the Minister of the Interior was, behind the ardent flight of the conquest, the methodical and mute calculator of forces of renewal, and also the engineer of forces of murder, unleashing the anonymous powers of chemistry and mechanics against the Yellows, with the coldness that he had once brought to unleashing them in the social revolution.

Claude Laigle sensed that active cerebral reserve behind him, the shudder of the express exalting him to the point of the vision of the hordes of brutes that he would soon see face to face in the land of the sun—and his thoughts bounded with the drunkenness of the hectic course, launched as rigidly as the train into the night, coherent, exact and dense, similarly ensured by couplings, gliding toward destiny with its rectilinear energy constantly multiplied of its own accord, frightfully, with a clouded dream occasionally illuminated by a flash of lightning above their irreversible momentum...

Dawn paled over the landscapes of Saxony and Bohemia. In the rainy capitals, amid the popular acclamation, Claude Laigle verified publicly what he had come to see in secret several times before: the condition of the arsenals and the troops. Everything was ready. Armies were descending to the points of concentration. He turned southwards, traversed Italy in its length, visited the ports of war, crossed the sea and found himself on the soil of Egypt.

Everywhere he found the immense black and uniform crowds of the civilized world, the cavalries, the artilleries and the regiments performing their sinister geometry. The squadrons of the Mediterranean were heading at full steam for the Red Sea; they crossed it by night, with their fixed beacons and their electric fans, stars of a sky of science and death, proposing to consciousness a new and palpable ideal.

The yellow and black oriflamme writhed symbolically at the top of the mizzen-mast of the transport ships. In Syria, Damascus and Baghdad, the accumulation of Europeans troops massed before his eyes in the dazzle of the sun. And in spite of the white costumes of the soldiers ready to depart for torrid climes, Claude saw them still black, abstractly black in the modern color, black and exact, black in accordance with the strange irony of the pirates of old.

Pirates! He smiled at that word, and Ménières smiled too. "Everything is cyclical," the latter said. "We're bringing the spirit of intellectual creation with the hue of death."

In Claude's heart, however, the Idea persisted: he saw it as a svelte and supple statue, which black suited perfectly. "Not the hue of death," he said, "but that of mourning. We're displaying our mourning, Ménières, for the old ideas of the old world. We're wearing mourning for the errors of yore: the Idea will only be dressed in joy later, when all of these things are finished. It's good that everything is reduced to a single hue, like our soul, the hue of exactitude and energy."

Complex dreams visited his heart, and he fell silent.

A vast series of ironclad squadrons attained the Persian Gulf. They were to spread out along the Hindu coasts, land floods of men there, and then go on to the seas of China to gnaw at the east of the immense enemy empire, gripping it in a semicircle of iron and fire, to establish a blockade and, reaching all the way to Shanghai, seize the yellow power from behind.

Great shocks would astonish the naval Orient—but the principal effort had to be directed on the continent. Through Persia and Afghanistan, the European armies would penetrate into northern India, joining up with the divisions disembarked in Bengal. It was there that the tactics of General de Trénan would be concentrated. It was there that his strategic thought would combine with the abstract genius of the dictator. It was in India, revolted, armed and resuscitated with its antique fatalisms, that it was necessary to kill the energy of the old world.

There, truly, the essential danger rose up. That first country, more than China and more than Japan, harbored the devouring soul and the ambitious reprisal of the future. Japan, clinging like an England to Manchuria and Korea, was incessantly pouring through the Celestial Empire its mechanical genius and the dynamic inspiration of its modernism, but India was the advance-guard toward Europe, it was the terrible peninsula where all those inert forces, shaken from the north-east, were coagulating.

Claude's plan was to avoid the immensity of the Chinese plains, to cut Orientalism in India, in the very place from which it might pounce on Europe by awakening Arabia and perhaps the Negroes, to isolate Japan in the distant seas, maintain it there with fleets, ruining its commerce—that was the essential thing. Between an India seized again and vanquished and a Japan blockaded, the immeasurable swamp of yellow men between the Altaï and the Himalaya could become inert and vegetative again for thousands of years. Destruction would have been vain and unrealizable; Claude did not even think of it.

Since the beginning of the world the belly of the Orient had been stuffed with stagnant and pullulating hosts; it was like the humus of humankind; it had only been possible to nibble at its edges; civilized power, attacking it sideways, had been annulled by numbers and extent, like a shell launched into the void. Merely to contain those masses, to plunge them again into barbarity and darkness by suppressing their points of mental revitalization was to decapitate that body, severing the neural connections.

Claude Laigle knew full well that civilization is only born of destruction, that the intellectuality given to those agglomerations of beings was incompatible with that of the Occident, that it was necessary to kill one in order that the other might live. He had chosen.

India and Japan, one giving birth and the other concentrating: Claude Laigle always returned to those two fixed points, around which all his thoughts revolved. Across the Chinese plains, the transfusion of the ideas of the yellow lands operated slowly; ideas of rectitude, the grouping of brute forces, of barbaric socialization, of cohesion with a view to a tidal wave rushing over Europe in future, circulated with difficulty, like overly bitter blood in swollen veins, but they did circulate. In India, they found the support of the old Aryan genius;[11]

---

[11] When *L'Orient vierge* was written there had been a veritable glut of works in the previous three decades devoted to the scholarly fantasy of the Aryas [Aryan Race], the supposed original speakers of the ancestor of the Indo-European lan-

they became almost similar to those of the peoples of the West; they suddenly contemplated their power over an extremely refined land from which corteges of masterpieces had once emerged, and where a tenacious and admirable magic still burned.

After atrocious struggles, India had once again rejected the English; at present, it belonged to no one, it was dreaming of a reawakening. Newly emerged among its rajahs was a race of cruel and brilliant princes in whom the penetration of modernity had only rendered more precise and more sagacious the ancient ambition of Nana Sahib. It was not for nothing that, seeming to yield, those men had come to Europe with the sons of the Samurai, to bring their assimilative intelligence into the schools, to take from the Occidental world its discoveries, to ripen energies there.

Claude knew that it was high time to stop that interior movement. Japan and India were the brains of Asia; China was merely the reservoir of brute forces, the domestic and armed hosts on which they counted on drawing one day in order to realize their autocratic and ferocious ideal, their hateful feudalism, their eternal dream of dominating migration westwards.

The fleets would contain Japanese power, but in India, it was more than surveillance and diminution that was required; it was a conquest, an absolute submission, a sterilization of thought, of the terrible Oriental thought incompatible with ours. It was there that the land armies would act. It was at the very foot of the Himalaya, in the Punjab, in Kashmir, in Nepal, in Bengal, at the sources of the Ganges and the Indus, that

---

guages,. The most notable French titles included the oft-reprinted *Les Origines indo-européennes ou Les Aryas primitifs* (1859) by Adolphe Pictet and *Origines indo-européens: Le Berceau des Aryas* (1861), one of several books on the subject by Joseph van den Gheyn. Mauclair's subsequent adoption of the term *Berceau* [Cradle] suggests that he might well have read the latter.

the real war would be concentrated. The army corps coming from the south via Mysore, Nizam, Gujarat and the lands of the Rajputs, had orders to join up with the troops coming from Persia. The triangle would close in the Deccan, and via Allahabad, Cawnpore and Delhi, over an immense riot of blood and fire, the forces of two worlds would find themselves in a supreme contest. Everything indicated that with a luminous clarity.

The direction of the naval war, Claude Laigle left to the admirals. What impassioned him, what he wanted to see, was the collision in the primitive earth of the ancient Aryans and the new Aryans, turned against their ancestors. It really was a war of races, a family war, of which he dreamed. The action of Russia in Mongolia would drive the Chinese masses back toward that central conflagration. The true war, the war of ideas, would unravel there, in the Himalaya, in the Hindu Kush, near the Pamir, in the eternal places where the germination of the Occident had poured forth at the origin of the worlds,[12] and to which the transformed Occident was about to return in order to confront its enemy brethren, to put in parallel their fateful inertia, their immutable gods, and its own ideal of active and atheistic energy. It was in the very cradle of the race that the great question, which Claude called "the Dream," with his entire faith in the superiority of the new Occident, was about to be settled once and for all.

---

[12] The idea that the Pamir mountains were the point of origin of land-based life, and hence a kind of focal point of evolutionary radiation, can be traced in France back to Benoît de Maillet's *Telliamed* (1748 in a drastically censored version, third augmented ed. 1755), which proposed an evolutionary theory based on the notion that the Earth had once been entirely covered with water, but had slowly dried out, gradually exposing more of the surface. It gelled conveniently with the theory of the origin of the Aryan Race in the same area, as scholarly fantasies sometimes do, offering esthetic satisfaction and an illusion of logical support.

Behind the walls of Tibet, behind Burma, the yellow masses could sleep. Claude had no fear of them once the enlivening force was removed from them. The immense series of equatorial archipelagoes did not worry him either; what was required there was to kill the consciousness of number, to sever the link between them and the occidental world, prevent contagion via Arabia and Africa.

"The third age will be the age of Negroes," he said. "We are only on the threshold of the age of the Yellows. Later, the civilized will make arrangements. The black continent will sleep too."

In the heart of Africa, no visible ferment had been born. But the sacred land of the old spirit, Hindustan, was seething with fury and convulsed, ready for extraordinary destines, and behind it, driven by methodical and implacable Japan, the yellow rabble, irresistible in its pullulation, was rising. Claude Laigle could not detach his dreams therefrom. What obscure and passionate dreams tormented his thoughts on joining up with the black armies traversing Iran!

The dispatches arrived one after another, and at each of them his heart leapt in his breast. The envelopment of the fleets was closing around the Asiatic littoral. In the gulf of Bengal, on the coasts of Siam, along the Philippines, the European cruisers were prowling, seeking the enemy. Claude followed them instinctively on the map. They went around the seas of China, leaving to their right the vast and fantastic archipelago with fabulous names: Sumatra, Java, Borneo, Mindanao, Celebes, Luzon; islands crouching in the ocean like clawed monsters, twisting their savage volcanic sequence, vestiges of a catastrophe and an original tearing.

The fleets reached Formosa. Weeks went by without news. Eventually, it was learned that in the first encounter, near the passes of Chusan, five Japanese ships had been sunk. The news was like an electric shock, coming back toward the capitals of Europe. At the same time, the land armies were advancing. It seemed to Claude that he could hear, beyond the deserts and the expanses of water, from rainy Germany to burning Syria, the formidable subterranean sound of one world marching against another. Distances no longer existed; everything was linked.

At Kelat, Claude learned that the disembarkation of the southern divisions had commenced. The squadrons had reached Goa; the troops had been landed after a three-day bombardment. Europe was beginning to bite Asia; the latter's silence was profound. Nothing was known, or almost nothing. It was said that immense forces coming from Annam and Burma had joined up in Nepal and were concentrating there. The Asiatics were waiting on their own ground, fatalistically, perhaps counting on the immanent forces of the primordial divinity.

The dictator followed on the maps the realization of his hypothesis, and General de Trénan, impassively, not paying any heed to his lyrical and uneven speeches, showed him with a smile the mechanical means of his dream. Everything was coming together rapidly, fortune was visibly favoring the Occident. Fleets and armies were unified by the genius of a few tacticians. And suddenly, Claude Laigle, pale and excited, sensed the approach of the supreme impact, sensed that the heart of a race was within him, living in his breast, ramified in him alone; in him, one mere man followed by a little shadow over the sand, millions of souls and blades agitated at his signal.

What a dream! he thought. *There are no more distances: we're going!* He sought the face of the Adversary in the invisible. For him, the continent almost took on a human face.

Toward the end of September, it was known that the Russian forces had descended upon Mongolia, driving southwestwards the disorganized masses of the yellow race, which were falling back to Tibet. Everything would be decided in India. The will to destruction was one.

IV. The Asiatic Heart

Immobile on his horse, Claude Laigle tranquilly removed his cigar from his mouth and gazed at the horizon bathed with light. Smoke was rising up in the distance, tangled with clumps of palm trees.

Suddenly, there was a ripping red flare; the atmosphere was dislocated; at the foot of the mound where the dictator was standing, a shell burst. The battle began.

The day before, the first cadavers had appeared, White, Hindu and Yellow, sparse at first, and then in heaps, amid horses and broken chariots. Over the leagues, the cavalries had filed past the sinister vestiges. Finally, Claude Laigle's escort, launched as an advance guard, had recognized the enemy positions. Near Lahore, after a series of rapid countermarches, the first decisive contact was about to take place.

A sound of horses' hooves and the rolling of wheels caused the master's bright eyes to turn round. Along a sunken road, coming toward him at a rapid trot, through the black pennants, was General de Trénan's caleche. He was ill; his pale and glabrous face, with glacial eyes, emerged from the flank of the vehicle, a gilded arm whose thin hand was clenched, agitated among the officers galloping alongside the vehicle's door.

A second shell fell, in a spray of blood, frightening the animals in harness. Claude Laigle urged his horse forward, leaned over, and shook the fingers of the terrible old man. They smiled. An acclamation grew, abruptly broken by the thunder of a nearby volley, and the air rumbled deafeningly; a few hundred meters away, the European batteries responded to the signal in kind.

"The junction is made!" shouted General de Trénan. "The southern corps has come up the Indus! I have excellent news of the Rajput region! A good day today and we'll be marching on Delhi! You have your war!"

"Yes," said Claude Laigle. "Let's make the dream with blood—it's time. Do you remember the Franconia campaign,

Trénan, the dawn when the German emperor, wounded and covered in mud, passed before us between his hussars? That was another family quarrel; the present one will be bigger!"

He laughed, proudly, on his huge horse. The thunder boomed again to the right; the escort moved off at a gallop into the wind. Claude Laigle followed the caleche, shouting words of joy punctuated by the wind of the gallop. The landscape burned his gaze. The black lines of the divisions undulated in accordance with the hillsides, the massed cavalries crowned the crests. A blue river curled in two bends toward a pink plain extended to infinity, drowned in the vibrations of a magical vaporous light. White villages alternated with clumps of trees. Two were ablaze, vertically plumed with thick smoke, striping the azure.

Suddenly, Claude heard a clamor. "Vive l'Aigle!" He saluted.

Mounted batteries crossed his path tumultuously; the escort was obliged to pause; the mass of metal, dense and growling, filed past tumultuously, filling the road. The artillerymen, standing in their stirrups, brought forth a scintillation of sabers, extended toward the master with a joyful gesture. The svelte gray steel cannons stretched out among the rumps and the wheels, jolting in a sinister and exact convoy.

General de Trénan's attentive eyes followed the guns with a strange tenderness. In the din, the dictator tried to orientate himself, to divine the secret destination of the ensemble. The geography of the battle astonished him; the imperceptible vermicular movement of divisions perceived in the distance, almost non-existent in the immense roseate landscape, filed him with a singular sentiment of uncertainty. How little space the effort took up! The living idea animated those black worms crawling over the plain. It became almost theoretical; it seemed to Claude that he was still in the previous night's council, consulting his maps.

Everything was distant, everything was geometrical and devoid of humanity, everything was reduced to those few lines scarcely added to the panorama, quashed into a mutter beneath the sun. And nearly two hundred thousand men were confronting one anther! The swarms on the facing heights quivered sand shifted.

And suddenly, the gallop resumed. Claude threw himself to his right, following the banners. A vast semicircle indicated the edge of a wood, and the divisionary lines curved in accordance with it, spreading into the thickets, moving in mathematical harmony with an implacable slowness toward the final engagement with the adverse positions, from which smoke was still rising.

The stridency of a volley of shells passed over the riders' heads. They whistled hideously and heavily. Flies seemed to be dancing at the zenith, blossoming into red bombs, raining down beyond the blue river and disappearing. The interminable batteries assembled. Harnessed vehicles flowed toward them incessantly, swerving sharply, detaching more guns, long and slender. Claude watched servants hastening around them minuscule in the distance. From that uniform series, stretching toward the horizon, no smoke rose. The powder of the civilized was invisible in its volcanic blaze; only wan flashes sparkled. And on the grassy slopes, descending in shelter toward the river, the general staff overtook the artillery.

As the viewpoints shifted, the orientation of the battle appeared more sharply, the cohesion of the forces becoming evident. Near a ruined pagoda, Claude saw regiments rising up that had been lying low since the morning. The acclamation was guttural; they were troops from the States of Central Europe, a division of Austrians whose voices and faces alone revealed them beneath the unification of costume.

Suddenly, Claude Laigle had a singular memory. He had seen those faces in Silesia once, during the Franco-German war. Contingents of Austrians had taken part in it; then he had followed the French army, as a simple officer, anxious about the issue of a conflict on which the sociological future depended; he had seen those men, heard those voices, but in the evenings, in the villages taken during the attack, in the files of prisoners. He was gripped. How things had changed! They were marching with him now.

He had seen Trénan taking the French revenge to them, and he found himself alongside the aged commander-in-chief again, having become the agitator of a world, the ideologue leading crowds, the master of triumphant Anarchism! He looked at the old man, attentive in his caleche. He had scarcely changed, the pale, bony and glabrous face smiling thinly, with the same fixed smile. And he, Claude Laigle, felt solid on his horse. He thought about his own face, the hair scarcely graying, and behind the mask burned a soul just as incendiary, shining in the luminous pupils, as of old. He had the vertigo of the illusion of time; the abstraction of years, places, life and death rose up with a single surge in his devouring mind. The idea appeared to him again over the Oriental landscape, ignited, and undulated in the overheated atmosphere, in the open sky.

Everything is nothing but an idea, even conquest and its real bloodshed, he thought. He smiled; the sentiment of harmony radiated, the expansive law that, with is ace, had driven him from Europe to India, convulsed his nerves and thrust him even further forward.

"Vive l'Aigle!" The cry sprang up as he passed, the impulse of an aide-de-camp saluting him, going past the general's vehicle at a frantic pace, bearing away the dictator's name in a flash. But his name no longer existed, or his form; he felt himself truly the ideologue, cerebral, an abstract force, a number.

How scantly one exists! he said to himself, astonished to find himself thinking lucidly although his body no longer belonged to him.

A number! He thought about Médion, "the living number," glimpsing him across the immense journey, the burning plains, the seas and mountains, still in Paris, the other number, the other god of the world, responding for more than a quarter of the world, creating back there the fatal energy that would decide the material result here. The sensation of the abolition of distance dominated everything.

At that moment, a new corner of the landscape was revealed to the west of the plain. The snaking lines of black men reappeared, swarming in a vermicular movement—and this time, Claude Laigle understood why they no longer existed, why they summarized, in the distance, by their impassive and exact graphic form, from which death emanated without being visible, the mental conception of effort. The idea remained sovereign, matter was abolished.

What beauty! Claude said to himself. *The war of brutes has finished with the old times; modern warfare erases like the stroke of a philosopher's pen. Beautiful warfare without barbaric heroism, without muscles and strangulations, beautiful calculative and synthetic warfare! The intellectual is everything here. The destructive idea remains sovereign, everything is accomplished at a distance, and the hideousness of the human clearance is subsidiary.*

And he thought about the bombing of the Parliaments ten years before, and the sentiment of integral power, infinite in a small volume, overflowed his voluptuous soul. Those black streaks out there, and that crystal ball that a hand could grip, were the same reduction of matter to the minimum, the same silent geometry of Energy...

The cannonade was propagated throughout the extent; over the ten leagues of the plain it burned intensely, for hours. The Yellows held firm, their distant lines did not buckle; the dispatch of shells was regular. The horses of the general staff were leaping over cadavers. They went on and on, going around the hills, traversing the thickets with difficulty, getting bogged down in the sparse marshes, following the curves of the blue river. In front of the entire army, the fortune of the race passed, as the pale and ailing commander-in-chief's caleche filed through the battalions.

The sagacious gaze fell scrupulously on the ranks of men, and next to the leader's vehicle Claude Laigle bounded, black and simple, devoid of weapons his attitude amused and enthusiastic. A cry ran behind them, banners flapped, the flow of cavaliers passed in a swell of manes and flashes.

From time to time, General de Trénan made a sign.

Claude leaned over, and the old man, with his whistling voice, designated a point: "We'll go there…the east is occupied as I wished. It's going to plan. Another two hours of artillery, I think… I'm waiting for news of the Southern corps; the road they've taken is long; there are three large villages to take. It's there, look, over there, that they'll appear, there that they'll seal the final circle…"

His bony hand simulated a strangulation in the void. In an abandoned village, they stopped. It was necessary to change the horses. Everyone drew breath.

"That's good, rest," said the chief of the army, briefly. "Shells from up there will protect us." Ironically, he added: "Under that volley of iron that I unleashed behind us this morning, we'll be sheltered. The people over there will leave us tranquil. The shell has its merits, Master. Do you remember our conversation on the eve of the departure, in Paris? You'll be able to argue again with Médion about metaphysics and sentiment, thanks to my servant. In the meantime let's eat; it's necessary to take advantage of a respite, the day will be hard, and perhaps the night too."

They are, cheerfully, side by side in the carriage. The radiation of the midday sun was terrible, but their nervousness was too great for them to suffer from it. In the host of assembled soldiers, a violent magnetism was active. Near the river, troops of armed men were sitting down, waiting. Ranged behind the batteries, the infantrymen watched the artillerymen work. The volley of death wrote its definitive formulae in the open sky, designing the Idea, geometrical and light, borne upon the parabolas of the shells; frail gyroscopes launched rockets, splashes of fire soared.

Enemy projectiles suddenly fell in the joyous river, and then decreased; the facing cannons, unable to extend their fire any further, drew away, dislodged.

From time to time, General de Trénan, ceasing to eat, stood up in the carriage, leaning on the shoulder of an officer, afflicted by rheumatism but calm, his face almost blissful. The telescope shifted; he was following in thought an invisible equation.

"Look, Master," he said, "here's where we are. The figure is simple; all this is just an abstract problem, fundamentally. There's your war, it's going in accordance with your wishes." He explained with his finger on an improvised map, pronouncing Hindu names tranquilly, and the lucid speech, never embarrassed, of the man of war, enlightened Claude Laigle. The dream took body. Messengers ran up, shouted sentences, corroborated a hypothesis with a word and departed again with the order that would make it real. The immense agency of the battle was becoming clear.

At about two o'clock, Ménières came hurrying from the right, among the generals, and embraced Claude violently. He was unrecognizable, superb, regenerated by the war into which his restless energy had thrust him, reanimated and revivified by a sap of charity and blood.

"Oh, Claude," he shouted, "how beautiful it is! Everything's coming together! All the theories, all the intellectual complications, to arrive here, at this communion! To this law, because it's decidedly a law of the universe! A hundred thousand men with a single heart!"

He straightened up violently. A rumor circulated. The Southern corps was approaching; the direction of the cannonade indicated it, and the retreat of the Yellows moving back to meet it. The Asiatics sensed that they were being cut in two; the hour had come!

In a building of mud and straw, the council agitated. The black men soberly fringed with gold, consulted one another one last time. Heads leaned toward the commander-in-chief. In the middle of the group the dry voice sounded, the white hands ordered.

Claude Laigle went out. Busy soldiers were raising the poles of a field-telegraph, unrolling the wires, briskly disentangling the hollow iron beams and the coils, all the scientific apparatus involved in the intellectual war. Again the fire drew closer, the movement of batteries bringing them forward, and everyone mounted up again, Ménières following Claude Laigle. General de Trénan's vehicle turned and disappeared; the dictator found himself in the middle of the armed host that was racing to cross the river, moving off *en masse*, shouting, toward the invisible conjunction with the Southern corps that had finally arrived.

The black lines modified their position, became concave, now crawling from all points of the plain toward the water, toward the opposite heights. Leafy islets filled up with men, the cavalry descended in a crowd into the turbulent water, breaking cover from twenty different places. The swarm of the civilized interlaced its vermicular network everywhere, under the hurricane of the batteries.

Suddenly, a hallucination seized Claude Laigle. He was at the Asiatic Heart, at the core of the enemy organism, entering into it with Occidental Modernity, with the terrible rectitude of a plunging rapier, and the black lines, sinuous and insistent, were gnawing like mortal worms the rotten flesh of the old world, digging, sterilizing, orchestrating its death-throes.

A frenzy shook the dictator; the gallop accelerated; the magnetic drag of the army condensed in his soul, and, with the torrent of men, he charged, an anonymous black force, a flame in the blood.

Howling up the slope amid the charge of the cavalry, they entered a large burning village. The clutter of carriages halted the surge; there was confusion. Claude Laigle and his escort were dragged toward a partly-demolished temple. The white columns were dislocated, jets of sunlight were falling through the cracks in the roof, piercing the shadow; around a gilded Buddha still standing at the rear, an unusual pile of cadavers appeared, and Claude finally saw the Yellows!

They had been machine-gunned in a group around the effigy, the bronzed or grimacing faces emerging from somber garments like those of the Civilized; the dead flesh was hideous, with a hideousness identical to ours. The dictator looked up at the idol, which a jet of blood and brain-tissue had splashed amid the fade gilt of its cheeks. The enemy Idea became incarnate, springing forth against his cold and sure gaze. The sentiment of triumphant force invaded him.

A hand touched his shoulder; he turned round and saw Ménières.

"Do you remember, Claude, the massacres of Bajazet[13] in the cathedrals, or the monks of Saragossa?"

"Yes!" shouted Claude, feverishly, "But we're doing better—here there's a thought! Matter for matter, this crushing will serve nobler ends. There's a superior meaning in the death!"

A clamor caused them to go out, stepping over the Hindu and Japanese cadavers, the guided chests and faces with hooded eyes and prominent cheekbones.

"Masks, masks, all that!" said Claude

Outside a tumult burst forth, arms extending toward the opposite hills, and clusters of men climbing on to straw roofs in order to see better. Circling the crests, black masses were perceptible, streaming like ants.

"The Southern corps!" The unanimous cry rose up from the army, as the hour sounded in the surge of blood to the hearts of a hundred thousand soldiers. "The Southern corps!"

Finally, they appeared; it was five o'clock. The immense embrace of two armies crushing a third definitively closed its arms of fire.

Huge clouds of smoke flew eastwards; the artillery storm raged behind the mountains; the whistle of shells almost ceased where Claude was. The enemy turned toward the other battle in order to pierce a way through and retreat in the direction of Lahore. Suddenly, anxiously, the mass of the divisions poured torrentially toward the new echo, stumbling in their

---

[13] The French version of the name of the Ottoman Sultan Bayezid I (1360-1402), popularized in a play by Racine that had very little relation to actual history.

entirely over the crests of the hills to the far slopes, in order to see.

Below the horizon, a frightful turbulence of vapors hid the collision of the Southern corps with the Indian rout. The Yellow army finally unfurled before Claude's gaze; the zone of the cannonade surpassed, the geometry ceased, the demon of war was within reach. The momentum of the charge of a brigade of hussars passed directly ahead of the general staffs escort, streaming over the slopes and fell into the gulf of fire and smoke. In spite of the distance, the dry and lucid atmosphere of the admirable day allowed the minuscule humans to be seen perfectly.

While troops erupted from a blazing wood in a flock of mantles and manes; the Punjab cavalry collided with the Europeans, a sinister quarrel of iron birds entangled over the foothills of the mountain. Black lines broke up, convulsions ran along them, glow-worms folded up, were tied in knots, unstrung, hideously chopped up, but then reformed; as n the threshold of a voracious ant-hive, and infinite agitation of black or bright dots covered the extreme landscape.

Near Claude Laigle, upright on his horse, a row of gyroscopes was aligned; the deadly rockets leapt into the sky, then fell amid pink and violet fire, and the black dots moved more violently still beneath that strange rain. Voids formed, patches of blue terrain, previously covered with men, became visible again. In the little circle of his telescope, Claude enclosed the massacre, and then lifted it up, aiming higher and further, beyond the deafening inferno.

Beyond the undulations of the ground, a bright city appeared with brilliant domes: Lahore! Beyond that, the unfathomable blue of the firmament mingled with the azure, almost unreal crests of the Himalaya: the sanctuary, the heart! And turning toward the west, Claude's ardent gaze sought Delhi, as if he might discover, beyond the primitive rivers, the odious sacred country, the odious eternal azure...

Suddenly, warning clarions dryly vibrated; toward the slopes rose a confused agglomeration of horses and curved blades; banners fluttered, a fusillade rang out, the petty screech of bullets, like a buzzing of flies, was heard in the hurricane, its special ringing not arriving at the ears but touching, one might have thought, the nerves themselves.

A cry of astonishment went up. A hectic charge of Hindu cavaliers, cut off from their division, was racing toward the general staff, blindly and unwittingly, in a supreme surge of brutality toward inevitable death. Against all probability, they were coming up at the gallop. Hussars hurled themselves in front of them.

Pale and resolute, Claude Laigle drove his horse to join the crowd; standing up in the stirrups he watched the Hindus arrive, sun-bronzed faces with ferocious golden eyes, fists clutching scimitars, a riot of plumes and sashes whirling in the dementia of immolation. And among the admirable wild beasts of the Punjab, little men with flattered viperine heads raised straight sabers: Japanese cavaliers mingled with the others, a disorderly residue of dislocated armies attempting the impossible.

The old absurd heroism rose from Claude Laigle's heart to his lips, in a rush of instinctive blood. "A sword!" he cried.

No one heard him. Horses were bumping into his, the backs of men were interposed. He tried to jostle, to see, but he was trapped in a defensive circle; the savagery of hand-to-hand fighting arrived close at hand like a tornado, and between the heads the flames of revolvers mingled with the flashes of blades. A terrible swell crushed in its undertow a mass of bewildered and furious beings; a severed head leapt bloodily on to the haggard Claude Laigle's saddle; a slain general slid against him, the braided arms grasping at his for a second; and black and bearded faces appeared, crested with plumes and white turbans.

Everything dissolved into a red fracas; he could no longer see, no longer comprehend, and his nervous hands hooked on to the saddle-bow of the stallion, which, mad with fear and fury, was oscillating in the living wave, throwing back its mane into his face.

The moment was abominable. *Am I going to be killed? The idea...* In the depths of his soul, become as barbaric as those of the brutes facing him, the supreme anguish imposed itself with an indescribable rage. And he only understood the amity of destiny when he felt himself being drawn away, while cries of "Vive l'Aigle!" sprang from wide-open mouths.

A bloody head on golden shoulders loomed up before his own, howling: "We're saved, Master! There are no more of them."

And at the same moment, a cluster of plumes, steel and draperies, from which protruded the feet of a horse beating the empty air, fell against the flank of his mount, brushing his leg: the cadaver of an enemy chief, maintained until then by the strangulation of the crowd, collapsing horribly toward him.

He nearly fell, but found himself standing up among lacerated officers brandishing swords. In a flood of blood, a heap of wounded bronzed figures were gasping, fallen in a dense triangular mass, driven like a wedge into the general staff and hacked to pieces.

That was all that remained of the Yellow charge.

Two hours later, as night was falling, Claude Laigle found General de Trénan at the extremity of the battlefield. The circle was closed, the Indo-Japanese army cut into two stumps by the immense scissoring of shells, and one of the two stumps was fleeing toward Delhi while the other was being driven back to Lahore and the northern mountains.

The pale face with the thin lips greeted Claude with the same terrible smile. The exhausted dictator could not say anything; the day of triumph commanded silence; only the eyes were alive. Avidly, they wandered over the army. The first fires were propagating along the slopes, the artillery units were returning, swarms of infantry ere filing the streets and fields. The odor of humanity rose over the landscape along the odors of cannon-fire and conflagration.

In the distance, already obscure, enemy hosts were retreating in fits and starts; detonations persisted, spaced out; the stridencies of machine-guns striped the atmosphere at times. The agitation of the general headquarters brought Claude back to a sentiment of the real; the activity of the war gripped him again; he got back on his horse near the caleche, as in the morning, and passed along the front of the troops. Pools of blood interminable wet the feet of the panting animals; the profusion of cadavers in the red mud was extraordinary, piled up in shell-holes, walls sustaining rows of men shot by rifle-fire, sitting up and grimacing. The horror was nullified by dint of reigning everywhere.

Long escorts of cannons crossed their path, returning from the battle, and behind them Claude Laigle encountered convoys of prisoners. The first torches lighting their impassive faces, the general staff, from the height of saddles, watched them pass between the rifles. They advanced slowly, arranged in a column along the road.

General de Trénan, ever correct, raised himself up and saluted lightly, in accordance with the ancient habit of victors. Claude Laigle and Ménières, pensive, imitated him unconsciously. The captives looked at the embroidered Civilized and the black master without responding. Claude's eyes scrutinized them intently as they passed by Hindu chief, wrapped in colored loincloths dully stained with blood, were rubbing shoulders with semi-naked Nepalese couriers, Rajputs with gilded helmets and faces barred by nasals. Between them were little men in European dress were glimpsed, their centurion in good order, his shoulder-knots retied, strict and elegant, raising flattened heads. They were Japanese officers. One or two Chinese garments surprised by virtue of their yellow silk embroidered with a dragon.

The confrontation of Asia and the old world unfurled thus, interminably, but Claude only paid close attention to the Japanese. He ordered that they be separated for interrogation; hussars pushed them out of the ranks and brought them to the quarters.

They had been part of contingents come via the Ganges from Indo-China and Annam, allied corps that the Ministry in

Tokyo and the vice-regent of Formosa had sent to the rajahs. The council questioned them; they stood still, mute and obstinate. Claude Laigle thought he recognized some of them, once seen in Paris, when he frequented the special schools himself, and General de Trénan also murmured, before one of them: "I've seen that man during artillery maneuvers, I don't know where."

The prisoner looked at him strangely, and then smiled. He it was who had, for six hours, directed the batteries on the enemy right wing, the last to hold out, and his method had been that of the commander-in-chief. Claude Laigle might have cried: "Join us!" but the thought of the gilded idol glimpsed in the afternoon, the vision of fatalism, of the hateful revenge of the Orient choosing our weapons for a retrograde design, passed through his mind. The logical war came back to his memory, and he contained himself.

"Messieurs," he said, "the sociological struggle is turning to our advantage. Let us think about Europe released. I raise my mind this evening toward modern science, toward the idea of superior life consecrated by blood and the bomb to Anarchism. The Confederation of the Occident will be saved."

The clear voice rang in the striking silence of the generals. Night had fallen. The innumerable fires designed in the obscurity the vermicular lines of the encampments; they were still eating away the Asiatic heart. Soon they would crawl toward Delhi, toward the sacred summits, toward the sanctuaries; the heart would be emptied of blood, inertia would descend again for centuries in opiate dust over the stagnant masses of the uncultured.

Claude's soul opened beneath the heavens; the conqueror dreamed. A cannon shot expired in the darkness, on the road to Lahore.

V. The Descent from the North

Some time after the battle, important news reached the general staff. The cannoneers coming up the branches of the

Indus confirmed it in part. Hyderabad had surrendered after dogged resistance, to the corps disembarked in Gujarat along the chain of the Vindhyas. There was talk of a great unresolved conflict outside Allahabad. Cruisers returned from Surat announced the destruction of two Japanese fleets and the investment of Hong Kong. In Indo-China, grave dissents between the Burman princes and the Japanese generals were paralyzing the Yellow action.

Time passed; the immense installation of military telegraphs was completed. They ended up receiving god news from central India. The other Hyderabad, the antique Golconda crazy for precious stones, was occupied, Nizam invaded. A dissent between Thugs and allies had neutralized the terrible sect of stranglers there. It was thought that in Bengal the route of the Ganges would be open to the Civilized. Nothing essential had been modified in the original plan.

Extraordinary stories were running around. Parsee troops were coming over to the Europeans; their anarchism, in revolt against the autocracy of the rajahs, threw them into the lap of the men of the West. The intrusion of the Japanese also irritated them; between the power of Tokyo and the opposed power, sects that could not choose were agitating dully; popular Hindustan was beginning to seethe of its own accord.

The heritage of its gods and its fatalities could only be stolen by the regulars of one invasion or the other, and the authoritarian advent of the Sino-Japanese in the sacred territory insulted multiple fanaticisms, united in an ambition of autonomy. Placards bearing images circulated; passwords were discovered. The people murmured that it was superfluous to have expelled the English only to see Japanese hordes and European hordes quarreling on the sacred soil. A detestation of uniforms, engines and tactics was excited in the anonymous crowd. But the success of the civilized rallied the instinctive servility of the lower classes.

Dessort, arrived from Europe, stimulated these secret conflagrations with his genius. In a few weeks, he penetrated the mechanism and multiplied its importance tenfold, finding the simple forms that it required to propagate them in India. An association of indigenous couriers took adroit instructions from him, and spread swarms of men into his provinces, bearers of false news and promises. The Japanese armies that were stationed in the region were irritating, by virtue of their exigent arrogance, by their costly presence and the fear of remaining that was visibly established within them, by their European weapons and the cold discipline of their manner. The quarrels in Burma were reported deceptively; the scorn of the Japanese generals for the leaders of the Thugs and the irregulars of Nizam was recounted from one brigade to another.

With a lucid diplomatic subtlety, Dessort propagated the seeds of dissent between Orientals and Yellows, creating racial conflicts in the very bosom of the enemy. The Parsees aided him powerfully; cruel and intelligent, held in suspicion, they were the very soul of oriental cunning, the enemies of castes and rajahs, the mental advance guard of the egalitarianism of the West.

Gradually, the leader of crowds, the perverter of masses, pursued the work of disorganization, continuing under the sky of India his work of psychological decomposition, as he once had against the socialists and powers of Central Europe. Alongside Claude Laigle, ideological strength, and General de Trénan, mechanical strength, Dessort was analytical strength, the terrible solvent of the modern world eating into the ancient one.

The conversations of the three men quickly came into accord on the necessity of simultaneously pursuing the work of death by those three means. With the war of the shells and the war of the incompatibility of ideals, the war of the fermentation of suspicions was juxtaposed. Perhaps for the first time, Claude Laigle glimpsed that his hatred of the Yellows ought not to be uniform, that there were two Orients. The Japanese Orient was, for Europe, the danger of an armed civilization, with similar equipment and methods. The Hindu Orient was the danger of a vast stagnation of anti-progressive and fatalistic ideas in the middle of the world. One danger was active the other inert. And above those two dangerous worlds was the great dormant swamp of brutes, the reserve of unintelligent muscle ready to lend itself: China.

A diplomacy of division could intervene between those two potential initiators of the great barbarian flood. Their ruination might be consummated mutually, their cohesion into one will of hatred against the Occident could not yet have overcome the multiple suspicions between peoples. Claude's ideology was delighted by that idea: the struggle was no longer purely military; it appeared abstract, the hour of the first truly sociological war having sounded in humankind's midst.

In dreaming of the unification of Asia against Europe, the genius of Japanese politicians and the rajahs of India had, as always, imitated the races of the West, accomplishing their unification by the anarchism of the State; but that genius had gambled too soon on ideas, the immense distances had not permitted that, from Punjab to Burma, from Indo-China to Japan and from Tibet to Mongolia, a leverage of intellectual contact could be operated at will. Reciprocal incomprehension would last a long time yet; the method of the cabinets of Tokyo and Peking was superior but too theoretical, and the Europeans had arrived in time to paralyze it.

Claude Laigle understood how indispensable the work of disaggregation pursued by Dessort was; the two methods of the West and the Far East were about to engage logically, over the stake of crowds, in a combat of ideas dominating the artilleries. In spite of everything, matter was decidedly subsidiary, colonial interests were eclipsed by the idea. Only a conflict of consciousness remained, and Claude Laigle, during the vicissitudes of the war, amid the forced slowness of military occupation, began to dream about the duality suddenly revealed in the enemy.

His innate hatred of the people of the sun was no longer unique; two distinct hatreds were intensified. There were times when he could almost have wanted to reach an understanding with the Japanese, so much was their goal worthy of his own, so much did the avid intelligence of their psychology of races force his own to esteem. There really were two spirits of modernism grasping the Asiatic host, from one end of the old world and the other—but the obscurity of the Far Eastern soul threw Claude Laigle back upon the determination to annihilate it. The surprising borrowings of the inventions of Europe served to protect an ungraspable barbaric dream; that brain of the new Asia would refuse the brain of the new Europe; it was necessary to attain it and kill it; there, decidedly, as the real peril.

"What a pity!" That cry filled the dictator's soul. A kind of mental tenderness sometimes took hold of him: the singular tenderness of logicians and those familiar with abstraction for those that they sense to be "strong."

Claude's nervousness was troublesome; he had the sincere ingenuity of the thoughtful man who does not demand to be right as long as reason prevails, and who finds a secret contentment in its triumph even if he has to sacrifice his own argument to it. But those reversions did not last long; the man of action was decidedly predominant in Claude Laigle; the war exasperated that side of his character, effacing the other, and he threw himself back brutally into his cold conception of annihilation.

As for his hatred for India, no intellectual esteem tempered it; there, everything was hateful, especially the conception of an inactive life, the constant determinism—horror itself for Claude Laigle. For the somnolent Chinese masses of the Himalaya and the Altaï, out there, so distant, he only experienced a scornful pity, the disdain of the constructor of refined hypotheses for an embryonic protoplasm.

About those, we'll see later, he said to himself, *whether to imprison them forever or make use them, as we choose. That's fallow material, not even seeded yet. It's necessary to breathe into that colorless paste, as glass-blowers do; the molds are to be found. Or perhaps leave them to their slumber and their abdication, behind the mountains. They existed before...will they still exist, at our whim? We shall see...*

In his soul, the obscure clouds of the north-east sometimes cast vacillating and confused shadows, but disgust for those stupid and sly agglomerations chase away all other thoughts; the nauseating odor of the Chinese repelled him; his overheated imagination sought luminous points, and always came back to the determination of Japan, the obstinacy of India, the resolution of Europe. On those three points, Claude Laigle calculated the ideological circle of the situation.

Insinuation, thanks to Dessort, disorganized India. Significant facts were abruptly learned: desertions were occurring in Nepal. The defeat of a Japanese squadron appeared to be due to the probably-deliberate inaction of a division of cruisers equipped by the rajahs. Mutinies were repeated in Nagpur; a Japanese general was assassinated by the Thugs following an overexcitement of fanatics; the Princes of Mysore made it known that they were disinterested in the struggle.

At the same time, however, it was known that grave checks were slowing down the progress of the Civilized in Bengal. A three-day battle had turned to the advantage of the Yellows. At Midnapour, frightful massacres had given a bloody actuality to the sinister tradition of the well of Cawnpore stuffed with cadavers; a surrounded division, cut off from the rest of the army, had been almost annihilated, and the other corps, led stray by a false strategy, heading for Assam, had been separated from the coast and driven into conflict with superior Asiatic forces.

General de Trénan's anger was extreme, his plan might have to be adjourned for several months.

The alternative endured; there was no good news permitting an advance for a long time. It would have been imprudent to relax the gigantic line linking the European armies, via Kelat, the Indus and Afghanistan, with the infinite series of supply-points set up between the Mediterranean ports and India. At the other end of the chain, Médion, invisibly active, poured a torrential flow of resources. The army remained around Lahore; the distances were immense; the unknown of leagues and crowds was the essential peril. It required cunning, to wait, to commence the war of patience against Oriental tergiversation.

Dismal weeks went by, wearing away the master's feverish activity. The economic establishment, the turmoil of war budgets, the accountancy of the effort, created a painful period. The concentration of forces was pursued with difficulty; results were no longer perceptible; everything was secretly composed without apparent profit. In that phase of the Adventure it was Dessort who took the leading role, his qualities of dissociation priming everything, the annexation of indigenous consents becoming the essential condition of success.

Claude Laigle suffered from that solvent psychology; it was a weapon whose necessity he understood, but because he had not wanted to lead Europe against the hypocrisy of enemy races, his lyrical pride revolted against it, his vision of beauty was diminished; he was no longer anything but the introducer of evil ferments among the evil ferments of the enemy. The perfected Occidental modernism that he had, and which provided the noble goal that he had set himself, carried to barbarity inevitable ruses and perfidies of another order than his own, but the moral level was similar. The sociological war was using base means, like the others; the man of the West, like the man of the Orient, revealed flaws of consciousness.

Claude Laigle sensed something inferior therein; he was gripped by melancholy; each of Dessort's results touched his heart with a vague bitterness; beneath the contentment it persisted, and he disinterested himself in that part of the struggle. He isolated himself with Ménières. Ménières, in his disillusioned soul, retained a keen intuition of its nuances, and pointed them out to Claude. They both appeared to be invalids of heroism gone astray among calculators.

The impassive General de Trénan did not come to them; he was waiting for better news, for the machinations of Dessort to permit the decisive recommencement of the campaign, the re-entrance on to the stage of the artillery. That was definitely all he saw in the conquest: his murderous rigidity shocked the master, conversations that were almost irritated took place.

Claude Laigle rediscovered the impression of the evening in Paris, the sensation of solitude in a dream not accepted by others. For them, the face of the Adversary was different. Dessort was continuing in India his demoralizing experiments previously tried on the socialists of France and Germany; Trénan was killing scientifically in the Deccan as in Franconia ad Bohemia. They were really mechanisms devoid of consciousness and discernment, scientific forces of modernity serving, with the most ingenious methods, the eternal human instinct of domination and blood. The Anarchistic ideal had not touched their active souls; action always crushing the sentiment of a superior morality, it was necessary to choose between that and ideology.

And bitterly, Claude Laigle rediscovered that contradiction in himself; he evoked his speech including the declaration of war with a dolorous irony; he had thought he was formulating at that moment the establishment of a mental progress, but he had only been formulating his desire. Fundamentally, everything remained to be done, the glimmers of the revolution had only illuminated at intervals the supremacy, so ardently desired, of morality over instinct. The solidarity of economic interests had contributed a hundred times more to determine social union than the vision of a world of individual responsibility and mental nobility. Had Claude Laigle's dream put too much hatred into trying to prove itself by action?

But no! said the dictator to himself. *My calculation is accurate, and if it isn't yet, it will be. The conditions of security before all! It's for them that we're here. Later, when the Oriental peril is averted, we'll have to work in Europe, on our return. There will be years of moral education to embark on. It's always necessary to commence with blood: that of Europe flowed to commence the work, that of Asia will flow to fortify it, and afterwards, it will be necessary to perfect.*

Long perspectives of intellectual labor haunted his soul, filled the vision of his old age.

210

It won't finish with me, he told himself, *but everything is ordered and logical. It's necessary first to make the crowds understand that one can imagine a society with ne consciousness; I've cleared the way for that. Now the crowds have the material means to be themselves, it's necessary to repeat to them that it's accomplished, and they'll end up being obliged to believe it. It's necessary to retouch, to prune, to use cunning, to create methods, develop the sentimental current alongside the scientific current, which serves, but harms if it gets the upper hand. The equilibrium of means and conceptions, that's the formula.*

He dared not confess to himself that his present conception, in spite of everything, surpassed his means. Perhaps he did not perceive it. For long days he came back to it...

They traversed the rainy season thus. The agglomeration of armies had become immense. Journeys took Claude Laigle from one camp to another, through Hindu populations contained by posts or indifferent. It seemed that India was disinteresting itself in the great war between the men in uniforms and its tactics, seeking itself in the infinite extent of its mountains and plains. From the mouths of the Indus to Lahore the Franco-German divisions lined up; they were linked via Gujarat to the sea and the fleets, the filing of transport ships across the Persian Gulf created an incessant flow of supplies, a connection with Europe.

A second army, half-Austrian and half-Italian, was in Nizam, while toward Bengal, creeping obstinately along the Ganges, surpassing Benares and extending all the way to Oude, a third army, mostly English, formed a triangle around the center of Hindustan. All the nations of the Occidental Confederation were there; internationalism reigned, simplified by the adoption of French as the diplomatic and military language. Telegraphic networks submitted almost all those corps to the will of the general staff. It was an encampment of peoples of unified initiative, which was incessantly augmented.

Indigenous defections were numerous. After the neutrality of Mysore, the adhesion of Kashmir was announced. Dessort's campaign succeeded; rivalries between the rajahs and the Japanese became manifest almost everywhere. Finally, the setbacks in the west were repaired; a battle fought near Darjeeling and an unexpectedly successful retreat of the corps gone astray in Assam had changed the face of things.

The fine season was approaching, and the war could resume.

At sea, it was virtually finished. Amazing destructions of fleets had annihilated Japan's naval forces; the squadrons could limit themselves to the blockade of the coasts and the protection of European cargo ships. The last hecatomb of the Gulf of Siam was disastrous; four Japanese battleships ran aground after a pursuit of several days before being destroyed at a distance by torpedoes launched from balloons, which testified to European genius. The skyborne fleet had annihilated the marine fleet; an unexpected magic of war was beginning.

Finally, the new from Kashmir brought the echo of the Russian action. Hundreds of leagues away, the Chinese mass had been dislocated, reduced to inertia, driven impotently back to the high plateaux and the infinite sterility of the desert. The noise of the war was drawing away from its slumber, and it was stagnating.

Again, Claude Laigle's heart was convulsed by joy, and the renaissance of active energy effaced his doubts. He found himself the master once again, and determined.

Then, descending through the Hindu Kush, coming from Asian Russia, there were immense emigrations of strange men. The North, moved by an ethnological magnetism, ceding to an instinctive pressure, came to see the strangulation of fateful India, moved by the obscure, by the planetary rancor of creatures of the snow against creatures of the sun!

The Arctic Circle was displaced toward the Tropic of Cancer; one half of the hemisphere rose up against the other; the ant-hive of races tore itself out of its vegetative existence and the passivity of its destiny to experience and upheaval unprecedented for centuries. Distant peoples appeared in the three camps; unusual faces even astonished the Civilized. The immemorial cold of the steppes had fixed a special soul there. From beyond Lake Balkhash they came, and from the regions of the Yenisei, and further still, from the semi-annual obscurity and pallor of the poles, from places where nothing is known and where dreams themselves expire, for want to warmth and consciousness...

The emigration of the North was frightening. A new crusade was born, but it was also a Children's Crusade, so utterly unknown were those human troops, save for the fact of their descent. It was necessary to suspect them, to give orders to keep them away from the army, to reach an understanding with the military governors of Aral and Irkutsk in order to stem that irrational flow of witnesses running to the division of Asia's flesh.

They arrived, without knowing why, quitting the commerce and the muted existence of the snow-fields, the darkness of Asiatic Russia; they too were barbaric, in fief to a blind cult, to the Northern god who detested the azure swarm. They had returned to the cruel simplicity of primitive humans, to the generative hatred of forces, to the babbling instinct of differing climates creating different souls. An odor of blood was rising from the middle of the world in the overheating of the central light, and humankind steered in that direction.

Pensively, Claude Laigle and Ménières considered those quiverings of races, the eternal magnetism of three or four physiological currents that ordered humanity, beneath the varied modes of mores, beneath the illusory acquisition of the refinements of civilization. The reduction to the simple was striking. There too, as in the fundamental causes of the war, as in the geometry of armies, everything was number, abstraction and polarity; everything happened by virtue of mental reciprocities, everything was scientific evaluation. Dynamism was god.

"In the final analysis," said Claude, joyfully, "is ideology a vain word? All this is the play of ideas—we're philosophizing."

Smiling, Ménières replied. "All this is also poetry. The décor is beautiful."

There was a period of joy for the two men. Among so many beings with various languages and visages, their detestation of old fatherlands and their faith in individual internationalism was reborn.

"I almost believe in progress, in seeing how these people understand one another," Ménières said, one day. "The absurdity of frontier conflicts is decidedly dead; ethnological war at least has an intelligent meaning. These spectators coming from the Urals, and almost from Lapland, have one thought, which pleases me. The men of the cold hate the men of the heat; that's logical, natural and plausible; it's a climatic division that has a reason for being.

"This is the first war that I don't find imbecilic. It's like an instinctive gesture: and what beauty! It's not even a matter of killing to colonize, to install merchant thieves in an exotic land and cheat poor brutes without risk. The governments of old only saw that consequence of their visits to the Asiatics or Negroes; this is better, more noble and saner. The Northerners who are coming to the army have no material interest for coming; it really is a thought that guides them, a mental interest. Your lyrical modernity exists, Claude."

The dictator approved. "Yes, these are symptoms that touch me. The Idea is acting on crowds, the act of killing is beginning to prove worthy. We're going to see more killing, Ménières: blood is the promise of life." And the visage with the luminous eyes contemplated the fatigued and fine visage. "You'll live to see all that, Ménières. Have I've brought you far enough? Is there enough air here for your dreams? How vast our hopes in Paris have become! Here, one acts and thinks together..."

Claude Laigle's enthusiasm infected the army. It expanded everywhere in words of ardent exhortation to energy.

Reviews took place, proclamations circulated; adroit guarantees to the population calmed the effervescence produced by the resumption of the campaign. The legations of the Confederated States brought testimonies from Europe of any absolute confidence in the dictatorship. Capitals lit up; the socialist union, from the shipyards of Glasgow to the workshops of Bohemia, voted further credit. Médion's organization was monitoring everything; they could march.

More delays occurred; typhus disrupted the Nizam army for some time; it was necessary to wait and carry out effective translations. But fortune was definitely favoring the Civilized. Victories on the Ganges permitted a rapid march of the third army. Cawnpore, the sinister city, was taken, the queen of Oude capitulated, the rajah of Bundelkund had to yield in his turn.

Everywhere, the Europeans were advancing; the English divisions reappeared on the blood-soaked soil of the ancient Sepoy revolt. The horrors of 1856 were renewed. Terrible things were seen: the burning of Lucknow; six thousand Yellows surrounded in the great pagodas and exterminated by batteries moving through the streets; a broth of humans and horses streaming in the fire under the shells; the terror of the massacre extended for fifty leagues, in the heart of sacred India. General de Trénan's lieutenants pushed their advance-guard all the way to Gwalior. The army of Vindhya came toward them; the triangle tightened around central India; the struggle attained its maximum of atrocity.

The news of the conjunction at Gwalior arrived one evening, brought by Indian couriers in Dessort's service. Those bronzed, semi-naked individuals conferred mysteriously with the chiefs. A frisson passed through the army when the aged commander-in-chief suddenly appeared in the camp. The bony white hand made a sign to the summoning clarions. The generals ran hither and yon, the streets were filled with messengers coming and going, and silence fell.

The old man spoke: "Messieurs," he said, simply, "we're marching on Delhi."

The long-awaited name burst forth. The great war was approaching its end; the supreme effort was about to be attempted; a breeze of relief rose.

In the glare of the fires that sparkled in the night, Claude Laigle saw once again the vermicular snaking of the Civilized, as on the eve of the Battle of Lahore. The Asiatic heart was about to feel the rip of the sword. The sovereign Idea would live! It was exactly fourteen months since the solemn declaration in Paris had awakened its electric resonance had awakened...

An infinite gratitude to destiny, for assuring the triumph of modernity and choosing him to be the leader of that triumph, penetrated Claude's soul. One grandeur was about to annihilate another; he had the intuition of a consent of the part of the world to the supremacy of the North. And, responding to an interior voice, he said:

"I accept. I submit. I shall serve the Idea."

The rumor of the bivouacs approved.

A few weeks later, the investment of Delhi was accomplished. An Indo-Japanese army was surrounded under the walls of the city. Inside, the fortune of Asia, its princes, its gods and its age-old fatalism awaited the end. The times of Nineveh and Carthage were about to reappear in the evolution of worlds.

VI. The Assault on Delhi

From the lines of circumvolution in which the guns of the siege were thundering, the armored cupolas of enemy forts were clearly distinguishable. The reflection of the sunlight from their white paint made them into strange domes of buried temples. They emerged from the soil at regular intervals. A plume of smoke rose up rapidly, and then they were effaced in the undulation of the grassy plain, and the shell arrived.

Delhi was somnolent behind its cupolas, staged on the bank of the Jumna. No sound was born there; it was scarcely visible. Heavy vapors floated in the blue sky; the landscape was desperately serene. The days and nights succeeded one another, with the monotony of an infinite agony, while the batteries thundered. The timetable of death was mathematically regulated by those giant pulsations, which responded to one another in the extent, alternated by the positions of the three armies.

The Yellows riposted with furious cries that were increasingly widely spaced. The aerial exchange of flies of iron and fire spun its turbulent and ferocious network high over the camps and ramparts. The slaughter was invisible; the sonority of the discharges was the only sign of the vast confrontation of men. They were propagated regularly in the direction of the plain, convulsive and intermittent in opposition; the shriveling of the enemy race was detectable.

From time to time, the crackle of machine-guns and the stinging dryness of fusillades, mingling with the throbbing echoes of the cannon, indicated a sortie, a furious impulse of the imprisoned army. Rapid movements carried masses of cavalry and infantry forward; the black ant-hives orientated in the distance an incessantly deformed geometry; the vermicular oscillation of the Civilized designed trapezia, curves, parallelograms, diamonds, broken, remade and dissociated in sudden fractures. The rain of ardent iron fell, and then the clarions sounded the halt, casting everything back into silence. Convoys of wounded moved back; the inertia of the wait imposed itself again.

In the nascent darkness of the night, profound and vague melodies rose up over the odor of blood: the bands of the army corps played symphonies and hymns. The chanting of the Hindu couriers joined in, stridently or languorously, and a strange sensation of intensity took hold.

Above the lines, in the open sky, oblong aerostats floated, their aluminum spurs shining. They drifted, enormous, casting the elongated shadow of their course on the ground, like artificial clouds. They were seen soaring over the city. Their pale lights striped the obscurity, and one might have thought that a squadron was scrutinizing the impalpable waves of a sea of darkness; they sought one another and appealed to one another, the life of the siege continued in the sky; and above the luminous interchange of bombs and the violet light of gyroscopes, their enormous pale stars maneuvered in a phosphorescent rotation, expending the tentacles of blue-tinted squid over the suddenly-illuminated domes of Delhi.

Sulfurous jets leapt up toward the monsters, were extinguished without reaching them, and extraordinary nocturnal combats hallucinated the army. Torpedoes fell from the balloons; their suddenly-stifled crepitation created whirlwinds of stones and flames; vibrations broadened to deafening pitch convulsed the atmosphere. The living stars wandered over those cataclysms, ironically converged their oblique radiations, and then disappeared.

One evening, an unforgettable spectacle caused three hundred thousand men to look up. Two similar balloons rose up from the city and floated; Japanese genius had succeeded in equipping them, and suddenly they too launched torpedoes, at an artillery division. A clamor went up; awakened, the regiments assembled tumultuously, emerging from tents to gaze at the two monsters that were swimming rapidly and casting lights over the camp. The signals sprang into action and a confusion of messengers filled the roads; the anxiety was terrible.

Before an order could be given for the airborne scourge to be driven away, however, other stars converged, coming from the depths of the horizon. The electricians and aerostatic engineers of Europe were alert! A gyration of white rays passed over, the two enemy stars were effaced, atmospheric frictions created an artificial breeze, the supernatural beasts pursued one another, darting dazzling jets in the darkness. The breathless troops sought them at the zenith, a human frisson vibrated from the army to the invested city. And suddenly, in a colorless splash, two of the stars collided, and both were seen to fall, one of them disemboweling the other. They fell on a grove of palm-trees in a horrible collapse, a quarrel of bolides burning over the agony of India, while toward the west a fiery spark fled, pursued by others.

The evolution of the hours seemed a flight of flaming gems; a crown of diamonds sparkled in the night, burst into flames; multicolored rockets rained down from the aerostats, announcing the end of the battle. The two enemy machines had been destroyed.

Long bleak days followed that supernatural drama. It seemed that the soul of the new India, having momentarily raised itself into the sky in order to escape, was dead, and that fatalism was stagnating forever. That effort was the last. The slow strangulation of famine and despair commenced for Delhi. The black belt of the Civilized circled the white city narrowly. The mediocre horror of the artillery battle, assassinating individual heroism, propagated its long-distance devastation methodically. The three camps awaited the moment.

For two days, a frightful battle brought them to their feet; a Japanese army arrived from Bengal, the last that had escaped anterior disasters, tried to force the blockade, attacking the circling forces. The Civilized fought, caught in their turn between the newcomers and a sortie by the besieged. The battle was fierce; one German division was almost annihilated, eight generals were killed—but the third dawn determined the European triumph. The Yellows had nothing to sustain them in the interior of the region; cut in two, they retreated, decimated, and broke up, toward the upper Ganges to rejoin the mountain tribes. The circle reformed around the city; the huge stone beast, after its final death-throes, was no longer shivering...

The division of the flesh could begin.

On the forty-seventh day of the siege, the electric signals, the semaphores and the flags announced the assault.

The enemy forts were mute, their ammunition exhausted; smoke no longer rose up above their cupolas. The debris of the invested army went back into the city; despair descended silently behind the sanctity of the walls. The military bands struck up; the besieging army advanced in five columns.

For hours the cannoneers on the river bank sent shells into Delhi itself, having forced the passes and the chains of torpedoes established under the water. The invasion was devastating and simultaneous. The infantry crossed the war zone without anything in front of them giving any sign of life. A frightful taciturnity reigned. They passed the extinct, abandoned forts, hardly daring to believe that no surprise would emerge therefrom.

Revolver in hand, colonels went into them. A few luminous bulbs were still shining here and there; the tiled courtyards were empty, the guns dismantled and recumbent, the bunkers collapsed, the armor-plating holed. Broken carts littered the military roads, smashed by the erosion projectiles. A few cadavers were lying in their congealed blood, at the crests of the round walls. Wooden sentry-posts maintained half-burned skeletons upright. Everything was deserted; they advanced in terrifying silence.

Sometimes the general staff halted, almost expecting a distant group to appear, to negotiate; but nothing transpired. Finally, the jagged ramparts of the city appeared, vast extents of glacis, sometimes mingled with old carved masonry, doors with sculpted corbels, vestiges of primitive epochs. And suddenly, as the columns were about to attain it, a furious cannonade burst forth, a blaze of turbulent lightning, volleys of bullets arrived at ground level, breaking the first battalions. The anger of the final day rose up.

Fearfully, Claude Laigle and Ménières were watching the spectacle from a distance. They ran toward it, no longer able to hold still, gripped by the crisis of the irreparable. A swarm of black armies rushed over the crests, twisting into stumps, punctured by red fore. Mines exploded, with clusters of burning men. The engulfment of the rigid Civilized disemboweled the city with a mad violence, the clarions persisting in the extraordinary tumult of explosions, their curt sonority ripping through the air. The mounted batteries raced, oscillating, trying in vain to install themselves. The cry of the charge finally annulled the monotonous ferocity of the cannons; European nerves were exasperated, and the rush of the white army killed all tactics.

The dictator galloped into the outlying districts of the city. An immense crowd filled them, driving back the artillery vehicles, tipping over the ammunition trucks, the wheels of which dug into the flesh. Dazed clamors shook those human swarms, hurling them into the streets in swarming masses, under fire from houses and terraces.

The assault ran from street to street, house to house, room to room, increasingly specialized in its horror. The confusion was total, gallops of cavalry traversing the accumulation of infantrymen, entire sections of causeway opening up in wells of flame, entire companies falling into them in frightful collapses, and severed heads leaping into the air with bouquets of blood.

In the thick smoke, swirling in enormous spirals, perspectives full of eddying humans and horses and tangles were perceptible, entangled beings with faces convulsed in the wan light. The officers shouted in vain; the order of the assault was dislocated; human force regained its mastery; and unknown magnetism carried the armies away.

Claude Laigle appeared in that tumult without anyone paying any heed to him. Only the odor of blood guided him through that vast city, gripping his throat and his stomach. The five assault columns sought one another, puncturing the mass of stone in every direction. The excitement was as fervent as dementia; there were indescribable scenes.

The dome of one of the great sanctuaries split in an explosion and collapsed on the besiegers; entire colonnades were felled, smashed by batteries, porticos vacillated and fell, in clouds of dust.

Finally, Claude Laigle saw the Yellows again. They were swarming; the city was crammed with them, their variegated bands were surging forth from all directions, the terraces were crowned with semi-naked men. Against the embrasures of galleries, against the angles of courtyards, repulsive crushes launched red spurts; blind alleys were heaped with cadavers, their heaps rising up along the walls. Cannons filed along the avenues, at the end of which seethed floods of human beings.

Women fell from balconies, clung on to soldiers, raised daggers above their heads.

The accumulation of flesh was prodigious; the arms of men raising rifles could not find the space to shoulder them; mounted officers were pitching in the human tide along with their horses, howling as they stumbled. Bombs coming from other parts of the city suddenly crashed down from the sky; deadly rockets departed at random; the crepitation of revolvers and the clash of sabers were drowned in the tumult. And from gardens, houses, cisterns, from everywhere, new troops continually surged forth.

Clumps of palm trees were burning, the flaming trunks falling; horses with flaming manes ran madly through the crowd, the impact of their hooves stamping blood-soaked flesh into a hideous pulp. Bands of madmen were murdering one another in corners; naked stranglers leapt at the throats of soldiers, bounded on to the saddles of officers. At one intersection, among clumps of trees, long railings opened up, and tigers released by the slaves of rajahs hurtled into the midst of regiments, mingling their wild cries with the frightful human clamor.

Turbulent agglomerations of men filled the large squares; voids suddenly appeared, filled in by lines of black beings emerging from the streets. The concentric fusillade accumulated amid pyramids of cadavers. In the bazaars and ground-floor rooms, bloody crowds mingled the Civilized and the Yellows; scimitars and bayonets clashed. Murder fumed with splendor.

Hours passed thus.

Livid, the dictator allowed himself to be borne along by the crowd.

Ménières follow him, his eyes dilated, ultimately contenting himself with an unsuspectable dream, a monstrous imagination of his unhealthy genius.

"Carthage!" he shouted to Claude Laigle, in a rare moment when the fracas allowed him to speak audibly.

Claude Laigle remained silent, crouched on his horse, amid the gestures of frightened officers. They moved forward, in spite of everything. House by house, they reached the heart of Delhi, the lines of the battalions reformed in the midst of the burned quarters. The heads of the columns met; one appeared, the other came to intercept it. Cavalry charges freed the streets.

In a vast conquered pagoda, amid the heaps of the dead, the smoke and the red mud, the general staff gathered. General de Trénan arrived. Night was about to fall; in the obscured sky, the flames were beginning to appear formidable and luminous. It was necessary to organize the definitive effort before it was completely dark. The gesticulation of the generals deafened Claude Laigle.

The commander-in-chief seemed as calm as usual. He arrived at the head of the third column, the two others carrying out a massacre on the river bank; on the far shore the machine-guns could be heard in gusts; they were forcing barricades to the west and south of Delhi. Reserves were entering behind them; the plan of attack was being realized. In the confused atrocity of the carnage, the old tactician saw clearly, orientated himself, rediscovered harmonies. He barked orders, the lieutenants dispersed, the geometry reappeared. From the milieu of swirling smoke the reinforced columns prang in a fan, precipitated by the strident cry of clarions sounding the charge. The terrible old man disappeared with one of them. Claude perceived his gilded arm agitating its white hand amid the rifles.

The assault rushed backwards; already brandished torches were making the horses of the escort snort. The dictator galloped. Around him bounded a black legion; the crowd was dislocated by a volley of bullets; yellow faces leaned over terraces; the clash of blades and the curt cry of revolvers alternated in the chaos. A white horse passed by, carrying a man whose hair was soaked in blood. He almost threw himself upon the mater's horse, but disappeared. Others followed; they fell into the midst of the running infantry. Some were waving cords and strange daggers—stranglers! Thugs! They were killed in short order, though, and they passed on.

An inert general was carried to a street corner, his swollen head vacillating; a cord had seized him by the neck in passing, and Claude Laigle, bending over him, had a sensation of horror even more intense than before blood, in the presence of that green-tinted face from which the blackened tongue was protruding and the eyes were repulsively tumefied.

"Forward!" he cried, madly, and, dropping the cadaver, he ran toward blinding death, crimsoned by fire, chasing from his mind the image of the sly death.

"In beauty, at least!" The key word of all his morality rose incomprehensibly to his lips.

The furnace-like heat created a nightmare. Was it from life or the dream that the pandemonium of flames sprang? The conflagration of the old world was surpassed, and former Anarchist vengeance; it appeared to Claude that a gigantic vertigo was about to roast him like a despicable dust-mote in the convulsively flamboyant heart of India.

Scarcely had he recognized that he was not mad when the immense walls and domes were heaped up to the summit of the sky in a scintillating bouquet of rockets. The sacred pagodas and palaces of the center poured out springs of fire over a square black with people. Cannon fire converged and the porticoes were smashed in the explosions, the galleries of gods shattered. The human tide gesticulated, jostling the batteries, plunging under the vaults with the machine-gun fire; the lines of bayonets undulated; people stumbled in pools of blood.

Breathless, Claude Laigle raced into the first rank, in order that he too could enter, with masculine brutality, with all the males he was leading, into the detested virginity of those parvises. They opened up, ogival and somberly tortuous. The odor of age-old incense sprang abruptly from the holes in walls staved in by shells, the sacrilege of the rape of the old gods leaping with the soul of assassinated India, in blood. Oh, those palaces, those retreats of fatalism, those golden matrices! The rigidity of the European column, stiff and terrible, entered there with a single atrocious thrust, like a black penis, all the way to be depths, in the crushed flesh, in a red dampness, in the tearing of blades and the lust of fire.

Claude Laigle almost fainted as he shouted into Ménières' face, emerging by his side: "What joy! We're in!" He laughed, obscene and sublime in the giant rut. His eyes were hallucinated by the scintillation of vaguely visible Buddhas, rising up into the vaults, licked by gleams. His race was violating virgin India, spattering its soiling there with death!

And suddenly, a pale light rose up from the depths of his being, effacing the gilded specters: the Idea appeared, the unreal metaphysical enchantment that, above the armies of modernism, led the Adventure and his genius. Under the blank gesture, he fell from his horse into the arms of frightened officers, raised his hands, and sank into the unknowable...

A bullet, puncturing his garments without penetrating him, had thrown him down. When he reopened his eyes, the fusillade was drawing away to his right. The great pagoda was conquered; sappers were bringing down the gods with axblows, drunk on an instinctive fury, enraged by the terrible war, falling upon the great bronze monsters as if on mute and responsible masters. The eternal surge of the ancient mind armed them; the Idea was crushing the Dream!

"Wonderful!" shouted Claude Laigle. "Smash those dolls for me!"

He forgot the assault, the time, the necessary orders, entirely in the present, gripped once again by lyrical verity, his mind reeling from the collision of worlds.

Ménières' voice shook him. "It's very beautiful, though, Claude. You're scorning the genius of an extinct era. You're killing art!"

Very pale, Ménières stood up, almost revolted. Claude turned round; their blazing eyes met.

"Art! Oh, we don't care about that, in the end, Ménières!" the master cried. "It gets in the way of everything:

I hate it, do you hear! It's the artificial, the absurd, one more dirty religion that degrades humans. Their art, in the blood and under the ax, is like them, like everything that comes from them! You can pick up the fragments for our museums, if anything remains and it amuses you. But break those faces of the gods first! Their art, that servility to their fetishes! We'll make one more beautiful when we're rid of theirs: a human art, a true art! Their art! Oh, no pity, no more for the beings as for these forms of error! It's lies and obscurantism that I'm snuffing out here in the presence of sixty centuries. Yes, yes, break!" he cried to the soldiers.

"You're doing as they do!" said Ménières. "Mohammed at Saint Sophia—and to come so far, for that! You're not new, you're imitating. As barbaric as the rest, definitely!"

"Well, yes, let's be Barbarians, as you wish. Barbarians—so be it; you'll understand later, you who were an artist yesterday!" Claude Laigle replied, bursting into nervous laughter. "Art! Are you going to try to stop me with that word? Only the Idea counts here! Obey!"

"I said so," Ménières riposted...

His voice was cut off by the din of an explosion. Side by side they were thrown out of the enclosure in a whirlwind of men, shouting irritated phrases without being able to make themselves heard.

Outside, a flood of cavalry separated them. The confusion was insane, the assault flooding back from the center toward the east of the city, Delhi entire resplendent with terror. The standards of the fifth column were visible in the avenues; the conjunction had taken place, the quintuple star of the European army entangling its branches. The blast of the fusillade arrived from all sides simultaneously.

Claude Laigle, in the midst of the general staff, climbed up on to a terrace, drunk with the unfurling of the battle, which descended all the way to the river. Obscure emplacements indicated a surcease in the combat; from the southern districts luminous signals sprang announcing the victory. The blue lights of aerostats radiant in the black sky, and the direction of the cannonade was clear. There was no more fighting except in the center and the west; the holy city was palpitating in the final spasms of its death throes.

"Vive l'Occident!" cried the crowd.

"Vive l'Anarchie!" replied Claude, dazedly.

Barbarians! He thought, angrily repeating Ménières' word. *Barbarians, to kill barbarity! He doesn't understand any more, and doesn't understand because of art, as the others don't understand because of science! Anyway, we shall see...*

He saw the diaphanous light again, the phantom of the Adventure, smiling in a dawn of linked verities, in the open sky above the world, the mystical obsession floating. He smiled, sensing the indefatigable and devouring genius of a leader of armies, at the divinatory gesture. His soul dilated in extraordinary abstract wellbeing, and he shivered.

To live this is to be! Is it credible?

No man or god had ever been so great, and as the word *die* passed through his mind with the parabola of a bomb flying before his eyes, Claude Laigle straightened up.

I shall not die! he said to himself.

The sentiment of that seemed to him to be insignificant, in any case, his body and his fear annulling it, cerebral intoxication stiffening his nerves above the horror. He searched with his eyes for Ménières, in order to speak to him again, but could no longer see him. It was the glabrous face of General de Trénan that appeared.

The god of shells! thought Claude, and he ran toward the bearer of present Verity to embrace him fervently.

"Yes, yes, it's done—the beast is dead!" said the commander-in-chief. Behind him, a battery escort undulated at the gallop; the pale and blood-stained artillerymen saluting with their sabers, the guns and ammunition-trucks rumbling; and an immense cavalcade was seen racing from along central avenues at the gesture of the pale hand agitated outside the golden sleeve. The man with the ivory head was leading his hordes thundering, with pride, the Angel of Dynamism, with him, toward the old world.

"The assault has succeeded," he said. "You're the master; the living force is neutralized; China will sleep for centuries more beyond the Altaï, metaphysical and mental Europe is yours, Claude Laigle."

The general staff looked at the two men mutely; in spite of their inexorable soul they were trembling with joy; the moment was decisive in the history of human energy, and their eyes expressed an emotion so rare that the generals lowered theirs.

The cannonade over the river ceased. The searchlights of the aerostats indicated that the outlying districts were conquered. In the gardens of the north of the city, the last defenders were being crushed; three of the five columns were returning to the center. Delhi was in the hands of the Civilized.

General de Trénan took the dictator to one side. "I've contained the army," he said. "Mathematical war is admirably passive. It would never have been thus in the past, but the enervation is too great. It's necessary to let the men's nerves relax; these silent troops surpass the human. I ask for my soldiers a feast of blood, the ancient drunkennesss of evenings of victory, atrocious and lyric drunkenness, as you say, Master. Those thousands of living beings have been perfect machines; let them live instinctively for one night. You understand my thinking: it's necessary that the animal feeds occasionally."

Claude Laigle acquiesced with a sign. Ménières' recent remark went through his mind: "Barbarians, like the rest!" He smiled bitterly, effaced the ironic memory of a surge of prideful will, and waited...

The light of burning pagodas illuminated the army. Suddenly, the file of artillery became enormous, from the height of the streets all the way to the Ganges. The heat of the fires and the battle excited the delirium of the blood, the age-old soul of triumphs smoldered. The cannons rolled, the compact divisions lining up at a gallop toward the northern encampments, as Claude Laigle sat down, exhausted, on a balcony spared by the bombs, his gaze passing into a dream.

Ammunition trucks filled the streets, brushing the walls, and on them and the gun-carriages, lugubriously illuminated by torches brandished by human hands, naked bodies were tied, tossed about by the jolts of the course. Seized from apartments in houses whose doors had been forced, stolen from the harems and palaces of the old city, howling women were writhing under the cords, their arms twisted above their heads and their legs tied to the gun-carriages, showing their white abdomens, their obscene sexes, their breasts violent amid the floods of hair or shining with jewels. Jets of blood spurted over them when the wheels crushed heaps of corpses, a red mud debasing that white flesh, above which the faces of men sniggered.

The teams of horses were covered with precious cloths piled up and tied; the squadrons were in a hurry, ferrying that lust and that theft, the nostrils of the harassed horses were sneezing fire and drool on the terrified faces of the captives. The infantrymen ranged against the walls, brushed by the rapid wheels, extended their hands toward the women, feeling flesh at hazard while laughing. The interminable gallop of the artillery units drew them into the dark night, the light of the illuminated porticos and domes casting on the steel, the manes, the loins of the women and the bestial faces of the men a terrible alternation of darkness and gold.

That passed like a great dream of horror, and Claude Laigle dreamed dazedly of the sack of Carthage, the burning of Agrigente, the convulsions of ancient capitals, the faces of Scipio's and Titus' legionnaires, the beautiful evenings of Attila and Genseric, the burning of Constantinople, the lusts of the cavaliers of Timur and the Amurats, the frightful magic of Latin, Persian, Tartar or Mohammedan conquests reverberating in the ancient world, from the deserts to the mountains to the oceans, from Syria to Gaul and Rome to Scythia, its tumult splendid with flowers, flesh, metal, thunder and blood.

Claude Laigle had an intuition of the eternal recommencement, of primordial sentiments, of the brutal beauty of instinct suppressing time and details, returning everything to simplicity. The nausea was extinguished within him beneath ideological joy. Matter was nothing, decidedly; forms were always similar; only the Idea...

Yes, he said to himself, *they're like the others, but it's necessary, in making use of them for something else, to make with that human dough another bread of life, that's everything. No need to change them, even if that were possible; only to understand them, and do with them and I wish. And what is it that I wish? That which hasn't yet been tried, to extract even from this a beauty...*

Above the sprawling and sobbing women, bare flesh and sabers, the diaphanous specter rose again, floating, the white idea of an unaccustomed heaven hid everything, and the dictator was absorbed in the deafening jolting of the squadrons.

The arriving booty passed, and after it appeared the carts in which strange prey was piled: statues, fabulous or obscure faces, the violation of a population of ruined gods, the ferocious idols of Juggernaut, the figures of man-eaters and devourers of fire, the mysterious deities of fatalism and death; the entire heritage of contemplative Hindustan summoning the great offended shades of Rama and Sita, the singular allegories of fecundity and oblivion, coupled in derisory fashion in the pillage, dragged and knocked down on the bank of the primitive holy river before the rubble of the glory of princes; a long lamentable file of assassinated beliefs passing before the gaze of the new Europe. The distant cannon, at intervals, underlined their desperate march.

And after that came the processions of prisoners, the desolation of wounds, the sumptuous and ragged rajahs, the naked thin stranglers, the sepoys brutalized by rage and fear, pushed toward the stakes of the fusillade, amid the gunfire of platoons heard in the nearby streets. The cavalry were leading them; they ran, hastened by the breasts of the horses, all of them—fakirs, soldiers, insurgents—mocked by the mob of

Parsee and Mahrattas adherent to the European cause. The Yellows followed, a compact host painting in front of Claude Laigle, raising hooded and prominent faces amid the bare cloth. For two hours they passed by. All of Asia seemed to be dying that night!

In the distance, the clamors of the soldiers could be heard, resting in drunkenness and rape, laboring with bare arms in female flesh and the stolen objects, as in the blood and fire before. Suddenly, a rumor spread, wounded Europeans arrived from all directions; the odor of field hospitals gripped Claude to the point of frightening him, the exaltation of victory having faded. A group of cavaliers appeared, in disorder, surrounding a litter, which was pushed into the middle of the general staff. Exclamations sprang forth, heads turned toward the dictator, officers interposed themselves.

Claude Laigle advanced to look.

On muddy straw and carpets, braided cadavers lay: generals. And in the middle of them, Claude Laigle saw a head of golden hair protruding from a roll of cloth.

Ménières!

He had been killed with the others, an hour before, in the east, when an exploding mine had hollowed out the ground beneath an attack column.

The master's hands parted the cloth; the head vacillated and rolled in a sinister fashion; it was no longer securely bound to the body. A mass of burned flesh, filthy, slashed by splinters of stone, bristling with shards of beams, appeared in the dirty serge like a repugnant item of butchery. Blood clots were drying on the shapeless mass. Only the head had not been afflicted; the golden hair surrounded it; the pale lips were closed; the eyes devoid of thought, remained vitreous.

He didn't believe in the work of life, Claude Laigle said to himself, pensively. *He didn't believe. He thought we were barbarians, like the others. Not to have talked to him about that again—what fatality! However, however, he was wrong, he would have understood... He was wrong?*

He raised his head and looked at the impassive face of General de Trénan, the weapons, the fire, the blood—and a strange mist covered his eyes: the white Idea vacillated with a disenchanted smile in his soul, and he was troubled. Doubt in the adventure descended from the sky...

He sensed that his anxiety was visible, anticipated the curious eyes of the commander-in-chief, and shivered.

"I loved him," he said gesturing toward Ménières' cadaver.

He was lying; was not trembling because of that. The certainty of destiny and he beauty of the Forces escaped him, for the first time.

His heart sank.

The army band suddenly burst forth; the triumphant harmonies of *Lohengrin* floated over the blood, and the tottering will of Claude Laigle plunged into the thunder of the orchestra.

Book Two: The Obsession

VII. The Crisis

For two months, a torpid soul vegetated in Claude Laigle.

Had the white Idea touched him that evening with a bloodstained finger? A kind of paralysis gripped him. Transported by the campaign, he lived almost unconsciously, in the midst of his lieutenants, developing the Adventure. Their multiples cares were employed without him paying any heed to them.

Across the world a confused murmur rose up, the organic stirring of an immense stupor, quivering in the skeleton of mountains, the veins of rivers, the structure of plains and seas. The weapon plunged into the primitive heart of races vibrated from pole to pole; then the torpor stagnated. It seemed that humankind, frightened of itself, no longer dared trouble the silence of the murder.

Delhi bled disastrously in the middle of India, like a beast forced from its lair that the armies had torn apart. The sharing of the flesh had not taken place visibly; calm was almost established.

The great war was over, the final encounters in Nepal and Assam made no noise, and the joy of Europe was too distant. No more was heard about Russian action in northern China; an irremediable silence reigned beyond the Himalaya. The news from the Yellow seas was bleak, confirming the blockade, preventative maneuvers, slow and devoid of beauty, useful but monotonous measures.

The sentiment of a universal weariness floated over armaments and peoples, and above all, an uncertainty appeared. No one yet took account of what had just become the extraordinary and capital fact in the evolution of the Old World. The malaise of relaxation thus extended for a long time before the organization of the conquest was settled. People watched.

Claude's malady coincided with the duration of that indefinable state; not because it was an obstacle to the progress of the Europeans, but it seemed that it symbolized clearly the general alternative. The collapse had been too devastating, and in the same way that the master's brain had almost given way under the pressure of exacerbated will, so the nervous tension of humankind turned abruptly to inertia now that the things had been accomplished. In spite of everything, however, the immense consequences of the stiffening of the West against the East were perceived, one by one.

Asiatic power had been definitively cut in two. The great swamps of yellow beings beyond Altaï and Annam were about to fall back into mental obscurity before having had time to emerge from it. Perhaps for centuries, the vital spark was extinct there; ideas and passwords did not cross the mountains, the empire of somnolence bogged its hordes down in poverty and primitive unconsciousness; that mass of human substance would not take any direction or form.

Japanese supremacy was ruined, two hundred years of brilliantly energetic politics wiped out beneath the crush of Occidental shells. Surrounded by the Confederate fleets, Nippon, exhausted of money and blood, could no longer act or spread out on the yellow continent. India was tightly gripped, the rajahs were dissociated, the junction of their forces with those of Japan no longer existed, and in accordance with General de Trénan's plans. An insurmountable barrier was about to be established in Indo-China and Burma.

The Tokyo cabinet no longer had any armies; the last, which had carried out the campaign in the Deccan, had been obliged to retreat after the taking of Delhi, to break up and fall back to the Ganges. It was learned, when Calcutta was reconquered, that the army in question had been almost completely annihilated, and the European cruisers in the vicinity of Singapore and the isles of Sunda closed the route forever to the debris of the Far-Eastern squadrons. The rivalries of the Burmese princes and the Japanese generals did the rest; the success was unhoped for, the cables and the supply lines brought the acclamations of reassured crowds from Paris, London, Berlin, Vienna and Rome.

The unification of Anarchism was consecrated, the sociological world was free to fortify itself internally; dynamic expansion had found its route. At the same time, the repair began of the coalition's losses.

They were grave. The invasion of one world by the other had not taken place without an atrocious shock; the framework of Europe was cracked; the losses of money and blood were revealed to be enormous. But the disemboweling of the adversary was total and irreparable; it seemed that the colossus of the North, tottering itself, was holding out in its clenched fists the sumptuously dislocated cadaver of Asia and lifting it up painfully before breaking its back definitively and laying it out beneath its impassive sky alongside its mountains and its seas. With one hand it was holding Japan by the throat, surrounded by its ironclad fleets, and with the other it had grabbed the belt of India, and within the span of that frightful embrace, that he magnificent body had finished gasping.

The colossus was able to rest, and needed it. Those twenty epic months had nevertheless extracted for Europe the major part of its vital strength. The conscription of men had been excessive, the displacement of finances had almost overturned the markets; everything had truly been wagered against everything, with nothing held back. International organization had saved everything; no alliance in the diplomatic fashion of old could have sustained a similar effort. The Confederation had shown an admirable cohesion; maintained and indoctrinated by Dessort, the industrial masses had poured toward Suez and the Persian Gulf inexhaustible accumulations of food and weapons, without hesitating over a sacrifice, genuinely stiffened by the evidence of an abstract principle.

Médion, finally arriving, depicted for Claude Laigle the enthusiasms of the North and the Occident. The word of beauty had germinated back there, the peoples had understood the

Adventure. Through the Minister's coldly lucid formulae, the convalescent Claude glimpsed intellectual landscapes that reanimated him. How great the return would be: not the trumpeted grandeur of military triumphs and illuminations, but the certainty of an ideological future finally illuminated by the virgin fire of an intellectual responsibility, a modern consciousness simply raised!

The odor of blood faded in the master's soul. He looked at Médion hopefully, completing his dry phrases with an interior lyrical exaltation, interrogating him less about facts than about ideas, scrutinizing him less with his words than with his eyes, searching the mineral irises for the European expression almost forgotten during the twenty months of Asiatic sojourn. That face, as rigid and geometrical as the thought that inhabited it, almost pleased Claude; he rediscovered therein a certainty, an order, after the delirium of sun and carnage in which his great voluptuous soul had been maddened for some time.

Ménières face was erased from his languid memory; he no longer saw it vacillating above the infamous serge putrid with red mud, among the golden hair; he sought in vain to remember is expression of disavowal and anger during their quarrel in the great pagoda. The artist's denial was extinguished beneath the din of victory. "Barbarians like the rest!" Ménières' last words seemed to Claude less violent, distant and incomprehensible.

There was an element of truth in it...yes undoubtedly, an element...but he went astray. What a pity that he died! He died for not having believed...now he'd see, he'd understand...

For slow days, among the gardens and the white minarets, in the unconscious enchantment of the light of Asia, Claude Laigle's fever was calmed by the precise discourse of Médion. He almost liked him, and the terrible logician, as if he had understood the master's crisis, seemed to incline toward him, to invent a kind of affection, a careful persuasion, a concession of his exactitude to the unquiet lyricism of the leader of peoples. By an effort of his dry intellect, did Médion admit that Claude's romanticism was an organic necessity?

Singular currents of the soul were established between the two men; Claude gradually recovered his strength, became anxious about details, interested in the economic and financial labor that would complete the work.

The news received from General de Trénan confirmed that renaissance. The commander-in-chief, departed for the South, indefatigable in perfecting the mission of his artillery, announced the pacification of provinces. It was known that the squadrons were cruising without encountering adversaries; the rumble of cannons was decidedly vanishing from the midst of humanity, the effort was becoming mental.

I'm still here, Claude said to himself. *It's now that it's necessary to stay here, now that it's necessary to create.*

He understood that the essential was now to be accomplished after the necessary, listened internally to the noise of his vitality, and felt strong.

To stay here, to finish everything, and after that and only then, to go home and resume working, he thought. *Manipulate the brute, organic matter here, and then triturate the thinking matter back there. I'm still young; I can do it; I'll only be able to prepare, but now is one of those hours when the main thing is to prepare.*

The vision of a Europe developed on his givens, impulsive with regard o his future action, shivering like a child in the depths of his flesh, the eternal pride of designates raised him up again.

How much there is to do! It's necessary...

His convalescence was thus completed by surges of impatience life. The gardens were opulent in fruit and flowers, everything was weighed down by fecundity and sap; the vital example was universal. In the sunlight, Claude Laigle saw his blue shadow trailing behind him, small and bizarre, and smiling; thus his memory would trail behind over the thinking world, but it would be an immense metal shadow, a true shade, a haunting of consciousness, a visitor of souls. Would that shadow be the diaphanous sister of the white Idea, linking his truths with the open sky of adventure?

He saw it again, dreamed it, slowly, with a sentimental enjoyment, a sweet sentiment of mystical espousal leading his glory and his energy to the eternal altar of human destiny. Thus he was cured, amid the efflorescences of parks, and close to him, without impatience, Médion waited, with his firm and insensible soul.

The descent of the Ganges was delightful for Claude. In the vicinity of Benares, the affirmation of his compromised energy was completed, in sensations of beauty.

The voyage proceeded under triumphant blue skies, between the giant banks ornamented with white temples, sometimes disemboweled; the traces of the war remained. The cries of soldiers, from the top of ruins, saluted Claude Laigle; the dusks were gripping in their majesty, the grandeur barbaric; ancient ostentations were evoked in the landscape and the firmament. Within him the dictator bore modern grandeur, the abstract ostentation of the master spirit: the comparison was pleasing.

He disdained the voluptuous beauty of sites, was scornful of the confines of Hindu empires. Convoys he encountered impassioned him; they were dragging away the debris of the heritage of fatalistic arts—steles, statues, stolen gods— carrying them to European steamships to relate in the museums of the Occident the further collapse of a race, to put their gilt to sleep under the dust of time, next to the dusts of Assyria and Egypt. The white man reigned.

The arrival of Dessort changed everything. He came to take account of the recent organization of the conquest, the task of moral decomposition being complete in all the provinces, due to his cares, and again Claude was gripped by the awkward impression he had experienced after the Battle of Lahore. The socialisator calculated coldly, in accordance with an ensemble of psychological laws, the decline of humanity; his immense and singular endeavor acted from the north to the south, exciting the Indian princes against one another, dissolving the fermentations of the people with the acidity of a politics of hypocrisy and concessions, troubling the crowds, paralyzing communications, flattering sects, creating everywhere a vicious mental respiration that anemiated the soul of the great peninsula.

There was, beneath the military cataclysm burning cities, a slow and progressive fissure through which that soul was escaping into the depths of the earth, and Dessort, an evil workman in the shadows, in the cellars of the magnificent collapsed palaces, was enlarging that insupportable rift. The thought of India was broken under the ground as the skull of a man struck on the head is sometimes fractured beneath the intact skin. Claude sensed that singular swarming, that work of undermining, in the cities through which he passed and he was horrified, although accepting it.

Dessort's face frightened him; clear, with its sharp contours, the caesarian head with the persuasive years appeared immutable; the long, then, feminine smile of the socialisator had not changed. His administrative genius was enunciated in harmoniously simple phrases. While he was explaining his plans, Claude listened to him, almost seduced by the charm, the famous charm that had once coagulated the massed workers of internationalism. It really was the same method, applied to human matter in effervescence, the eloquent insinuation, the speech adapted with admirable hypocrisy to the instinct of crowds. And if Claude Laigle turned to Médion, the impression was similar—and if he thought about the active force of old General de Trénan, if he reread his messages, he found one again the same systematic impassivity.

Those three individuals really were the regulators of a world: a universe of chemistry, socialization and organized murder; their three ideals were very modern, inaccessible to any sentimentalism, noble or puerile. Between the three of them, Claude divined that he was quite alone, sensing that they were strong and strict, strangers to him, excusive and marvelously contrived. For them, there was neither morality or amorality, no sensitive datum existed; everything was nothing but continuities, polarizations, directions, antinomies, balances of forces, energies, currents, associations, amplitudes and categories. Those names replaced the ancient names of the affections of the soul; they were the names of future virtues. Admirable moderns, odious people!

Bitterly, Claude thought about his speech at the declaration of war, his extraordinary flight toward a directive metaphysics of races, and he perceived how unrealizable that prophecy still was. He had been allowed to say it and he understood why. In the eyes of those men, he had only agitated great phantoms before the legates; but those men were too intelligent not to understand how a Head of State, a responsible word-bearer, had to make use of phantoms in order to give a relief to public decisions.

A hundred years before, the scientists had shrugged their shoulders, shown their public scorn for those hollow images; at present, truly developed in their concept of modernism, Dessort, Médion and Trénan, sociologists of the first order, admitted in their "balance of forces" the value of "verbal illusionism," and were content to make it a scientific element, a force auxiliary to their exact ideal. They made use of Claude and his decorative speech; they made use of his prestigious power. He represented in their calculations the love of crowds, an element they needed for the task that they did not disclose.

And Claude Laigle sensed them around him, the ardent constructors of an epoch to come, obedient to obscure ethnic laws, yielding to his will and nevertheless drawing him; as minuscule insects crushed by a great blade of grass move beneath it, dragging it to their lair while seeming to submit to it; those men were working without dreaming, silently edifying around him the terrible constructions that only the obstinacy of subordinates, the anonymous army of men in the background, can lead to a successful conclusion, when the most imperious genius is exhausted therein. In India, as in Europe, they were continuing to be themselves, to apply their systems on a larger scale, to satisfy their respective manias.

Dessort, with a keen comprehension, created clubs everywhere, gave substance to the demands of coolies, tolerated democracy, divided everything into groups, used the sects against one another, enervating everything by clemency and half-measures, talked to populations "for their own good," won them over to a communist ideal while taking account of their heredity.

Médion acted upon the Parsees as on the class of university malcontents in Europe. He assembled around himself those intelligent and wily individuals, graduates of Bombay or Calcutta scorned by the castes and armed against them by modern method and knowledge, and made them into the natural leaders of Anarchism in Hindustan.

And thus everything was about to recommence, on the model of the Occidental Confederation, and that was good; it was only for that reason that Claude had wanted the war, and everything was normal and logical. And yet, deep within him, an indistinct, confused, almost organic distaste was beginning to arise: an infinite and unformulated disavowal of his *double* regarding the intervention in the extraordinary heroism of the Adventure of the obstinate force of banality, of utilitarianism, the planed and the ordinary.

Those systems transported to other climes, that clockwork cerebration, dismantled and reassembled like naval machine-guns and campaign telegraphs, that impassive transposition of methods into the collapse of an age-old fatality, made Clause Laigle feel slightly sick. He was subject to the crisis of the man of war and clamor brought back to a job as a bookkeeper; the insipidity of the useful disturbed him.

By acquired habit he occupied himself with details and arrangements, presided over meetings, straightened out the surprising entanglement of the politics of conquest, and muffled the profound and embryonic rumor that was had been born within him, but his soul had been touched; a reaction to the effort was beginning, and he had to admit that to himself regardless.

Am I, then, above all the familiar, the lover of Forces? he asked himself, on certain evenings. *Am I not, as much as I was before the man of the Idea? The Idea is slow to separate out; all that labor, all those categories and formalities veil it;*

241

plunging in the sword is seductive and clear, drawing it out again is less interesting, it's true, but nevertheless, nevertheless, the Idea exists. It was to arrive at this gray period that I constructed the whole of the red period passionately; now the intermediaries are here, that's the hardest phase to pass through for people of my kind. But I have faith; it's necessary...

He evoked the unreal face, the white Adventure reeling off its future promises in the metaphysical sky. In spite of everything he thought of it like those who maintain in amity a woman they have possessed, and claim no longer to love, and tranquilly see someone else cherish her: something very beautiful and untrue intervened, he no longer kissed the diaphanous form on the lips, and shivered to admit it to himself.

The period was difficult, almost terrible. He no longer loved the Adventure as much; it no longer appeared to him entirely in the future, desirable; it was partly realized, he was living it. The sovereign Idea of his existence was already partly detached from him, misted by reality, extracted from his brain and his dreams by time. He was living it, but would he be living it much longer?

The hypothesis, taking on substance, was beginning no longer to belong to him; other men were taking possession of it, burrowing into it like termites. He still loved it, but it was beginning no longer to love him, like a child who, growing up, goes his own way, separately, trying the arms of will that have been given to him—and he sensed that he was going to have to resign himself to no longer loving the Adventure exclusively and jealously, although could not see anything else as yet that he could love, nothing great enough, and in any case, it would not be the same thing. Thus, those who detach themselves from a rare woman cannot imagine that a similar power can ever arise in their life.

And he was alone, the sole passionate individual among the comprehensive individuals who could, even if the Adventure had not existed, employ their energy and their systems to some other construction. For the first time, the crushing majesty of the Oriental sky, instead of being a harmonious decor for Claude's proud will, oppressed him like a mute menace. Was the counsel of fatalism born of those colossal landscapes the revenge of India on the violator of its destiny?

Does this land still conceal sorceries that impress me regardless—or am I growing old, or missing the air of Europe?

In his mind those questions came together, and to all three he responded negatively; there was, however, a element of verity in all three, and he dared not ask himself the fourth question, the real one: is modernism truly unassailable? He skirted that without formulating it; his animal being sensed that it was deadly; in the depths of his being, the very cells protested darkly against that mortal seed.

He thought he was fatigued, avoided returning to those things. *I'm overcomplicating*, he said to himself.

Perhaps, however, he was simply beginning to see.

The crisis developed further. Everything aided it. The aspect of scientific modernity, under that admirable sky and in the hectic lushness of overheated nature, definitely repelled Claude Laigle. The artifice of practical reason revolted his dreams. The establishment of fiscal regimes and confederative modes appeared to him to be derisory in its slowness.

An event! Something...! He could almost have wished for a revolt, the disembarkation of a Japanese army. Risings occurred, but were too easily repressed. There were serious anxieties for a week, because of a retaliatory offensive by the rajahs of Kashmir, threatening to cut off the route to a European division that had imprudently advanced too rapidly. Claude Laigle was regripped by passion for the Idea—but the news of the victory arrived almost at the same time as that of the trouble, and everything fell back into calm.

The forces were decidedly complicit, the repercussion set in, and after having struggled joyfully against events, he had to struggle coldly against the lack of events, against the quotidian, against the trivial...

The identity of methods and formulae depressed Claude, and filled him with remorse against himself.

Do I no longer want the same things, then? What am I complaining about? Everything is in conformity with my aims, and yet I'm discontented. I want something else...what? It's childishness, perhaps fatigue. How terrible it is to pass through neutral periods! I've supported others, though...

This one did not end. Everyone around the dictator seemed to consider it not as neutral but as definitive; they had conquered, they were organizing, incorporating, annexing: a perfectly natural period, the evident corollary to a great effort.

Claude attempted a few insinuations on the subject to Médion and Dessort; they did not even notice them. Médion was absorbed in his doctrines of scientific diffusion, creating faculties and courses, choosing in the Hindu mind the assimilative fractions and groups them together. Dessort was systematizing labor, talking about disciplining the masses "for their own benefit." Their own benefit! The face with the persuasive eyes and then thin and feminine smile was troubling in endlessly repeating that formula, in which Claude sensed an unfathomable irony.

Around those men a legion of lieutenants strove to second them, all intelligences avid to exercise their mechanism, beginning to triturate this new substance like Europeans substance, butchering the immense cadaver, commencing the autopsy after the murder. Everyone was occupied with the Orientals. That led Claude to take an interest too, to see at close range what they might be.

Fundamentally, he had never formed a very serious psychological idea of them, he had only envisaged them collectively as enemy powers. His hatred had denied them any moral existence outside fatalism and contemplation—which is to say, two notions irrespirable in the Europe of his dreams. In repose and inaction, however, he had the time to admit that that analysis, sufficient to lead the war, became absolutely superficial in the period that was now inaugurated.

His lieutenants seemed to have known that far longer than him. What struck him was that they did not appear to detest the Orient, as he did. One might have thought that they glimpsed the possibility of linking themselves to it, of reaching an understanding with the subjugated peoples. Were not crowds and their laws identical in all climes? The hatred had faded away; it had only lasted as long as the war, while the "yellow peril" existed. Now affinities seemed to be born; people were less occupied with sterilizing Oriental military force and preventing its offensive return permanently than with trying to insinuate occidental principles there. By virtue of a singular attraction, the two parts of the old world, violently divided, appeared to be seeking to join up again.

Claude's thoughts were abandoned. Who was in the right, his ministers or him? Was it the attractive baseness of masses that was active in that, or a law of human alliance higher than hatred? He did not know what to think, and doubted.

Certain facts, in the countless reports that were submitted to him, astonished him. Unexpected links definitely attached the Oriental world to his own. Japanese prisoners were affiliated to freemasonry; it was observed with surprise that the field hospitals of the Yellow army belonged to the society of Geneva; armbands with white crosses were found on cadavers.

A hundred facts of that sort accumulated; something that was almost a comedy took form: a cold comedy of Japanese in suits, mandarins using telephones; the comedy of anachronism becoming an ethnological verity. Claude Laigle perceived that they were ready to reach an understanding with his ministers, having been unable to devour Europe: modernism had identified the contraries, industrial leveling was the master, transportable methods had penetrated everywhere, and the conception he had formed of Orientals had, after all been very romantic and behind the times. Metaphysics and his lyricism had made him see falsely in the detail.

He became impatient. *Oh, let the others occupy themselves with the detail; they're excellent for that,* he said to himself. *I'm alone in synthesizing, in dreaming the moral aspect. I'll make use of their fragmentary remarks to construct my abstract edifice.*

He relived the epoch of extreme socialism in which Anarchism had been elaborated in Europe fifteen years before. *It's a malady, the leveling*, he thought. *It's good for the formation of active forces; afterwards, the notion of the superior individual is detached by disgust; it's necessary to endure that confrontation with detail first. It will recommence here as it did back there. Fundamentally, is it always the same thing? But if the modification of souls isn't accentuated, is it worth the trouble of disturbing ourselves so much? It will be necessary, if this turns out like that, for me to intervene. Médion, Dessort and Trénan seem to believe that we've simply warded off a material danger; that's only half the Adventure, and I'm at least as committed to the second half!*

In spite of everything, the Orient attracted him. To have something to do, in order not to return to Europe to occupy himself solely with European affairs, but to leave mental traces after the traces of the war—that new concern gripped him without him being aware of it. Once he had thought that, once the yellow peril was averted, it would not matter to him what the vanquished would think; now that worried him and amused him; conquering avidity caused him to emerge from the frontiers of his race.

Immense and torpid China no longer occupied him; he still thought of it as a repulsive swamp, far in retreat from life; but Japan and the new Hindustan, the Parsees, the curious elements…perhaps there was something to be made of all that. He did not see that his initial conception, brutal and unjust but clear, was beginning to be falsified in the dangerous solicitations of inaction, and that psychological interest was breaking it down.

The pacification decidedly accentuating, Claude Laigle resolved to confront the unexpected question that had come to his mind, and he departed through the provinces. He went northwards from Benares, relived the horror of Cawnpore and it well full of stranglers, reached Lucknow avoided Delhi, went along the frontiers of Rajputan and the deserts, and reached Lahore, studying, interrogating, and making his hypotheses more precise.

In Lahore, Médion, who had gone with him, parted company in order to rejoin the Indus. Claude stayed in the Punjab with an army, determined to fathom the soul of the mysterious region. Weeks went by in the sumptuousness and enchantment of the landscapes.

The extraordinary beauty of India, sank like a fainting woman into the depths of Claude Laigle's heart; in spite of everything the beauty of India gripped him, an irresistible sensuality born of the soil, and Claude finally began to glimpse how that sensuality, that annulment of thought before love, might, in alliance with the spirit of contemplation born of peace, create the fatalistic mysticism that, in Europe, had irritated his energy so madly.

The hatred of the soil united in him with the hatred of the sons it bore, but it was no longer a hatred founded on antipathy and ethical theories; he no longer found that way of life repugnant; he sensed that it was dangerous, but complete and appreciable in itself, no longer inferior to the scientific way of life of occidental modernism but juxtaposed, parallel and, in sum, equally legitimate. He already admitted that the danger had a right to exist. He no longer had within him the sudden start of the civilized man warding off, with a direct strike, the abject offensive of the uncultured, but the rational envisaging of a different race. The struggle became abstract, one mentality against another.

The enemy rose in Claude's esteem. He understood now that the remarkable individuals among the enemy were not, as he had once lightly assumed, those who had adopted methods from Europe, but those who, obscurely and tenaciously, conserved the primitive soul.

Well, so much the better; one can reason with them as equals. If I had believed them equal during the war, I might have weakened; now, it's worth the trouble to think about it. I no longer hate them in the same fashion. They don't disgust me; they impassion me.

He did not admit that they had already conquered him a little, by virtue of the very fact that the desire to conquer them intellectually had taken the place of his original desire to kill them...

Claude Laigle quit Lahore to visit Kashmir, the sources of the Indus and the Hindu Kush. He had decided to go back to the ultimate origins of the white races. Everything was in order; the latest correspondence determined him to devote six months to the ethnological investigation that he wanted to complete before returning to Europe.

Already, for a year, he had heard talk of vast mystical communities that had been established in the far North, toward the plateau of Pamir. Information regarding them was vague, even the indigenes knew almost nothing about them. Semi-legendary rumors circulated on the subject of those citadels of fatalism, buried in gardens in the hollows of the mountains. Prophecies were propagated; only widely-spaced pilgrimages brought news of a life mingled with strange oracles, in the retirement of those sacred convents.

Claude's instinct quivered within him; from those mountains and those cells perhaps descended, like spiritual rivers, the terrible contemplative ferments spread throughout Hindustan. It was there that he had to go; he signified his desire. At the head of the Punjab divisions he headed toward that region. Couriers spread the announcement of the European intrusion, and India experienced a secret frisson.

At Peshawar, the dictator, centralizing the forces, awaited a deputation of communities. The negotiations concluded amiably, as he desired; women appeared, bringing on behalf of the convents the acceptance of the European visit. Their cortege arrived in the camp; the master received them in a little wood. They came accompanied by servants, but without equals. Their vast agglomerations had become autonomous fifty years before; the colleges of fakirs did not meddle therein; and the meditative power of women in coalition radiated a singular mental clarity from the depths of their retreat. Claude

Laigle gradually formed an obscure and great idea, sensing there an axiomatic verity, an unknown role.

One woman led all the others, a mystical empress, of abstract and vast power, about whom Claude Laigle knew almost nothing except for her Parsee origin and her entirely European origin. Mrs. Freany Teema had been, for many years the astonishment and admiration of the university of Calcutta, having traveled in Europe and then, in the era of the expulsion of the English, retired into the mountains. An immense occult influence was attributed to her in the organization of Hindu feminism. Silence had apparently fallen over her. It was known that, abandoning all the prerogatives of modernism, as if touched by an indefinable resolution, she had renounced showing herself in the peninsula, cultivated secret studies, and even abdicated her family name, living in the mystical communities under the name of Erodia.

Interested, Claude awaited that enemy priestess.

She was the last to appear. He was astonished, having anticipated something different. Her black robe made her indistinctly Oriental and modern; tall, with an energetic, passionate and weary visage, she opened large moist and bright eyes. The extension of feline pupils and the undulation of her hips signaled exoticism more specifically; a noble secret force emanated from her.

Salome grown old, Claude thought.[14] Her forty years spread a spicy and strict prestige.

They looked at one another, immediately alone among the ceremonials. Claude was not afraid, and was not harsh.

---

[14] This reference emphasizes the analogy between Erodia's adopted name and that of Salome's mother, Herodias, although it seems equally likely that the name's primary significance relates to the same root that produced the English word "erode". Mauclair was fascinated by the character of Salome and her relationship to the myth of the *femme fatale*; one of his several essays on her symbolic figure is reprinted in *Les Clefs d'or*.

The first exchange of glances did not inaugurate anything special. They spoke. She expressed the consent of the communities with hauteur and abandon; he acquiesced. Their two black and sober forms were allied in the radiation of the palms and the azure; they secretly understood one another, and esteemed one another.

"You shall see our sisters," said Erodia. "They have singular thoughts, modes of the soul that you do not know in Europe. Conquest has not shown you everything."

"I sensed that, and that is why I have come to see," said Claude, simply. "I have set down the sword in order to contemplate."

"Yes," Erodia murmured, "yes...an exchange of forces. You have violated the Orient, but as yet, that is not finished. It is necessary that you put down the sword; it will not be of any use to you for what remains to be envisaged..."

"And that is?" Claude replied.

"Oh, I don't know how to put it...exactly. It is...yes...the *virgin Orient*."

Claude eyelids fluttered. He glimpsed, in a flash, the face of Ménières on the evening of the council in Paris, saying: "Perhaps the being you seek is among them." He shivered; she sound of the voice had been identical.

Straightening up, he looked Erodia proudly in the face. And the leader of souls suddenly illuminated in her large and luminous pupils a strange landscape of pure fire. Then she lowered the lashes very slowly, a mute promise of the invisible. And with her lashes, Claude's lowered too, and he sensed at that precise moment that, following the curve of their eyelids, he was *redescending* the other slope of the adventure.

VIII. The Cradle

They departed for the sanctuaries of the North.

For a long time they traveled side by side without looking at one another, black and haughty forms meditating dissimilar worlds and enemy beliefs. When they brushed one another the friction of irreconcilable thoughts vibrated between them, and the waited mutely, very calm, savoring the rare voluptuousness of estimating one another as parallel forces. They did not feel, at first, the need to talk.

At the hazard of encampments, Claude Laigle glimpsed Erodia among her women. Her svelte somber silhouette passed back and forth between the tents. In the evenings, she returned to her quarters, beneath the foliage or in the rocks, and no sound arrived from the direction of the Hindu recluses. In the mornings, she appeared on horseback, joined the dictator's escort, and they went on.

The master treated her as an equal; she accepted with a strict and easy simplicity, habituated to living in the European fashion, speaking a very pure French, responding to the salutes of officers with a tranquil elegance. No woman was any more familiar to her than any other, she marched ahead of them all, alone. The caprice of the roads brought her close to Claude Laigle during the marches, or drew them apart; for orders, runners went to one or other of them alternately, the corteges separated out or mingled.

An immense peace descended from the zenith with the heat of the azure. Claude Laigle meditated, and did not know what special thoughts were alive behind the forehead and eyes of Erodia. The soldiers were astonished by her; she galloped in their midst at top speed, with an indifferent flexibility, casting a cold and arrogant stare over the infantry. Litters followed without her reposing thereon; nonchalance was scarcely revealed in the corners of her long eyelids, signed with oriental circles. Claude found her singular and very modern, without saying so to anyone. She was not at all what he had expected, but secretly, he was not surprised; it seemed to him that he had imagined her thus once, obscurely, in indefinable dreams.

They arrived thus is the heart of the mountains, on the extreme slopes of the Himalaya, amid the prodigious accumulation of pink rocks. The exaltation of the natural beauty gripped Claude Laigle. Erodia seemed, as she approached her refuge, to relax her suspicion somewhat and to rediscover her sovereignty. They isolated themselves from the troops, spoke to one another more, and then made definite contact, soul to soul, proudly.

Claude Laigle was impressed by the admirable intellectuality that the tall woman revealed, discovered her logical and lyrical, like himself, perceived treasures of mental refinement, resolved to study the leader of souls before exploring her realm. Since Ibsenian creatures, European women had made a great deal of progress in a hundred years, and Claude Laigle, although having had little contact with them, had glimpsed enough complexity and nobility in them not longer to hold them in systematic and vain scorn. Sociological anarchism had taken very useful root in women and had opened wide the doors of intellectual life to them, while liberating them from their instincts and their unions—but this one surpassed any that Claude had been able to see.

He only perceived the modernism in her; the other face, the Oriental face, was mysterious; Erodia seemed to be reserving it for the terminus of the voyage—but the modern face impassioned Claude Laigle's mind. That intuitive Parsee, sprung from a detested race, fortified in its genius by the reprobation of castes now ruined, truly had surprising gifts, a faculty of scientific comprehension infinitely developed.

She's evidently artificial, like everyone, the dictator said to himself, *but she'd delight Médion! I'll put them at odds when he rejoins us.*

As he was thinking that, smiling, he did not see the long blue-tinted eyes, the torsions of the indolent and muscular hips in total, the torpid lightning that was Erodia. He saw her beauty poorly, like all those that souls interest first.

He told her about the revolution in Europe, the parliaments blown up in the middle of the capitals in a single night, the defections of armies, the flights of sovereigns, the social masses docile to the information of free consciousness, the intoxication of the triumph of ideas. She had seen some episodes, as an anonymous visitor; she had scented the odor of the new times among the people of the Latin race.

252

She spoke about her childhood and adolescence of study, her late nights in the laboratories of the University of Calcutta, her theological research in the sacred cities of Hindustan, strange meetings with the fakirs, her revolts of consciousness, her abstract joys taming sensuality, her exile in the hidden country, her initiation into silence and dream. And Claude, in listening to her, found common methods, analogous elaborations of the soul, with a scarcely-dissimulated surprise.

Sometimes, ardent enthusiasms colored the clear voice of the Oriental. *I don't know, after all, whether she would delight Médion*, Claude then objected to himself. *She isn't as dry as he is. Dessort would accept her better.* But immediately, he thought that Dessort's persuasive and ornate eloquence did not have that passionate gravity. The woman decidedly persisted beneath the intellectual, and in a mixture so accurately dosed that the conqueror found an indefinite charm therein.

Erodia was strict, not without languor, but without insistence; she was not seductive, and Claude appreciated that reserve, approaching the mind very closely, without being solicited by the flesh. Otherwise he would have been suspect, as a male. He only savored the charm of pure reason there.

An exchange of forces slowly united them; the esteem grew, they measured one another more deliberately; in the oppressive enormity of the landscape, their humanity increased; the mutual sentiment of active consciousness became more precise before the magnificent inertia of locations. In the evenings, when Erodia went back to the Hindu camp, among her women, Claude Laigle savored, pensively, the magnetism of the nocturnal summer. He scarcely saw the strong face amid the hair with profound reflections, but he heard the grave and musical voice, lent to the lyricism that he loved so much.

That priestess is truly astonishing, he confessed, with a half-smile. And a pleasant disturbance, the joy of finding in those solitudes a soul at the height of his own, froze on his lips the specious and facile reflection by which his irony was about to try to safeguard his superiority as a man. He did not even perceive that that was in play. After the discouraging period of his convalescence, the intellectual voyage delighted him.

I have India by military power, and now I'm visiting my conquest, scrutinizing the living force of the hostile Orient. I'm the master.

That security vivified him; nothing in the landscape disconcerted him any longer. He was about to enter the sanctuaries curiously, but without dread, with an armed mind, ready to experience anything without weakening. The unknown of those populated deserts attracted him without fever; everything was normal.

Reassuring news still reached him from the armies of the Ganges and the Indus. Then they plunged decisively into the escarpments, toward the Hindu Kush, toward Pamir; they were reaching the end of the long journey. Claude and Erodia arrived there almost friends; the leader of souls became more mysteriously serene.

Finally, the first convents appeared. Vast quadrilaterals of white buildings were staged amid palms and fountains, spacious farms and fecund fields announced them. Claude and the army were astonished. The region was reputed to be uncultivated; the maps said nothing about them. Rare explorers had passed through them a long time before; a few had perished there, the sun had drunk their blood and nothing more had been heard of them. Had that blood enabled these white constructions to germinate? It was, rather, the mind of Erodia that had created everything. She seemed to Claude to be suddenly transformed, smiling at an interior certainty.

The Europeans made contact with the luxurious communities. Where they had expected a savage life, masses of huts, and primitive hermitages, stood perfectly grouped edifices in which a spirit of modernity was allied with Orientalism. Series of brightly-illuminated rooms opened on to gardens; outcrops of rock suddenly rounded unmasked others, infinitely. Their organization was logical and simple; the ventilation was good, isolated pavilions served as retreats for the sick, and a comfort inexplicable in these remote regions was revealed. Erodia took the surprised dictator to visit them, anticipating his questions.

"All this is the work of patience," she said, "and the scorned Parsees are rich. Fortunes have accumulated what you see here, by means of immense transports. The work has been slow and secret, the rajahs have had no suspicion of it—they were so uncultivated from that point of view! The precious stones of the heirs and the money of the merchants of our race have aided it, along with the tithes of the poor. For the order that there is here I spent ten years in the laboratories and the hospitals of Calcutta, and I had memories of Europe. We're not so far away from you. I've told you that the Orient was not what you thought—and then again, this is a special Orient." With her eyes half-closed and in a soft voice, she added: "The virgin Orient."

"I thought," Claude said, "that there was nothing here but wilderness."

"There was," she replied, "but fifty years have sufficed, since the English quit India. And there was a long time when everything you see was dreamed, for what you see materially is trivial. Your emigrants to Australia and America have done more astonishing things. But we were not seeking what they were seeking; our goal was dissimilar. It's not what you perceive that is important, but what these installations and locations permit to our dreams. We have stopped in time, my sisters and I, on the road of material progress. In any case, it was necessary."

"Why?" asked Claude. "Was the difficulty too great?"

"No. We could have done more. You can't imagine the tenacity and fidelity of my associates. This land has its unknown routes, its undetectable means. You can imagine, in any case, that it was easy for us to perfect the details of our installation, since we were able to bring it to its present point without being troubled by the rajahs—and the monetary resources could be multiplied tenfold tomorrow, if we desired.

"If it had pleased us to establish ourselves beside the sea, we could have equipped a fleet, surrounded ourselves with torpedoes. I thought about it. It would have been an autonomous and impregnable State. Then I recognized that isolation would defend our white buildings better than cruisers or melinite, and I believe I saw accurately. Do you know that I'm the mistress of more gold than the queen of Oude or the princes of Bundelkund? Not to mention will-power.

"The electrical networks linking your armies to Europe animate crowds less rapidly than the mental magnetism that animates my affiliates. My messages go from here to Travancore or Assam more slowly but more surely than yours. Our cables can't be cut. During all your military operations last summer, I never ceased to receive my information through your sieges, your blockades and your marches. I even had news from Delhi two days before the assault.

"The beings and plants in this land concur with superior wills. With regard to slowness—which, in any case, is relative—it has been sufficient for me to organize my intellectual calculations in a special fashion in order not to be thwarted. Time is only what we imagine it to be, and my curiosities are no more hurried than the mental phenomena that they monitor. What we await is not enclosed in telegrams and cannot be intercepted."

"There is, however, the question of delays that paralyze all action," said Claude.

"All…visible action," Erodia replied. "But there are orders of dynamic acts."

"I understand. Your *influence*. But that's a preparation for action."

"Or a conclusion…"

Astonished, Claude looked at the smiling Erodia.

"That's true," he said. "But given what you've just told me, why did you stop at a certain degree of material progress?"

"Because it's always necessary to stop in what you call the *material*, and limits are indiscernible," replied Erodia, tranquilly. "And as we didn't come here to stop, we have, to a certain degree, quit the form that would have failed us one day or another, and taken a new one."

"A moral form of progress?"

"Mental—because moral form also has its evolutionary limits, and that also is finished for us," said Erodia.

"And you believe that the form of mental progression of your race isn't limited in its turn by natural laws of ethnology?"

"Of our race? What race are you talking about?"

"But...the Hindu race, or even the yellow races fused with yours.

"And what tells you that we're limited to our race?" Erodia pronounced. "Do you take us for recluses concentrating the soul of their native land?"

"Do you claim to be concentrating the soul of other lands?"

They looked at one another.

"But why not? You've come here with your people, and with your European ideas, bringing the soul of the Latin races, meditating a mental conquest. Why shouldn't we go to your homeland?"

Claude, amused and a little proud, said, softly: "For that, you lack certain means of...visible action, especially at present, and we have...traveled a little rapidly for your actions to be truly such."

"I understand you; I've understood what is called irony in Europe, although I haven't wanted to retain it for my own usage. But there's an error in terminology at present. You speak about the *yellow peril*? You have brought that to a conclusion, after having made a very ingenious theory. But a theory comprises several aspects, and several conclusions. In other terms, there are *indefinite* theories, like certain mathematical solutions—and in mentality, all theories are like that."

"What does that mean?"

"But...that you have, by means of your *voyage*, concluded by the assault on Delhi, brought to a conclusion what you envisage as a solution, but that that doesn't forbid us a parallel and dissimilar solution by means of another order of…voyage," said Erodia, placidly. "You spoke of race, of my race? Observe that I haven't told you that our communities are linked to the intellectual development of Hindustan, according to itself. You made allusion to your suppression of the yellow peril? I also have not told you that anyone here is meditating a new phase of the war. I've spoken to you of mentality. What your generals do does not disturb me. Believe me when I tell you that I have seen all that as a spectator. I have a horror of the Japanese, and the Hindustan of the rajahs doesn't interest me. I'm a Parsee, but I haven't even taken pleasure in being avenged by you for the ancient persecutions of my sect. The question is distinct from those nationalizations, for you as for me. I won't even say that you helped me."

"You're not a mystic?" said Claude.

"Not at all, and nor is any of my sisters. There's no trace of religion here. Do you believe, then, what you've been told about our communities? The vulgar think that we're simply recluses guarding the traditions of the Vedas, but I thought you were better informed. The Vedas suffice for the moral current of my women, but we have other concerns."

"Political concerns?"

"Even in the mouth of the leader of Occidental Anarchism, the word 'politics' isn't clear to me," said Elodia.

"In sum, the object of your meditations is a force of expansive mentality?"

"Yes," said Elodia.

"I have an analogous objective—and that's the reason for my presence here," said Claude.

"I knew that."

"Oh? Then you also admit that, next to my first solution, I place another, parallel, like yours?"

"Yes."

"And you're not anxious about that? You don't imagine that it might render your…expansion superfluous?"

"Not at all, for your solution will be mine."

"Do you mean that you accept my views?"

"I didn't say that your solution *is* mine, I said that it *will be*."

"You're speaking obscurely."

"And you a little too quickly."

They fell silent, considering one another gravely, with esteem. Singular sentiments were born in Claude Laigle's soul.

He said: "You're closer to me than I thought, in certain respects. I understand you better here, in your home, than on the road. You seemed to be expecting me. Was I mistaken?"

"No," Erodia replied.

"You mentioned dynamic acts, secret messages, magnetism. I imagine that your expansion requires abstract means. Should I understand occult forces?"

"It's evidently not the force of the shell. The shell is only an idea for me."

"For me too, believe me."

"I do believe you."

Claude shivered, remembering that he had made a similar reflection on the evening of the council in Paris—and the ivory face of General de Trénan appeared in his mind's eye, and like the terrible old man, he rectified his remark: "But the shell is a guarantee."

"I haven't prevented you from adopting it. As I told you, the work of your generals doesn't hinder me; it doesn't help me either."

He became irritated. "In sum, you have a goal? And a goal that you avow to be expansive?"

"Certainly."

"And you think it identical to mine?"

"Yes."

"And what if it isn't? What if you get in my way?"

"I'm astonished," said Erodia, impassively, "that an angry thought should come to the mind of a leader of sociological anarchism when he thinks of sedentary individuals. You only have to displace a soldier and his mentality is free, according to your own principles."

"I was joking," said Claude, surprised. "You're strangely focused."

"Like a woman, like the notion of the present that she incarnates."

"I thought I conceived that you were expecting me in order to be my ally, that you're preparing here—you, a Parsee educated in modern science—a new cerebrality, made to accord with my conquest..."

"After you have obtained your...guarantees against the rajahs and the Yellows? And that I would be a kind of intermediary between Asia and you?"

"Yes." Claude Laigle was struck internally by the clarity with which he had pronounced that word. So, his primitive conception really had been modified! He no longer wanted to sterilize India between Europe and the Japanese power. Decidedly, the country interested him; he no longer hated all the so-called uncultured. How ideas changed! How the action of shells ended in unforeseen hypotheses! He was resolutely dreaming that new dream. And he waited almost with certainty for Erodia's acquiescence.

But she pronounced, with an imperceptibly disdainful mildness: "I told you that our solutions were *parallel*."

"I said *alliance*. You understood an *exchange*?"

"A mental exchange, yes."

"And it can take place, now that the war is materially terminated?"

"Certainly—and only now is it possible, since we finally find ourselves on a level, on the same plane of intellectual dynamism, with the same instruments. At present, you're more than a logician, like me. You know that I'm disinterested in the ancient Orient, that there can be no antagonism of ideas between us there, and that I'm applying abstract methods toward a goal coexistent with yours. Why should there not be an exchange?"

"You're truly disinterested in the ancient Orient?"

"Certainly. It didn't hinder me, but wasn't useful, any more than your armies. I'm thinking of other things."

"You're not an Oriental, then?"

"I believe that we'll soon find, together, a clearer definition of that word, and even of the name Occidental, for it's necessary to understand one another. I'm not a dissident, and I'm not an intermediary between Europe and this land I'm here, and more so than this conversation might lead you to think, but I'm not what you think I am. I repeat that we're acting in concert, but separately. I believe in the Orient, but my faith is not in that to which your hatred is addressed."

"Yes," said Claude Laigle. "I'm beginning to glimpse what you mean. 'The virgin Orient.' You're guarding a rite of which I'm ignorant. Three months ago, I would have thought it irreconcilable with my ideas. Today, I'm waiting. But what are you brining to the exchange?"

"Simply the idea of this," said Erodia, indicating the white constructions.

Dusk was falling. They separated.

In the garden, in the bright halls, in the white rooms, lived a small population of women. They were not veiled; their faces were placid and imprinted with an interior liberty. Many were, like Erodia, former pupils of the Faculties, educated in the European fashion, and had worked in that fashion. In laboratories and clinics their adroit hands had manipulated retorts, leafed through tomes, touched sick people subtly. There was no trace in those communities of religion or of art. The concentration of mentality alone created something holy and harmonious there. Discreet and inoffensive disciplines appeared to regulate the recluses easily; nothing concerned them but the employment of time. Extreme isolation, the natural mildness of the vegetation and the days, simplified the detail of living.

Few men were perceptible—servants circulating. Muscular and handsome young men lived separately, hunting and guarding the enclosures, almost all of them Parsees and whites. At night, the women received them in their homes. Some did not receive them, limiting the satisfaction of amour to reciprocal kisses, and that question was not the object of public reflections. Liberty on that subject was identified with various tastes for one dish or another, a contestation would have appeared anachronistic and negligent. The exaggeration of appetites, matched to the inspiration of the climate, contained by that very fact their accepted legitimacy.

Children were invisible; as soon as they were born they were sent to hidden places, some in the cities of modernized India, others remaining in the mountains. Informed progressively of the conditions of their birth by affiliates disseminated from Kashmir to Bengal and from Kabul to Calcutta, they opted freely for a life to their taste, returning to the communities or serving them at a distance, or, if they wished, disinteresting themselves in them, receiving civil estates permitting them to present themselves to the world with a suitable identity—but they were dead to their mothers. Those defections, in any case, hardly every occurred.

The economy of the material resources of the recluses, their information networks and the surveillance of convoys was regulated by special services via consultation. Nothing apparent distinguished the association of a free convent from a phalanstery of intellectuals cooperating, by mean of their fortune, in an ornate, mutually agreed retreat. Similar societies did not astonish Hindustan or surprise the Europeans, among whom the first form of anarchism had been thus revealed by private initiative. The tradition of mysticism and the retention the sacred principles of India sufficed for the indifferent respect of neighboring rajahs; rumors of discreet debauchery contented superficial opinion and the skeptical curiosity of the vulgar. A fear of sorcerous sciences created the respect of anonymous crowd. The authentic idea of the grouping remained unsuspected. No one talked about it outside, and the messages seized by the complicity of a few faithless couriers in the early years had not revealed anything to the governors of the province—and calm had descended on the subject.

Visiting the various communities, Claude Laigle observed those apparent details, similar everywhere, of a minuscule civilization whose harmony seemed attractive to him, but whose essential reason was not obvious to his mind. The astonishment of finding such an organization of mental forces in this wilderness struck him; the idea of his initial error on the subject of the Orient was increasing fortified, effacing completely his former conception of the enemy race.

What surprised him even more was not finding any trace of fatalism, and the conversations he had with the women convinced him of the absence of that detested sentiment. They lived, thousands of leagues from Occidental Anarchism, with an absolute intuition of its principles, and went further in several respects. Their active intelligences scrutinized sciences and sociologies in silence, and their morality was liberated without being dismembered; the equilibrium of individualism and the strength of association was perfect; that State of women had no faults.

They're truly very superior, and very sympathetic to my ideas, the master said to himself. *Is it because women, unlike men, understand what the present is, and are nascent with the energy of cohesion?*

But he could not understand how that unexpected revelation of a sensitive intellectual Orient could be of use of him. He was far from any hatred against the recluses of the Pamir; they were no hindrance to him and they pleased him, but they seemed to exist apart from the ancient Orient and the new Europe. What exchange had Erodia meant, and of what did that ambition of *expansive* force consist, among these wise beings, who seemed, on the contrary, to constitute an end, to be complete in all respects?

"The virgin Orient" Claude certainly perceived, and he thought about Dessort's astonishment and Médion's suspicion when they came to know in their turn the little concentrated group, proud and white, retrenched in the Hindu crests. But in what way could that "virgin Orient" second him? Behind the first secret, was there another? He could not discover it, and considered Erodia, seeking the enigma in the frown of the clear forehead and the long, circle eyelashes—but she remained impassive, watching him. Since their first veritable encounter, she appeared to be waiting, keeping out of his way with a measured courtesy, as if her consent to explain herself depended on an evolution in her adversary's mind.

That evolution, irritated curiosity, the majestic sensuality of the sky and the landscape, intellectual satisfaction, the odor of an unknown soul, and distance from Europe all activated in Claude Laigle.

Have I before me the last refined Orientals, all that the sumptuous and ferocious imbecility of fatalism has been able to spare in this punished land? Are they the creatures the penetration of the modern mind has been able to awaken some beauty? Are they our intellectual children? Or have I before my eyes the first witnesses of a regenerated Asia, as Erodia seems to understand, beings formed in the depths of the Orient, of its very blood, not forgetting it but mingling it with the acquisitions of the Occident, and meditating an unknown future, pagodas raised to the cerebral god? But that would change the question infinitely! Is it the result of an infiltration of the west into the ancient Orient that I perceive, or a reaction of that Orient awakening to march toward us with our abstract arms? From which side will the exchange commence?

I sense that, although we have the appearance of having arrived as masters, there is something here that is also commencing. And that woman affirms positively that she is heading toward, outside of my control, by parallel ways, to a solution reconcilable with mine! And yet she doesn't solicit an alliance!

What, then, is the virgin Orient? Who has left it virgin— the rajahs of the ruined regime, or my armies? Erodia says that I have not saved it, that Orient, by coming, nor have the rajahs saved it. They did not kill it in the egg, and nor have I. How, then, does it exist between those two contrary forces? Is there an Orient that is neither the ancient one nor the one of whose transformation I dream, which is developing at its own whim?

That's the question to which I always come back. One might think that Erodia is eluding it. Is it because there's nothing there but a void, and she's guarding an imaginary secret? No; that ruse wouldn't lead me astray. It seems to me, rather, that she's waiting for me to find the answer in myself.

These alternatives filed Claude Laigle's mind.

Deep down, he glimpsed more clearly with his sensibility than with his reason a mental empire, concentrated in a few groups of buildings, just sufficient to nourish the bodies of its inhabitants: an abstract empire, a floating manifestation, a college of concentrated beings, summarizing in a simple frame the dynamic accumulation of the world and acting by insinuation in the ideological universe.

It was necessary not to search for the virginity of the Orient in this communist State founded in the distant mountains, nor in the safeguards of that State against the rajahs and the conquering armies. That primary virginity was surprising, made to impassion; but there was a second, and that must be the true one, the essential one. But would it dissolve, that unassailable virginity, in the age-old traditions of the Hindu soil, or a new comprehension of the intellectual future? Did she think it could be saved forever by the inertial resistance of ancient Asia, always prostituted and always intact, or by the admiration of Europe? To what did it tend?

Thus turning, in an attractive series of hypotheses, Claude's reasoning blossomed.

At that moment, Dessort and Médion rejoined him. He observed them increasingly affirmed in their idea of civilizing the conquered country, of creating in India a current sympathetic to Europe, to fashion it into a future obstacle between the Occident and a possible reawakening of Japan and the Yellow masses. They would give prerogatives to the people, develop industry, open wide to all the facilities of obtaining rank, of socializing.

Claude explained the situation to them, his research and his curiosities since the beginning of his travels, expecting anger or scorn. On the contrary, Médion and Dessort seemed delighted by "the virgin Orient." They were interested in it.

"An excellent center for the propagation of Europeanism," said Médion. "You've found a precious force here, Master."

And Dessort added: "This Erodia is one of ours. She's working for us. These intellectuals will help us, even though they'll forbid themselves to do so, and you know what a growing force the intervention of the new woman will have."

They fell into accord on the fashion of considering the mountain communities: a group of intermediate intelligences, renovating the Orient, opening it up to Europe. They immediately attached themselves to that utilitarian formula, easily. Claude Laigle wanted to believe them, and then was almost shocked. How simplistic they were, those men with theories! Erodia's eyes sometimes signified things that truly further complicated the question that the arguments of the two ministers would not admit.

"A few more months, Master," Médion assured him, "And we'll return to Europe with everything set in place. Our agents will only have to continue on our givens."

That tranquility, instead of convincing Claude, left him doubtful, in the malaise of an increasing incomprehension. The aggravation increased of finding Médion identical, faithful to his "universe of chemistry," and Dessort, with his dreams of organization, his irritating administrative genius! They had not changed; the extraordinary Adventure had passed over their heads without surprising them. A year before, Claude would have seen that as an admirable strength of soul; at present he discovered therein a narrowness of mind.

There are, however, combinations of circumstances that overturn living beings, unless those beings are atonal, having only the appearance of dynamism, are mediocre! he said to himself.

And in a second, he glimpsed as mediocre those he had before him, ordered and sectarian, and Trénan with them, and the entire world left on the road to Europe…that limited technologists! The ideal of the future civilized Orient broke in him the image of the society of engineers in which he had lived.

Useful, yes, certainly, but second-rate all the same! Have I made the conquest with those men, for those men? And he cried: *No!* internally with such force that he was alarmed by it.

The image of Ménières, almost ironic in the council in Paris, almost revolted in the assault on Delhi, passed through his memory, reappearing very visible. How haunted that dilettante had been by strange prescience! Claude sensed that he was less distant from him than the others, and suddenly he had a crazy, absurd idea, a fugitive flash of the radiance of superior truth.

Erodia is Ménières resuscitated!

Implicitly, he loved Erodia. The strong visage with the noble eyes, the pale face surging from the blood and the mud from the infamous serge, the two heads of hair, everything mingled, in a single embracing image, so violently that Claude, dizzy, clasped his hands to his torso, seized by a neuralgia of the heart.

He thought: *If he revived, if he saw her, we'd all three of us understand one another, in opposition to those men!*

He shivered, having spoken aloud without taking account of it, but he was alone.

From then on, his soul let go.

The diaphanous visage of the ancient Idea floated in his dreams, untying his bouquet of verities in the open sky of the Adventure, as before, but so fluid, so frail, that he could only now discern in those brilliant curls the tresses of Erodia and Ménières, confused...

By means of successive short journeys, Erodia drew Claude Laigle into the mountains, to visit all of the communities. During that period their intimacy was accentuated. The leader of souls was smiling, the serenity of the sky remained marvelous and the long-contained lyricism rose once again to Claude's mind, and calmed it. Everything collaborated in that calm: the echo of the immense catastrophe was distanced, quivering now in the confines of the habitable world; European power soared. They were consoling and decisive days. The reversion in the dictator's thoughts attenuated the wait for a new route, perhaps broader, more surprising, and everything depended on Erodia's secret.

She did not seem to be in any hurry to speak, but revealed herself luxurious and gentler, as if soothed by an interior harmony, Claude finally saw her, savored her beauty in the spacious landscapes. She seemed more Oriental, always black and strict, but the surrounds of her elongated eyes beneath her luminous hair were more emphatic.

Salome grown old, Claude had thought at their first encounter. At present he did not see Erodia's forty years, Salome was no longer perverse or a little girl, but the torsion of the hips and the languid gleam of eyes crying youth and triumph.

One evening, she announced the final voyage, to the heart of the Pamir.

"You'll understand all my ideology then, Master," she said.

They left, with Dessort and Médion, who esteemed Erodia, counting in her a future force and support, but keeping their distance from her and Claude, with a secret base design. They reached the great plateau thus. The last buildings were visited.

"But there's the landscape," said Erodia. "It's necessary to come."

They went; she guided the men and the camp, with a sign and a smile, almost like an elegant excursion, became entirely a woman, free and cheerful.

They camped on the plateau of Pamir; Claude Laigle waited.

And there, placidly, the annunciatrix, drew him away and showed him the solitudes. And she said: "Do you know what we call this desert, surrounded by our communities? Our supreme windows open over it. I sometimes come here to consider it. This is what matters, this empty space, circular, hollow and defended..."

"I don't know," said Claude.

She half-closed her eyes, and pronounced, in a very low voice: "We call it the Cradle."

Her voice was strange, changed, as if born from the depths of the Earth. Claude shuddered. Erodia had taken his hand, touching him for the first time.

Very rapidly, she said: "It's here that the first races were born. It's from here that they radiated out over the world, that they descended into India, and toward the Occident. It's here that you were rendered possible, you and yours. There is neither Orient nor Occident here, there is neither right not left, nor north or south, do you understand? Here, humankind was cradled by the unconscious song that rose up when chaos was finished! When all the white men had departed westwards to solicit destiny, it remained solitary, the curbed and sad plateau, with its arid soil, beneath the sky. But under the clear earth human imprints were still germinating the eternal seed. Why did they all believe that the Cradle was empty? They went away without looking back, out there, far away, beyond the mountains and sea, in millions! They went into exile as if they were going to conquest!"

She stopped, appeared to repress rapid words, and only repeated, softly and sadly: "Why did they all believe that the Cradle was empty?"

"This time I understand, Erodia," said Claude, very pale. "Behind those who departed for the Occident, believing that they were only leaving a desert, the Cradle didn't remain empty. Souls reformed, and if the hosts had gone, that was because it no longer mattered that their temporary mass, anonymous and vain, remained there. A thought sufficed."

"Yes," said Erodia.

"And that thought, you've heard living for centuries under the ground, and you've drawn living beings from it, and you maintain it in silence."

"Yes," she said, again.

"And what the rajahs and my generals haven't been able to attain or fortify, is that thought of the fecund Orient guarded by your recluses. What you come to contemplate from the extreme windows open over this plateau is that thought, dormant in that curved and hollow Cradle of the men of the white race..."

She lowered her head, smiling pensively.

"And now I understand what you mean by the virgin Orient. And I also know what you're waiting for and why you were waiting for me."

"Say it," murmured Erodia.

"When all the white men had gone, without looking back toward the empty Cradle, that which you have thought, firmly hoped for, was what they remembered. What you're waiting for, Erodia, is for them to *come back* to the virgin Orient."

She looked at him proudly. "You have understood, Claude Laigle."

"And I understand why you're women gathered here," he said. "It requires gentle hands to guard the Cradle; you're obeying the immortal instinct of *gardiennes*,[15] and you're cradling the cherished thought, in order that they will find here the uncompromised source of life, saved by your cares while waiting patiently for them to come back."

"Yes," she said.

"*I have come back*, Erodia," said Claude, softly.

She let go of his hand, shivering. They considered one another. The sun was setting obliquely; violet shadows and red enchantments of an infinite splendor filled the curved horizon.

In the mute Cradle, the central point of races and thoughts, Claude Laigle sensed a new man born and palpitat-

---

[15] Because all nouns in French are gendered, many words referring to human roles come in distinct masculine and female forms, only a few of which are reproduced in English. Here, *gardiennes* is employed in a special sense, essentially restricted to women, and it would be misleading to translate it as "guardians."

ing within him. And he attached his eyes to those of Erodia, upright and immobile; he moved very close to her; in those two magnetic pupils millions of lives dwelt, outside of dates and countries, outside ages, purified in the permanence of time.

"Erodia," he said, "now that I've come back, would you like, in order to guard the Cradle and raise the thought-child, for there henceforth to be a man and a woman?"

She acquiesced silently. And he was perhaps about to say something more, but their faces were so close that the kiss came more rapidly than the words.

That evening, in the obscurity of the sleeping camp. Two shadows cautiously leaned out of a tall tent. A glimmer of light colored the curtains. The silence was total. A few paces away, on a carpet, soldiers were asleep. The two shadows suddenly shifted slightly, together.

"The kisses of a woman through a closed door," one of them said, and added, ironically: "The virgin Orient."

"He'll weary of it," said Dessort. "It's dangerous when, having passed through what he's passed through, one starts to occupy oneself with that. But it's something, all the same, isn't it? And then, it might be useful to us. In any case, I think it'll pass..."

"No," said Médion. "He's lost. It's not the woman yet, but...I sense clearly..."

"What?"

"He's made an error of calculation."

They went away without adding anything.

IX. The Visitor

She said:

"You have not come in vain to the calm Orient. The echo of the cannon is dead. Rest. Here, among the high palms and skies as open as young hearts, there is a thought that time will never trouble. I have waited for you patiently beside the Cradle, and now you have come back from the confines of the world, with your artillery, your crowds and your wrath, as I hoped. O son of my race, long distant! Who spoke to you of Orient and Occident? Mingle their names on my lips; I love you with tranquility; our bloods are not dissimilar. Here, among the mildness of instinctive plants, the distinctions of tribes are diminished.

"Those you have brought with you no longer understand you, Master, but the word of truth is valuable in itself. One seed is sufficient to summarize the crop. Your conquest is secret; it is virginal too, as was my silence; now it belongs to you alone; in you it will open and slowly flower, at your whim, unknown to your armies and our ministers, now that you truly dispose of it, you think it, it no longer has anything material; it lives behind your forehead, is transparent in your eyes.

"How I have waited for you! You are almost unchanged; you have the signs of the primordial man, the surprising heir of a long series of masters. You are simple: your unprecedented enterprise is simple too. You thought to conquer, and you came back. Thus, those who raise dreams in dreams only do so to rediscover their veritable being and to recover their wellbeing, and you have only come back to your authentic childhood. Now the second period of your power is accomplished. I am with you in order to dream of the past beauty and to edify the future beauty.

"Alas, Master, do not think, because I am a woman, that I am triumphing over you. I am beside you; our means are different and our thoughts parallel; here, no one is above anyone; the gardiennes are not triumphant women, and this soil has not known, like that from which you come, the idea that woman is evil. You do not believe that, for you are not of that land. You are of this one, which does not belong to anyone, and you know that it is the only fatherland of beings like us. It has remained empty of men and women, and we shall not repopulate it.

"See, even I remain on the threshold; I only contemplate it from the extreme windows of my convents. There must live, alone, the original thought of races; that is what it is necessary to guard. What does it matter to me what the vulgar believe, thinking that I have retired here with my women in order to conserve the Vedic traditions? Here, beyond religions, something holy palpitates that surpasses the secrets of rites, a pure and inviolable evidence.

"You have come back, you have touched it; and you have never forgotten it, in the depths of yourself. You have only forgotten the name; it is of this that you were thinking in standing up against Asia a vast apparatus of war. All forms are good to return to what one guards in the depths of oneself. I have waited for you; I have waited for you ardently and confidently. The echo of your approaching cannons already brought me the voice of the return. I heard therein the joy of solemn salvoes that also saluted peace by the howling of the beasts of death.

"You came here to force the final secret and you thought that I ought to hate you; I am smiling at that now. I have detested the Yellows that the stupid rajahs summoned here to stop you; I have feared for a long time that they might go to your Europe to take you a false and abject idea of the beautiful primitive Orient. Your captains, ignorant as they are of the real nature of things, have seen in my eyes how I rejoice in their work, and they love me without understanding me, as they will love you now.

"You tried in vain to distract yourself from the meaning of the truth. In vain you thought to depart in anger against what you called the yellow peril, the indolent fatalism of Asia. That Asia is not what you imagined her in your mind to be. You were only able to vanquish those who misunderstand her, the Mother. Now the figure of peace is rising up for you, and these desert plateaux disdain the passage of armies. It is thus that you have returned to the first place of the white races, and my kisses, for years, have reached you beyond the mountains and the seas.

"I had glimpsed you during my voyage, out there; but the time was not yet ripe, and I could only speak to you here. I glimpsed you, out there, without you suspecting me, an anonymous passer-by in the rumor of capitals. How necessary it was to contain ardent and rapid dreams! The truth worthy of you did not want to be spoken, and when I found you again in Kashmir, until I brought you here, into the presence of the excellent earth, I clenched my teeth upon the words the cried on this side of my lips!

"Now, love me as I love you, for the long patience of my great desire. I have infinite and multiform souls within me, living souls of blood and aromatics, ripened for the leader of old and grave souls..."

She kissed him, smiling, the strong face with the circled eyed paled by voluptuousness beneath the somber tresses, and they gripped one another ardently.

Claude loved her like a dream finally clothed in visible flesh, beneath the opulent sky of the wild country. The svelte diaphanous Idea, autumnal with her tresses of semi-loosened verities, and her pale promises, the svelte Shadow of the Adventure, thinned in the dusks of Europe, finally descended into his arms, and he found her stronger and prouder, drunk like him on solar savors, nourished by light and calices in all her supple gilded flesh. His fingers likewise modeled the dream of his life; the animate statue was real, he savored her with greed and fervor.

The secret exchange burned in both of them; they enclosed it between their twin lips, and in the middle of the kiss they drank it like an extraordinary fruit. While, joined at the mouth and their hands clutching hips and shoulders, they aspired it in the same convulsive or calm rhythm, Claude penetrated Erodia's elongated pupils with his eyes. Half-closed in the blue-tinted torpor of the great rings, among the reeds of lashes, they unveiled verdant water in which appeared a transparent sky; shadows passed therein like clouds, immemorial shadows; thousands and thousands of voluptuous and pensive faces emanated from the earth and sanctuaries.

The warm odor of breasts rose toward those eyes, a feverish perfume of juices and aromatics, phantoms floating in the pupils hallucinated by them, spinning indistinctly; and suddenly, the blue-tinted curves of the eyelids narrowed, and the moist gleam of the irises was annulled, rolling the specters and the clouds into sudden obscurity—and Claude, alarmed, felt in his shoulders the mute bite of fingernails gripping more tenaciously...

The lips tightened then in their nervous flesh the word ready to spring forth, caressing it, tasting it with the cynical tongue, then strangling it, preventing it from mingling with the breath, driving it back into the depths by the penetrating and voracious advance of kisses between the teeth. The alternating beat of their hearts arrived through the flesh, harmonized with the quivering of the lips, and alone remained alive in the silence and the sweat of the embrace.

The inappreciable time passed, followed by the surge of two breaths; then they yielded, exhausted by the exchange, and Claude's fixed and empty eyes saw, slowly reopening between the unclenched lashes, the stretched and glaucous pupils...

At other times, in the totally sexual play, they suddenly became motionless, savoring the secret contact, the head upstanding and free; they looked at one another, drew apart, only vibrating imperceptible in the centers. The irritating intoxication exasperated by the wait, they did not yield to it, smiling, a smile taut over cold teeth, hands open and swinging, holding back the wild desire to seize one another; and they considered one another with a refined care, he savoring himself alive in her, she savoring the shiver of masculine strength. That double invisible vitality was as if separate from themselves; they allowed it to exist apart; their thoughts, really vaulting above the act of their bodies, floated lightly, happy and hollow, borne between them on the odor of amour.

It was an immaterial and delectable moment.

Then, the enervation of inferior life rose up, attaining them all the way to the hands that sought one another, the eyes that dilated, the mind that was maddened; the woman with the erect breasts undulated first, and they threw themselves upon one another, sighing.

They made love in the remote gardens, in the dusk, waiting for the enormous azure to become very deep, and for forms to become indistinct. Desire made the fingers haunting their waists almost cold; she, pliant, offered the calyx of her mouth while murmuring very softly; an incomprehensible clarity remained scattered around her hair, which suddenly slid, rolling, down to her hips, defining her with a savage and sulfurous contour. He sought the loins of the great feline woman, and his arm was lost in that warm and fugitive fleece. He became irritated, parted it in handfuls, threw it back like a curtain, and burrowing in the heavy waves divided them, uncovering the nape of the neck and the hollow of the powerful shoulders, kissed that odorous flesh in the darkness, relentlessly, until Erodia, half-convulsed, turned, gave her mouth above the shoulder and the hair, with a sharp gaze whose magnetism reached him in spite of the obscurity.

They walked thus, staggering, linked by the center of the visage, mingling their legs brushed by palms. The army bands and the somnolent recitatives of the Hindu couriers reached them through the woods and the rocks, a melancholy softened their hectic souls; and, releasing one another in order to take hold of one another cautiously, they kissed one another on the cheeks and the eyes like children who have been afraid together, and ended up going to sleep in the even warmth of the Oriental night. And the roseate fire of dawn touched their unconscious eyes.

Beneath her grave and passionate head with the profound and weary expression, she displayed a perfect body, whose svelte flight tapered desirably toward the abdomen, and which, suddenly curbed for amour, softened a golden flesh into unctuous folds, elastic and subtly nourished by aromatics, sometimes coppery, sometimes very white, as pulpy as the heart of warm fruit and resistant under the dampness of hands; a full and highly cambered cleavage made the warrior more womanly and more amorous. The torsion of her hips was sovereign.

Claude contemplated that body pensively and discovered there all the Orient of dreams, Judith and Herodias, Balkis, Queen of Sheba, the great Semiramis, and the recluses of the pachaliks, and the unknown dominatrices of the emirs, and the Persian princesses living in the crystal, and those who, in tales, entertained themselves with genies in subterranean caves were their tremulous lamps illuminated bones and treasures, and those whose nudity was heightened by the sun in the bazaars of Basra, in the gardens of Golconda, on the white stairways descending to the Ganges from the heights of the palaces of Benares.

Then he returned to the face, touched by abstract thought, marked by secrecy, sensuality, dolor and dream, with the long reticent and meditative eyes, to the bitter mouth, the round white forehead, the lubricious and tenacious chin, and he rediscovered the Occident, determination crowning passivity, the dualism of worlds conciliated by that head and that body, the one able to be queen in the dusks of Europe, in the nuanced air of intellectual modernism, the other made to be ambered and candied in the sunlight and the languor of roseate countries.

It seemed to Claude that the link between two worlds was clear, signified between that head and that body by the neck, robust in its birth at the bosom and shoulders, and suddenly tapered, bearing like an undulating stem the visage-flower weighed down by the hair; that the great tresses, winding around the noble statue and enveloping it with life, also linked the two strange landscapes of flesh with the hectic wave of its strongly perfumed curls, of which secretly warm memory persisted obscurely in the groin.

The gardienne of the Cradle united the two races, revealing one alone, primordial, the age-old race of the white beings descended from the mountains of the original earth, toward the Occident and toward the South...

Together, Erodia and Claude wandered on the edge of the desert Cradle, and their kisses never had more moral and voluptuous savor than in the presence of those dry rocks and sad sands, to which the sun gave the color of the body.

They loved that primitive flesh, asleep for eternity among the sharp stones. Their limbs were harmonized in amour by the thousand indescribable attachments that, above inclination and sentiment, magnetize one body toward another for life. It appeared to them that that illusory flesh of soft sands was also similar to their own. They were unified with that soil. Their fingers took up the sand and allowed it to filter through; it was a singular caress. Soon, they lay down upon it, naked, their great musculatures of tamers of men imprinting themselves upon it, and they believed themselves to be three in the embraces.

The warm body of the desert bore theirs; they possessed it, inert beneath and between them; the flamboyance of the azure made them delirious; they cried out spasmodically in the middle of that arid wave, and swam in it as if in living water. There were unusual delights for them, a confusion of sensualities and ideas, equally exalted by the sky, the impression that they were rediscovering one another after a voyage of many centuries, as at the awakening from a dream, not having budged since the origin, beyond dates, places, history and death.

The virgin Orient effaced all the simple and naked prestige of its blond sands; they fell asleep there in silence.

Sometimes, in the repose of fine afternoons, they lay somnolently beside one another on the beloved ground, hearing nothing but the quiver of the mysterious Idea that rose within them, which rose through them from the depths of the quivering earth with the oblique sunlight, and which penetrated their bodies and their souls in the vibrations of the heat. And Claude no longer thought about the skies of Europe. The fever took hold of them, and with pleasure they watched the women advance, bearing cold sorbets and precious fruits to their dry lips.

In the morning, amid the cares of councils, in the middle of the troops, in conferences with the ministers and the visits of the communities, Erodia passed by, svelte, clad in black, devoid of jewelry, having become intellectual and strict again, attenuating the sentiment of the immense exile in the heart of the Europeans by means of conversations and modern mannerisms, a free and expert talker at meals or a disdainfully elegant amazons in rides through the camp and excursions. Her savant and incisive speech born of a scarcely indolent voice, she truly became once again the torpid flash that Claude had vaguely suspected at their first encounter. And he considered her with amazement, remembering the night.

Their eyes met without retaining anything of recent hallucinations; she brushed him tranquilly, with neither perversity nor reticence. Only the Oriental body hidden beneath the somber silks revived the luminous head of thought, constrained by the long luxurious tresses, now tightened in narrow torsades. Claude rediscovered the woman born of the Cradle but departed, like him, for the Occident; the duality of the body and the visage was affirmed, and yet, by imperceptible signs, he perceived that Erodia was one.

But, suddenly alone, the kiss rose up from their flesh and seized their heads to join them violently to one another, in the torsion of loins and the collapse of sumptuous hair, the male lover recognized the orgiastic female lover with the seeking hands, and there were rare and equivocal attachments, the intellectual attitudes of the queen of the recluses and the leader of armies yielding abruptly to naked sex, faun and satyress clasped like beasts of prey, with joyful bites...

When they were talking one evening about oriental princesses born of the Cradle and famous among men, she smiled without saying a word, went out and reappeared. A ribbon of precious stones circled her forehead and her cheeks were illuminated, making her ringed pupils darker; straight and slender, she swayed thus, at the summit of a heavy rigid robe, a bouquet of blue jewels, lamps on the floor casting her shadow on the drapes of the tent, and she danced, extending her strong arms, the wrists of which were brilliant. He was silent, astonished by the game.

She did not look at him, gripped by an ancient rite, her gaze fixed, her entire body attentive to the ceremony. All the India of warm seas, forests, pagodas and deserts inspired her silent dance; the implacable claustration of the harems of Asia, conserving voluptuous secrets, seemed to have meditated its most astonishing inventions in that moving statue. Claude, frightened, recognized Salome, the eternal indifferent dancer; the feline odor emitted by that great living calyx, followed by an exact or deformed reflection, awakened desire in him; he felt desperately human, perceived, in a flash, the eternal conqueror subjugated, startled by fear and lust.

But suddenly, tearing off the precious stones and kicking over the lamps, she threw herself on to him in the darkness and he felt tears among the urgent kisses, and she took him in her arms, murmuring:

"That's a game; I detest it; I wanted to show you one of the forms of our soul, one of the forms that you hated once; I wanted to show you, since we were talking about past charmers, that I too knew...

"Forgive me, don't think about it anymore; love me in the present; I'm present; I'm your sister in thought and the flesh, we have no need of extinct grandeurs. That which is dead is hateful, we shall edify something else...

"I was playing, I was playing with the past..."

An overturned lamp threw of a last and more vivid flame; he gripped Erodia's visage between his hands and turned it violently toward the light. And he suddenly perceived the eyes. They were grave in the scintillation of tears, the Oriental lie was no longer revealed there, they opened as pure as Northern lakes. He rediscovered the north, and shook the evil cloud from his soul.

Then, he adored Erodia without reserve.

She visited his mind and his heart with the gentle and admirable psychology of loving gardiennes.

She was not only gentle with him in the physical sense. She approached him with a perspicacious soul expert in sounding wounds. They hugged one another for long intervals. Their thoughts remounted the stream of time, bound to one another by a fraternal lust; it was a spiritual nuptial voyage beneath a perpetually serene metaphysical sky. They drifted together on the canals of the invisible, leaning over cisterns filled with marvelous thoughts, finding in the depths of sensations the salt of strength and the jewels of meditation, and climbing once again, souls laden with discoveries, spacious grottos in which ideality sleeps like a child in a supernatural light. Their mutual grandeurs confronted one another with wisdom in the simplicity of the Cradle. In that central place, it no longer seemed to them that ideas could escape toward the North or the South, like races; they rebound their essential bundle, and they both contemplate them without difficulty.

What lofty hypotheses exalted them during the nights when, insomnia reigning over their flesh liberated of amour, they considered one another, quivering, bewildered to be mastered by one another. Claude, especially, was animated, finally returned to himself after years of political cares, studies, anxieties and actions, thrown back into his native lyricism, bathing therein at his ease. The past and the future no longer haunted him; he became a being of the present; here, only the present had any meaning, like the place, like the woman. He had the sentiment of finally grasping something essential, of no longer waiting, of no longer preparing, but of holding, and whether it was Erodia's mouth, or the intuition of moral plenitude, he *possessed* it.

His conqueror's soul savored those beautiful preys; he was happy.

Pensively, Erodia listened to the indefinable murmur of that happiness within him, studied it, and watched over it. Solely by the sentiment of the tradition of the race, she had acquired the plenitude of the imagination for which all others beings seek in the exceptional of the universe; she had found her central and real point, the very landscape of her certainty, which other individuals only glimpse in dreams, and her joy was fortified in being shared with Claude.

The Occidental returned to the Cradle brought her thoughts transformed, an original bouquet in which she recognized the species, but whose calices had become paler, as of diaphanized by the damp and tender skies of Europe. She mingled slowly therein the odiferous crimson of the flowers of Asia; they rose, nonchalant and heavy, above the astonishing spray, and they both placed those offerings on the edge of the rediscovered Cradle. Erodia continually collected new ones in Claude's soul; she discovered tremulous heroisms there; the leader of races was worthy of surprising destinies.

There was no longer any question of time, nor of customs, nor of ancient or modern details; everything was unified—and slowly, slowly, the visitor allowed herself to elaborate her future projects.

"Do you see," she said, "how admirable the words are, since they have led you here? And do you see how detestable the words are, since they almost caused you to stand up against me with hatred, in return? What do you discern now, Master, between the Oriental and the Occidental? Between brother and brother is there any other distinction than that of their very duality and their double dwelling, and does that lead to irreconcilable anger? Is fratricide inevitable, by virtue of the fact that they are two? They are united in the mother, and you are in the Cradle here. The words right and left, up and down, only have meaning relative to the human being, who is central.

"What are we, you and I? Do you not see that we are central beings, a man and a woman, children of the central place? Oh, Master, Master, between the Orient that you hate and the Occident that feels threatened by that Orient, there was an unknown land, a little desert patch, a seed from which ours grew, and that was the virgin Orient, which belonged to no one.

"There are no directions here; everything is stable and meditates continuously in the present; there is no progress here, Master, there are only dissimilar forms, multiple signs that color the world variously. The mechanical progress of which your armies and your people confederated in their modernism are so proud raises up clever machinery *in relief* over invariable sentiments, over an amour, a beauty, a death and a silence that never changes. That progress is accomplished in parallel here, but *hollowed out*, in the mental domain, among my reclusive gardiennes—and you have discovered that with astonishment, and now you are no longer astonished and you find it natural that I am here, with my dreams and my kisses!

"You have come back, you have come back to the homeland of the men of the white race. I don't know why I said that I detested the yellow peoples and the Hindu princes who summoned them; on reflection, I almost love them. Without their coalition, perhaps you would not have come for many years—and perhaps I would have grown old, you would have found me too late, a white-haired gardienne, her eyes burned by waiting!

"Turned in the direction of the West, my desolate face would have visited your dreams, you would have suspected me vaguely as a specter throughout your life, and we would finally have confronted one another with a flesh deprived of charms, and our elderly kisses would not have been able to reanimate the bright virginal Idea that we can still seize with our warm lips. But our secret god was alert, and here you are, arrived in time.

"The man returns, when he is mature, to primitive pilgrimages. You were in exile, my love; you have returned to obtain the counsel of your ancient birth, and later, you will obtain the counsel of what was before it—for is what we call death before or after life? There are no directions there either; there too, everything reigns in the present."

"The present," said Claude. "That's true...that is all I have really conquered."

"And there was nothing but that to conquer. What will you call progress now, and what meaning will you give to that word, which suffices for the rudimentary ideal of your ministers?"

"None, it's true…their science is foreign to me."

"I have fathomed it too," said Erodia. "It is utilitarian. Admirably ingenious, but utilitarian; it cannot serve us; it is false, no more than a unification of analytical faculties with a view to knowledge. It is not cosmic; it is killed by empiricism; the industrial triumph of applications holds it back; it is local."

"I've tried to take it back to its sources…it was more intellectual in the Middle Ages. I've tried; I thought, since Anarchism, that it would reconnect with metaphysics. That was a dream that they didn't want. Metaphysics, the great insulted! Oh, Erodia, if you knew what hatred that name still awakens back there! Half of the detestation of the world is focused on that name, as if it specified a racial remorse!"

"Remorse? No, Claude, regret—the regret of having quit for damper skies the country of the observers of the stars. You are their leader, you see, but perhaps you're not for them. Here, I am the queen of a small white people nourished on the central thought sand augmented in solitude, but you, you're too elevated for them, or are you dissimilar to them? Alas, my love, the authority of the prophet surpasses all the others, but his renunciation is universal. They want to raise a hand against their mother, and you have led them, but you have recognized and saluted that mother; will they forgive you? You have raised that immense horde of men; will you be strong enough to drive it back to the other side of the mental world?"

"Do you hate those I have led?"

"I don't hate them at all. I'm waiting for them to understand, and I adore them as one adores imminent forces, for they can do what is necessary now. I'm waiting for them to understand, and I hope that they will understand, through you. Their cannons are futile. Science is futile. But they love their cannons and their science. Will they find in themselves, in the obscure memory of origins, a more powerful means than the ones that delight them? Will they conquer the virgin Orient, will they carry away this desert landscape in their souls as the visible image of the promised land?

"Oh, let them remain in India if they wish, or return to Europe, provided that they retain that vision! I hope that the astonishment of having found an unknown State in these reputedly arid mountains will be a sufficient sign for them. With the memory of my white communities the Idea will be enclosed—and you will tell them that, won't you, Claude? You will tell them that? Since the yellow peril is no more, which might have threatened their interests, they won't refuse to admit the idea? They won't create that frightful divorce between themselves and the Cradle, they won't be unjust enough, insane enough, to separate themselves, the white people, from the birthplace of the white race! They'll rally Hindustan, they'll make it the extreme barrier against the hideous swamp of coppery men dormant beyond the Himalaya and the Altaï, won't they, Claude? It's the same thought, in sum, but broader, than the one that guided you here, and of which they approved!"

"Yes," replied Claude Laigle. "I've thought of that, and I believe instinctively that they'll come to it. They've already reached an understanding with the southern provinces. The primitive conception has been modified, but not contradicted."

"Ah!" exclaimed Erodia. "You see clearly! I'll help them; I'll bring them my secret allies! You don't know what I can do in India, what obscure webs I've woven during the years of voluntary reclusion. It really is a question of Vedic fatalism; I've occupied myself with the gods of the Ganges and the sanctuaries of the upper Indus, and all the old Hindu thought that the rajahs retained. A new India can be born through me, Claude—a modern India, an India of genius, young enough to astonish young Europe.

"Oh, if they wish, your people will see! They'll see what the Idea of the virgin Orient has been able to prepare! The face of that country is weary of dreams, like mine, but its body will surprise you, as mine has surprised you! My body is its body; you have embraced it in embracing me; it will give itself to you as I have given myself! Benares and Hyderabad are its breasts, the Pamir is its pensive head, Gujarat and the Oude swell like its hips; with the tip of its foot it plays with the marvelous Ceylon, and within the complete triangle that it forms, the warm and odiferous triangle, saturated with light and aromatics, you have sensed your male strength quivering, as within me.

"You will retain my body as a symbol; to your people I give the body of this country. I shall render the Cradle to all. Then, perhaps, they will understand that under various climes, the same life palpitates. Tell them that, Claude! Is it for nothing that the highest mountain in the world separates us from the yellow people? Is it for nothing that the extraordinary limit of the Himalaya contains those masses? Dormant Pamir leans against it, like a sleeping head. The wall of the white world is there; there commences the vast series of thoughts unfurling all the way to the Occidental ease. Is it not logical, is it not simple?"

"Perhaps I can explain it to them," said Claude. "Perhaps they'll follow me. But it's an almost total change of direction. I'm frightened myself by the change that has taken place in me. Oh, Erodia, you really are the great gardienne of the Cradle, responsible for our race, and however warm our kisses might be, it's still from the lips of an abstract mistress that I suspend my lips when I touch yours. The diaphanous phantom of Anarchism and conquest has put on flesh. But you are above all a Visitor of Souls.

"I don't know any more whether it's you or what you guard that I love. Will I be alone in talking to my people or will you be with me? I don't know. It seems to me at times that if you went away, the Idea would be sufficient, and yet you summarize it, and to possess you is a repose for me. I touch in you the earth that renders strength. And it also seems to me sometimes, Erodia, that if the Idea were annulled, your presence would retain for me a sufficiently clear reflection to guide me. You are the Visitor of my Soul, and my soul is not different from the one that you have guarded in the Cradle. Thus, indissoluble mixtures are produced in me."

"It will be necessary for you to speak alone, Claude. You are the Master and they don't trust me. I no longer ask to speak; the influence of the woman will live eternally, but it must remain occult. I have deliberately renounced all public life and chosen, in order to act, the mode of solitude and secrecy. And I would no longer be the same in your Europe, my friend, my Master; I would only be the attentive traveler who once perceived you in the crowds, whom you did not suspect. It is thus that, growing old, I will come back to your capitals to consider the completed work. There are only various forms, Claude; I am one form, nothing more. I have told you: although I am a woman, do not believe that I am triumphing over you. I will be the latent form of your actions. Gardienne I was, gardienne I shall remain. Of the two of us, the one whose hands are gentler befits that role, and the Cradle does not want to be alone. From the extreme windows of my convents I shall watch over it as before. Its sunlight will be happier over its sharp rocks, and over its sands, the color of which is that of the body."

"Are we quitting one another, then, Erodia? Can I not act from here?"

"They would not listen to you, Master. I love you, but what does it matter that you see the distant capitals again, now? You have come back in thought, and I have no fear that you will forget that return. Your actions might be produced out there, but I know that you are here, because our reason for being, the reason for our intercourse, remains enclosed here. I will rejoin you when the time comes, when your people know what they need to know, when the Idea has given a goal to their science, a framework to their quest for progress. They would think that I have shackled you; back there, decked in the prestige of the false return that they believe to be true, they will listen to you without suspicion. I have waited for you here; out there it is you who will wait for me, and I will only come when they have forgotten my name, our adventure extinguished in the din of the triumph."

"You're right," said Claude, going pale. "How you live the Idea, Erodia!"

"You are the Idea now, and it's necessary that it goes to the Occidental countries. The two of us have savored it, but no one ought to be deprived of it. If you stayed, we would be inferior; I would be bad for you. Here," she said, sad and smiling, "woman is not bad."

They embraced, drunk with a kind of joy; and in the hasty kisses, speech died, aspired by their breath, stifled in the flesh of their lips.

The next day, in the council, Claude Laigle announced curtly his resolution to depart for the South. Médion and Dessort started in surprise, which made him smile internally.

"The voyage that I wanted to make is finished; I know what I wanted to know," he said, loftily. They inclined, anxiously, and communicated the latest news. General de Trénan was waiting for the dictator and his minister in Delhi, which he was fortifying as a stronghold. The last uprisings in Nepal were extinct. It was known that the blockade of Japan had determined the cabinet in Tokyo to negotiate a peace-treaty. It was the consummation of the enterprise commenced on the evening of the declaration of war in Paris.

The dictator agreed the measures taken. Erodia appeared next to him for the last time, careless of insistent stares. The ceremonies of farewell were exchanged. And while the "boots and saddles" was being sounded the impatient ministers approached Claude Laigle, speaking in low voices.

"These recluses...what plans?"

"Everything remains as it is," he said, coldly.

"Will they help us? It appears that they really can," said Dessort. "I know that from my couriers. A number of them obeyed them before obeying me. You've surely understood, Master, what these women can do, the secret reason for their grouping. Your voyage of convalescence had a goal."

Claude smiled. "Assuredly."

"Is the alliance made?" Dessort asked.

"Will you take coercive measures later?" asked Médion.

"I shall not take any, at least as you can think of them, Messieurs," Claude declared. "The alliance is made...mentally," he added, with an indefinable nuance.

Disconcerted, they said no more. Médion followed him with his eyes for a long time, dubiously, his hard face contracted with concern, but Claude Laigle was already drawing away, saluting Erodia. She and he, observed, stiffened; on the threshold of the white communities, the laboratories and the gardens, the solitary Intellectuals gazed, amid the troops and the horses, at the two svelte black forms of the Masters. Above the palm trees staged on the extreme slopes of the roseate rocks, the plateau of Pamir opened its shallow curved horizons in the even and silent light. The violet shadows moved over the ground. The European clarions sounded.

Toward the occidental South, Claude Laigle, bearing a new soul, descended from the Cradle.

X. The Denial

In Delhi, the dictator, listening to General de Trénan's explanations, was astonished by the fortifications commenced—recent grassy slopes, white circumvolutions bristling with multiple piles—and the geometric impression of modernism gripped him. The hammering of foundries and the screech of saws rose up from construction-yards, alternating with jets of steam; carts cluttered the roads; an army of workers lined up in squads at a gesture from the engineers; flying cranes gyrated on the edge of the Jumna, encumbered by barges and dispatch-boats.

Claude did not recognize anything of the burning city into which he had once hurled himself on horseback, with the diaphanous Idea leading, in the madness of the assault, amid the red smoke, the fulgurant destinies of the Adventure. He had left a place of terror and he came back to factories. He traveled through the city, confusedly evoking the route followed on the eve of the battle. At the crossroads, ruined pagodas and palaces appeared, patched with fresh plaster over the traces of the conflagration, held up by stays and embankments.

The great gardens of the rajahs displayed rowed of charred tree-trunks, mostly lying on the ground, fissured domes open to the sky, colonnettes remaining upright with fragments of entablatures. A dung-heap of rubble and mud, thrown out in heaps, bordered the avenues. On that debris, among the palisades, the huts and mattresses of sepoys were agglomerated, along with improvised shops, all the miserable flora of demolitions. A busy population filed the canteens and the tents, a repulsive life born from death; the cries of merchants were odious. From the top of rattan miradors, European bells rang. Children were swarming obscenely in the harsh sunlight.

Claude Laigle went past the construction-yards, reaching the northern districts; their bleak streets extended clay walls; the rare windows were closed; violet and languid shadows loomed up interminable between the houses, furtive and earthen Hindu faces surging from wretched loincloths on the thresholds. And Claude thought about the communities of the Pamir, spacious and cheerful, with their slender women with bright eyes, under the palm trees next to fountains. Here the ancient Orient was veritably rotting.

The obsequious greetings of people were disagreeable to him; he would have liked to detect hatred in a face, but the listless people, won over by Dessort's concessions, and above all by the idea of cannons, sickened him. And yet, many of the men he saw in these side-streets must have seen him on the night of the assault; nothing apparently remained of all the horror. The soldiers and colonists were circulating among the shops, fraternizing with the Hindus. For the dictator, it was an impression analogous to that of the days after the revolution in Paris, and he saw once again the stalls erected in the debris of the Parliament, the drinking-dens and popular gossip-shops, the curious attitudes of women, the rubbish, the newsvendors, the recommencement that followed the thunderclaps, the eternal people who always ate lunch, as if the sublime and the terrible had not raised their heads: life, in short...

Life...

But here the sky was dissimilar, and there was no longer the strange black anger, the contraction of faces charged with thought, as at the dawn of Anarchism. Here, people were clearing up and tidying up; everything temporary, all the multicolored mediocrity that there was in the word "colonial" was becoming manifest. And it would be necessary, after the thunderbolts of shells and torpedoes, to insinuate the thunderbolt of the virgin Idea into that industrialism...

Claude was troubled, a trifle weary.

Dessort, satisfied, explained the plans: Delhi, reconstructed and fortified, commanding central India, with a retrenched camp, and all the Deccan in fief to the military power of the Europeans as an advance guard, a barrier, against the Yellows., if they ever reformed.

"It's coming along; General de Trénan's organizing everything admirably—see what he's done! This country will serve us."

Claude listened, embarrassed. They reached more formless rubble, and in a vast quadrilateral of blackened walls, the dictator recognized the great pagoda where he had seen Ménières' gilded head alive for the last time, raised up in revolt against the violation, crying his disavowal. He shivered. And the idea of the violation rose up again, the savage sensuality of the bloody penetration, the ogival wombs dilated by the rigid assault columns, engulfed with brutal clamors. He was no longer vibrant, sought the enjoyment in his flesh, was astonished, and suddenly felt reborn, but gentler, more profound, under a distant firmament, among rocks rosy in the sunlight, on sand the color of the body...

Erodia...

And he considered the dislocated arches with a confident sadness. Through them, and beyond the hysterical stiffness of his male loins, he had touched something eternally virginal;

the buildings had become kisses, and the kisses had become almost-maternal caresses, up there, toward the curved and flat cradle.

Claude looked away, and closed his eyes. In the vibrations of light persisting beneath his eyelids, a dear head lived, a strong face with golden hair, and that head emerged from muddy and bloody serge. Ménières and Erodia were a single being. Love had spiritualized the death of the one and the life of the other, he perhaps having died in order that she might appear...

A profusion of debris strewed the soil, confused heaps piled up against the walls. Claude wanted to see. Old rusty weapons, scimitars and helmets with nasals, rifles with their twisted metalwork bristling next to stacks of cannonballs, spiked guns, torn coats of mail, cartridge-belts: an entire set of ancient armaments snatched from cadavers and thrown away scornfully. Ragged clothing lay in heaps, sometimes swollen by the semblance of bodies under their heavy dusty folds. Brown patches splattered them, stiffening the cloth, and an atrocious odor of cooled and insipid blood rose from all that wreckage.

Through the breaches, on waste ground, regular undulations of the soil could be seen: symmetrical blisters, revealing the recent excavation of trenches. A word from Dessort explained. They were the vestiges of mass graves dug in haste the day after the assault. A great many had been burned, the Hindus having demanded it. These had been filled with the Japanese, officers and soldiers, pell-mell, decomposition threatening under the torrid sky. They had immediately set to work on that repulsive clearance.

Claude imagined the scenes, like those back there in Europe once, after the bombs: all that meat in linen, the stretcher, the spades, the stink, the entire harvest of war...

He shrugged, drew away, and then smiled. It was necessary. At least it was the wherewithal to make admirable triumphs of ideology, especially now that he knew. It was over bodies, inevitably, that one pursued and caught up with the Idea.

But that cold flesh, carried in armfuls by the soldiers...

He thought about the warm and supple body of the Visitor, weakening under him, against him, experienced a frisson, and abruptly quit the rags, the weapons, the broken Buddha, the lamentable display of the ancient Orient. It was necessary to efface all that, to live in the present.

The present! To attain a certainty, the instant one knows that it must be, that it *is*, not *will be* or *has been*. The exhausting and unique research of the superior human being standing up in the incessant unfurling of the images of life! Claude had just had a certainty, and already it lacked continuity; it was important that it endured. He looked around; people were still preparing, it was still the intermediary of the temporary. When would they finish elaborating? He sensed disorder everywhere, a poorly equilibrated soul, like those palisades, those banks, those heaps of debris, those carts, those gesticulations of carpenters and laborers. And always, however, always that European method, exact, geometrical, applying uniform frames, transporting systems for the mind as for the body, that method served by impassive executives, believers in number and dosage, manipulating, planning, regulating, with closed faces and stiff hands, chemists, electricians, artillerymen, the surprising and icy wires of Modernity and Dynamism!

To them it was necessary to speak. Would they listen, occupied with successive ideals, to elevated words of long range, the synthetic words of effort?

Decidedly, on seeing them again, Claude rediscovered his disappointment, the anxieties of his convalescence a few months before, and the very evening of the declaration in Paris, when he had only tried to insinuate a minimal idea compared with the one that haunted him today. How alone he had felt that evening! But then, nothing ideological can be discussed essentially before one knows the fate of the forces of war, and in the deployment of those forces all controversy had calmed. Since then nothing: universal contentment, the intoxication of the ends of battles, the fever...

One single memory: the prophetic cry of Ménières before his disappearance in the mine blast...

And then, the virgin Orient, the Visitor moving, with a simple finger, all the genius of the leader of the Occident...

And how to make himself understood? How, first of all, fully to understand himself? For the contradiction was resident in the master's soul, and considering himself, he was frightened; regripped involuntarily by the spectacle of his own people, by the thousand attachments of habit, sobered of the intellectual dream of the virgin Cradle and a Statesman once again, he felt keenly that his conception was as yet only mental, and that its practical communication was not ready. Up there, when his gaze had met Erodia's, the essence of the idea had been sufficient for them, but here? The gray and insistent ideas of Médion, the ambiguous pupils of Dessort, the unknown of those men, their suspicion, surely, perhaps their enemy calculations, something finished between them and him, the alliance exalted in the battle and untied with her...

Those companions in murder might not follow him in the idea. They had followed him once, and remained as before. One ought not to change one's soul when one is a leader...

"The authority of the prophet always surpasses the others, but his renunciation is universal." The dear mouth that had said that!

"Prophet?" Claude confessed, smiling bitterly. "Fundamentally, what faith? I don't know anything."

A singular and perilous juncture! Was it necessary to return to Europe, to hope that the credit of the triumph, the magnetism of the soil, would cause his new thought to be accepted? But that was to isolate himself from the parallel action of Erodia. Beyond the seas, the Orient would seem so distant, the Cradle so theoretical. And there would be other projects out there, other constructions, other progress! No, it was on this bloody earth that the word had to be born; everything ought to be consummated here; it was necessary to return with all the work, with the coronation of his thought as with the triumphant sword, to say everything at once to the hosts of Europe, to return with an army won over to India, to change the soldiers into messengers of the good news, instead of meditating alone a project whose delay would be mortal.

I shall speak here, and everything will be decided here, Claude Laigle said to himself, proudly. *It's up to me to find the necessary words. After all, I have been further than all men, and people have followed me. They only understood gradually, but they obeyed first. The annexation of India, the union of the Aryan races, India no longer hated but allied, a sister against the Yellows, that is what will nourish their activity. Erodia will elaborate the conversion of the Hindus; I shall decree it in Europe. It is necessary that people understand that we are not going to kill an admirable force.*

He resolved to explain himself without delay.

The magnetism of the Visitor made him tremble; something holy drove him toward the peril; he rediscovered his lyrical energy; the inertia that had followed the conquest and had extenuated him came to an end. The great mental period of Anarchism, the first of his life, and the great period of the detestation of the yellow races, were about to be followed by a third, and definitive one: a period of love and ardent intellectuality, more beautiful and broader. And what grandeur there would be in the annunciation of the return, if he succeeded! It would no longer be the triumph of the illustrious Killer, the age-old and atrocious triumph; the man with the red hands would bring life! He would rediscover once again the voluptuousness of seizing the present, once again before growing old...

I'm going gray, and there's much to do, but am I strong enough?

Yes, since I believe! Claude avowed. *I see what it is necessary to say, and I alone can say it. In any case, it's simple, like everything abstract. I have detested the Orient, because of the yellow peril, and because of ideas opposed to the European world. The yellow peril is annihilated, and I recognize that my beliefs were ill-founded. I no longer hate India; I want it to be ours. Behind the Orient that I hate I have found another; where I imagined sterility there is life, and perfect life, mental life as developed as our mechanical life. At one end of the land of the white race there is an active force, at the other a meditative force. And the latter is the essential one, for it safeguards the common tradition of both, the Aryan tradition.*

The limit of the modern world, which I placed on the threshold of Hindustan, I shall extend to the Himalaya. I have tamed the land that was opposed to my present conception; now that the Yellows and their allies the rajahs no longer constrain these people, what I want from them is not passive obedience but their comprehension. Erodia will help them to understand. I must help my people to understand that new idea. I left with hatred, and because of her, I'm returning with love. That's clear.

My ministers see nothing here but colonial expansion, annexation, industrial profit and indemnity of war; it's up to me to make them see more nobly, to explain to them the ideological value of the recluses grouped in the Pamir. The Idea of the white races guarded by them, the virgin Orient that cannot die and which is the true one, above that of the Vedas and the revolutionaries of 1856. That is a politics based on a lyricism. Perhaps they'll smile, but we shall see.

He isolated himself for a few days, meditating haunted by the diaphanous Face, strong beneath the luxuriant hair, the face of Erodia, of Ménières, unified into that of the Adventure. Now it relaxed, that svelte figure, in the metaphysical sky of sprays of bright and colored verities, and those verities wanted to flourish in the open azure, between the sapphire of the zenith and he blood of the soil, powerfully...

He was decided.

Everything, in any case, seemed to be soliciting a denouement. Claude Laigle's internal fever left him all the lucidity of observation. He noticed the preoccupied expression of Médion, the subtle and attentive manner of Dessort, their reticence, their questions retained with difficulty, their coldness.

They were too intelligent not to sense the transformation of the master's thought, and in spite of the moral hierarchy established in Anarchism and strictly respected, the long sojourn in Hindustan, the immensely extended vice-regency and the enervation of the war and the organization gave them a liberty of appearance greater than in the councils of Europe. They too had developed, affirmed in their theories, they too were forces, adjacent but individual, and the interest of the difficult contest impassioned Claude.

He understood that he had been more the master before the declaration of war, when it was only a project that was in the mind; since those men had contributed greatly to its success, they had appropriated the thought and action of a promoters; the Adventure belonged to them as well as to him. What he was about to present to them was authorized less by a prestige now shared as the mystery of another conception still virginal in his mind. Thus the second stage of the conquest would be elaborated.

After the passionate rise of the departure, until the assault on Delhi, the descent of the Adventure, glimpsed in Erodia's eyes during the first encounter, had plunged into mental regions under the apparent inertia succeeding the war, and then stopped at the Cradle; now it was about to rise again, the Adventure having become ideological, and return with the army to the Occident having touched the unforgettable earth.

Days passed in cautious consultation, in urgent regulation, in diplomatic concerns, as if he adversaries were drawing away before the decisive words. They observed one another in the councils, and as before, the impassive General de Trénan remained silent among them, with his cold and ironic expression, interjecting rare polished and mordant remarks.

The terrible old man was worn away internally, the life was retreating from that ivory face; the long precise hands no longer trembled but were placed flat, as if dead, on the pointed knees. The shaven head with the cruel blue eyes was decidedly that of a priest—the priest of a religion now abandoned. A carriage ferried the old man continually through the artillery batteries, along the rows of cannons; he was almost incapable of getting down, but he leaned out, extending his arms, touching the breeches of the guns as he passed by, handling the rockets and detonators, obsessed with ballistics and explosives, dying of his passion for the shell now that that frightful idea, his idea, no longer sprang from his will toward the horizons.

Claude considered that man with an indefinable pity. And Dessort and Médion had changed too; the socialisator's feminine smile was twisted; his velvety eyes were tarnished, and the face of the engineer had thinned, the temples hollowed out, the forehead striated, the bone-structure of the nose more curtly prominent. Claude felt weary himself, although younger; the neuralgia of the heart recurred from time to time. Only the voices remained the same.

Oh, the aftermath of conflicts in middle age! And Europe was so far away!

They all considered one another with esteem and dread, not daring to commence, to say the thing that would ignite everything. But it was said, however, of its own accord, among the futilities, one evening, as they were regulating an arrangement of colonization, of permissions to set up trading posts and establish manufactories on the cost of Gujarat. Dessort insisted, showing certain economic and industrial advantages and several times already the dictator had replied: "Accepted," in an indifferent tone, his mind absent, when a remark by Médion caused him to raise his head.

"And then, for the posts in the valley of the Indus, the location designated in excellent; it requires an entrenched camp, surveillance is important. The populations are still restless, we're already having enough trouble establishing ourselves in Bombay, which became a Hindu city again a few years after the expulsion of the English. It's necessary that all that ceases once and for all, that the Europeans are the masters; and I'm also thinking about the upper Indus and the Kashmir region. There are germinations of ideas there, in spite of everything, that it's necessary to render impossible. In addition, the profits to be extracted from the mines and restricted salaries..."

"I no longer accept," said Claude, curtly. "Your expressions, Médion, are those of a dominator. My thought is different; I want allies. I only want to take advantage of the restriction of salaries as a measure compatible with the simple life of the indigenes, not as exploitation. We haven't made war uniquely to enrich merchants. And then, we no longer understand one another, I fear, with regard to the 'germination of ideas.' I don't perceive those ideas as you perceive them."

"However," said Médion, "these tribesmen..."

"They aren't 'tribesmen,' Médion. You're neglecting ethnology. They're Aryans, like us, and I desire to treat them as such, with commercial laws analogous to ours, and established rights."

"Your conception of Europeanism had been greatly modified, then?" Médion replied.

"And your conception of anarchistic individualism?" retorted Claude Laigle. "Return to it—you're forgetting it somewhat."

"I've helped enough to render it possible politically..."

"Morally."

"No. Morally...that's your affair, but mine is political...in order not to forget," said Médion, coldly. "But until now, I only considered it applicable to the Confederation of Central Europe, not to it enemies."

"You mean the Orientals?"

"Evidently, since it's to safeguard anarchistic individualism against the enterprises of Oriental fatalism that we've followed you here."

"It was primarily to safeguard the material interests of modernism against a coalition of Yellows that you accepted the war, and it's in those material interests that you've always thought and still think," said Claude.

"So be it—I was talking about your abstract point of view."

"Resume yours, Médion. Mine has changed. I no longer consider the Orientals in the original fashion, and I separate the Hindus clearly from the 'yellow peril,'"

"They marched against us with the Japanese, summoned by their rajahs."

"I'm not talking about the Orient of the rajahs. That's finished, and the fatalism too. I'm talking about a new Orient, with a thinking more appropriate to serve and enrich our colonists. I accept that thinking today, and that's why, far from being frightened of 'germinations of ideas,' I oppose the creation of entrenched camps, especially in the upper Indus."

"I'm beginning to glimpse," Médion said, tranquilly, "that this...thinking and its penetration are doubtless the result of your recent voyage."

"Yes," said Claude, rising to his feet, pale but also tranquil. "I haven't traveled, personally, uniquely to study where camps or factories might be established in the upper Indus."

"I have no intention, however, of establishing any higher up—in the desert regions of the Pamir, for instance. There's no commerce possible there, and it might trouble the communities, whose ideas are agreeable to you, metaphysically speaking."

Médion's voice did not reveal any sarcasm, and yet there was a terrible silence. After a few seconds, Dessort intervened, as a conciliator.

"In any case," he said, "it's a matter of mining exploitations to protect, and there can't be any question of the Pamir. The projects concern lower regions..."

"The mines don't matter to me," Claude Laigle put in, dryly.

"As for entrenched camps," Dessort went on, "it's a matter of emplacement very different, in sum, from the upper Indus, half way between the coast and Kashmir..."

"Distant or not, I don't see any real utility in them," said the dictator. "The posts distributed from Gujarat to Delhi and to Cawnpore suffice for a military supremacy that the northern provinces aren't disputing with us, having no armies. The sources of the Indus and the Ganges can remain free of surveillance, and as for the surveillance of ideas, since that expression has been pronounced, I've already said that the ideas coming from the Pamir or elsewhere don't appear to me to be contradictory to ours. It's pointless to want to isolate central India from them by a military regime, whether it's installed in the regions themselves or lower down, between them and the Deccan. That constraint, disguised or avowed, doesn't suit me."

"But it's not exactly a matter of a constraint of that sort," Dessort objected. "The project simply concerns the anticipation of offensive returns dangerous to the security of our industries."

"You know full well that those offensive returns can't be produced in the high regions," said Claude Laigle. And I know how that material surveillance, costly and superfluous in itself, could rapidly be combined with another, with your prefects and your theories. Do you think that I don't sense your thinking—yours and Médion's. Do you think that I haven't divined the mental preoccupation that's been haunting you since my voyage, and which reappears in your attention to detail?"

All three of them looked at one another.

"There's certainly one that's been haunting you since the same voyage," said Médion, curtly. "Well, yes, we have something to say to one another: your idea is rubbing against ours too closely, I imagine, for us not to come into confrontation."

"I'm ready for that, although I don't know if you are," said Claude Laigle disdainfully. "I could speak only in Europe, to the legates of the Confederation, but I'll content your curiosity sooner..."

He interrupted himself, considering the two men. They were sitting down, their gazes cold, their attitude defensive and contracted. Something tragic was occurring. Claude shrugged his shoulders,

"Is it your curiosity, or your summons, that I ought to say? You seem to be waiting...do you intend to judge me? I don't know what indefinable expression astonishes me in those eyes that you're raising toward me. I can shut up."

"You ought not to count on the assembly of legates," Médion replied, simply.

"That's true, but I believe I'm speaking here to collaborators, to friends...." Brusquely, Claude Laigle said: "Come on, Médion, Dessort, let's drop this tone between ourselves. My thought is entirely peaceful, and if we're not in sympathy, at least let's esteem one another and let's not talk of accounts to settle. You were much closer to me during the conflict, because our logic was in accord; but now it's a matter of continuing, of accomplishing intellectually, and your support is perhaps more precious to me than ever. Forget the dictator, see the man. Yes, we have something to say to one another. You've thought apart from me and I've thought apart from you. Let's bring our conceptions together, let's bring our legates a unified system, a moral result after the material result. What my voyage has revealed to me, I'll tell you, and afterwards, we'll examine together what the future might be."

He stood up, resolutely, and spoke. He spoke for a long time, with an enthusiastic eloquence, the energy of a lucid conviction, an infinite unfurling of images and thoughts ornamenting one central idea: the idea of the Cradle orientating modernism, taking away its hatred and its dryness, creating, above the cult of mechanical progress, the cult of the Aryan race, giving the war a higher conclusion, am expansion of sensibility and love, a tradition of ethnological simplicity finally sustaining a certainty for all, a return to the primordial laws of evolution. With broad violent and ardent strokes, he depicted the modern ideal, safeguarded by the recluses of the virgin Orient, and without pronouncing Erodia's name, his words, addressed to the beauty of the forces of life, trembled with passion and tenderness as if he were holding, in his empty open hands, the very body of the Visitor, become the immaterial envelope of the Adventure. At any rate, his heart overflowed his mind, one vivifying the other—and he did not feel that the voluptuous expression with which he was ornamenting the logical truth undermined it.

The two ministers, pensively, listened to him less than they considered him, pale and enthusiastic, entirely vibrant with that great interior sonority that rose from the depths of his being, and of which the burning jet came to crystallize on their cold and impenetrable souls. He sometimes had an intuition of that, and, excited in all his combative and fervent nature, wanted to vanquish that mute antipathy to his lyricism with even more lyricism. Suddenly seized by the demon of speech, making an abstraction of himself, of the persuasion undertaken, of the hostility sensed, he yielded to the superior perversity, and said everything, because a prophet ecstasized by beauty in itself, with the exclusivism of the man of dreams who always opens an abyss between the world and his vision.

Asia entire took its revenge in his fatal and admirable intoxication, reappeared alive in that son finally returned, incarnated in him its contemplative centuries, the immensity of its torrid skies, the immortal renaissance of its metaphysics meditated among the palms. And the two moderns, through the master's words, glimpsed her, their enemy, the luxurious queen of the ancient world, rising up once again to face the irreconcilable Occident in the person of that pale man who had led them to the idol and had become her priest, seduced by the ancient world.

An excitement gripped them too, but inversely, the intuition that above the three bodies, the invisible drama was playing out of two essential and contradictory verities. The original antagonism of the act and the dream, which only the abstract laws of the universe can resolve, and which it is not given to human beings to unite. And each of Claude's phrases awoke in them an echo of a dissimilar consciousness, augmenting the irreparable sentiment of an antinomy, separating the two conceptions emerged from the same fact of conquest further and further.

The eloquence of the master operated upon them, but by making them remember the very foundations of their adverse life, and the fracture that had been snaking for months in those three arrogant and silent souls suddenly burst, becoming a gulf. Speech acted above them, simplifying the situation by the divorce of the individual paths. And between the two seated men and the one who, standing, was pronouncing the definitive rupture by invoking union, the sensation of intellectual death rose and floated, inertly, like the great exhausted old man who, his material strength extinct before that conflict of mental forces, listened mutely in his armchair, waiting for the decision to be made for him, the hands falling, the glabrous face with the cold gray eyes leaning over the golden collar...

The dictator fell silent.

For several minutes no one moved. One might have thought that they were all waiting for an invisible being to leave. And Claude, confusedly, sensed that it was the old amity that slowly vanished with the vibrations of the irreparable words.

The faces of the two ministers remained glacial, fixed in attention. Claude's insistent pupils sought theirs in vain. And as the unreal specter dissolved, the eyelids were raised, as if relieved. The eyes finally met; Médion's lips parted, and he said: "Is that all?"

"Yes," said Claude, accepting the terrible doubt.

Dessort raised a hand, swung according to his custom to the rhythm of his nonchalant voice.

"The very considerable conception that is yours, Master, seems to me, whatever luster your eloquence adds to it, to deviate singularly from the very meaning of our initial effort, and is perhaps founded on a...shall I say hasty?...appreciation of the Oriental mind. I don't contradict the utility of the hypotheses, without going so far as to summarize them in a fact—and it's a matter here of such a considerable modification of ideas that it would lead us almost immediately to facts, privileges conceded to the Hindus, even participation in federative consultations—for in sum, if I've understood you correctly, it wouldn't only be a matter of material rights, but of rights of mentality.

"Now, I confess that the soul of this country, even directed by the occult influence of the communities of the North, does not appear to me, at least for a long time henceforth, sufficiently clearly compatible with the European soul for us to be able to present to the legates, on our return, a guarantee permitting the immediate concession of intellectual rights. I will even add that that eventuality is distant, and that in any case, it is necessary to wait for a more complete assurance, on the part of the communities, of aims identified with ours..."

"Wait...gain time...," said Claude. "No. I wouldn't have spoken if I didn't feel that this matter ought to be settled immediately. There are links, by the very fact of the mother-idea of my project, and the longer we wait, the more difficult those links will be to retire. It's immediately after the ruination of the ancient India that we ought to awaken the sentiment of the new India and quit the enemy attitude in its regard. As for the communities, I can pronounce that I will answer for them. I told you when we quit the Pamir that the alliance is made, mentally. What does Médion think?"

"It's quite simple," said Médion. "I think that there's nothing here but hypotheses and more hypotheses, and that we can't return to Europe, which has been bled white for two years for an idea proposed by all of us, in order to declare that that idea no longer suits us, and propose in exchange a hypothesis."

"I thought I was expressing a verity," retorted Claude Laigle.

"A verity of what order? A factual verity?"

"No, a verity of mentality."

"It doesn't involve, thus far at least, a factual verity; and that kind of verity, I call metaphysical—which is to say, interesting and seductive but worthless. Yes, worthless, and it's clearly evident that it was born here, in this land that can't produce others and which has died because of that, as much and more than because of us."

"It isn't dead, and it's that very new life that I'm bringing you."

"Yes, I know, the virgin Orient…but the experience has been harsh, for centuries. This land propitious to enchantments charges forms easily; the Occidental consciousness will see the ancient monster behind the new face. It will see that your 'mental verity' is the dream of a summer, and that it can only make those kinds of dreams."

"The dream of a summer?" said Claude Laigle proudly. "I hear you. Are you insinuating that I'm bringing the counsels of Erodia here? Go on, dare to say it!"

"I shall not bring into such a grave discussion the consideration of a woman, who is, in any case, intelligent and who, if well-directed and carefully monitored, might be useful to us later."

"Useful to *us*? Who do you mean by *us*?"

"I still mean Europe, you and all of our people."

"But I don't mean that anymore."

"Us…and you—so that makes two, now?"

The simple and terrible assertion fell between the three men. In his corner, General de Trénan shuddered weakly. Médion and Claude measured one another with their gazes, enemies now."

"That's one statement too many, Médion."

"You forced me to pronounce it, Claude Laigle."

"You misunderstand me. I spoke too soon, I believe, just now. As for Erodia, this is the respect in which *we* and *you* make two, as you put it. She will not be *useful* to me as you think she will be *useful* to you. She is outside utilizations, she will not propagandize your idea or mine; she is and will remain free. But it happens that her thought and mine are in accord, and will act separately.

"That's fine, with regard to your hypothesis. But as for facts, if the communities and their leader are not the couriers in India of the Occidental modernist spirit, they are indeed of no use, to you any more than to us. They will vegetate. And Europe will find it good that they are monitored—oh, not rigorously, simply to avoid the singular attempts to which inertia can push overly searching consciousness, the possible…materializations that minds overheated by solitary metaphysics might attempt."

"Is it in your name that you speak?"

"I believe I am speaking, this time, in the name of the entire Confederation, of its need for peace, of its fatigue with dreams succeeding dreams and throwing it into adventures when it ought to be fortifying its position."

"Still your refusal of general ideas, then? You haven't advanced since our conversation in Paris on the eve of the war?"

"I've advanced in my direction, and you in yours."

"So, your 'universe of chemistry,' your science, your exclusive Occidentalism, and nothing more?"

"So, one is an ideologue when one is Head of State?" pronounced Médion, dryly.

"Well, so be it. We'll see whether one can be both. It's my very idea that you're refusing?"

"Europe will refuse it too, I assure you. There's no point in going as far as a disavowal. It's Anarchism itself that you're compromising if you persist."

"What is it, however, if not an ideology?"

"It has become a State, and demands facts. The Parliaments have been blown up; that's a fact. We have ruined the yellow peril, in order to be able to work tranquilly at home; that's another fact. Don't excite us to emerge therefrom at the very moment when we're about to go back; that would be a third fact, which would annul the other two. That's what Europe will say, and you can't go against her will; you're the master but you won't be any longer if she refuses to follow you."

"She has had faith in me."

"She won't any longer. I regret having to tell you such things."

"Don't insist, Médion. I sense—I know—what your regret is worth."

"It's sincere, Claude Laigle. But you're taking us too far, and I can only attribute it to the influence of this pernicious sky and this accursed soil, where abstract systems have germinated a cerebral aberration to which a woman is no stranger."

"Ah! You're coming back to that!"

"I repeat that by 'a woman' I mean the detestable Idea that she represents. The rest doesn't concern me."

"But admit, then," cried the dictator, "that you hate the virgin Orient as much and more than the old, because you're afraid of it!"

"Yes, I'm afraid of it, of the ancient monster with multiple faces, since it can deform a man like you. The Occident is irreconcilable with the State you dream of aggrandizing. Whether or not we set out from your Cradle, we won't return there in thought; out there we've made a new life. May it remain desert! And may its reclusive metaphysicians, whose secret correspondence is so zealous, not talk too loudly about the security of their phalanstery! You ask whether I hate it, this poorly killed Orient that is reborn and is absorbing you? Yes, I hate it, like the abstract laws that oppose the active will. And you—am I mistaken?—confess that you now hate the Occident!"

"Médion!" Dessort intervened, alarmed.

But Claude Laigle, startled, cried to the minister who had become a judge: "Well, yes, I hate it, if that's what it is! I hate it, your modernism, your labeled world, prostrate before I don't know what mechanical progress, what ideal of exact science torturing thought, edifying and order and a harmony on silence and blood. After the kings, after the bourgeoisie, after the tyranny of money, now there's the tyranny of Dynamism, and I shouldn't detest it? But it's like the others, it kills egotistically like the others, it has the number for a fetish as the others had the crown, the ballot or the check-book, and what you call progress is putting a hideous plaything in the place of those who have served too much.

"Your science is killing sensibility, and I don't want it, your life fragmented into formulae, I don't want your aluminum cities where firm and inexorable faces go by beneath electric lights—I don't want it! Your Occident, with its regu lated barbarity, deprived even of the free instinct that is so beautiful here, I refuse it; you can arrange it as you wish, with your compasses, look in your retorts to see with what oxides you'll transform its rottenness into wellbeing! But if I've had to accept power and all the responsibilities of my life to be the great leader of your mechanisms, the accountant of your derisory equations, I shall go away laughing, so ridiculous, even more than odious, do I find you all, engineers, the bizarre population of geometry that I shall treat as Gulliver did!

"Has it taken you until now to understand that I wanted to do something extraordinary with you? On the evening of the declaration of war, when I said that the sublime of a politics was the realization a dream, you didn't understand, and you threw yourselves immediately into the Adventure in order to give a fine role to your torpedoes, your telephones, your gyroscopes, to all your means, which you made into ends, and also to enrich the merchants, you offer yourselves colonial theft on a grand scale, to carry to other skies the prestige of the modern as you understand it, the strict gentleman with his pince-nez, his notebook and his syphilis!

"And you think, perhaps, that after having led you to ideological war against the Parliaments, I'd compensate you by permitting your avidity this vast gallimaufry, under the pretext of protecting yourselves, permitting you the reflective elaboration of a new consciousness? Get away! You haven't understood anything of what I see, but I'm bringing you forces more elevated than your technical perfections, and you'll understand, or you'll yield; those forces won't be belied; they'll hold sway in spite of you; I shall use the rest of a life, not caring whether it ought to be yours, in crying out to them, in prophesying to them.

"I shall address myself to that which is eternal in humans, the heart, the instinct, and I shall address myself to the baser parts if the mentality has been too poisoned by your dogmatism, but it's necessary that your fetishization of the number, you who speak of mine, goes with the others into the red mud were the obsolete ideals stagnate, the dung-heap beneath humankind!

"Oh, you persist until I speak for myself, you want me finally to say what I've thought for a long time about the fashion in which Europe, at least as you've shaped it, uses the Anarchism that I gave it, and you think that I'm going to accept that everything continues to go on as before, the petty trafficking, the petty formulae, the transportable methods, all your apparatus of progress? Well, now you know what I think.

"We had, in coming here, a stake, India. We'll have another out there, and we'll see which of us, you or me, will raise up that great mass of human beings bogged down in error and throw it back into the current of the river of life. In the meantime, I'm still the master, and I know where I'm going. You'll silence your suspicions, you'll give way until my return to Europe, and you'll obey me!"

He stopped dead, terrible. Médion and Dessort inclined impassively.

And suddenly, a voice that they scarcely recognized rose up behind them, stammering: "The shell...the shell...was a guarantee... It was worth the trouble..."

They turned round. The bloodless face of General de Trénan, leaning over the golden collar, showed vitreous eyes, the pupils half veiled with gray under the narrowing of the eyelids; the thin lips were colorless. The tall, thin old man was weakening after the work done. They drew closer.

"A guarantee..."

His mouth formed a rictus, and remained inert. Outside, a sudden racket burst forth, a dull rumble of mounted batteries passing at the gallop; the ground trembled, and the dangling hands of the cadaver, long waxen hands, stirred slightly with that vibration.

XI. The Ellipse

The veritable funeral of General de Trénan was to take place on the return to Europe; no ceremony, beyond an embalming in the presence of a few mute witnesses, announced officially that the master of the artillery was dead. The hasty building of forts and the multiple cares of administration attenuated the effect of that loss. Already, the idea of the reintegration with the Occident, the conquest terminated, was floating over the army. The soldier stood aside before the civil element, the colonist and the engineer taking up their roles, and the disappearance of the commander-in-chief had less impact on minds. There was no funeral eulogy, except for the orders of the day and an imposed silence.

Claude, self-absorbed, left the expedition of current affairs to the ministers. With the great murmur of material disarray that was agitating everywhere, his determination faltered, sensing a disaggregation brewing. In order to get a grip on himself he shut himself away.

The accumulation of decisive circumstances rose around him, stifling him and keeping him upright at the same time. The demonic Adventure, alive and shrill in itself, demanded its solution, developed to the extreme without concern for interior ravages, and he sensed it stirring in his flesh like a child, or the millions of microbes of a disease ready to burst forth. There was nothing more to defer; everything was imposing; everything was coming to term; the hypotheses had expired; life had simplified things terribly.

The unreal bouquet of verities, unbound by the Idea from the metaphysical sky, had let its flowers fall, their germination had blossomed, insistent and devouring, and it was necessary to die in the torpor of those perfumes or to uproot the spray once again with a masterly fist.

The situation was complex, but so synthetic that Claude's mental system adapted to it with an absolute precision, and he had the sentiment of being confronted, without the hope of escape but also without deception, by a double obstacle, material and intellectual. At least that clarity of the peril stiffened him now, with a clear gaze, to envisage his despair; in the midst of his anguish, the perversity of logic created within him a strange joy, the intoxication of living intensely, exceptionally, a drama of unknown proportions in which he as the essential actor. The cerebration was killing him as it exalted him. He felt driven into a corner, concentrated in himself.

What should he do? In bringing about the irreparable argument between the ministers and himself, had he clarified the situation or sealed it forever? The problem had at least been posed, but had not the negative solution been pronounced at the same time? Was everything finished, or was everything about to begin? It had been necessary to speak, evidently, and Claude did not regret anything, sensing that evasions, unworthy in themselves and repugnant to his nature, would in any case have been futile or even harmful.

The new Idea was one that did not admit petty means, and which had to be presented in its totality or never. It was, therefore, in accordance with his nobility, his logic and his future that Claude had acted in speaking—but he also sensed clearly that the ministers' refusal was decisive, and that the European soul, progressive and modernist, had passed in their response; the quarrel with the ministers was not a difference of reasoning but a formal antagonism of races. Europe would not ratify his position; either it would be necessary to force it to do so, or resign.

Dictator, having served in their interests, resign when it's a matter of explaining to them the mother-idea of so much fatigue? Get away! Claude said to himself, revolted. *I'd be too forgetful of the ancestor Nietzsche and "the aristocracy of masters." I shall fight—like the sovereigns of the old times, but as a true anarchist. Deep down, these people are still socialists. It's the mental habit of the masses that is standing up against me.*

And he avowed that he would anticipate them. The face of Erodia appeared to his mind's eye. "The authority of the prophet surpasses all others, but his renunciation is universal." Well, yes, a prophet, and a modern prophet, choosing between authority and renunciation. He accepted the alternative internally.

What can that do to me? I have nothing left to lose if I lose my conception. They'll understand and give in or I shall...cease.

Life, with its violent forms, as in the time of the bombs, as in the taking of Delhi, raised a pitiless landscape in his soul.

After all, I've struggled alone, or very nearly, against the Parliaments, when I was young; I'll begin again, as an individual leading the collectivities. And will I be without adherents? That remains to be seen.

The revolution of the masters, then, after that of the people?

Well, if they don't understand, regardless...why not? It seems to me that I'm only now recognizing myself as an anarchist. The masters, that was what the bosses once called themselves, but I'm against the material bosses and for the ideological bosses. That's a religion in the fashion of the positivist calendar; it's a trifle silly, but people only find it so when others want to impose it on them, when it's in a silly form...

He smiled, sadly, listening to two contradictory voices, the mass, isolated, the brutes from which everything germinates, and the sterile, who understand and lead the brutes, the antinomy that had rotted all societies since the primal era.

And then what? There'll be blood again, they'll kill the masters; they always kill the masters, and yet it's the instinct of every anonymous individual to be a master. Is it my fault if they led me there? It's not me who's demanding, it's the Idea that wants it, and ideas are more powerful than men, more powerful than them and more powerful than me. Except that it's always necessary to attain them through the flesh, to extirpate them messily, like children, in blood...

Always that red glue, which sticks, and also causes the forces to skid into one another...

It's never tidy, as soon as one acts. But it's that, or submit, with a heap of thoughts in the belly that want to get out and call you a coward...

He sensed that he was not the master of the choice, that within him the Idea was identified with instinct, which could only be stifled along with his respiration.

Too bad, too bad—it will come out. It's up to me to see that it doesn't cost too dearly, that the childbirth isn't too messy. They're expecting, back there, another infant, which I've promised them. Well, one can be mistaken. I'll explain, that's all. Will they disinherit the child because the physician anticipated another? I'm very much afraid that they won't want to hear anything; with their modernism, they imagine that the Orient is antinomic to them...

All that's still a matter of customs. Modernism, to them, is still frock-coats and phonographs; understood like that, how stupid modernism is! To think that I believed in it—me! Yes, I believed in it, in spite of everything; I realize that I was a prisoner of the habits and the décor of Paris. Oh, the décor! But at least I'm liberated from that now; they're still there.

They want to give machines and top hats to the Orientals, and that doesn't worry me, but as for admitting the Orientals as their own, never! They invoke the rights of conquest, the money to be made from colonial trafficking. They'll nobly grant the telephone and the black suit to the Hindus, while making the observation that it's an act of generosity, but it won't be out of the desire to give them something better than they have, but in the spirit of domination, of leveling, of socialism! And they'll believe, because they're dupes themselves that they've brought the Occidental soul here.

Oh, businessmen, accountants! And the foundation of all that is always the old hatred of ideas, always the execration of those secret leaders that inject them, like sperm, into the bourgeois belly, prepare their descendancy, and are always obliged, in the end, to emerge violently, with blood...

All that turns in the same circle. And there isn't any reason for it to finish, that's the grandeur of humanity, it's with that that they want to make things!

He plunged himself into successive projects. To fight head on if Europe was obstinate? Dangerous and impractical.

It was necessary, then, to assemble the aristocracy of masters, to found a State within a State? Might as well found it here, then! He glimpsed the whiteness of the communities among the roseate rocks and the palms, the sand of the Pamir with the color of the body, Erodia, an inaccessible realm, conserving the traditions of the white races in their very Cradle, and felt the desire to let go of everything out there, the land of mechanism, to fade into the dream of happiness—and then started.

Oh, no! If I return to the Cradle, it won't be as a prodigal son, alone and naked; Erodia would ask me what I had done as a son, she'd reject me; that would give the lie to the Idea, the laughter of Europe would arrive here, and if we resisted, the Idea wouldn't resist. Not to mention that the posts of the upper Indus and Médion's plans wouldn't leave you tranquil in decline for long...

More blood, decidedly, whichever way I turn...and then, if I fail, at last Erodia will remain intact. She'll continue, her recluses will choose another, later. Blood for blood, it's better that it's shed back there...

Everything pressed him to return to the Occident. After the real forces that he had led away, the abstract forces that he would take back, the ebb and flow of the same red tide.

His conquest had become exclusively cerebral. From a group of facts, it had become a group of ideas, and all those ideas, born of a desire to bring him back morally to the Orient, united nevertheless to take him away from it materially. There was an inexplicable contradiction there.

I'm really quite disorientated, Claude said to himself, and suddenly burst out laughing. *Disorientated! Oh, words and their justice! Yes, I've 'lost the Orient' in wanting to 'lose North.' Disorientated? Of course, since I'm a man of the Occident! Is Médion right, then? How droll it is!*

He interrogated himself, almost amused.

So, he said to himself, *everything is lined up to take me away from here, and yet I came here and found here my true reason for being; so, what led me here in spite of everything? Was it some absurd law? There are no absurd laws. It wasn't*

315

colonial politics, nor the annihilation of the yellow peril; they're apparent and circumstantial reasons, now laws. What is that law? I realize that it isn't my personal will. Oh, yes, Claude the willful, tell yourself that it was you alone! You wouldn't have been sufficient, you'd already be dead if you wanted to offer yourself to that dream of your own accord. It's a law that's amusing itself in leading you and giving you the necessary strength of endurance...but what is it? I can see that it's what's leading me, but where is it taking me? And yet they have to be reclusive! What a singular thing! In the first sense, I can conceive the Adventure very clearly, and in the second I perceive it even better. But between the two slopes, in the present, where I am now, what am I, who is asking the question, going to do?

The obstinate mutism of destiny confronted Claude like an extraordinary wall.

It's annoying! If I occupied myself with theology it couldn't be more unknowable—and yet these questions have a material basis; it's an ethnological matter, after all, there are methods! Oh yes, methods! They lead to contraries, and the contraries form identity. And to think that moderns of Médion's sort live in tranquility dreaming of a universe of methods! What a pity! How petty that is! Do I believe in God?

He smiled.

No... Yes... I don't know any more. It depends. And to think that I'm not skeptical and that I'm bursting with faith in the midst of all these people...

He was crazy for days, like a metaphysician constructing a theory. But if a theory is false, it remains interesting, and it is only a matter of making another while awaiting a third. That is dilettantism. Whereas, given that the situation was complicated by too many material interests, and active energy, how was it permissible to be mistaken? Misfortune was waiting at the door, and he did not have much time in which to decide. The ministers must be studying their plans too, and as their theory was much more rudimentary, they would move more rapidly in the examination of the measures to be taken.

Pensively, Claude walked the streets of the poor quarters, obsessed with the Idea, gazing around him vaguely, almost as Newton must have been gazing the instant before the apple's fall.

One evening, at dusk, cries caused him to look up. Children, having taken possession of a large empty barrel, were climbing on top of it and amusing themselves by making it roll, maintaining their equilibrium by means of a continual tread. Suddenly, one of them, unable to maintain himself, slipped and fell, and the heavy barrel passed over him, half stifling him. At the moment when Claude looked up he saw the little body caught under the curvature of the thick staves, lying underneath the round mass, which continued to rotate. An image struck him and he went pale.

Already, the other children were lifting to the weeping and bruised child and taking him away, amid the remonstrations of the women who had hastened forward. Claude drew away, almost running, and went back into his apartment, pushing past the sentries.

That child is me, and the great round mass that passes over him, that throws him underneath simply by virtue of the fact that it continue to rotate...is the earth!

Slowly, the idea awakened by the analogy rose up symbolically, took form, became a specter, the specter of the Adventure itself sitting facing the frightened dictator. A certainty emerged from it by degrees.

But that's it! Imbecile that I was! he suddenly exclaimed. *What have I come to do, what idea has led me here in spite of all the circumstances that are now taking me away and casting me down? What did I see descending again with Erodia's eyelids in our first meeting? But it's quite simple! It's the movement of the earth continuing. It's the hemisphere that rises around the axis and descends again, and I'm descending again with it! And I'm caught underneath! In the previous rotation I rose with it toward the Orient, and now it's necessary that I follow it and pass underneath it, in order to reappear on the other side. And if I remain still, like that child*

317

whom the ground stopped and prevented him from making the compete rotation, I'll be crushed, like him! There's no fixed point!

What have I come to do? I can see it clearly now. I've come as Napoléon wanted to do, but he stopped in Egypt, and I've succeeded, I've been as far as India, like Alexander. And how is it that I've succeeded materially where Napoléon failed, where Alexander's attempt had no serious duration, where the domination of the British East India Company was broken in 1856? How is it that I've succeeded materially? I understand the pride of my ministers; that fact consecrates for them the right of the Occident to tame Asia. But what they can't comprehend, the poor fellows, what it will be necessary for me to explain to them, and what they'll never admit, is that my material success is an irony greater than Napoléon's failure, for if the destinies of the Orient have permitted me, against all probability, to come here, it's in order to be caught by this very country. The Occident thought it was sending a conqueror but it has only sent them one follower more, a hostage! I've come here, yes but to change my soul, and it's once again that the Orient is obtaining the upper hand. Once it rejected the men of the West; now it's welcoming them, but modifying them!

The law that has pushed me here is the terrible law of evolution—not the evolution of races, but astronomical evolution. And that's where we'll never understand one another, the Europeans and me! What has brought me is the Ellipse, the fleeing curvature of the Ellipse, which governs the course of terrestrial evolution, and I'm making the tour! I've been brought, I'm being taken away! And I thought I was led by the natural expansion of the Occident! No! That was an illusion. The movement of the world has thrown me into the Orient; that's why I've succeeded where my predecessors failed, and I can't maintain myself any more than the child n the barrel just now!

He stopped, bathed in a cold sweat, a sudden idea opening up.

"Also, it's not natural," he said, in a low voice.

He went on, slowly:

"What's happening is just. My conquest, such as I undertook it, wasn't natural. The failure of my predecessors ought to have shown me that. I thought that modern perfection would enable me to succeed; I was short-sighted, and the immediate political interest hid the abstract consequences of my contact from me. I made an error. The perfection of weapons and the State wasn't in question, they only served to drive me further into an impasse, and instead of succeeding more than Napoléon or the English, I've simply taken failure to its extreme. My conquest is *abnormal*."

The decisive words were born, one by one, from his mind, hesitated on the edge of his lips, and then emerged— and his life went with them.

He said to himself then:

Abnormal, yes. I understand now the unknown disturbance that hasn't ceased to haunt me since the departure from Paris, and which reappeared as soon as the racket of the war eased and let me think. But I couldn't see; it was necessary for me to go to the depths of the error, from me to come here for that. What irony! My conquest is abnormal, because it's contrary to the movement of forces, which is from East to West. Like the child on the barrel I've leapt on to the world at the moment when it was passing in one of the directions of the ellipse, and now, by virtue of the natural force, I'm falling again.

I knew full well that there was something contrary to nature in that success. The movements of conquest are always produced from the Orient toward the Occident, in a quantity infinitely superior to the others; and neither Alexander nor Napoléon, nor the Crusades nor the British, have been able to succeed. They were going against the Ellipse, and the rotation had brought them back. I've made the movement of moving closer to a hearth, and that made me think I'd succeeded; it has taken me much further in the inverse direction, but I've been thrown back all the more rapidly in the true one.

The Europe that is drawing me back might well install it-self here materially, but mentally, she can't; it's still the Orient that will come toward her; and she senses that obscurely and hates it. The Oriental descends toward her from the height of the plateaux, and arrives by the conquest the old Aryan genius brings it: the flood of Tartar, Hunnish, Finnish or Mongol hordes created the Franks, or the Russians, or the Slavs, but the contrary current is impossible. The Aryan genius doesn't move back toward its source; that makes no sense.

He interrupted himself, pensively:

"Was Erodia wrong, then?"

No. She isn't asking us to come back. Her idea is greater, and unassailable. She's simply asking that we remember the Cradle, that we don't forget that we're the sons of the virgin Orient. She told me that: our coming is neither a hindrance not a help. She isn't afraid, nor desirous, of a real presence, but she wants a mental presence. There are neither Orientals not Occidentals from her point of view; there are Aryans. It's because of that idea that she also told me that I'd come back. She's right. I came back to the Cradle, but it wasn't with my armies, by way of them or for them that I came back. I was reasoning politically, to prevent the yellow peril and destroy the India of the rajahs, which had also forgotten the Cradle, but I was wrong to give Europe the hatred of the Orient.

I've broken, by my attempt, a cosmogonic law, the immutable law of the Westward evolution of the East. That's why my conquest is absurd and can't last. The more my lieutenants try to consolidate it, the more they'll be obstinate in the error. If they try to annihilate the virgin Orient, it will be them who become the Barbarians, Oh, Ménières told me that in Paris: perhaps we are the Barbarians, and the being we seek, which Médion and Dessort declare to be impossible, is here! It's Erodia who incarnates it.

And even if that were maintained, if I installed the Occident here by force, as my ministers wish, wouldn't the secret counter-direction burst forth one day or another? There would

be a latent voice, and it would develop as a direct conse-
quence of its opposition. No, no. Nothing can be founded on
an initial error, and this one has already lasted too long. It's
something anti-natural. I only occupied myself with the politi-
cal interest of my conquest, but now that the facts have fallen
silent, where's the why of it all? A revulsion toward the moral
origins of Europe, yes, but not a material installation. The
sociological divorce of the races, yes, but not a mental di-
vorce—and it's exactly the contrary that I wanted, and that
Europe, drawn by me, still wants! It's necessary to repair that.

He let his head fall into his hands, overwhelmed.

Repair that! Oh, I've moved a sphere that's too heavy!
How superior the women of the virgin Orient are to me!
They're in the right; they've understood the eternal movement.
They've remained at the Asiatic center, at the Cradle, and in
the midst of the incursions of Europe and the despotism of the
rajahs, they've safeguarded the idea of races. We believed,
stupidly, that behind our exodus we'd left a desert, and that
there, where our race was born, everything was finished. As if
there were no more fields when the crop has been harvested!

They're taking responsibility, the silent ones, for showing
us the contrary. They'll remain behind us, they'll reform, in-
tellectually behind the emigrants we were, they'll use our sci-
entific inventions and our moral and theological liberations,
but rejecting that which stains them with error. They'll re-
main, they won't go in the counter-direction, they won't try
like us to throw themselves Eastwards—to regenerate the Yel-
lows, for instance. Turned toward us, their forgotten brethren,
they'll remain in conformity with the Ellipse of the world, of
which they're one of the focal points, and they'll wait! "I was
waiting for you," Erodia said to me.

And now, now that we've come back, as enemy brothers,
they remain unassailable to fratricide; they've summarized
their power in a system that doesn't even need a representa-
tive ideological material, and which an army can no more
annihilate than, for instance, the idea of weight. The enemy
brothers have come back to lose everything , and now they're

redescending, changed in me, and with them the mother-idea will redescend, Aryan thought once more affirmed by those who wanted to kill it. The eternal conquering exodus of the East toward the West, it's my armies that will undertake it, unconsciously. Oh yes, we are the Barbarians, in every fashion! We were Barbarians in the atrocious fashion, in coming here to exterminate, and we shall be in the vivifying sense, in retaking the road of Attila and Timur with a fecund thought!

He raised his head proudly.

I shall lead them! Come on! I'm a man of the Orient myself, a son of the Cradle, an Aryan who remembers! I'm at home here, and I've felt it keenly. Perhaps alone of all European armies, I've been logical in returning, I've been right. But all the rest were wrong to return with ideas of hatred. Fortunately, I haven't been killed by an imbecile bullet before understanding that. Ménières sensed it before dying, and it's necessary that the thought lived on in someone, since Trénan has died of consumption after the cannon was killed that kept him alive, dead like the hatred that I brought from Europe, which he incarnated.

I'm a man of the Orient, and I'm only beginning to be a man of action, a conqueror, in returning, with the next rotation of the Ellipse, to the Occident with the idea of the virgin Orient. I ought to have departed alone to seek across the mountains, away from Paris, the central idea of Anarchism, the true new religion of which machinism is just a parody, but if the armies have accompanied me, it's as an ambassadorial escort. There's been nothing here but the simulacrum of a conquest; the veritable one is about to commence.

Oh, I really am an Oriental, yes, since I'm now going to return with my troops against Europe! But I won't return like Attila or Timur, for theft and murder, as my ministers have done here; I shall summon mental Europe in order to give it the faith for which she is searching! A continual exchange takes place; everything that has passed Westwards has passed inversely and exactly here; Europe has sent a Timur in my person, as Asia once dispatched one; Europe had sent a

Pierre l'Ermite against Asia; the virgin Orient will render her another, and it will be me! There was a Sepulcher to deliver? There is now a Cradle to recognize!

Everything balances: but why is it necessary that the exchange seems treacherous? The Europeans led by me were traitors and fratricides toward the Orient, and now I know that Médion, Dessort and all the others will judge me a traitor and a fratricide toward Europe! Is the exchange impossible, then, without violence? Always the childbirth in blood, always the Idea attained through the flesh. What fatal misery!

Come on! Have I truly arrived at the bottom of my idea? Let's see, let's see...yes, now, I'm confronting it totally. But have I the strength? It's frightening. I understand, I see, what has to be done, but...but what? What's wrong with me? What's retaining me here, sitting down with my head in my hands?

He was gripped by a contraction of the heart. He stiffened himself, haggard, his hands flat on his breast, immobile.

The pain passed.

Poverty of the body, poverty of the soul! There—that's because I see what has to be one and that I no longer have the desire to do it!

Is it because I'm growing old, because I feel that I'm alone, sick with the neuralgia of the heart that will carry me off one of these days? Is it because I'm afraid of the consequences of my second conquest? Is it rather because, now that I've clearly satisfied the idea, my soul is satisfied and no longer finds it interesting to realize it? Yes, that's it! Intellectual perversity, then, but in reverse! Instead of doing something because everything indicates to me that I shouldn't, I no longer want to do it because everything indicates to me that I must. But that's absurd, absurd, and I sense that the absurdity, born within me, is growing, devouring all the rest. Let's see...I'm tired, I'm going astray...

He listened to himself, livid, and murmured:

"To go against the Ellipse...to force the initial error to its most extreme consequences...make it a verity...maintain oneself in spite of everything until the next rotation of evolution will perhaps put things back in place...to be obstinate in Napoléon's dream...that would be grandiose too! Very grandiose, very extraordinary! And Europe, this time, would consent, while in the contrary case I'll have to take possession of everything again, assuming that I can...

"To go against the Ellipse...to struggle against the ethnological laws, the cosmogonic laws—what a terrible ideal! There it is, the abstract struggle, the intoxication of the geometer and the astronomer applied to the material power..."

His arm described a series of ellipses in the air.

"Yes, there are the focal points, the curvature...to struggle with that sign, face to face, to tame that... That sign, which my arm follows easily, that's my enemy..."

And suddenly, he shivered, and almost shouted: "Oh! But what about the virgin Orient, and Erodia, and my faith, and what I said to the ministers, and everything? I'd be denying all of that for the desire for power! But that's insane, that's inviable, that's false...and yet, why is that what I've thought, after all that I've promised myself? Perversity or fatigue? I know full well that if I go against the Ellipse, it will succeed for a time and end up by failing, while the other conception, almost impossible at the outset, will inevitably grow into verity. Is it, then, that I don't love verity enough? Is that I'm an Occidental all the same? Truly, this is becoming madness; a man can't touch what is simple without going mad..."

And, prostrate, with cold tears trickling between his fingers, stuck to his face, Claude Laigle let himself go. The energy overtaxed for months, for years, finally abdicated, leaving him inert, on a swell of sobs.

I dare not, I dare not, that's all...I'm not sure... Oh, Erodia, how far away you are! But it isn't you who's troubling me and driving me to despair; your Idea is just and calming... It's the Ellipse that frightens me. Ought I to yield—and what labor before the disavowal of odious Europe! Ought I, impiously, violently to remount the course of the movement of races, disavow the eternal order! Do I even have the strength before that abominable, infamous and despotic thought? It's tempting me, Erodia, it's tempting me! It's because I lived for too long out there, before knowing you! If I'd come here younger... No, no, I'm lying. It's out of cowardice that I want to go against the Ellipse, because I wouldn't be alone, because the others would help me, because it's easier... *What shame!*

In a low voice, he called: "Claude Laigle? Where are you, Claude Laigle?"

He laughed, bitterly.

It's really the Idea you believed to be alive that's killing you, Claude Laigle. You thought you were an ideologue? But you've never been strong except in action, always weak before ideas, fundamentally. You really are a conqueror, an active man, you're only good for that, you see. You're the Timur, the Genseric, the stupid and grim leader of brutes who demolished in order that his people can install their petty systems, devote themselves to their tasks, satisfy their manias and their habits, as if at home.

You've taken a bath in blood here, months ago, and now your soldiers and your engineers are building, arranging, leveling, applying their methods. You can see that you've taken a great deal of trouble to do exactly as the others did. You're good for nothing before the Idea, you can see that you're too small to do anything with it...

At least your rivals couldn't see, and were quite tranquil. You've sought your doom, Claude Laigle. You've pushed the round machine in one direction, like the children you saw, and now it's turning, without paying any heed to you, and you're falling, and it's the entire world that's pushing you to make you fall...

And you're not accelerating the movement because you'd be alone in trying, and you won't go in the reverse direction because your people wouldn't suffer that either...

You're an ordinary man, an episodic, and moreover, you have the misfortune to perceive it, and to perceive that you've run out of strength.

Claude Laigle, Claude Laigle...oh, who can envisage an essential Idea without terror?

The phantom of the Adventure, untying the unreal flowers, got up, threw them away, dead, and left. And Claude, exhausted, watched it draw away through his tears, with an ironic face laughing over its shoulder.

XII. The Supreme Evening

There was no further mention of the violent conversation at the conclusion of which the commander-in-chief had died. Médion and Dessort remained strict in the councils, and outside the regulation of everyday questions, Claude Laigle enclosed himself in an absolute silence.

Some time having gone by, he received a message from Erodia.

Have you spoken already, or are you waiting for the return to Europe? she wrote. *I have been working on my side; the Idea is steadily gaining ground. I have good news of adhesions throughout the valley of the Ganges, attachments in the Oude, an almost complete consent in Mysore and Nepal, which, in any case, have secretly favored you rather than detesting you. Many marched by force, under the orders of the Japanese and the princes. Do your ministers know that? My associations are gaining power and making contacts everywhere; the Aryan Idea will be saved. I need to come as far as Lahore, with a large escort, a party of my women, and a number of affiliates that I shall bring with me. It is useful that we see one another again. Can you leave Delhi and come to meet me?*

He hesitated, and then decided. Delhi was odious to him, doubly so, by virtue of the obsession of blood and the broken idea of the Ellipse that had just attained him there. He announced a plan to inspect the camps in the direction of the Kashmir frontier, and departed for Lahore. The ministers were to accompany him there, and then quit him to travel through the provinces. He acquiesced to that measure of solicitude, in which he divined suspicion, and made the voyage indifferently with them. In any case, they avoided him discreetly when their presence was not indispensable. He isolated himself in the marches, ill, suffering from his heart and of a kind of dull stupefaction only glimpsing confusedly a reawakening of his intelligence by means of the confrontation with the Visitor of Souls.

Perhaps I'll recover at a stroke, on seeing her...

Familiar landscapes struck his eyes. They were following inversely the route they had taken from Lahore after the great victory, toward the investment of Delhi, and he rediscovered impressions, the sentiment of decisive action, the sentiment that had once hastened his gallop alongside the terrible old man's caleche. But a world of dreams had risen up since then, and how dissimilar!

They traversed vast encampments. Everywhere, on the military roads, the dictator observed the preparations for departure, which the ministers had hastened. Divisions crossed their path heading toward the valley of the Indus and transports were moored on the river. Others astonished him that were heading northwards, parallel to his escort. He interrogated Médion; evasive pretexts although quite plausible, were given—except that one morning, Claude no longer saw the troops whose direction seemed menacing. They had disappeared, traveling behind the woods and hills without him being able to suspect their presence.

All around him, in the villages and the forts, the mobilization was stirring for the exodus to the Occident, with a surprising activity. The force was withdrawing too precipitately not to cause Claude Laigle anxiety; it seemed that Médion and Dessort had quickly renounced their ideas of surveillance.

Convoys of artillery cluttered the passages. The Occident was decidedly commencing the reflux of its tide of men; everything revealed the breakage, the slow attraction of the lands quit, drawing the sons of Dynamism away after the completed task.

In the approaches to Lahore the impression was accentuated; the military quarters were no longer empty, but an immense quantity of carts had accumulated there, all overflowing with piled-up baggage. Europe was taking back her own. Claude was struck by that.

To maintain them here, against the movement of Ellipse, in a contradictory effort? he said to himself. But they're the ones who seem no longer able to hold on; they're leaving with urgency. Is the solution I wanted the one that they're ultimately adopting, mechanically? Evidently, Médion and Dessort are stimulating all this, pressing the departure; I can't see their intention clearly; one would think that it's been modified since our conversation.

Yes, but the point isn't to go back as they departed, but to go back with a changed soul, and their soul is the same. Morally, they haven't learned anything or forgotten anything, and it's there that it's necessary for me to intervene. Come on, I shall act! I shall act! I was mad to think of maintaining the effort in the counter-direction; I don't know what moral depression came over me. It really is the other solution that's necessary, the Idea of the virgin Orient remains; I'll no longer be afraid when I've seen Erodia...

He felt reassured, hopeful. As they got closer to the North and the Cradle, the Oriental he was recovered his strength.

He reached Lahore observing and meditating. Nothing suspect had appeared to him, however. When he arrived, there was news of Erodia. A few more days would be necessary yet for her to join him. He decided to wait, quite calm.

In those few days, amid external cares, the encumbrance of the troops and the preparations for the departure, an extreme confidence took hold of him again. He was almost joyful, reanimated, not by the imminent presence of the Visitor, but by the sweetness of the Idea, reappeared in his mind after months of doubt. The spectacle of the reflux of the Occidentals penetrated him with the conviction that it was necessary to act before that reflux carried him away, a more important unit, but dissolved in the mass.

He was ill, but his mind was clarified by the illness itself; he had arrived, beyond the anguish of his logic and his energy, in the relatively calm regions in which one enjoys an idea abstractly for its own sake, without tumult, like the areas of calm reflective water at the center of a maelstrom. The contradictory rotation of forces gripped him and maintained him in a relative equilibrium; he was in the depths of the cyclone but believed that he was floating above it, out of reach. The strange illusion of moribund individuals who talk about voyaging in fresh countries sustained him in an ideological wellbeing. One last start brought him upright, and he believed at the first moment in a rejuvenation of energy. Thus, he waited for the Visitor.

And suddenly, he became anxious. His happiness, as it resumed a tangible form and drew nearer to him in the appearance of an individual, seemed to expose him to a peril that he could not define. Was it the magnetism of amour that warned him in that fashion? He recalled the suspicious and prepared attitude of the ministers, Médion's closed expression, Dessort's taut smile. Perhaps they were meditating some surprise...

Get away! I'm the master, no one here budges without my wishing it!

In spite of everything, he would perhaps prefer it if Erodia were not coming at that moment. He dreamed about her still up there, inaccessible, the enigmatic deity of the virgin Orient, with her recluses ready, when she grew old, to ripen the conserved Idea, if she had not yet enable it to flower. He almost thought of telling her that, summoned couriers, and then sent them away without a message, revolted by the thought.

What would she say? Decidedly, I'm still weak, to have such scruples. I'm like a mistrustful tyrant; it's ridiculous.

An anxiety remained, which irritated him fully without him succeeding in chasing it away or defining its causes precisely.

The rainy season had returned; stifling storms floated, bursting in warm torrents; the odor of plants and the overheated earth caused malaise, and the electricity in the air exasperated thought. Claude attributed that vertigo of doubt and suspicion to that.

The days passed; Erodia did not appear, delays evidently due to the season held her up on the route. At the same time, Claude Laigle observed singular troop movements in the vicinity of Lahore. Taking advantage of a calm in the rains, he left the city, and recognized with surprise and dread the divisions he had seen following roads parallel to his since Delhi, which had suddenly disappeared on the way. They had not, then, veered eastwards toward the Indus? Why had they come as far as Lahore, openly at first, and then secretly?

A terrible suspicion went through his mind. Médion was playing with him! What was the objective of this convergence of troops? He recalled that those divisions had disappeared one morning, after a question posed by him, and interrogated Médion distractedly, and then the commanders of the corps. The responses were vague...he must have been mistaken about the numbers of the regiments...these troops were partly destined to replace the forces that were about to quit the city and Kashmir. The confusion was quite understandable in the great upheaval of the mobilization. Then again, half the troops that he saw really had quit the other half, which ought now to be descending the Indus toward the transports...

Reasons of management and administration were established, precise in themselves, but tedious, obscured by the multiplicity of details. Claude Laigle renounced seeing clearly, and then turned away, gripped again by the Idea that effaced everything. He remained on his guard, but judged his anxieties excessive. Between and undeniable ill will and a direct assault there was an abyss that no one dared cross. The Dictatorship, in any case, with the terrible discipline of Anarchism, created a right for him, protected him. Médion and Dessort, even if they dared, would not ruin their own cause before the Confederation—and there would be an immediate court martial...

No, it was too improbable. Their hatred would only be free to express itself in Europe, after the decision of the council of legates. Absorbed in the Idea, Claude gathered his strength again for that alone. In any case, Erodia's arrival was announced. One more day, and her free escorts would be camped south-east of Lahore. Claude received the news in Médion's presence, observed his face, but only saw a sullen indifference, the expression of a discontentment on seeing something stupid occurring about which nothing could be done—and he smiled internally.

His rank, and the ceremonial customary before the Hindus, forbade him to go to meet Erodia and her cortege. He waited for them to arrive. The next day, the establishment of the Hindu encampments was known at three o'clock, but a new storm abruptly burst, frightfully; the streets of Lahore and the military quarters were inundated by tumultuous rain; an immense whirlwind developed with unusual violence, and disorder followed. The reception could not take place; it was necessary to wait.

Claude was irritated. At four o'clock the storm attained its greatest intensity. In the dictator's house a crowd of officers and dignitaries had gathered for Erodia's coming, anxious about the weather. Everyone was mingling, leaning out of windows or over the edge of the terraces, talking animatedly.

Suddenly, Claude Laigle, in the din of a thunderclap that shook the house to its foundations, felt his arm gently touched, and looked round. A sepoy officer saluted him ceremoniously. When the man's head was raised again, the eyelids fluttered. Claude shivered, recognizing one of Erodia's servants, seen beside her once in the Pamir.

The man spoke, very rapidly and quietly.

"She has been here since yesterday evening, and it is not the storm that prevents her from coming. She is anxious. There are cordons of European troops south-west of the city;

they have replaced the sepoy troops of which I am part, and are ready if you have need of them. Know that orders have been given for that."

He drew away; a new clap of thunder burst, and fell as much upon Claude Laigle's soul as on the city. He tottered, dazzled by rage and terror, and leaned on a balustrade. People hurried around,

"Nothing," he said. "A fleeting pain in the heart. The repercussion of the thunder. It's nothing."

His eyes sought Médion and Dessort, saw them calm and impassive, seemingly bored.

"Messieurs," he said. "the reception is decidedly postponed until tomorrow. You're free to retire at the first calm."

Haughtily, with a brief salute, he disappeared, went back to his apartment, a surge of violent ideas leaping up in his soul as if to break it, and at the same time stiffened by the danger, which finally saved him from his doubts. Anything rather than doubt!

The blood was rushing within him like the seething of a cataract. He dug his fingernails into his palms, and stammered: "Oh, I knew full well... Act! It's necessary to act! So they dare! Well, I like that; we're going to settle this right away!"

Anger convulsed him, and for a second he became the Claude Laigle of Anarchism, the conqueror of Delhi, the Master.

"We're going to see whether I have the army or not, whether subordinates..."

A thousand plans jostled furiously in his mind. He thought about having Médion and Dessort arrested immediately...

But no—they're surely not alone; they have affiliates among the troop commanders. That would alert them; I don't know anything... and then, let's not rush; there must be evidence. An arrest would give the others time to destroy the evidence. Then these orders would be explained slyly... no, that's not the way. First of all, it's necessary to save Erodia, to find a pretext, a ruse, to prevent the troops from...

What luck that this storm prevented the meeting! Everything might have been irreparable by now. I have until tomorrow to think! What a filthy mess! But I'll save her; there's still time. I'll be there; I'll talk; I'll lead the army, even if I have to make use of indigenous regiments to be in with to prevent a skirmish. Would they dare assassinate her, all the same? But what about me, then, who also has the Idea? No, they'll want to use cunning, gain time, simply invent I don't know what delay...

Then again, perhaps they believe that it's me who's meditating some violence against them, and they're being wary...

What alternatives! But first, first, see her! Oh, how that Occident weighs upon me! I've had enough of it! To quit everything, yes, to live up there, at the Cradle, with her, as an inaccessible emperor, and slowly conquer by mans of books the world they're disputing with me in deeds! Yes, but...that would be to retreat, all the same. They're acting, I shall act. Tomorrow, I'll be north-west of the city, with Her, with her women, and her genius, and the sepoy troops, and tomorrow I'll bring that elite of the true civilized down on Europe, on Dynamism! I'll bring them back to Europe with me to direct my crowds and sow the Idea there, and we'll see whether anyone will dare to raise a hand against me! This is a minute that will decide everything; I'm no longer hesitant. They wanted it; it's not longer as equals that I'll bring back the Orientals—it's as masters!

The fury that was strangling him burst out as a terrible joy, with a brutal change of direction, and he stood up, ready.

Two hours later, in a wretched cart hitched to the team of an artillery ammunition-wagon, Claude Laigle rolled through the suburbs of Lahore, heading for Erodia's encampments.

He had got out without any difficulty, the house empty of visitors, the ministers disappeared. Under the torrential rain the streets and courtyards were deserted. No vehicle in harness remained there; he had had to go as far as a neighboring post and requisition horses from an artillery battery; the artillery men had had great difficulty finding a cart with a tarpaulin cover in a hangar, which he had adapted as best he could.

The four horses were galloping among the jolts and the splashing mud. Darkness had fallen; it was almost cold now; the extreme humidity intense. The downpour had relented, but the roads were in a parlous state.

Wrapped up in his martial cloak under the rough, soaked tarpaulin, Claude Laigle, exasperated, expecting the unknown, was no longer thinking, almost unconscious, living a purely physical existence, gazing at the bounding rumps of the horses, where lantern-light vacillated, the dark landscape, the palm trees broken by the storm, and the city's lines of firelight. At the advanced posts he leaned toward the officer of the guard, showed a abruptly-illuminated face, snapped "Secret mission!" and the horses galloped on amid the jolts, under the whip of three drivers whose large cloaks were flapping.

It resembled a flight, that departure toward the triumph of the Idea, and a bitter irony sometimes gripped Claude Laigle's heart. The night, the downpour, the wretched cart: all the sinister and pitiful aspects of the Adventure were thus denounced in mud after being born in blood. But tomorrow, perhaps an unreal Sun would rise!

Images passed vaguely through his mind: Louis XVI on the road to Varennes, an old engraving contemplated in childhood...the boulevards of Paris on the evening of the explosion of the Élysée...the assault on Delhi...Ménières' face over the dirty serge...Erodia, the roseate rocks, the opulent horses, the curved Cradle...Trénan inert, fallen on the arm of his chair...

And the Idea rose up, floating in the improbable sky of metaphysics.

"Are we getting close? I can't see anything. Are we nearly there? Nothing can be heard."

The suburb was deserted, sulfurous gleams trailing on the pools of water. The carriage, bogged down by the mud, swerved on to a round road; distant lights appeared. Claude started. Was that the camp of the recluses and their escort. Yes, that was the direction. The lights became more precise in the curtains of rain, which were become less dense. Erodia! Erodia!

Distant rumbles of thunder rolled over the plain; the storm was resuming, but dryly; the downpour cleared, almost stopped.

Suddenly, a more precise noise mingled with the rumbling thunder, in abrupt spasms—a noise that Claude thought he recognized, but almost indiscernible in the storm. However...

No!

He leaned over the edge of the cart and shouted: "How long before we reach the lights?"

"Another three-quarters of an hour," replied a servant, half turning.

"Hurry, hurry... Are they so far away, those lights? We're almost there..."

"There's no air, but it's some way off. And the road..."

"Can't you hear anything, apart from the storm?"

"No," said the man. "It's making a noise like machine-guns...one might think, but...."

He shouted, in gasps, in the jolts of the cart and the whistling of the wind: "The sound of machine-guns?"

"Well, yes...there's no reason.... But I heard it said in camp today that there was a sepoy mutiny, and that it might get hot. One's never sure with these people. It's already arrived..."

"But the sepoys have been moved; they're not in that direction. If there were trouble, even so far as necessitating cannons, the noise wouldn't be coming from that direction..."

"Perhaps...I don't know..."

Claude threw himself back into the shadow. *And no one's following me! What does that mean? Another three-quarters of an hour! No one's following me! Is it because they believe I won't do anything? They must have seen me leave—I didn't hide. Or is it already too late? Would they dare? Erodia! Erodia!*

Time passed. The artilleryman closest to Claude turned round abruptly. "There are cavalry ahead and to the side, but I don't know what it is..."

"Cavalry?"

"Yes—listen, you can hear..."

In the calm, there was a dull and regular rumble.

"It's not sepoys, at any rate...they aren't mounted. There's no danger..."

"It's a guard unit!" shouted the voice of the driver at the front. "They're ours! No danger!"

Is it them? Claude wondered. *No danger*, he added, bitterly...

The sound of hoofbeats grew. From the depths of the darkness indistinct silhouettes separated into two masses coming to met them, one head on, the other obliquely.

"Don't stop!"

The team kicked on, enveloped by whiplashes; the carriage rolled furiously, drawing Claude, both frightened and calm. If it's then, everything's finished...

And suddenly, the horsemen seemed very close; he heard distant cries, a "Halt!" The password was ready to leap from his lips, but the others did not should anything, and broke up. The carriage flew. The great shadows wheeled, drew aside to let them pass, and then came alongside at a rapid trot, on both sides of the cart.

Suddenly, in a gust, shouts overlapped:

"Confederates!"

"Who are you?"

"Confederates!"

One, two vivid flashes shone to the right of Claude Laigle, surging from the tarpaulins. A cavalier almost brushing the cart stretched out his arm; two revolver shots rang out, and then three more. A terrible jolt stopped the cart dead in a muddy skid; one of the horses fell, a lantern smashed. The driver nearest to Claude uttered an oath.

"Confederates, you were told! Are you deaf or mad?"

A face leaned over.

"You didn't respond, either!"

"A horse killed! Now we're in a mess! And urgent service!"

The horsemen surrounded the vehicle. Claude stood up, resolved. He was about to shout: "Another horse, quickly!" when the words froze on his lips. By the light of the remaining lantern he recognized the man who had fired.

It was Médion.

The latter pronounced, very rapidly: "No need to continue. *We've come back*."

Claude stammered: "You've dared...!"

"The idea remains to you," said Médion, with a sneer. "You can use it as you wish, alone. As for the people *up there*, they were superfluous. Europe will approve. Anyway, *she* was hit by chance..."

In a mist of blood, Claude heard the thunderous voice of Dessort.

"What an error! After the skirmish just now, that disorder...understandable. We didn't hear you when you shouted. Hitch up another horse. Service of the dictator!"

Claude's hand clutched at his belt, seeking his revolver. Médion saw the movement, threw himself backwards, and Claude, with a single movement, braced himself against the edge of the cart, his arm extended to kill. But suddenly, in the effort, an abominable pain seized his heart, a decisive rupture of life.

His hand shook, the revolver fell, and his body, folding in two, collapsed, spinning, the neck dislocated, the arms outside the cart, in the void.

Médion leaned over.

"The Master has fainted!"

Heads approached. Claude's tongue, between the parted lips, stirred.

Médion shouted, very loudly: "An accident! His neuralgia of the heart afflicted him again this morning. That storm favored it. He wanted to go out all the same..."

"Yes," shouted Dessort, "to see the skirmish with the sepoys. We dissuaded him, but he went out in spite of his condition. And that alert just now…the shock…"

Claude's tongue was no longer moving. Everyone shut up. There was a frightful silence. And suddenly, the cart shifted, the dictator vacillated, and the poor inert head came into the light, displaying the revulsed eyes.

"The Master is dead!"

The soldiers bustled, terrified, a disarray of horses and men clattered, drowning out the ministers' words. They came close together, driven toward the cadaver, gesticulating.

"It's necessary that no one knows," said Médion, in a low voice.

"Assuredly."

"An accident…a sudden and fatal crisis…"

"The consequence of so much fatigue for the cause…he died after the work was done…"

"His work…ours…that of the evening of the declaration of Paris.…"

With a cold gaze, they understood one another.

Claude Laigle, his body folded in two, was still hanging over the edge of the cart, his arms outside, dangling.

As the rain continued to stream over the soft face of the cadaver, they tore the silk lining out of a hood, and someone covered it.

January 1895-February 1897.

PREFACE TO THE 1897 EDITION OF THE VIRGIN ORIENT

The present book exposes, in the course of a singular political and social hypothesis, the spectacle of an active elevated will, having reached the limits of power by the force of arms and the assent of destiny, but nevertheless thrown into dementia and disarray by the irony of invisible laws. These laws are discernible beneath the actions of individuals; there is but one drama, that of their struggle with our mind, and before all the variegated and feverish characters in novels, they are the essential and living figures. This story, in its various episodes, renders further homage to those abstract laws of the soul and the mind; they exist there more veritably than the men and the woman that will be seen to appear therein.

An elevated will, I have said. Undoubtedly, when the book is closed, it will be thought that there is a more authentic and more noble one, and it will be felt that that one does not content me any more perfectly. There are several degrees of will, and if one understands by that word the play of the soul seeking its plenitude, how much more accomplished the effort of a Marcus Aurelius, a Pascal or an Immanuel Kant will appear than that of my conqueror, dazzled by a brutal dream amid the whinnying of war-horses That is because philosophers and mystics, who are the foremost of men, raise themselves without difficulty above the will that I have been careful to name *active*. They rectify within themselves the grouping of circumstances by means of a logic that is proper to them, and thus obtain an interior heroism that surpasses all others.

Fable shows us Bellerophon, Perseus or Siegfried, strangely silent, penetrated by the knowledge of their destiny, and clad, under the appearance of divine armor, in a certainty so impenetrable and so innate that it would be incomprehensible if it were forgotten that their exploits have nothing material, but allegorize abstract conquests. Also revealed in those heroes are feats that are the faithful followers of pure thought; thus it is necessary to envisage what is known as calm of mind as the mark of very superior wills.

That is not to say that the existence of philosophers and mystics is exempt from discouragement and sadness; that is necessary for the nobility of the soul, and research in those arid and almost uninhabitable regions of knowledge also encounters ironic gulfs and sudden landslides. But those interior disasters never efface the serenity of the meditative; it is as if they are illuminated by a constant light of joy that comes from their very consecration to pure thought and its perils. They study as conditions of life what others curse as catastrophes, and they do not panic.

Men of merely active will, on the contrary, do not expect, in composing the order of their ambitions, the intervention of those great laws of intellectual direction, which are the spiritual climatology or meteorology, and the reflective prevision of which will perhaps be the religion of the future. Or, if the concern occurs to them, they perhaps also fear losing faith in themselves and enervating themselves with hesitation by thinking too much about it; human actions have always seemed to demand for their success the forgetfulness of certain mental conditions, even some narrowness of mind, a violent and somewhat brutal aspect.

My character provides an example of one of these wills applied to the things of material life; scarcely conceiving any but one goal, which is the domination of others. His desire is to be above others, without thinking overmuch about what he will be. And it is precisely because of that forgetfulness that he falls, when the second part of the narrative leaves him free in confrontation with his dream; his force of expansion only having been employed in preparing for the advent of a will of a higher degree than his own, he perceives that many of the efforts he has expended have ended in an infraction of natural laws, wants to return abruptly to his conception, but cannot: having departed without having discovered a logical idea of his attempt, he finds it surpassed, and conceives an upheaval that leads to delirium and kills it more surely than an aneurism. That initial error in the calculation of his own effort vitiates the entire psychology of the willful man of the first degree, of which the adventure of a dictator appeared to me to comprehend completely enough all the avatars, and to fit comfortably enough into a novel, since that discord of a life of action suddenly paralyzed by the abstract is a very modern case, in spite of the hypothetical and futuristic fabulation of the book.

As for what happens herein, in so many external and episodic accidents, given what I have just said, it might be sensed that I have not intended them as anything more than excellent pretexts of psychology, and that I have not presented them without have put into them what I could of ornamentation in the style and lyrical liberty in the arrangement. One might contest with as much right the scant arbitrary merit that fills these pages and disposes therein of events, countries and races; so I pray that I am now granted full license, because I would not care about ethnological and chronological verity in a work of art—and this book is neither a realistic novel nor a political prophecy, but uniquely a work of art—if I had renounced giving the imagination free play therein.

That is for me the prerogative of fiction, and I am only taking the opportunity to issue an immediate warning that I have not wanted anything to be exact; it is even my desire to make it felt unequivocally what has in part determined the situation of my story in the future. I do not see how, or why, I should hasten to defend the possibility of such upheavals of the indicated States or admit anything further; I concede in that regard all that a historian or politician might demand, since there is nothing here to please them and I am not making any claims at all. It is evident that this Europe to come, this Latin dictator, this change of direction of the Occident against the yellow races and all these conflagrations of peoples, sieges, battles, are not equivalent to any diplomatic prevision and are only a poetic game.

It has pleased me to suppose that considerable events will astonish the close of the twentieth century. I have admitted the establishment of Russia in Constantinople and its disinterest in Central Europe, the mental separation of the Germano-Latins and the Slavs. I have arbitrarily constituted an Occidental Confederation, and it was necessary for that for me consider as accomplished facts, firstly, the ruination of the hegemony of the Hohenzollerns and the Triple Alliance in the wake of a new Franco-German war; secondly, a general disarmament due to socialism; thirdly, a political effacement of the latter before the advent of an anarchistic internationalism; and finally, an ideological cohesion of Central Europe after the collapse of constitutional monarchies and parliamentary regimes.

Those are serious and risky hypotheses; I had to advance them for the very essence of my book. And I have only said what is strictly necessary for the intelligence of its real subject, which is the drama of a man of will at grips with an error. The rest is décor, and I do not put much weight on it. To tell the truth, if pushed, I would argue that this terrible fantasy is nevertheless not without support in a few previsions of general history, which do not seem to ne to be absurd, and that I have not severed all connections between my book and what the future might plausibly bring—and in the end, everything comes about, even dreams...

But I shall not strive by that means to regain what I have just abandoned, and it remains to be determined whether a writer has a right to construct an absolute fiction about the real society of contemporary Europe, by conserving some elements and suppressing or disguising others. Who determines the rights of the author, and where to they run out? If I have concerted my epic developments with the soul of the man who engenders them, I shall consider myself acquitted by that from further plausible resemblances to life; I will have satisfied one of the forms of verity, altering the others to the sole advantage of that one, and if the concert remain harmonious, I shall have created no disharmony from the artistic point of view, It will be realized, however, that this novel, with the appearance and frame of a social novel, is nevertheless entirely chimerical, a book of general psychology and invention.

Is it not necessary, in any case, to take issue with what is called historical truth? In what I have turned upside down here, I might seem to pass judgment on and contest that notion, but in truth I contest it with excellent minds who sense clearly today, after the accumulation of documents and memoirs, that history is nevertheless a sentimental science. Even leaving aside the details of erudition and décor, only to attach myself to minds, I do not discover anything in archeological tomes more veridical than the Queen of Sheba, or Salammbô as depicted by Flaubert. No monograph by the most well-informed compiler disturbs in that regard the sentiment inspired in me by that great man, and I think that sentiment has a right to be cited in history as validly as the most reliable document, that it contains a mental authenticity, that interpretation has inalienable prerogatives, and that there is an infinity of fashions of being certain.

I can, in sum, only reserve the same scruple for the rapid sketch of moral civilization of *The Virgin Orient*, which the aspect that I agree to be the least satisfactory, if I am allowed the secret contentment of not having wanting to avoid check, I sense that more might have been demanded, and that would have merited another book. But I am restricting myself here, not to all I could say about it, but to what my hero has to perceive usefully in order for doubt in his work to come to his mind; and the words of Erodia are those of a temporary being, which serve precisely to hasten the drama of that man in combat with new phantoms, and the singular country ruled by that Visitor of Souls ought not, to my mind, to be more real than it seems in the story.

I might be more seriously challenged on the condition of the future in which I have situated my history. And since I perceive myself confessing in this preface a quantity of doubts regarding what I have done, I shall also renounce protecting myself on that point. It is the most vulnerable, and the anticipation of what might happen is a convention in which the arbitrary might shock, especially in our period of analysis, in which one holds to facts and modern milieux; but is that convention much more wounding than that of that of the theater, for example, which assembles in one character a host of traits and generalities? And would it not have been even more insupportable to disturb the past in order to introduce my fiction into it?

It is only a procedure, and I have constructed everything as fiction, without the support of more reality than was indispensable. I will add that the logical relationship between a man and his adventures remains entire and possible outside all question of epoch, without the intervention of scruples regarding dates anterior to the moment of reading or contemporary events. That fortuitous but entirely veridical reason is especially relevant to this book, which was conceived in its entirety several months before the Sino-Japanese events of April 1895,[16] the prelude to an alliance of the yellow races, the anxiety of the Occident and the project of a European league against "the Asiatic peril," arrived to corroborate historically the basic idea, which will now seem to the reader to stem from them. Without taking pride in that foresight, I can extract enough force from it against the distinction between what happens and what will happen for it not to worry overmuch about having arbitrarily determined dates and events.

In any case, I am only concerned with evoking an emotional reaction, and it will be my entire satisfaction to have impassioned a few individuals with all kinds of elements, true or fictitious, if they tell me that I have succeeded in that. Is not that emotional evocation the entire reason for writing, as soon

---

[16] The first Sino-Japanese War lasted from 1 August 1894 to the signing of the punitive treaty of Shimonseki on 17 April 1895; the latter event must be the circumstance to which this remark refers

as one becomes disinterested in informing? Literature is the formulation of thoughts and sentiments under the pretext of telling stories, and that always underlies the interest of "stories."

Why, finally—in concluding these commentaries and reticences—should I forbid myself to confess that I have attempted this book, perhaps too vast, by virtue of an instinct of protest against the narrowness of present-day novels, in the desire to introduce individual lyricism into the very bosom of contemporary spectacles, in a great and violent sentiment of weariness in the presence of the illusory "verity" that serves today to excuse the impotence of invention and limits art to copying?

It is, moreover, odious to me, that servitude to date and fact; it has nothing to do with true verity; the authentic verity is that of expansive genius. In the novel more than anywhere else, events are the fruit of character, and I have only wanted here to try to liberate myself from a vision restricted to that which sees around it the infinity of life and the soul. Such books, I know, do not often succeed, but what is necessary is to make the attempt, and there are times in which the nobility of art is less a matter of perfecting small things than going wholeheartedly toward a larger one.

This is a dream that is not contained in my own time, but my mental time is not the interval between my birth and death, it is which has had life since limbo, and I feel that I am contemporary with all passionate and interesting beings, from the first century to the last. The others might rub shoulders with me, but they seem to me to be cadavers, and art is absurd if it does not address itself instinctively to elevated figures, to "representative human beings." Otherwise, it is the fare of gossip.

You will not find herein a practical verity, a historical painting, a documentary depiction, pseudonymous portraits or all the attractions of realism. But what you will find here are images, dreams, appeals to a broader life, toward exaltations of human energy; perhaps you will also find, beneath the poet-

345

ic and improbable fabulation, the intuition of a truth that does not need to be dated, the only one I love, the only one that touches me in the work of the dead and the living, the only one that does not shackle us to the quotidian, the only one that is the source of grave, fecund and permanent thoughts.

C.M.

PREFACE TO THE 1920 EDITION OF THE VIRGIN ORIENT

This novel was written in 1895 by a young man of twenty-three. That consideration, if it does not excuse anything, will at least explain to the reader the weaknesses he might find in a work on a subject as vast as it is ambitious, uniting action with dream.

The Virgin Orient presupposed a certain number of political and social hypotheses, some of which have been realized and other contradicted by events, or have remained in the realm of pure imagination. It would be ridiculous for the author even to seem to obtain vanity from a certain gift for prophecy, attested by several data in his book, and due to pure intuition. He was then only a debutant trying to compose a novel of adventures around a symbol. After a quarter of a century he reviews with the melancholy and irony of experience a work of which Alphonse Daudet, both interested and scolding, said that "when one has had the luck to find a theme so extraordinary, one abandons everything else and devotes to it, in order to extract a masterpiece from it, the ten years that *Salammbô* required of Flaubert."

The Virgin Orient is not a masterpiece, and did not cost ten years. The man who conceived it is not absolved. But he is giving the work again as it was composed, as an effort doubtless too great and too hasty, but above all with the entitlement of a rather curious anticipation. Scientific warfare has appeared to us entirely other than it could have been foreseen in 1895, before the automobile and the submarine. We can still discern the premonitory symptoms of the European recasting that it supposes to have been accomplished in the year 2000 by an anarchistic internationalism and an Occidental Confederation. But this attempt to display the circulation of a living Idea in the crowds, and this ardent curiosity about future transformations, are very characteristic of an epoch in which literary youth was extremely passionate and inventive. This novel can, therefore be considered as one of the most striking evidences of that state of mind. That will suffice to give this new edition its exact significance.

C.M.

THE POISON OF PRECIOUS STONES

The semi-naked slave lifting up the bronze lamps stopped, hesitantly on the threshold of Prince Sparyanthis' bedroom, and her charming breast quivered, for the young man who was asleep in there, on a pile of carpets and silks, was so handsome that all the dreams of the young women of the kingdom had the form of his body. Blond and white, he appeared unclothed in the warm penumbra, displaying a slender nudity. His head inclined over his folded arms like an overly heavy fruit curving its branch; a necklace of emeralds sparkled at his neck, and from his neck to his feet the shiny and nacreous waves of his flesh, scarcely animated by a slow and even respiration, flowed over somber fabrics, displacing subtle shadows.

Sparyanthis was eighteen years old. He loved dreams, the silence of parks, slumber, music and reading, and consecrated a sumptuous and nonchalant life to them, while his elder brother, Prince Cimmerion, robust and bellicose, sought glory in distant battles and bore the military renown of the Etesian people, whom both of them, since the death of their father the king, bent to their will, as far as the savage regions of the Orient.

In the depths of the vast palace-citadel whose walls enclosed celebrated gardens, lakes and basalt cliffs the color of night and blood, and where an abyss opened, in the bosom of which, it was said, the dazzled eye could reflect the burning waters of Hell, in the depths of that palace-citadel, where an army watched, Prince Sparyanthis had already been distracting himself for long weeks with his jugglers and his women, while awaiting his brother's return. Announced by signal fires on the summits of mountains, the first combat chariots were finally about to appear at the gates of the city, where an immense rumor quivered, stifled by the massive walls and the vast labyrinths of porticos preceding Sparyanthis' apartments. A band of pale light extended at the limit of the horizon and the sky, and in the intervals of tapestries suspended from the arches, oblique glimmers slid.

The young woman with the naked breasts dared not awaken the young man by sprinkling a few drops of perfumed water over him, as was customary, because he was smiling in his sleep, at a continuing dream, and his lips were parted as if for a kiss.

However, the profound sonority of bells summoning the guards to the interior courtyards became faintly audible, and the amorous and pensive slave was just about to tilt the golden bottle suspended from her waist over the handsome face of Sparyanthis, when, with a great sigh, the sleeper moved and opened his eyes of his own accord. Between the rings of blue-tinted make-up, his long gem-like irises glittered.

Smiling, he murmured: "What do you want with me, girl? Leaning over me, are you only coming to wake me, or to offer the reality of your flesh to the prolongation of my dream? In truth, I was dreaming that a woman was coming toward me compared with whom your beauty is only a vain shadow—but I could not grasp her. She came from a distant country, her desire responded to mine, but something separated us…I don't know...

"Perhaps, by closing my eyes and touching the freshness of her body, I might recapture the illusion, and if you wanted me, you whom my waking caprice would reject, hasten to take the place of a shadow in the deceptive sleep of Sparyanthis, come and be silent..."

But the slave sighed and said: "I am yours, O my master, disdained or chosen. Only the order of the hours has caused me to dare a presence that dread would have forbidden to my desire, for do you not reject the most beautiful and the most worthy, who, like me, suffer from your pride and kiss your memory on the lips that violate them? Prince Cimmerion is approaching, his army is at the gates, and that is why I am here with the bronze lamp and the golden bottle.

"I was waiting in the dream for a woman," Sparyanthis exclaimed, "but the gods had reserved me another joy. My beloved brother is returning: the mighty warrior, whose brown breast is covered with bronze scales and whose head shakes the tawny crest of gold and plumes above the crowds of the war! Let me be dressed in my most beautiful silks, let my jewels, from the diadem to my slippers, make me scintillate like the drew, and I shall wait between the standards of my terrace, gladly, for the man who is the strength of my race and the pride of my eyes!

At the slave's gesture, the women who were to dress the young man hurried forward. In their midst, as naked as a statue, laughing and cheerful, he offered his arms and his neck for adornment; a flood of embroideries weighed down with gold and gems undulated around his limbs; bright flowers were mingled with his blond hair.

Impatient, he scarcely permitted the followers to close the precious clasps of his crimson buskins, for the strident sounds of the clarions of the royal cavalry entered the palace with the sunlight, and the sonority mingled with the light so joyfully that one might have thought them the same flight of golden arrows mirrored in the reflections of the marble basin into which the prince had just plunged.

The sound of songs and acclamations made the colonnades resound, and drew a groan from the shields suspended in trophies, as if those spoils of ancient victories were protesting against the new joy of the vanquishers.

"Someone take them away!" cried Sparyanthis, "and let them be buried in the crypts of our arsenals! They shall no longer moan their plaint and their reproach here, and if at least a fraction of the souls of those who bore them persists in their metal, let them lament in a night as profound as the one in which their bones lie! My brother Cimmerion is bringing a harvest in his chariots rich enough to garnish these spacious galleries anew!

Among the spread drapes, Prince Sparyanthis appeared on the terraces, from which the city and the edge of the mountains of Etesia could be seen.

The roofs were covered by a crowd no less immense than the one that filled the streets and the squares, and a triumphant tumult rose up in gusts with the great swirls of smoke exhaled by the perfumed braziers and the torches aligning their avenues of flames in the somber masses of foliage in the gardens.

In the distance, the weapons of the cavaliers and infantrymen gleamed, like stains on the robe of a colossal sinuous serpent extending its multiple heads, crawling over the crossroads and advancing toward the majestic gates of the palace, from which pathways bordered by ramparts of palms rose in spacious curves, all the way to the splendid staging of the supreme terraces, at the summit of which, a svelte idol of diamonds, stood the youthful stature of Sparyanthis, extending a golden laurel into the infinite space, in the glory of the sunlight. Alone, at the limit of the azure, on the rim of white stairways where his shadow vibrated, he left behind him the variegated group of women and musicians, and his gaze was lost in the consideration of the landscape.

Black yew-trees were standing up like swords next to the basins of the parks, like silver shields. A frisson of light refracted by the torsos of guards designed the crenellations of the successive enclosures, and at the base of that throne it made an accumulation of walls and the domes of the great city fume, as if in an assault, palpitating with cries, while it was gripped more violently with every passing minute by the enlacement if Cimmerion's army penetrating through the five Oriental gates and losing its sinuosities in the foothills and defiles of the distant mountain, bathed by a blue-tinted vapor.

But what Sparyanthis' gaze was particularly anxious to discover, in that sparkling triumphant host, causing the crowd to seethe between the white banks of houses, was the war chariot on which his brother was standing. For Sparyanthis loved his brother dearly. Their souls were narrowly united.

Sparyanthis was effeminate, weak and dissolute, but sagacious and knowledgeable; the safety of the kingdom reposed on a few magical secrets that the ancient kings of Etesia had obtained from the gods, and only Sparyanthis knew and fully understood their sacred value. Cimmerion, made to bear arms, recognized that he was less subtle than his brother, and they loved one another mutually for their weakness and their strength.

The elder, rude and almost chaste, cherished like a spouse the sage counsels of the frail adolescent with the brain filled with visions, and affectionately excused his lust and preciosity. The younger was enthused by the fraternal strength, and between the two of them, they were the masters and the leaders of a submissive people.

At night, on seeing the extreme galleries of the palace light up, where Sparyanthis shut himself with the mages as well as women, turned toward the heavens amid the instruments of an unknown science, and pursued, out of love as much as dreams, the research of firmamental wills, the Etesians knew that the tutelary soul of their race was on watch in the midst of the orgy. And by day, inclined before Prince Cimmerion, ordering all things, standing like a statue of war, they were able to salute without abasement Etesian force incarnate in its superb son.

The recent conquest of the only neighboring kingdom that might conceal a genuine peril, a conquest of which couriers had brought news a few days before, assured the prestige of the reign definitively. This day was the promise of a total glory. The situation of Etesia, at the heart of a country surrounded by colossal mountain chains, would isolate it perhaps for centuries, from the covetousness of distant nations, occupied in subjugating the coasts of interior seas by the force of their fleets, and scarcely knowing what existed beyond those sheer mountains.

Those glad thoughts filled the soul of the meditative prince, lulled by the songs of viols, and as everything in the soul of Sparyanthis was referred to the feminine form of beauty, as all of his joys resembled more or less the softness savored in a bodily embrace, he mingled confusedly with the image of the triumph, in that bright morning succeeding the dreams of the dawn, the memory of the woman glimpsed in his sleep—and the memory of that tall white form undulated before his pupils, dazzled the dancing mirage of the spangles of the sunlit sky.

Finally, the golden mail-clad torsos of guards raising curved buccinas surged on to the terraces; inflated cheeks squirted out howling blasts of military music, blasts and bronze identifying their splendor, as if the fanfare itself, materialized in the metal, were shining in the fists of the men taut with effort. A thunder of drums rumbled; bearing two sheaves of blue-fletched arrows fixed to the pleats of the belt, turbaned archers appeared, as supple as women in their scaly half-breastplates, and the octagonal crests of the ax-bearers, haloed by their steel disks, were already emerging from the steps. A thicket of spears starred with red tufts of feathers, and a flock of princes in short mantles of white hide, clad in white reflections of their mantles over their silver armor, raised a semicircle of brandished swords to salute the child of diamonds and emeralds extending his hands in their homage, and then parted.

Alone, a gigantic scarab of somber metal, devoid of insignia and jewels, his long brown hair overflowing the helmet on which a single sheaf of golden leaves trembled, throwing back his cape of war, Prince Cimmerion smiled at his brother Sparyanthis, who, with a great cry, threw himself on his bosom, crushing his embroideries upon the breastplate and the chain of the heavy sword, while the fraternal arms squeezed him.

The unanimous acclamation fell silent abruptly to respect the majesty of that kiss of princes; then, when they finally came apart, burst forth more formidably still, magnified by fanfares. The cortege of captain united with that of mages and women, and the princes, after a last gesture of adieu to the people, thousands of whose faces were crying out toward the double silhouette dominating the horizon, went into the vestibules strewn with flowers.

The luxurious vessels of feasts were already clattering, and the enchantment of the gardens and porticos was the prelude to an intoxication of beauty more captivating still, in accordance with the ingenious and voluptuous genius of Sparyanthis, who had prepared for the vanquishers the most violent of contrasts and the sweetest of pleasures.

The celebrations intensified. Etesia entire was abandoned to joy and enthusiasm; before the eyes of the crowd, at tables set up in the streets, crammed with food by the care of stewards, filed innumerable chariots of booty and cohorts of captives, which astonished the women, and the singing and dancing would be prolonged until the following dawn through an immense night of amour.

Meanwhile, the mages, gathered around the altars, applied themselves by their prayers and their studies to ward off the future misfortunes that destiny could not fail to prepare to compensate for such a beautiful moment.

And on the high bed of repose that dominated the hall in which the generals and the dignitaries were assembled, disdaining to eat, Sparyanthis and Cimmerion conversed together fervently.

Lying on a mass of conquered oriflammes, beneath an awning improvised with the shields of vanquished chiefs, they savored the joy of seeing one another again.

Cimmerion recounted the conquest, the rivers crossed under a rain of javelins, the cavalries dispersed, the combats in forests on fire, the catapults opening breaches in walls, the assaults, the rapes, the blood, the sanctuaries forced, and his laughter oscillated his leonine face, striped by the fresh scar, still red, of a sword-thrust stopped by the frontal of his helmet.

Sparyanthis recounted his subtle thoughts, his meditations in the company of mages, his incantations, his lusts and his dreams. And suddenly, he smiled, because the image of the woman he had imagined a few hours earlier reappeared in is memory, and when Cimmerion asked him what that smile signified, he explained it.

"O my brother," he said, in conclusion, "that dream announced to me a happiness in the form of a woman; I did not know then that the army was so close, and that the happiness in question would be that of your return, presaged by that illusory messenger.

It was then Cimmerion who smiled, and replied: "O Sparyanthis, my young brother of the subtle mind, perhaps that messenger was not illusory, and if she announced my coming, perhaps she was not because of that separate from real life, and her face, Sparyanthis, only preceded that of your brother, without being less real than him. The moment has come to tell you something dear to my rude heart, something from which neither the shield nor the breastplate could defend me."

"What do you mean, Cimmerion?"

"Permit me, who does not understand magic," the prince concluded, still smiling, "to experience the reality of your dream."

He made a sign to an officer. A few moments later, a curtain was lifted, and a veiled woman appeared, and stood motionless.

"Know now, my beloved brother, the face that veil conceals," said Cimmerion, removing it without abruptness.

Surprised, Sparyanthis considered the unknown woman. Scarcely had he rested his gaze upon her, however, than he shuddered, and his entire soul changed; for the woman who stood before him, and whom he had never seen in any place on earth, was the very one that he had desired in his dream, as Cimmerion had said in jest, unconscious of the import of his words. And the coincidence of that marvelous beauty, here living and taciturn, with the beauty of the dream, had something mysterious and terrible about it.

"O Sparyanthis!" sad Cimmerion then, "this is my bride-to-be, and if your dream foresaw her at the very moment when my return was about to be announced to you, it is because the gods wanted, from that moment on, to associate her image with that of the brother whose return you had not seen. But was it really her of whom you dreamed?"

At that instant, an obscure intuition gripped the heart of Sparyanthis, a shadow passed over his mind, and he sensed for the first time the necessity of lying to his brother Cimmerion, without yet understanding why.

"It was not her, my brother," he said, laughing, "but doubtless some phantom issued from my imagination prompted by lust."

With these words he looked coldly at the unknown woman, but he read in her eyes a contradiction so singular, so violent and so impressive that he felt penetrated in the very heart of his lie with such acuity that he almost felt hatred, while Cimmerion, incapable of interpreting that exchange of glances, said:

"The destiny of war gave me this Alilat, a princess of royal blood, and her beauty moved me. I do not bring her here as a captive, but she will be your sister, Sparyanthis, if the one that is dear to me is dear to you. In her resides the hope of my race, and if I die, with you she will be the mistress of Etesia.

"Let it be so, Cimmerion!" said Sparyanthis—and he threw himself into the arms of his elder brother, and kissed him on the shoulder and the forehead, in accordance with the rite of the oath of fidelity, in order to hide the trouble that invaded him, while the marvelous stranger, standing before them, immobile, considered them in silence.

A few days later, the wedding of the Princess Alilat and Prince Cimmerion was celebrated, and the life of the palace resumed its ordinary course. Cimmerion devoted himself to hunting in the leisure time that the affairs of the city left him; Sparyanthis, among the mages and the women, continued his cherished existence of dreams and kisses. Princess Alilat was confined to her apartments very distant from his own. Their two palaces opened at the two extremities of a vast wood, dense and dark. They only saw one another in the presence of

357

the elder prince, at times of feasts or in the Council of the Etesian State, and they hardly ever spoke to one another.

For a long time, in the evenings, Sparyanthis interrogated
his magic crystals and his ritual tables in order to discover
whether his brother's wife had been able to divine that he really had seen her in a dream, or whether the heavy, almost provocative gaze that she had attached to his might only be due to
hazard. But he could not determine it. That Princes Alilat had
appeared to him, he could not doubt, but that she knew it, and
had discerned his lie, he could not admit.

Cimmerion's simple mind had interpreted that apparition
as a fortunate presage, and the deceitful response had, in any
case, reassured him. It was nonetheless true that two links of a
mysterious chain already existed between Sparyanthis and
Alilat; a dream and a lie commanded one to the other.
Sparyanthis knew that he had desired that beauty, suddenly
arrived, in his sleep, as if his brother had brought him a bride
announced by the gods.

Before the innocent joy of the warrior with the primitive
soul, introducing the woman he loved, how could Sparyanthis,
having had the imprudence to recount his vision, have certi-
fied a resemblance that would have cast trouble into the heart
of the conqueror? It was necessary that he dissimulated, and
did not repent having done so. But how had Alilat been able to
penetrate the dissimulation? There lay the secret, there the
cloud of peril.

Sparyanthis did not love Alilat, in spite of the desire of
his slumber. He applied himself to the study of her beauty. It
was extraordinary. Never had a woman so white appeared in
Etesia. The whiteness of her skin was more like that of a wa-
ter-nymph than a mortal woman. Lying on a silken cushion, or
on the marble pedestal of a statue, Alilat's bare arm seemed to
be leaning on a surface of gold or amber, and yet her pallor
had no hint of the tomb, but revealed itself living and warm.

There was in Alilat's stride and attitudes, in addition to a
harmony easy to divine, an ineffable nonchalance. She did not
walk so much as undulate, and when the memory had evoked

the swelling of the throat of a turtle-dove, the palpitations of the bodies of enormous serpents, and the inflection of certain reeds, it remained incapable of depicting that indescribable caress of flesh imbued with sap, the unfurling of the organism that, when Alilat sat down, seemed to pour her slowly, like a river of milk and lilies emanating from a mysterious and pure spring.

That whiteness irradiated the penumbra of porticos, and appeared to traverse the precious fabrics in which the princess was dressed. Finally, the visage itself was surprising without one knowing why. The Etesians were astonished by those close-set eyes, opening two gulfs of green water, beside a narrow and willful nose, beneath the twin arches of eyebrows casting a heavy shadow; and the unusual redness of her lips was disquieting in the immaculate pallor of that oval face. Alilat's oriental blood revealed to their surprised eyes blond montagnards loving women with pink mouths and brightly colored cheeks.

A suggestion of intense voluptuousness emanated from her, belied by the mineral coldness of her pensive irises and the harshness of her taut mouth. Passive to Cimmerion's desires, she maintained an almost fateful dignity, the secret of a passion whose labyrinthine ways no one knew, and which slept within her like a palace of black stone. Perhaps no one had been able to fill those abstract and lugubrious vaults with the echo of a name.

It did not seem that Alilat retained the memory and the hatred of her destroyed race and her body seized by the conquering prince; she passed indifferently from one land to the other, as insensible as a symbol that cannot be profaned, and which retains the same splendor in the vaults of temples where its vanquishers come to admire it as in the sanctuaries in which its worship gave the vanquished pride.

Sparyanthis was almost surprised not to be moved by the beauty of Alilat, toward which his long ennui of women obtained had, in the sweetness of dreams, expressed the ardent ingenuity of a desire. The fact that she was dear to his beloved brother contained the logic of his mind, but without explaining the singular aversion of his body, previously faithful to all carnal attractions, and making of amour the sole spring of actions and passions.

Was there, then, a dissemblance between her and her dreamed image? No, since there was no doubting that she had made Sparyanthis understand that she knew the correlation of the presage and herself, and that the taut pleat of her smile had signified that to him imperiously beyond the lie. Sparyanthis often thought about that. Perhaps alone among all the diviners of Etesia, he glimpsed the existence of a semi-celestial region in which unions were accomplished, where identities were established of which earthly beings only testified to the reality by their appearances. Linked to Alilat by the lie and the prescience, he even thought about breaking the bond by limiting its extension in the future.

Meanwhile, the days and the weeks went by. Among Sparyanthis' favorites the slave who had woken him on the morning of Cimmerion's return was now predominant. He had deigned to pluck that virgin flower, and amused himself in artfully fading the fresh charm in the stifling mystery of obscure and perfumed galleries in which his enervating life delighted.

Sparyanthis quit them occasionally to dress his body in feminine robes and go to breathe the fresher and more natural atmosphere of the shady woods that surrounded his pavilion. Escorted by musicians and young people who carried fans, screens and censers, he went along sinuous pathways where the art of gardeners had acclimated aloes, palms and Oriental flowers, as far as a basin in the form of a half-moon, completely bordered by a high wall of sculpted yews, in the bosom of which opened, like a gaze, the surface of an aromatized pool, silent and immutable. There. Sparyanthis diverted himself studying the reflections of the nudities that he invited to the liberties of the bath, and among which his young mistress excited admiration, until the prince, ordering the miming of a few amorous fables, took to the extreme of realization the frolicsome sketch of long-contained desires.

Those fêtes were the favorite amusement of Sparyanthis; Cimmerion never took part in them, disdaining the delicate voluptuousness that softened the muscles of a man of war, and people talked with precaution among the Etesians of those immodest synods, in which the naked adolescent, whiter and more beautiful than all the women, with his hair powdered with mica and his broad necklace of emeralds, a nonchalant god with painted eyelids, seemed to be pursuing in the contemplation of multiple enlacements the secret of curves, the rhythm of united forms, the point at which, from the friction of enfevered flesh, the very idea sprang forth of amour, of infinity escaping from the finite.

It came about that Princess Alilat desired to know those games and to charm her gaze with the mingled beauty of slaves, for in her land, as in Etesia, matters of the flesh were distinct from decency, a virtue reserved for persons of high rank, having no meaning relative to inferior beings, whose sensual caprices were devoid of importance. She appeared, with her women, grave in a long black robe with violet flowers, and while, on her orders, her followers associated themselves with the exquisite and impure ceremony of the bath, she sat down next to Sparyanthis.

The adolescent, in his soft chlamys, ambiguous by virtue of his jewels and beardless face, seemed a younger sister of that pale and serious princess with the grim eyes. Both of them, filled with a similar respect for the religious significance of lust, gazed without ennui and without smiling at the slow tournament of naked forms, young men and young women interlaced, surrounding the porphyry margin of the pool, or half-dissimulating in the water the sighing union of their forms, while, with their backs to the black background of the cypress wall, like so many bouquets of roses changed into statues, other slaves waited and a strange and gripping music rose up, amid panting or laughter, dissimulated by the foliage, of which Sparyanthis took pleasure in orchestrating the rhythms and composing the cadences himself.

At times, the imperious visage of Alilat turned toward his, and they considered one another coldly, without speaking, as if retaining a thought that they did not want to voice.

Finally, Alilat congratulated Sparyanthis on the charming beauty of his favorite's forms and asked him in what epoch he had distinguished her.

"It was," said Sparyanthis nonchalantly, "the day when my brother Cimmerion came back from the war, bringing you with him. She woke me up to inform me of his return, and her grace, combined with the good news that she brought me, appeared sweeter to me. So I decided in my heart to choose her among all those in the apartments of my palace who were awaiting my caprice. I shall spend a season with her until, her aroma wearying my curiosity, I relegate her to the ranks of those who are no more to me than forms, mingled with others for the pleasure of my eyes, but distant from my bed."

"She will be fortunate," Alilat said, in a melancholy fashion, "to have at least known the season of her desire." Ironically, she added: "For are you not desired by all your female subjects? How many of them, young woman of high rank, living free in the palaces of your dignitaries, destined to enrich the dwellings of glorious captains or renowned scholar, would gladly exchange patrician status for the honor of being slaves in your somber porticos, awaiting the hour to dissipate your ennui and perfume your slumber? All of them, surely, think you the most handsome of Etesians. But tell me, prince, whether that young woman, on the day when she woke you up to tell you the good news, did not interrupt you in the spectacle of a dream? It seems to me that your brother mentioned such a circumstance to me..."

Troubled, Sparyanthis considered the impenetrable visage of Alilat, and replied: "I was, indeed, dreaming; an amorous fantasy was visiting me. Perhaps, without my suspecting it, the presence of that slave had suggested it to me..."

"Was it not rather, Sparyanthis," said Alilat then, with a mysterious and menacing expression, "my own face that appeared to you, while I returned, soon to be espoused but still captive nevertheless, in a litter, amid the harsh clink of weapons? While I waited to see your frail golden silhouette appear on the supreme terrace of that gigantic palace to salute the fraternal return, had not my image already come to meet you, and to smile at you happily in slumber?

"Why lie, Sparyanthis? Why not reply to me and interrogate me further, and ask me how I was able to know your secret? I am of a race that understands the arcana, and disposes of powers, and if my image reached you, it is because I wanted it. Emerged from me, Sparyanthis, it has attached itself to your soul, and in spite of you, it will interpose itself in your kisses—for we are of the same blood, Sparyanthis, the blood of seers, and your brother's conquest has only served to bring us together; it was to bring me to you that he fought."

"You are forgetting," said Sparyanthis, irritated, "that you are my brother's wife, and that one word... Let it suffice for me to reply that I do not love you. Yes, certainly, I have seen you in a dream, and I lied in order to reassure my brother; but you would not dare to reveal that imposture and thus annihilate your pride. Moreover, Alilat, you are too beautiful and too profound for any vain resentment to subsist between us, and you know full well that, having desired you in a dream, I cannot make do with your reality, because, for the beings that we are, wearied by having obtained everything, reality is merely the imperfect décor of dreams."

"Insensate," said Alilat, brusquely, "you have desired me in a dream, but you have not had me. Your desire will avenge me for your ennui, and you will not dare to confess it to your brother."

"I love my brother Cimmerion," said Sparyanthis.

"But we are made for one another, above that gross intelligence that only understands the force of arms, and you know it, O Sparyanthis, young man inspired by the old subtle genius, violator and sorrow of my Orient."

Prince Sparyanthis shivered, but Alilat had already risen to her feet and, bowing to him with the affectation of ritual salutes, a long black and violet serpent trailing her satin pleats, she drew away among the porters of parasols into the shadow of the cypresses, while Sparyanthis, pale and anxious, considered her, surrounded by the white nudities of young men and women. And it was as if all the secret whitenesses of Alilat's body had materialized and remained in her traces, vain simulacra, imperfect sketches of a beauty that she drew away to the rhythm of her imperious stride, to the secret undulation of her closed robes.

At the moment when she disappeared into the shadow of the domes of black leaves, the water of the pool was stained by the supernatural blood of the setting sun, dying in the sky, intercepted by the branches.

From then on, a thought lived with Sparyanthis, lying among the luxurious fabrics of his bed, laying siege to him on nights of study, and it was like a shadow, and no longer went away.

That thought soon enfevered Sparyanthis, and, as if to break him, in moments of voluptuousness, it gripped with a malevolent violence the young torsos united with his own, tightening his lips for fear of pronouncing aloud the execrable name that he invoked silently. Sometimes it was the burn of a handful of snow placed in the middle of is heart and choking him. Sometimes it was a dancing image that substituted itself for his and came to meet him in mirrors, or designed itself in the bosom of the air in the myriad sparks of bright midday. Sometimes it was a slow and cold presence sliding errantly through the darkness like a divinity of an unknown land seeking shelter in frightened souls.

The omnipotence of his belief in the reality of dreams filled Spartyanthis' mind, and all his pleasures had always had for him the savage and inebriating avidity of fatality. Alilat's amour violated his subtle will and attracted him all the more because he had commenced by refusing her desire in the habitual form.

If his dream had been able to give her to him completely, perhaps he would not have remembered her on awakening. But the question posed in the invisible had remained in suspense on the edge of reality, and it was the response that the living presence of Alilat had brought him, appearing in the midst of the army, in the triumphant clamor of trumpets and the pomp of standards, in the arms of another that the dream had not chosen.

She knew that, and that knowledge gripped the mind of Sparyanthis and drew him toward her outside of his flesh. Henceforth, Alilat, beyond the porticos and the vast detours of the park, was like a magnetic stone, hidden but irresistible. As a woman, he had disdained her; as a symbol of a divine and fatal will, he wanted her, as he had, during so many astrological nights, wanted the unknown of which she had revealed herself to be one of the poles.

He used up his desires in vain on young docile flesh. They seemed to him to be savorous fruits—but over the alleviation of lust, in the weary hours of the afternoon, the phantom of Alilat floated, more tyrannically spiritual. The incantations he attempted failed. Several times, having invoked it in mirrors in which the apparition of a face announced the imminent death of the individual it shows, he saw the silhouette of the sorceress sketch itself, but the mirrors cracked, and he perceived a kind of ironic snigger.

Having designed, by the force of his science, the curve of that existence, and attempted to confound it with the lineaments signifying death, he saw the thin sinuosity invariably rejoin his own and entwine with it, on the magic tableau, the sign that is the figure of the indissoluble. Undoubtedly, shut away in her distant apartments, the Oriental woman was pursuing her mysterious work, invoking spirits more powerful than those of Etesia.

Sparyanthis was suffering. He thought about his brother Cimmerion, whom he loved, and who had brought into the palace a principle of death and despair, thinking that he was bringing joy.

At times, he thought of telling him about Princess Alilat's confession of love. Then he recoiled from the idea of this destroying his brother's happiness, and immediately savored, in a furious surge of remorse and covetousness from which he could not extract his heart, a grim hatred in seeing Alilat exiled or tortured by the cruel anger of Cimmerion.

Then a revolt was born within him against the unconsciousness of the soldier who came back from his favorite hunts in the evening, arched in his bloodstained leather coat, making his bronze leg-guards ring, surging forth, spear in hand, among his officers and his slaves, dragging slaughtered animals over the floor-tiles of the vestibules. Alilat offered him a cup, with her calm smile and her haughty grace, and sometimes, moving his captains aside with a gesture, the man with the muscular torso hugged his white spouse, and left red stains on her bosom, without suspecting the adulterous thoughts and the hatred concealed beneath that untroubled and splendid flesh.

Sparyanthis knew the sudden brutalities of the sword-bearer. He too had respired the odor of murder on that armored breast, with the intoxication of a puny child admiring strength, but without jealousy, and now his mind was imagining with an intense clarity the consummation of that desire, the tall pale princess tipped back in the disorder of drapes under the imperious kisses of Cimmerion, without her body revolting against them.

Alilat had subjugated Sparyanthis' thought completely, and the idea that Cimmerion would never possess Alilat's gave him an emotion of dolorous joy. She had spoken the truth, in the depths of her mysterious soul; they were both made for spiritual union, for the magic predominance orientating Etesia toward marvelous destines, making it the center of a talismanic world against which no raising of swords could prevail.

Thus, new sentiments gradually entered into Sparyanthis, which astonished his anxious soul, and it was like the discovery within himself of unusual forms of amour. A strange mysticism, long and vainly sought in voluptuousness, was revealed to his eyes; he would have spoken about it to his brother without hesitation if he known that he was intelligent, but Cimmerion could not have understood, and thus the amour of Sparyanthis for Alilat gradually rose above the flesh, fortified by the secrecy. It became almost legitimate to hide the union of souls that the blind fury of the husband would have crushed with an unjust murder.

In his solitary meditations Sparyanthis attained revelations that only mages from the depths of Asia encountered by voyagers in Greece, to whom he had listened avidly when they passed through Etesia, had allowed him to have any hint of their essence. Of barbaric desire, satisfied by the penetration of the flesh, was born, like a splendid flower, the intuition of a more efficacious and more profound penetration. But at the same time, the amity of Sparyanthis for Cimmerion died; he judged his brother, no longer able to consider their strength and science as two equal conditions; his soul dew away toward regions in which spirituality ought to soar without admixture, and he suffered from those struggles and those scruples.

Grim before his existence, invisibly drawn away, he languished in debaucheries, inactive. In vain the animally happy creatures who had once aided the ascension of his soul showed themselves to him; at present, having surpassed the sum of dreams that the excess of the spasm provides, he judged it superfluous. Instead of extracting from every woman the second of infinity that is contained, unknowingly, in the pure jewel-case of her body, he became irritated in finding all flesh limited and impotent; the mere thought of Alilat gave him a vaster intoxication, and the attempted to possess her in dreams in order to liberate himself from that fascination. He became somnolent, exhausted by perfumes, and his vain attempts were followed by crises of wrath against the pale enchantress who had take his instinctive Barbarian happiness and awakened in him the vertigo of the absolute.

He understood that he was isolated from everyone, driven by his genius and passionate impulsion to a series of thoughts unknown to all his race, and singular cruelties were born in him. He was seen wandering, preoccupied, becoming thin, pushing away the young women offered, and the taste of kisses sickened him. Consternated, his favorites lived in a bleak anguish. Sometimes he told his musicians to shut up, and sometimes he commanded them to play violent dances, and sent them to the limits of the park, as if to carry to Alilat the announcement of an ironic insouciance that was belied by the tumult of his soul.

The implacable desire of Alilat went out toward the young man with the extraordinary rectitude that the simplicity of fatalism gives. It pleased her, because it incarnated the two most delicious sentiments she knew, which are like two wings enveloping the entire brood of human emotions: hatred and amour. To obtain Sparyanthis would be to avenge herself on Cimmerion, and that vengeance, expressed by a kiss, would be the most exquisite of all. The pride of her destroyed race was reborn in the person of the last daughter of kings, humiliated and captive, thrown into the victor's bed and suddenly upstanding again, vengefully. Every conquest made over the soul and the senses of Sparyanthis would be stolen from the soul and senses of Cimmerion, and in Sparyanthis himself, by awakening joy and amour, she would make the brother of her homeland's conqueror suffer.

Alilat wanted that triumphant adultery; she awaited the propitious evening when she would kiss her vengeance on the mouth, and she loved Sparyanthis madly because her desire would be contented in making him suffer. She did not hasten to see him, certain of the progress within him of the poison that her audacious speech had poured.

Execrated as the son of a usurper race and brother of the armed brute to whose embrace she submitted, Sparyanthis, in

Alilat's amour, was identified as the hoped-for, adored, vengeance ripened in the depths of her ardent soul, and she sensed that to him, she would give herself sincerely and totally, as if to the vengeance that her defeat of the brother would incarnate.

At the same time, she allowed free speech to her thirst for that tender and curious beauty, made supple in the balm of voluptuousness, rare and passive to whom remorse would give a new savor, and whose effeminate character pleased her energy as a pensive woman revolted by masculinity.

The moment came when Sparyanthis could no longer resist the force of destiny.

It was in a warm dusk. Sadly, he had gone alone to a large pool where, in the bosom a stone architecture, seven jets of water sprang forth: a marvelous invention that a Syrian prisoner had once installed in the royal garden. Those jets of water were like the souls of the palace. They came to life at dawn and died away as night fell, when the last cry uttered by the guards of the hour announced the period of silence. Sparyanthis often liked to watch them die away one by one, with a supreme sigh, like white peacocks irradiating their diaphanous tails. For him it was the pretext for a thousand images, in which he compared them to flowers or swords or serpents, saw the symbol of love expiring at the limit of the impassive sky, or imagined them as springing forth from a subterranean mine of precious stones, going to enrich the azure with a myriad of new stars.

That evening, he sensed with desolation that the jets of water were the signs of his scruples, forcefully enlaced, scattered, dissociated, broken against the pearly pallor of a sky that had the marvelous color of Alilat's flesh, and then falling back with the soft sound of a sob. And while he was dreaming, one of the jets broke, was nullified, disappeared into the nascent darkness, and then a second, and then a third. And along the edge of the pool Sparyanthis walked, with his heart hammering, as if to follow the successive deaths; and all the splendid play of the jets of water was that of an immense clepsydra noting the supreme minutes of his consented crime, and they fell back with the heaviness of fatality itself, shattering the mirror of the basins in which a tumult of illegible signs was quivering.

And finally, the seventh jet of water, which rose up at the extremity of the banks against an arch of moist black verdure plunged in a vertiginous descent, and Prince Sparyanthis, raising his eyes, saw Alilat waiting for him, with the gesture of silence.

As it was completely dark beneath the vault, all that he could see of her was the whiteness of her bare arms, shining.

Taciturn, they committed the sacrilege.

At first their amours were those of unconscious beasts, furious and hasty, as if every word would have had to conclude with a bite rather than touching the secret reason for their contact.

With a single surge the flood of forsaken voluptuousness rose again in Sparyanthis with the fury of surf breaking against the indescribable pale languor of Alilat's body abandoned in the darkness. It was an unending and sinuously obstinate tide, unleashed by its very expiration and reformed toward the central point of the somber mouth, toward the twin glimmer of those long eyes filled with icy green water, unfathomable and unmovable, exempt from tears and mists.

Never before had Sparyanthis, previously master of his own pleasure, dosing himself with the reflective power of an artist, elevating a certain suggestion of disdain and insouciance, experienced the delights of that total defeat of the self, the disaggregation of the entire being in the exquisite stupor of consented crime, the progressive diffusion of the will and the senses in a kind of warmth similar to that of anesthetic poisons.

In the arms of Alilat, Sparyanthis became akin to the man who, having drunk hemlock, lies down to die and, little by little, no longer senses his flesh, and believes that he is floating, falling asleep between heaven and earth.

They met in the arbors during the slow dismal afternoons while Cimmerion was hunting or visiting the camps that surrounded the city. Their meetings were easy, for Cimmerion, incapable of being suspicious of his brother, encouraged his relationship with his wife. He wanted them not to be enemies, and saw in that amicable union a means of extracting Sparyanthis from his life of enervating sensuality, of which he secretly disapproved. The young prince had become so weak and indolent that Cimmerion had been alarmed.

There was between them, and in accordance with dynastic custom, an absolute principal of reciprocal liberty between Etesian princes; the violent genius of their line had always been manifest in the double form of war and refined debauchery. But Cimmerion's love saw in Alilat, so sage and so haughty, an opportunity for Sparyanthis to enjoy repose and peaceful conversations, and although they feigned coldness and almost aversion at times of common gathering, that precaution only encouraged Cimmerion to bring them closer together. He even asked that of Alilat, who was careful not to tell Sparyanthis, the idea of a possible peril able to contribute to the irritation of his desires and his caprice. They were thus able to see one another at their ease, and a feverish life unfurled.

They sent away the slaves, and savored together the cold of shadows, the glaucous caress of reeds, the mystery of thickets, where the changing mistress seemed a surprised nymph, or a young hunter with an arrogant visage carrying away like an indecent prey the pliant body of the adolescent with the painted eyes. She was varied, as supple in the soul as in the flesh, illuminated by joy and vengeance. At certain times, they enclosed themselves in rocky lairs where, naked and bestial, stripping of all artifice of toilette, every jewel, her hair tinted with red powder falling like a mane over her vibrant flesh, the amorous woman, with cries and words concluded by gasps, offered herself cynically, and almost frightfully. Then she forbade Sparyanthis to seize her, gave him a rendezvous in some other place—and he found her there coiffed in a tiara, streaming with gems, sitting among her followers, with a dignified smile, and his soul, warm with the memory of the writhing of the satyress, was sharpened dolorously on the cold stone of that ironic contrast.

Alilat often surprised him, slipping into the spacious silence of porticos far from the bed of the sword-bearer, a shadow haunting the vestibules and placing on the lips of soldiers awakened by her rustling, before they were able to make their weapons clink, the odorous flower that was her special sign, and which briskly elongated her white arm. She disappeared, and the leather-helmeted head of the man-at-arms slumped backwards against the wall, smiling with the indifference of servitude. No one, before that agreed sign, would have dreamed of speaking, the royal personage being the very image of death—which is to say, of omnipotence. Alilat thus succeeded in reaching Sparyanthis apartments. The silk drapes rose; he shivered, perceived a slender female form modeled in the garment of a slave, and closed his eyes again—but then the slave kissed his lips violently, and it was Alilat.

At other times, as he was passing along a gallery, a motionless young archer would suddenly put a hand on his arm. He arched his back, surprised, recognized the double green lake of the inimitable eyes, and went back to his apartment, where, laughing and dropping the bow and the quiver of blue-fletched arrows, his lover seized him with the audacity of a Roman soldier bending to his desire a soft conquered Syrian girl.

And at other times, when he was dreaming among his magical instruments, the accumulation of a strange science, black granite tables, convex mirrors, phials of blood, bronze armatures supporting globes in which the stars were reflected, a mute mage would come in, and trace on the ground, with the tip of a wand, the hieroglyph signifying the union of opposites. Then, shivering, Sparyanthis would discern, beneath the constellated headband and the fake beard, the eyes and lips of

Alilat, whose breasts would surge forth beneath her parted robe. Thus she mingled with his entire life, by turns princess, slave, magicienne and prostitute, she represented to him the principal images to which his corrupt fantasy had always limited the world.

But soon, to the amazement and anxiety of Sparyanthis, she incarnated another personality. She became almost maternal. In the excessive nervous tension of his pleasure, he lowered his face on to his bed, weeping, and sometimes raised it haggard, thinking about his betrayed brother, their childhood games, their former amity, their mutual thoughts, and the hatred of the enchantress returned to him; it was another excess of voluptuousness, the savor of remorse was a supreme aroma mingled with the bitterness of tears on his lips. Then, Alilat took him in her arms and rocked him, singing strange melodies in a low voice, which penetrated him with tenderness and dread.

Chaste, without perfumes, severe in closed robes, she evoked the gestures of puerility in that adolescent initiated too soon into science and lust, raised by slaves, having never know his mother the princess, who had died giving birth to him, so weak that there had seemed to be no hope of his survival. Alilat was able to calm those rebellions of the soul, set aside the remorse, but the next day she revived them, having become a courtesan and an adulteress again.

When he awoke after a long torpor, Sparyanthis saw the daylight again wanting nothing except to prolong the illusion of innocence, the forgetfulness of the crime. Alilat came to fetch him, and instead of the maternal and gentle lover, he met a capricious mistress offering to his fatigue, amid music and the fumes of violent perfumes, the ingenious assemblage of new nudities grouped with perversion among the songs, the laugher and the racket of celebrations, and the languorous ardor of the sun, flowers, flesh and sonorities returned to the unquiet young man the lascivious and malevolent soul that had been momentarily banished.

Alilat silently enjoyed her triumph.

And gradually, her soul, corrosive and omnipotent, decomposed that of Sparyanthis. By that means she avenged in the very bosom of pleasure the insult made to her race. The two brothers dissociated, one betrayed, the other tamed: that was her work. She experienced an infinite exaltation in thinking that for that work, amour had sufficed her, which summarizes the world and places that the center of everything the unconscious and tranquil woman.

In satisfying her desire she satisfied her rancor; the beloved was the enemy, the cycle was closed, and all the tortures of Sparyanthis nourished his joys, and on seeing him suffer, she did not suffer, even though she loved him, because she knew that love and suffering are the two faces of passion, necessary and indissociable.

It was Etesia entire that she was debasing, the Etesia that had set fire to her capital, murdered her brothers, dispersed her wealth, seized her person, and which she now dominated from the height of the seven terraces of the colossal palace-citadel, while waiting to lead it to the destiny decided by her evil genius, whether she would usurp the throne for herself alone, or, enthusiastic for the magical life in the solitudes of her Oriental deserts, she created a colossal cataclysm and fled under the coarse mantle of a woman of the people, taking advantage of the panic, laughing under her veil.

Then, after many days and nights of exodus, she would be welcomed, beyond the savage mountains, by the communities of mages who decree the magnetic destiny of the world on the plateaux from which the first humankind descended. As queen, she would live happily until the time of her reunion with the harmonies that brush the earth and carry beings away into the spheres of crystal and fire where future incarnations are molded.

Those dreams occupied Alilat. She reigned without contest over the mind of Cimmerion. Her speech in the councils revealed a profound and prevailing sagacity; inclined before her thought, which completed that of her brother, the conqueror adored her beautiful body, which easily feigned enthusiasm for his strength.

In the hours when Sparyanthis reproached himself for his treason, Alilat was able, with a glance, to give birth in his presence to covetousness in Cimmerion's face. Once, she arranged for him to surprise her, semi-naked, in the master's arms. Sparyanthis ran away; she did not see him again all day, knowing that he was suffering, and the following day it was him who came back, pale and ardent.

The seed of hatred for his brother had entered into Sparyanthis. He slipped past the sleeping guards. The almost-extinguished torches cast sinister unequal lights, striping the great expanses of shadow on the galleries, causing the corners of shields, crests and sword-points to glitter on the ground, between the carpets and the mats, and sometimes and abrupt gleam revealed a woman's hair, a white breast, a shoulder, a rounded hip, shining softly, rubbing against a martial belt—for the slaves, at night, joined the archers and the hoplites slyly. The frightful voluptuousness of the palace had ended up destroying the ancient discipline, an orgiastic suggestion prowled the vast domain, and the heaviness of warm sensuality softened the men. Sighs and stammers lived in the darkness. Heaps of cushions retained the forms of bodies.

Sparyanthis, furious and bewildered, nude beneath his chlamys, having taken off his sandals, advanced among all those prostrate beings, all the way to Alilat's apartment, without even thinking that his brother might be there—his now-execrated brother, of whom the lustful image, congested with brutality, strength and desire, shone in his memory and brought a murderous cry to his lips.

He parted the tapestries violently. A little lamp scarcely illuminated the retreat. Broken adornments lay on the ground, which bruised his heels, torn robes resembled cadavers, and he heard a slight sound of sobbing.

Alilat, extended, hiding her head in her hands and in her abundant hair, was lying like an abused slave in the disorder.

He seized her wrists, threw back her tresses, and forced her to look at him. Then he saw an expression so savage that he was afraid, and she pushed him away with a gesture so furious that he tottered, imploring and crazed.

"Why didn't you come?" he said. "I had to be very brave to come to you this evening, and my brother himself..."

"I shan't come again, I shan't ever come again," said Alilat, in a low voice. "Oh, coward, coward! How could you leave me the shame of telling you that I'm sickened by your brother' kisses? How have I been able to love you, you who abandon me? How have I been mad enough to obey ironic destiny, come to you in a dream, submit for you to the outrage of exile instead of perishing in the conflagration of my capital, and believe that you would love me? Viler than a common prostitute, more unworthy of love than the least of your slaves, you have played with me; your egotistical debauchery accept-ed me as a pastime, and what do you care about the quotidian profanation of your brother, soiling this body that I had des-tined for you? Corrupt and cowardly child, vitiated by the ca-resses of mercenaries, could you comprehend the grandeur of my dream, unite yourself with me, prevail by force? You pre-ferred to lie to yourself, invoking a fraternal love in which you no longer believe, enemy enough to betray, but not enough to claim me. Do you think that I fear you? Even if you were to summon the guards, and even if your brother came in response to your voice to kill me, what does my life matter to me? In death I would no longer be your double plaything, I would at least forget that I had loved you!"

Sparyanthis, bewildered, tried to embrace her, but she slipped away, and continued, shaken by spasms:

"Yes, I've loved you, because you had, like me, the se-cret of sciences that lead crowds, the knowledge of fluids and numbers, the love of the celestial unknown. And I came to-ward you confidently, and when from my litter I perceived your golden form at the limit of the sun, like an arrested star, I knew that it was you and no other, and I would have recog-nized you among ten thousand like you, and my soul and my flesh quivered, and without even perceiving the soldier who, riding to my right, brought me captive and destined me for the derisory nuptial honor, I breathed and thought I was free, happy! But now it's necessary that, limiting my sad, violated, mocked life, a prisoner of gilded ennui, envying the lives of the daughters of your mountains, I die in this palace, at least refusing myself to you, faithful to your brother whom you love so much! Oh, coward, coward!"

"I hate Cimmerion," said Sparyanthis, pale.

"You're lying!"

"I hate my brother! Alilat, I hate him. Something in me has broken. Like a reflection of the sun, a column of gold and crystal, reflected in the ripples of a black pool of water, your image rises up from the gulf of my former melancholy, a column of joy, light and warmth, the wine of life! I hate the man who touches you, I have known for you the love that yields and supports, I have banished will in desire, and what does my artificial kingdom matter, compared with the soul that you have torn out of me!"

"If you hate your brother, then let him die!" sad Alilat, slowly, putting into that word the stake of her entire life.

Sparyanthis shuddered, and she believed that he was about to die. But he straightened himself and murmured: "If you wish."

"It's necessary that you wish it."

"I wish it...no, Alilat—he's my brother!"

"Go away, then, or I'll call him myself."

Sparyanthis shuddered again. She was standing up, distraught, like a surprised adulteress, challenging him, her face turned toward the issue that led to Prince Cimmerion's apartments.

"Go away! Or with a single scream I'll wake him up, and I'll escape from you."

He took two steps, and then, lowering his head, he acquiesced in silence.

She embraced him, but a sound was heard in the vestibule. They remained enlaced, holding their breath. They heard the voice of a guard muttering in a dream, and then a kiss, a rustle of silks and metal. Everything fell silent.

Alilat threw a woman's robe over Sparyanthis' shoulders, and he fled in the obscurity, avoiding the maladroit clutch of a drowsy soldier, who thought he was seeing a slave, and wearily went back to sleep after having tried to seize the edge of her veils in passing,

He found himself back in the clear night. The fixed stars and the cold seemed to him to be new things, and a great deliverance welled up within him, born of the acceptance of the crime.

The city was asleep under a blue enchantment, and, thinking about the stupor that would seize Etesia, the adolescent dressed as a young woman smiled with an almost glad irony.

Alilat did not mention the promise again. It seemed that she had forgotten it. Long days passed. Their pleasures were gentle and appropriate to the spring. If Sparyanthis attempted an allusion to that terrible night, Alilat playfully placed a rose over his mouth.

One evening, when he was reposing with her, in the company of Cimmerion, in one of the halls of the palace, he thought he observed that his brother was pale and having difficulty breathing. His clear gaze was fleetingly veiled, and there was throughout that powerful and naïve organism a kind of painful astonishment, a mute surprise, a slowness.

Sparyanthis looked at the princess. Pure and pale, she respired flowers and smiled. The mildness of the evening was exquisite. Sooner than was customary, Cimmerion rose to his feet and embraced his brother, who watched him draw away with Alilat.

The following day, as Cimmerion was leaving to go hunting and Sparyanthis found himself standing next to him, the prince complained of a malaise, and smiled.

"I miss the war," he said. "Peace and amour enervate the body and indispose the mind of a man habituated to camps."

He drew away, amid his dogs and his valets.

When he came back, he seemed sad, without understanding why.

More days passed. Sparyanthis trembled that he might have divined the adultery, and interrogated Alilat, but she smiled and avoided any question. He was irritated by that.

Singularly relieved since his resolution to the crime, only living any longer for two or three sentiments, simultaneously fortified and undermined by obsession, Sparyanthis, for the first time, was counting the hours and desirous of action.

Finally, one stormy afternoon, as he was going to his brother's apartment, he learned from a captain that his brother was ill. He found Cimmerion devoid of color and thin, lying on a platform.

Before him, servants were lining up trophies of conquered weapons, standards and insignia.

"I'm distracting myself in peace-time," said Cimmerion, "looking at these weapons, which I snatched from valiant warriors, in the hot sunlight, in the great dust wind of battled, when the ground was a tempest beneath the feet of furious horses. I'm sensing something that resembles ennui. However, Etesia is thirsty for calm, and I cannot lead her sons to death."

His visage was grave, and les brutal than usual. He considered Sparyanthis, tenderly and attentively, which troubled the latter.

At that moment, Alilat appeared and said: "Why, Seigneur, don't you undertake some new conquest? Only the breastplate is light enough for your torso, silk dalmatics are too heavy, and ennui is a black bird. Your cavalries are ready, the catapults and onagers are waiting in your camps, their ironwork rusting. Whatever our displeasure might be, why not depart on a new conquest?"

"I don't know where to direct my arms," said Cimmerion, "and I have no conquest more beautiful than yours, and that of my brother."

Sparyanthis shivered, because his brother's gaze was fixed on his own.

Nothing more was said that day.

The melancholy of the elder prince was aggravated by the hour. He seemed pensive, touched by an unknown illness. He said things that he had never thought before.

Sparyanthis resolved to finish with it, because his brother's mildness exasperated his hatred by reminding him of the old amity that he no longer wanted to remember.

Alilat remained impenetrable.

One night, he got up in order to go to meet her. They had both reached the point of no longer caring whether they were discovered, and in the atmosphere of lubricious folly that had gained the entire palace, they met without anyone paying any heed to them. He slipped into Alilat's bedroom, but she was not there.

He seized a dagger and advanced toward his brother's apartment—but what he saw there chilled him; for while Cimmerion was asleep, sighing and feverish, the princess was standing over him with her arms extended, seemingly surrounding him with strange signs. He recognized the gestures that summon invincible death around living beings, and render those who know them all-powerful.

After a few minutes, Alilat went out lightly through an opposite door. Resolutely, Sparyanthis followed her. He thought that she was going to find him, but at the moment when he was about to speak to her he saw that she was heading for another part of the gardens. Astonished, he followed in her footsteps.

Their black forms brushed the foliage, descended staircases and reached the center of terraces that were hollowed out in the interior, so that the colossal palace was elevated like a well around a gulf.

Then Sparyanthis understood that Alilat was heading for the mysterious abyss in which the eye could reflect the burning water of Hell. The ancient Etesian kings had surrounded it with a circle of thick walls and progressively staged around the crater the domes and hanging gardens of the seven regions of the granite palace accumulated by their proud descendancy.

Sparyanthis had never descended into it, for the sciences of the heavens occupied him entirely, and no one approached it. He could not even imagine how Alilat could suspect its existence.

However, she went to it without hesitation, and soon reached the place where the red glow and the sulfurous hot breath revealed the edge of the infernal crypt. By leaning over, one could see changing black shadows designed on the red walls, shadows cast by the gigantic flames that rumbled like a river on the sinister bed of the secret earth. The first king of Etesia had hurled himself into it as an expiatory victim in order to save the besieged city, and the great rout obtained the following day by means of that sacrifice had marked the commencement of an uninterrupted era of conquests and power. Alilat appeared, in the frightful reflection, to be illuminated by an enigmatic and terrible smile.

Sparyanthis watched her from the shadows.

She cried three times, in a great muffled voice that he did not recognize: "Athana! O enchantress Athana! O powerful enchantress Athana, come!"

Then a sudden mildness appeared the growling rumor of the fire, and the color of the flames became pink, and then yellow, and then green, and then blue; and the tip of a larger flame emerged, and gradually took on the oscillating form of an azured apparition, which took on a body, a visage and arms; and those arms extended toward those of Alilat.

"O enchantress Athana, daughter of fire, my sister!" said Alilat, "I come back to you as to the queen of my race, she who reigns over the internal suns of my hot fatherland, of which the foreigners only recognized the visible suns! At all the openings of the primitive earth your altars are erected. All verity is in you, and not in the firmament that is adored in this land of exile to which my worship summons you. For I have known the arcana of fire and I am a daughter of the Orient! I have need of you for my work, O Athana! I love a vengeance and I am avenging an amour, O Athana!"

The silent enchantress raised her hands without replying.

Alilat unfastened her necklace of precious stones and held it out to her.

"O Athana," she said, "touch these stones born of you, sprung from the furnace where you live, and communicate to them your power of destruction and death. Poison my sapphires and my diamonds, enlace devouring death in my bracelets, in order that they become drops and signs of fire to burn the breast and desiccate the life of the man who holds me against him, while behind my smile, my soul hates him. Give me the fire, Athana, in order that Prince Cimmerion will die!"

The great form of blue flame vacillated, and touched the gemstones suspended from Alilat's fingers one by one; and it was as if the statue of night had poured into Hell the stars of an entire night.

Sparyanthis listened dazedly to the dialogue of the two enchantresses. The sparkling skein of jewels burning in that infernal conjuration was Cimmerion's very life! A sacred horror gripped his heart.

Abruptly, he leapt toward Alilat when the enchantress Athana had disappeared into the entrails of the ground.

"What are you doing?"

"Acting. I am decided."

"Then the poison...."

"Do you believe," said Alilat, "that since your promise, that man has touched me once without my pouring death into him? By the contact of my precious stones, the annihilating fire assails him. Furthermore, I am giving him the death that pleases him." With a bitter smile, she added: "Know that he prefers me naked, adorned with my jewels. My necklaces press against his breast, and my bracelets, on my arms clasped around his neck, by means of their venomous gleam, distil the mortal intoxication into his brain that he mistakes for that of amour. You have followed me, Sparyanthis; now you know why your brother is pale, and why he is wasting away."

"I would have preferred the dagger," said Sparyanthis, duly.

"Your arm is weak," said Alilat, softly, "and why is it necessary that he knows that death is approaching? It is sufficient that we know it.

She smiled, mysteriously, fatally and logically. In her eyes, a reflection remained of the gulf she had evoked. They went back up the nocturnal avenues.

From then on, Cimmerion grew weaker, afflicted by an unknown malady. The anxious city knew it, and suffered. The palace was bleak, the flowers suspended on the trophies faded, and rust corroded the suits of armor in the vestibule. The slaves obstinately hid their refused nudities under veils. There were no more fêtes by the varicolored pools; the jets of water died soundlessly in forgetfulness. A pallor reigned over Etesia.

In the consummation of the crime, the days went by. Now, Cimmerion only lived through one joy: that of possessing Alilat, who offered herself to him ornamented with all her gems, rubbed against the breast of the weary warrior. From all her gems an evil spell was born: the rubies discolored the blood, the sapphires and amethysts paled the veins, the diamonds tarnished the gleam of the eyes, the chalcedonies and the topazes faded the flesh, and everything that had touched Athana gave death to the man dazzled by that sumptuous spouse. The poison of the precious stones oozed out, the life of Cimmerion enriched the fateful minerals. At night, while Prince Cimmerion slept, bathed in a sweat of which every drop was a pearl from a necklace, Alilat met Sparyanthis, she unfastened the golden clasps of her ornaments, and her lover possessed her, rich in her pale flesh alone.

But that flesh was itself an irremediable poison for the exhausted prince, who spent his days in bleak attitudes, with the immense stupor of sensing his strength melt away. Sparyanthis, without any precise thought, observed the progress of the sickness.

He was exhausting himself, undermined by remorse, hatred and carelessness of destiny; his astrological tables and his crystal spheres lay, dusty or broken, on the platforms that he no longer mounted. Everywhere, his weary hand traced, mechanically, the sign of confusion, stars with broken and entangled points. He designed them in the sand and on the drapes. He sent away his mages, exiling them among the cowherds in the mountains. He became very weak, sustained by a single idea: the study of the fraternal agony.

A sinister ideal obsessed him, drunk by all the perverse avidity of his soul, born for all decadence. He dreamed of the extinction of the race, the fall of a people accompanying to the tomb the last Etesian princes and being buried with them.

The ignorant people gazed at the colossal palace erected on a mount in the middle of the capital, a temple of strength, where two beings were vanishing under the will of a third, solemnly, in the silence.

Cimmerion was resigned, and pensive. His thoughts were modified. The malady created a new soul in him; he opened himself to previously unknown delicacies, to tendernesses that had never brushed his mind. One might have thought that, with the poison secreted by the precious stones of the criminal Alilat, death was causing sentiments to penetrate him, as pure and incorruptible as their fires.

And he continued to demand of Alilat that she repose on his breast, ornamented, heavy with all her gems. Only thus could he sleep, bathed in a delicious moisture that was already annihilation, and which he mistook for calm. Those slumbers, loved as benefits, left him more exhausted every day in his soul, and more lucid in the divination of a mental world that his primitive violence of a man of war had never glimpsed. A future Cimmerion, astral and purified, was born in that vast brown body, which lay peacefully, politely refusing the futile balms that the physicians offered him.

He had ordered that his suit of armor be brought to him, and, assembled on a mannequin, it seemed to be his projected shadow. He gazed with a pale smile at the specter of bronze, gold and leather, impenetrable to external impacts, empty and dead inside, and it seemed to him to be the very image of the

Cimmerion that he had been, insouciant and reckless, devoid a soul, a stranger to everything save instinct. He became more distant with every passing hour from that vain portrait of himself, penetrated by a detachment that surpassed in pleasure everything that he had previously known of the pleasure of life, and when a friend thinking to distract him from the anguish of his illness attempted to tell him some tale of combat, he bade him to be silent with a simple gesture.

A superhuman force constrained Sparyanthis to watch, without permitting himself an absence, the phases of that strange withering, and also the flourishing of that new soul, which astonished him. By certain reflections on Cimmerion's part, he measured the immensely increasing separation of the man he had hated from the man he had loved, and yet, neither one of them was before him, but a third, of whom he did not know what to think.

He remained, during the slow days, slumped in his brother's room, sick with hatred, anxiety and ennui. Cimmerion's gaze attached itself to him fixedly, and then moved to Alilat. Soon, Sparyanthis no longer doubted that a secret was being elaborated between the three of them in the bleak interrogation of that already vitreous gaze.

Cimmerion was keeping something silent, something about which he did not want to speak: something that wanted to be said, with which he was struggling. His lips stirred, and then his visage froze, seemingly waiting for another moment; and there were times when Sparyanthis stiffened, ready to get up, to interrogate him, to speak the crime aloud, in order to finish with that intolerable torture of silence.

Finally, a weakness so great seized Cimmerion that he seemed close to death. And Alilat, at his bedside, ornamented in accordance with his desire, scintillating with jewels, white and immutable, already seemed to be his soul suspended above him. The prince sent away the guards and dignitaries, and extended his hand to Sparyanthis.

"My brother," he said, softly, "I'm going to die. You're frail. The fate of Etesia is veiled, an eternal cloud will devour

our ancient sun, and perhaps interrupt here the vast line of the men who edified this palace around an unknown, unfathomable gulf. That is why I must talk to you, my brother, in the presence of this woman who is here. The minutes, the color of the night, surround me like as many avid flies.

"I'm not afraid. I shall not die as I have dreamed of dying, my heart opening a large issue to the blade of a sword, or a spear, and I shall not come back from the hurly-burly of battle extended on my royal shield, lifted up by my soldiers in the bosom of bloody crowds like a ship tossed by the storm on the phosphorescence of the furious sea.

"My fate is equal to my patience, and new thoughts have been born within me since I have been languid. Sparyanthis, and you, Alilat, whom I have extracted from the massacre and brought with honor to my bed, do not flee my gaze with yours; listen to me, for I know your secret."

"You know!" cried Sparyanthis, frightened.

"And why," said Cimmerion, smiling sadly, "would I not know it? I have known for a long time that you love Alilat, and that you are loved by her, and I am not offended by it."

"What do you mean?"

"I mean, my brother Sparyanthis, beloved child, sweetness, that I sensed that amour. But why change the face of either one, and what is culpable about it, which ought to be hidden? I am going to a land where these things are natural, just, blessed by the gods of which ours are perhaps only the imperfect images.

"Give me your hand, Sparyanthis, and give me yours, Alilat, so that in this one, large and still roughened by the pommel of the sword, I might grip those two fragile flowers, the hand of a woman and the hand of a child, and die holding them.

"It is necessary that you marry Alilat, Sparyanthis. It is necessary that you marry Sparyanthis, Alilat. My voice is weakening, I'm going; call my captains, that they might know my will. Hurry!

"Both of you have loved me, but I have known the union of your souls, perhaps better than you. I waited for the last moment...

"Sparyanthis, call my captains. And you, Alilat, come to me, bathe me in the refreshing fire of your precious stones...one last time..."

Impassively, Alilat drew nearer.

"What are you doing?" cried Sparyanthis

"I am obeying the prince's desire," Alilat replied, smiling.

Then a superhuman wave sprang forth in Sparyanthis' soul, a nameless cataclysm like that of the sea pouting into the secret crypts of a volcano shook him, crushing his hatred, his remorse and his life, his fraternal love terrified by Cimmerion's sublime wish. He leapt upon Alilat, seized her and shoved her away.

"No, no!" he cried. "You shall not die against her! I have possessed her, my brother, her stones are poisonous; I knew it, and I let her do it! I have killed you. Kill me!"

He shook off the tall pale woman hanging on to his shoulders, and tried to hold out a naked dagger to the dying man, who raised himself up, haggard, and croaked:

"Don't strike her! I forgive—marry her! I love you, Sparyanthis, I love you. Let no one know..."

In a supreme convulsion, Sparyanthis threw himself on the fraternal body, embraced it, felt the two hands of the dying man placed gently upon his hair. But he felt another hand slide over his own and try to detach the dagger from his clenched fingers.

At the same moment, his gaze met that of Cimmerion, and saw it immobilize, close forever. Then, mad, lost, with a superhuman violence, he brought his blade back in the direction of Alilat with a terrible thrust, and plunged it into her breast, without turning round.

A flood of blood drenched him; he remained lying on Cimmerion, hugging him, and over that inert mouth, still open for the pardon, his frenetic love sobbed, screeching.

387

A tumult of weapons and clamors finally made him raise his head. Eyes wide with terror, the guards, officers and slaves who had come running dared not approach the royal bed, at the foot of which the hallucinated gaze of Sparyanthis saw the cadaver of Alilat extended in her scarlet robe, sparking with precious stones, bathing in the sinister splendor of red blood.

An unexpected strength sustained him. He stood up, and in a loud voice, addressed the crowd.

"The prince is dead," he said. "Your Prince Sparyanthis remains before you, alone, the master of the destiny of Etesia. I have punished that murderess, the hypocritical slave to whom my beloved brother's death is due. For myself, I have few moments to live. Let your strength be your guide; here are the faithful chiefs that the counsels of Prince Cimmerion instructed in their duty. Obey! Let the jewels that cover that sacrilegious body be taken from her neck and her arms, and let them be put on me, for it is necessary that I bear them on me for some time. When that impure cadaver is denuded, let it be taken from this hall and thrown into the gulf into which criminals are thrown. Hurry!"

He gave orders stiffly and grimly. Then the trembling slaves decked him with the poisoned jewels, and with a strangely soft smile, he kissed them and pressed them against his flesh in order better to impregnate it. He became again the pale idol, moistened by a dew of precious stones, whose debauchery had once astonished the palace and stimulated the flame of lust on the veins of an entire people.

He advanced, followed by the cortege, and he began to walk through the avenues and arbors in which the phases of his childhood and adolescence had unfurled. He revisited the pool of water next to which Alilat had come to find him, and ordered that it be drained. Then he came to the arch of verdure where the initial crime had been committed, and commanded that a black mausoleum should be built there.

Finally, he headed or the inferior terraces, and while he walked he dictated orders to the dignitaries for the funeral of Cimmerion, urgent measures and edicts, in a cold and authoritarian voice that was surprising in its majesty. He was still descending toward the center of the seven staged enclosures. Half way, he staggered, but continued, leaning on the shoulders of guards.

Chilled by dread, the Etesians did not know where he was going, and they all followed him through the foliage, in a great clinking of weapons, with sobs and stifled words.

Finally, Prince Sparyanthis reached the edge of the terrible crypt that opened into the entrails of the earth. The red glow was visible, and the racket of the infernal waters was audible. There, many of the witnesses went pale, and some in the last ranks drew away, trying not to be perceived. For no one dared approach that issue surrounded by an eternal silence.

Then the prince advanced to the extreme point where Alilat's feet had once posed, and, transfigured, he took of his diadem, his bracelets and his necklaces; by signs, in silence, he ordered that others help him. In his raised hands scintillated an inestimable wave of precious stones, which he caused to sparkle above the sifting gleams of the gulf.

"Athana!" he cried. "O enchantress Athana! O powerful enchantress Athana, emerge and come to me!"

In spite of the sovereign authority of the prince, the crowd recoiled then, maddened by terror. For the color of the flames became pink, then yellow, then green, then blue, and from the tip of a larger flame emerged the oscillating form of an azured apparition, which took on a body, a visage, arms....

"Athana!" said Sparyanthis, "these are the jewels of your daughter Alilat, the jewels of poison. I have added to them the rubies of fresh blood, and the offering of my life, disdainful of living. Take these jewels, O enchantress Athana!"

With a great cry of frightful joy, he let them fall into the great dancing flame, and, bending his knees, before anyone dared to retain him, he closed his eyes and fell backwards into the unfathomable furnace, which was abruptly extinguished and closed up, while the crowd fled into the black foliage, haggard, an exodus of phantoms vanishing into the darkness.

SF & FANTASY

Adolphe Alhaiza. *Cybele*
Alphonse Allais. *The Adventures of Captain Cap*
Henri Allorge. *The Great Cataclysm*
Guy d'Armen. *Doc Ardan: The City of Gold and Lepers; The Troglodytes of Mount Everest/The Giants of Black Lake*
G.-J. Arnaud. *The Ice Company*
André Arnyvelde. *The Ark; The Mutilated Bacchus*
Charles Asselineau. *The Double Life*
Henri Austruy. *The Eupantophone; The Olotelepan; The Petitpaon Era*
Barillet-Lagargousse. *The Final War*
Cyprien Bérard. *The Vampire Lord Ruthwen*
S. Henry Berthoud. *Martyrs of Science*
Aloysius Bertrand. *Gaspard de la Nuit*
Richard Bessière. *The Gardens of the Apocalypse; The Masters of Silence*
Chevalier de Béthune. *The World of Mercury*
Albert Bleunard. *Ever Smaller*
Félix Bodin. *The Novel of the Future*
Louis Boussenard. *Monsieur Synthesis*
Alphonse Brown. *City of Glass; The Conquest of the Air*
Émile Calvet. *In a Thousand Years*
André Caroff. *The Terror of Madame Atomos; Miss Atomos; The Return of Madame Atomos; The Mistake of Madame Atomos; The Monsters of Madame Atomos; The Revenge of Madame Atomos; The Resurrection of Madame Atomos; The Mark of Madame Atomos; The Spheres of Madame Atomos; The Wrath of Madame Atomos* (w/M. & Sylvie Stéphan)
Félicien Champsaur. *Homo-Deus; The Human Arrow; Nora, The Ape-Woman; Ouha, King of the Apes; Pharaoh's Wife*
Didier de Chousy. *Ignis*
Jules Clarétie. *Obsession*
Jacques Collin de Plancy. *Voyage to the Center of the Earth*
Michel Corday. *The Eternal Flame*

André Couvreur. *Caresco, Superman; The Exploits of Professor Tornada* (3 vols.); *The Necessary Evil*
Camille Debans. *The Misfortunes of John Bull*
Captain Danrit. *Undersea Odyssey*
C. I. Defontenay. *Star (Psi Cassiopeia)*
Charles Derennes. *The People of the Pole*
Georges Dodds (anthologist). *The Missing Link*
Charles Dodeman. *The Silent Bomb*
Harry Dickson. *The Heir of Dracula; Harry Dickson vs. The Spider*
Jules Dornay. *Lord Ruthven Begins*
Alfred Driou. *The Adventures of a Parisian Aeronaut*
Sâr Dubnotal *vs. Jack the Ripper; The Astral Trail*
Odette Dulac. *The War of the Sexes*
Alexandre Dumas. *The Return of Lord Ruthven*
Renée Dunan. *Baal; The Ultimate Pleasure*
J.-C. Dunyach. *The Night Orchid; The Thieves of Silence*
Henri Duvernois. *The Man Who Found Himself*
Achille Eyraud. *Voyage to Venus*
Henri Falk. *The Age of Lead*
Paul Féval. *Anne of the Isles; Knightshade; Revenants; Vampire City; The Vampire Countess; The Wandering Jew's Daughter*
Paul Féval, *fils. Felifax, the Tiger-Man*
Charles de Fieux. *Lamékis*
Fernand Fleuret. *Jim Click*
Louis Forest. *Someone is Stealing Children in Paris*
Arnould Galopin. *Doctor Omega; Doctor Omega and the Shadowmen* (anthology)
Judith Gautier. *Isoline and the Serpent-Flower*
H. Gayar. *The Marvelous Adventures of Serge Myrandhal on Mars*
G.L. Gick. *Harry Dickson and the Werewolf of Rutherford Grange*
Raoul Gineste. *The Second Life of Doctor Albin*
Delphine de Girardin. *Balzac's Cane*
Léon Gozlan. *The Vampire of the Val-de-Grâce*

Jules Gros. *The Fossil Man*

Edmond Haraucourt. *Daah, the First Human; Illusions of Immortality*

Nathalie Henneberg. *The Green Gods*

Eugène Hennebert. *The Enchanted City*

Jules Hoche. *The Maker of Men and His Formula*

V. Hugo, P. Foucher & P. Meurice. *The Hunchback of Notre-Dame*

Romain d'Huissier. *Hexagon: Dark Matter*

Jules Janin. *The Magnetized Corpse*

Michel Jeury. *Chronolysis*

Gustave Kahn. *The Tale of Gold and Silence*

Gérard Klein. *The Mote in Time's Eye*

Fernand Kolney. *Love in 5000 Years*

Paul Lacroix. *Danse Macabre*

Louis-Guillaume de La Follie. *The Unpretentious Philosopher*

Jean de La Hire. *The Fiery Wheel; Enter the Nyctalope; The Nyctalope on Mars; The Nyctalope vs. Lucifer; The Nyctalope Steps In; Night of the Nyctalope; Return of the Nyctalope*

Etienne-Léon de Lamothe-Langon. *The Virgin Vampire*

André Laurie. *Spiridon*

Gabriel de Lautrec. *The Vengeance of the Oval Portrait*

Alain le Drimeur. *The Future City*

Georges Le Faure & Henri de Graffigny. *The Extraordinary Adventures of a Russian Scientist Across the Solar System* (2 vols.)

Gustave Le Rouge. *The Dominion of the World* (w/Gustave Guitton) (4 vols.); *The Mysterious Doctor Cornelius* (3 vols.); *The Vampires of Mars*

Jules Lermina. *The Battle of Strasbourg; Mysteryville; Panic in Paris; The Secret of Zippelius; To-Ho and the Gold Destroyers*

André Lichtenberger. *The Centaurs; The Children of the Crab*

Maurice Limat. *Mephista*

Listonai. *The Philosophical Voyager*

Jean-Marc & Randy Lofficier. *Edgar Allan Poe on Mars; The Katrina Protocol; Pacifica 1, 2; Robonocchio; Return of the*

Nyctalope; (anthologists) *Tales of the Shadowmen 1-12; The Vampire Almanac* (2 vols.)

Ch. Lomon & P.-B. Gheuzi. *The Last Days of Atlantis*

Xavier Mauméjean. *The League of Heroes*

Joseph Méry. *The Tower of Destiny*

Hippolyte Mettais. *Paris Before the Deluge; The Year 5865*

Louise Michel. *The Human Microbes; The New World*

Tony Moilin. *Paris in the Year 2000*

José Moselli. *Illa's End*

John-Antoine Nau. *Enemy Force*

Marie Nizet. *Captain Vampire*

Charles Nodier. *Trilby and The Crumb Fairy*

C. Nodier, A. Beraud & Toussaint-Merle. *Frankenstein*

Henri de Parville. *An Inhabitant of the Planet Mars*

Gaston de Pawlowski. *Journey to the Land of the 4th Dimension*

Georges Pellerin. *The World in 2000 Years*

Ernest Pérochon. *The Frenetic People*

Pierre Pelot. *The Child Who Walked on the Sky*

Jean Petithuguenin. *An International Mission to the Moon*

J. Polidori, C. Nodier, E. Scribe. *Lord Ruthven the Vampire*

P.-A. Ponson du Terrail. *The Immortal Woman; The Vampire and the Devil's Son*

Georges Price. *The Missing Men of the* Sirius

René Pujol. *The Chimerical Quest*

Edgar Quinet. *Ahasuerus; The Enchanter Merlin*

Henri de Régnier. *A Surfeit of Mirrors*

Maurice Renard. *The Blue Peril; Doctor Lerne; The Doctored Man; A Man Among the Microbes; The Master of Light*

Jean Richepin. *The Crazy Corner; The Wing*

Albert Robida. *The Adventures of Saturnin Farandoul; Chalet in the Sky; The Clock of the Centuries; The Electric Life; The Engineer Von Satanas*

J.-H. Rosny Aîné. *Helgvor of the Blue River; The Givreuse Enigma; The Mysterious Force; The Navigators of Space; Vamireh; The World of the Variants; The Young Vampire*

Marcel Rouff. *Journey to the Inverted World*

Marie-Anne de Roumier-Robert. *The Voyage of Lord Seaton to the Seven Planets*

Léonie Rouzade. *The World Turned Upside Down*

Han Ryner. *The Human Ant; The Superhumans*

Frank Schildiner. *The Quest of Frankenstein*

Pierre de Selenes: *An Unknown World*

Angelo de Sorr. *The Vampires of London*

Brian Stableford. *The Empire of the Necromancers (1. The Shadow of Frankenstein; 2. Frankenstein and the Vampire Countess; 3. Frankenstein in London); Eurydice's Lament; The New Faust at the Tragicomique; Sherlock Holmes and The Vampires of Eternity; The Stones of Camelot; The Wayward Muse.* (anthologist) *News from the Moon; The Germans on Venus; The Supreme Progress; The World Above the World; Nemoville; Investigations of the Future; The Conqueror of Death; The Revolt of the Machines; The Man With the Blue Face; The Aerial Valley; The New Moon; The Nickel Man; On the Brink of the World's End; The Mirror of Present Events*

Jacques Spitz. *The Eye of Purgatory*

Kurt Steiner. *Ortog*

Eugène Thébault. *Radio-Terror*

C.-F. Tiphaigne de La Roche. *Amilec*

Simon Tyssot de Patot. *The Strange Voyages of Jacques Massé and Pierre de Mésange*

Louis Ulbach. *Prince Bonifacio*

Théo Varlet. *The Castaways of Eros; The Golden Rock.; The Martian Epic* (w/Octave Joncquel); *Timeslip Troopers* (w/André Blandin); *The Xenobiotic Invasion*

Pierre Véron. *The Merchants of Health*

Paul Vibert. *The Mysterious Fluid*

Villiers de l'Isle-Adam. *The Scaffold; The Vampire Soul*

Gaston de Wailly. *The Murderer of the World*

Philippe Ward. *Artahe ; Manhattan Ghost* (w/Mickael Laguerre); *The Song of Montségur* (w/Sylvie Miller)